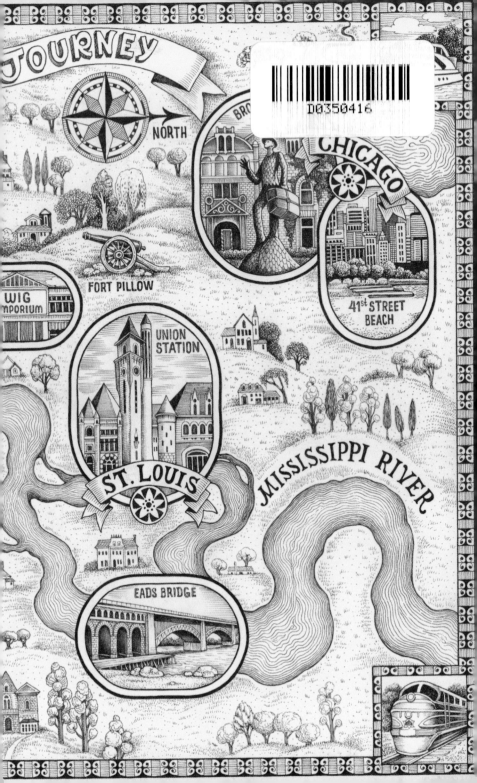

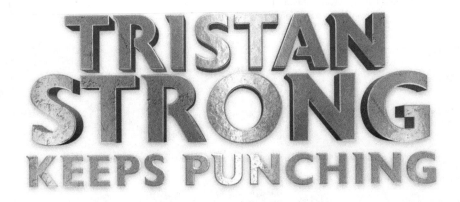

TRISTAN STRONG KEEPS PUNCHING

BOOK 3

KWAME MBALIA

RICK RIORDAN PRESENTS

DISNEY • HYPERION

Los Angeles   New York

Created in association with Cake Literary

First Edition, October 2021
1 3 5 7 9 10 8 6 4 2
FAC-021131-21232

Printed in the United States of America

This book is set in Minion Pro, Hoefler Text, Courier Std/
Monotype; Astoria, Bouledoug/Fontspring

Designed by Tyler Nevins
Endpaper illustration © 2021 by Sveta Dorosheva

Library of Congress Cataloging-in-Publication Data
Names: Mbalia, Kwame, author. • Mbalia, Kwame. Tristan Strong ; bk. 3.
Title: Tristan Strong keeps punching / Kwame Mbalia.
Description: First edition. • Los Angeles ; New York : Disney-Hyperion, 2021. • Series:
Tristan Strong ; book 3 • Audience: Ages 8–12. • Audience: Grades 4–6. • Summary:
The Strong family is having a reunion in New Orleans, and twelve-year-old Tristan
is supposed to be keeping an eye on his younger cousin Terrence when several things
happen at once: he sees his archenemy, King Cotton, and a mysterious girl grabs his
magic cellphone—her name is Seraphine, and she seems to know everything about
Tristan and the god Anansi (currently inhabiting the cellphone), and she has a mission
for Tristan, one that is going to lead to a final confrontation with haint King Cotton.
Identifiers: LCCN 2021013563 (print) • LCCN 2021013564 (ebook)
ISBN 9781368054874 (hardcover) • ISBN 9781368065993 (ebook)
Subjects: LCSH: Anansi (Legendary character)—Juvenile fiction. • African Americans—
Juvenile fiction. • Magic—Juvenile fiction. • Monsters—Juvenile fiction. • Adventure
stories. • Cousins—Juvenile fiction. • New Orleans (La.)—Juvenile fiction. • CYAC:
African Americans—Fiction. • Magic—Fiction. • Monsters—Fiction. • Characters
in literature—Fiction. • Cousins—Fiction. • Adventure and adventurers—Fiction.
• New Orleans (La.)—Fiction. • LCGFT: Action and adventure fiction.
Classification: LCC PZ7.1.M395 Trf 2021 (print)
LCC PZ7.1.M395 (ebook) • DDC 813.6 [Fic]—dc23
LC record available at https://lccn.loc.gov/2021013563
LC ebook record available at https://lccn.loc.gov/2021013564

Reinforced binding
Follow @ReadRiordan
Visit www.DisneyBooks.com

To the angry

CONTENTS

1 Stay Strong   I

2 A New Mission   15

3 The Return   27

4 Catch a Fire   43

5 Lectures and Warningsss   56

6 Mortar Over Bones   70

7 When the Haints...Come Marching In   78

8 The Kids Are All Right...for Now   87

9 The Ferryman's Warning   106

10 Angola   122

11 Haint No River Wide Enough   136

12 Haint Blue   151

13 If One of Us Ain't Free...   158

14 The Gods Must Be Cranky   168

15 Real Heroes Take Taxis   175

16 The Old Tricky Sticky   182

17 Gods in Grayscale   197

18 Spirit Utility Vehicle   212

19 The Rolling Thunder   223

20 Erzulie   237

21 The Redliners · 245

22 Patty Roller's Wig Emporium · 258

23 The Gods Hate Redliners · 268

24 The Hidden City · 282

25 Alke Is a Story · 298

26 The Boys Are Back in Town · 308

27 Breaker, Breaker · 320

28 Chicago Over Everything · 333

29 Beachfront Breaker Hunt · 347

30 A New Challenger Has Entered · 360

31 She Don't Miss · 372

32 The Gum Buddies · 383

33 The Final Fight of Tristan Strong · 390

Epilogue · 399

1
STAY STRONG

IT SHOULD BE PHYSICALLY IMPOSSIBLE FOR THE HUMAN BODY TO burst into flame. Aren't there rules against that? I'm pretty sure my Life Science class covered it last year. Call me old-fashioned, but I'm a firm believer that people aren't meant to be matches.

So that's why I stared in utter horror at the small silver flame popping out of my knuckles.

"I don't like that," I said, my voice sounding faint and distant to my own ears.

That was probably wrong to say. For several reasons. First, I was already trying my best not to lose my temper and attract attention. Our tour guide kept shooting angry looks at our group and shushing us. And we weren't even being that loud! No more so than anyone else on the tour. Still, I was pretty sure my bursting into flame would get us more than a mean look.

We were stuffed in the middle of a crowd in a tiny museum crammed with fascinating exhibits. Granddad called it the Pharmacy Museum. From that name I expected to see boring displays, like the history of headache medicine or something like that. Instead, I learned about century-old tools used to probe, prod, and investigate the human body. Pretty cool! But again, the place was jam-packed. Everybody in the French Quarter must've come for a tour. So I definitely didn't want to cause a panic because my fist had turned into a Flamin' Hot.

Yes, the Strongs were in New Orleans. One last adventure before I headed back to Chicago to start the new school year. It was bittersweet. I mean, I was looking forward to getting home, being back in my neighborhood, and seeing my parents. Still, I'd had fun with Granddad and Nana. I'd eaten a bunch of key lime pie, done a little boxing, fallen into another world with powerful gods and made a bunch of folk-hero friends.... You know, the normal summer.

I was excited to visit the Big Easy, but this trip had come with a few strings attached. And—

"What don't you like?" someone said over my left shoulder. "The artificial leech? C'mon! That's so cool! Apparently back then you'd jam that thing into your—"

"Thank you, Terrence," I whispered, covering up my burning hand.

The tour guide glared as Terrence continued to hiss facts

at me. I shot a glare right back, and the guide huffed and turned around. Then I looked at the walking encyclopedia behind me. Terrence was a short, thin Black boy with a red-tipped lightning bolt dyed into his close-cropped hair. He was also one of those aforementioned attached strings.

"No more ancient surgery lessons," I said in a low voice. "Please."

He shrugged and continued to mutter trivia to the stranger next to him. I shook my head. Terrence was my nine-year-old cousin, Dad's brother's son, and the second reason I had to keep things to myself. The powers that be (Nana) had decided that Terrence needed a buddy, someone to partner with as we toured New Orleans, and guess who that was?

Lucky me.

Terrence wore an oversize lime-green T-shirt with an icon of a flexed bicep on the front and STRONGS ON THE MOVE written beneath it in bold black letters. On the back, BLACK IS A RAINBOW arced over interlocking hands in different shades of brown. Yeah. Brown and lime green. The message was great! The aesthetics? Eh. I (unfortunately) was wearing the same shirt, and four or five others in the Pharmacy Museum were sporting it as well.

You've probably figured out what was happening.

It was a Strong family reunion.

Relatives I hadn't seen in years—and some I'd never met at all—had made the trip. Great-aunts, cousins, their children. I met my Uncle Jeff-Jeff and what he called his emotional support pug (also, strangely, called Jeff-Jeff). In fact, it seemed the only ones not here were my parents. They'd been unable to make the trip—something about car trouble—and Mom had stressed the importance of me representing for the Chicago Strongs. What I did would reflect on them. So, you know how it goes. Best behavior and all that.

Which brings us to the third reason I had to avoid making a scene. I was on a mission.

Two weeks ago I had returned from my second trip to Alke, the magical world where storied folk heroes like John Henry, heroines like Keelboat Annie, gods like Anansi and Nyame, and goddesses like Mami Wata reigned.

Unfortunately, it was also my last trip there. Alke had been destroyed, and the only way to save its inhabitants had been to weave the story of their world into mine. Now Alkeans were scattered across the country, and it was my responsibility to help find them and make sure they were okay.

Whiiich you can't really do when you're a line buddy for your cousin.

"Where should we visit next?" Terrence asked as we exited the museum. "I could use some dinner first." He pulled out his phone and started scrolling different travel websites, then gasped. "Tristan, look! There's a pizza parlor that gives you an oversize spatula if you eat a whole supreme pie!"

He looked at me with way too much glee in his eyes (could that be a medical condition?) and I shook my head. "We're supposed to wait here for Granddad, then we'll move to the next stop." The hotel, I hoped.

My phone vibrated. I froze for a second before reaching for it. Fortunately, the flame had disappeared from my knuckles, and Terrence was still busy reading about pizza. I pulled a sleek black smartphone from the back pocket of my basketball shorts.

The SBP, or Story Box Phone, was the magical treasure chest of Anansi tales. Nyame the sky god had transferred the stories from an actual box into my phone and then trapped Anansi himself inside with them. That hadn't stopped the spider god from bossing and heckling me at every opportunity. The plus side? Anansi had turned out to be a talented web designer and had added all sorts of cool apps, including one that alerted us to the location of Alkeans. I now had the most advanced smartphone in this realm or any other.

The spider god stared out at me from the home screen. His expression was impatient as he pointed to the Maps app icon. "What's taking you so long? We've got to get a move on!"

"Okay, where's the alert coming from?" I asked Anansi.

I wanted to tell him about the knuckle flames, but just at that moment Terrence moved closer to me. I turned to prevent him from being able to see the SBP's screen. *I'm on the phone*, I mouthed to him, pointing to the buds in my ears. He frowned but went back to scoping out which pizza he apparently wanted to cram inside his face.

"Hurry up, Tristan," said Terrence. "I've always wanted a pizza spatula. I'm going to be a chef, you know. Open my own restaurant and serve my famous teriyaki pizza." He licked his lips, and I shivered. Some food preferences should remain private.

I looked back at Anansi. "Well? Where should I send Nyame?"

Hey, I was only twelve. I couldn't exactly go gallivanting across the country by myself to find every Alkean. But the sky god could.

Anansi shook his head. "No, you're not listening. Right here, just a few blocks away. There's an Alkean who needs help in the French Quarter!"

I inhaled sharply. Yes! We could handle this ourselves! All I had to do was give Terrence the slip, and then we could—

A tingling sensation pricked the corners of my eyes.

That was weird. I squinted. Rubbed at them. Blinked a few times, but the sensation wouldn't go away. I had just turned to ask Terrence if there was anything in my eyes when I saw someone I recognized. He was whistling while walking down the street in the opposite direction.

Tall.

Neatly dressed.

Evil.

King Cotton was strolling through the French Quarter without a care in the world.

The way I figure it, no one is owed anything. Not an easy life. Not a happy ending. Nothing. I learned that from Granddad. Life comes at you fast, like a flurry of jabs and hooks, and sometimes the only thing you can do is learn how to take a few on the chin and keep on standing.

And not every story is neat and tidy, either. Sometimes pages are missing, ripped out by forces beyond our control. Sometimes the villain wins. Sometimes the villain wins by a *lot*. And not every question may get answered. I mean, there are a hundred stories unfolding without our knowledge every day, and the details will never see the light of day because we either can't or won't seek them out. So, tough luck, the ending to that chapter is forever shrouded from view.

Until someone comes along and tries to tell it. Tries to tease out the answers, give folks some closure. That's my role as an Anansesem—a seeker, recorder, and teller of stories. I didn't ask for the title—the title chose me when I was in Alke. In fact, I didn't want the job. I didn't think I'd be any good at it. But I was wrong. And despite my best attempts to avoid the responsibility, the magic of my people's stories didn't care about my objections. Since I was the reason the characters in those tales were now scattered around the globe, telling their stories was one thing that only I could do.

Maybe Nana had said it best the first week after we'd returned to our world. She'd been laid up in bed, recovering from being abducted, and the two of us were talking about Alke. And stories. When I mentioned it was hard to find the energy to speak about the world I had destroyed, she peered at me over the new quilt she was working on.

"You gotta find the pulse of the story, baby," she'd said. "Let the rhythm beat like a heart, and hold on to that pulse once you got it. Don't change it, no matter what anybody else says. Even if they call you a liar or selfish, or say you lucky to be here, or tell you to go somewhere else if you so unhappy, you don't let it go. Then speak those words. Tell the story."

Tell the story. I wanted to do just that. But how could I when King Cotton, the haint who had corrupted everything in Alke, now had his sights on my world? I had to stop him first.

"Hoo HOOO! Boy oh boy oh boy."

I'd shoved the phone back into my pocket and was two seconds away from tearing off after Cotton when Granddad walked out of a seafood grill a few doors down from the Pharmacy Museum. He was licking his fingers and doing a little jig, something everyone in the family called his *good-eatin' shuffle*. Nana followed him, no stranger to Granddad's apparent inability to say no to an order of battered clam strips. He had a bunch of take-out bags in his hand, and Nana was scolding him.

"Walter, you done stopped at every restaurant selling fried clams. You ain't supposed to be eating those! What you gonna do with all them, plant them?"

Before I could duck away, she spotted Terrence and me and steered Granddad toward us. Granddad didn't look up from his clam strips. He'd eat two or three, smack his lips and exclaim how good they were, then roll the bag closed and open another. It was like watching a squirrel eat nuts, except this particular squirrel knew how to throw a mean right hook and could ground you.

"Maaaaaaaaaan, let me tell you about these clam strips right here!" Granddad said when they reached us.

I rolled my eyes. Anytime he started with a *Let me tell you*, I knew we weren't going anywhere soon. Might as well unfurl a sleeping bag and put on your pajamas, you're going to be there for a while. Few things riled up Walter Strong more than a crisp, well-fried clam strip. Which would have been fine any other day (that's not exactly true, but what was I, a mere twelve-year-old, supposed to do?), just not when Cotton was on the loose.

My pocket vibrated twice. I checked to make sure Granddad was distracted (which was easy, since his eyes were closed as he bit into another clam strip) before pulling out the phone. Granddad hated how often I checked it. Meanwhile, Terrence told Nana about the pizza parlor.

The screen winked to life, and the worried face of a trickster god stared out at me.

On an average day, Anansi had a contagious smile and a twinkle in his eye. You never knew if he had your back or had a trick in his back pocket. He was the Weaver, the owner of all stories, from truths to tall tales, and his name was embedded in my title of Anansesem. But at the moment, the spider god looked far from his normal self.

I slipped in one earbud and his voice, normally melodic and lilting, was flat and strained. "Well, are we leaving or not?"

I peered around the crowded street filled with tourists just like me and my grandparents. It was early evening, but the Louisiana sun still beamed down on the French Quarter as if focused through a magnifying glass. My own reunion T-shirt (yes, still lime green) clung to my back, my black basketball shorts felt like they weighed thirty pounds, and my new all-black Chuck Taylors (*That's the second pair we bought you,* Granddad had grumbled) felt like their soles were melting.

Still, everywhere I looked, people were laughing, joking, shopping, eating, dancing, and carrying on their merry way through what was possibly the most vibrant square mile in the whole country. Music thumped from Bourbon Street a few blocks over while the casinos on Canal Street flickered to life. Adults and teens and children walked by with powdered sugar dusting their lips and fingers as they bit into soft, hot beignets and—if you didn't know any better—life was all good.

Yet a shadow lingered now, just out of sight. Cotton. The haint's specter hovered in my peripheral vision, waiting for the right moment to strike.

I shook my head. "Not just yet," I told Anansi. "But—"

"Time is running out, Tristan! We have to move!" There was resignation in his voice. He already knew the answer.

"I know," I said. "It's just... all my family is here."

Anansi didn't respond, and when I glanced at the SBP, I saw he was sitting with his back against the edge of the screen, slumped and depressed. I realized, too late, what I'd just said, and I opened my mouth to say more, but no words would bring back his family—specifically, his son—safe and sound, so I closed it. Sometimes condolences don't ease the hurt—they just make things worse.

"Hey now, what's with that face?"

Granddad's voice came from behind me. He cradled another container of clam strips as if it were a baby, but he wore a concerned look. Nana was speaking to Terrence a few feet away, both of them huddled over his phone as they picked the next destination for our Strong subgroup. "You look like you just got sucker punched, boy. What's the best way to defend against that happening again?"

I snorted, though there wasn't much humor in it. Granddad always had a boxing analogy ready to apply to any situation, and he'd quiz me at various points throughout the day to test my knowledge of the sport. History, theory, techniques—it didn't matter. He'd only let me go back to doing whatever I was doing if I answered his questions correctly.

If Gum Baby were here, she'd call it a Grandpop Quiz. I smiled, and then it faded from my face. The little loudmouth was lost out there somewhere, too. As much as I hated to admit it (and if you tell her, I will sing "The Ballad of the Gummy" nonstop outside your window), I missed the tiny sap monster.

"Well?" Granddad asked.

I sighed, stared into the crowd streaming past, and racked my brain. "Um, dodge it?"

"You take a sucker punch, you didn't dodge anything. Not for a good minute. Try again."

"Keep my head on a swivel? Make sure I'm always aware."

Granddad pursed his lips. "Better, but still not all the way there. Think about it. Sometimes an opponent will get the drop on you, and they'll send punch after punch at you. Those blows gonna land and land hard. Knock you back. Stun you. How do you defend against a flurry like that? How do you respond?"

I struggled to come up with an answer, but at that moment

the SBP vibrated. Three times in a row. That wasn't a signal from Anansi. That was an alert.

"Tristan."

Granddad's voice jerked me from my thoughts. He loaded me up with his take-out boxes and bags so he could place both hands on my shoulders. Then he pulled me close, into a hug. My arms were too full to hug him back, but I was too surprised to respond anyway.

"Sometimes," Granddad said, squeezing me tight, "you just have to hold on. Clinch, and catch your breath. The world is going to hit you hard, son. Clinch and don't let go until you can keep on fighting. Hear me?"

"Yessir," I said, my voice muffled by his shirt.

Sometimes I forgot that Granddad had been violently introduced to the world of Alke when Bear—under the poisonous influence of the haint King Cotton—had attacked the farmhouse and kidnapped Nana. Had Granddad felt helpless while we were gone? Sucker punched?

The SBP vibrated again. Granddad sucked his teeth and stepped back. "Boy, who is that blowing up your phone? Tell them Stanleys to give you a break."

I groaned. "No, Granddad, no, no, no. They're called stans. *Stans.*"

"Stans, Stanleys, Stanford Cardinals, you need to tell them to lay off." Granddad took back his clam strips and popped a few more golden-brown pieces into his mouth, chewing angrily. "I'm trying to teach here, and you, Mr. Popular, can barely focus. Go on and answer that, boy. I won't stand in the way."

I grinned even as I pulled out the phone and began to back up. "It's not like that, Granddad. I just need to check something real—"

"Tristan, watch out!"

Anansi's shout came from the earbud I still wore, even as the SBP was snatched from my hand. I whirled to see a kid running into the crowd.

"Hey!" I cried.

"Tristan—" Granddad began, but I was already tearing off after the robber.

"C'mon, Granddad!" I shouted and sprinted down the street.

2
A NEW MISSION

TAILING A THIEF THROUGH PACKS OF SIGHTSEEING ADULTS WAS
giving me a headache. Or maybe the pain was from the elbow
that clipped my head when a woman had tried to shake one
too many appendages to the street band's rhythm. I'd be
seeing stars and her not-quite-a-two-step for days to come.

Granddad kept one hand on my shoulder as we weaved
between people. Then we bumped into a cluster I couldn't
find a way through. "Did you see who took it?" he asked.

I hopped up and down to try to see over the throng. "No.
He was too fast," I said, scowling. "He's got to be around
here somewhere."

We scanned the area for several moments, but it was just
too crowded. A line of people stretched down the block to
my left and disappeared around the corner. A mouthwater-
ing aroma wafted from the open doors of a restaurant. My

stomach grumbled, and I sadly but deliberately turned away. *Another time, gumbo, my old friend. Another time.*

On the other side of the street, two kids played a complicated but catchy rhythm on a set of street drums—several overturned buckets, two plastic storage bins, and an old pot—while a third played a harmonica and a fourth held a brass horn to his lips. The beat snuck inside my head, and soon I caught myself nodding and tapping my fingers on my thigh as I searched. Finally, however, I sighed and gave up.

"Sorry, Granddad. Guess I lost him."

Granddad grunted and popped another fried clam into his mouth. "Not really supposed to be eating these," he mumbled to himself. "Your grandmother wouldn't approve."

I raised an eyebrow. Walter Strong, being irresponsible? Impossible.

Just then Granddad looked up and caught the partial smirk on my face. The stony frown he leveled at me could've cut glass. "Better watch them eyes, boy. You supposed to be the leader, so lead. Try asking some folks. What about them three boys making all that racket over there?"

I stopped and frowned. "Wait, did you say '*three* boys'? What three boys?"

Granddad looked at me strangely, then pointed with a half-chewed clam strip at the drummers and harmonica player across the street. "Them."

I whirled. The fourth member of the band was gone now,

and I realized—too late—that he had only been pretending to be part of their group. I muttered something under my breath and took off, sprinting past the boys and plunging into the dark side street behind them. "Come on, Granddad—we've got to catch up!"

"Hold on, boy—my clams!"

I raced down the street, among the cars in bumper-to-bumper traffic, and skidded to a stop. Granddad huffed up behind me, shaking his head. "You know I can't run and eat at the same time, Tristan. Did you lose him again?"

I punched my palm in frustration. Where had he gone?

Something hissed, and it took me a moment to realize the sound was coming from me. I'd been so close, *so close*, to finding my friends and yet I'd failed....

"Sorry, Granddad," I muttered. "Guess we ran all this way for nothing."

"Now just hold on. Don't go giving up yet." He sucked down another lungful of air and then straightened and began to examine the area. "You got fooled with the okeydoke once, ain't no harm in double-checking to make sure it don't happen again. Now, tell me what that boy was wearing, and let's see if we can't spot him."

I sighed and tried to remember. "Yes, sir. Well...he had on a T-shirt, pants with suspenders...A hat—one of those kinds Dad likes to wear. And he was carrying an instrument. A saxophone, maybe? No, a trumpet!" I was looking up and down the sidewalk as I spoke, trying to keep an eye out, when Granddad's hand landed heavily on my shoulder.

"A trumpet?"

I nodded.

Granddad pursed his lips and then jerked his head toward the other side of Rampart Street, where there was a big arch with a gate under it. "We can check one more spot—Louis Armstrong Park. Horn players like to hang out there."

I stared at the gates blocking the entrance, then turned back, only to see Granddad toss his empty food bags in a trash can and head for the crosswalk. That man really inhaled those clam strips. I shook my head and hurried after him. "Is it open?" I asked. "Do they close the park at night?"

Granddad strode up to the gates and gave them a shove. One swung open, and he smiled at me. "They haven't closed up yet. We've still got a bit of time. Come on, do you want to get your phone back or not?"

There was no way I was going to pass this up. Somewhere in Louis Armstrong Park, I hoped, there was a trumpeter with the SBP, and the sooner I found him, the sooner we could rescue the lost Alkean, and then I could focus on running down Cotton.

Congo Square.

That was the name of the clearing we entered. A sign on a pole near the path explained that the space had once served as a meeting spot for enslaved Black folks. This was where they had exchanged news. Exchanged songs. Exchanged solace, comfort, and hope.

And apparently, as I surveyed the plaza, this was where spirits now came to dance.

Seriously. Everywhere I looked, ghostly apparitions dressed in their Saturday night finest were hitting moves that made my calves cramp as I watched. At first I thought they were living people, but when I accidentally walked through an ancestor doing the two-step, I quickly corrected my assumption. There was a couple "walking the dog" and a child doing the foxtrot. And, if that weren't wild enough, as if on cue, everybody started doing the Electric Slide. And I thought my parents' cookouts were bad.

"Are you seeing this?" I asked Granddad.

He didn't answer, which I took to mean that he wasn't. Unlike me, he didn't have an Isihlangu bead to give him the ability to perceive spirits. But then . . . I hadn't activated mine. So how was *I* seeing this?

"Tristan . . ." Granddad started.

I was so focused on moving through the spirits, I didn't hear the rest of what he said. I sidestepped a woman with a baby in her arms, then squeezed past a couple swaying gently from side to side. A mother and father held hands as their four children stood in front of them, youngest to oldest, two girls and two boys. None of them paid me any mind. It was like I was the ghost haunting their world. That's an unnerving feeling.

And then I spotted him—the boy from the French Quarter, trumpet to his lips and eyes closed as he walked through the ghostly crowd. I thought he might be a ghost as well until his foot kicked a pebble across the square. He was coming my direction, his fingers pressing the valves and his cheeks bulging as he played a sad song that captured the attention of the spirits. The boy moved closer and closer. I leaned out, ready to grab his arm.

Suddenly he stopped right in front of me, lowered the trumpet, and opened his eyes.

"Tristan Strong. Ça va? She said you'd be here," he said, looking directly at me. "She said she wanted to meet you herself, but ain't no time for that now. Follow me, s'il vous plaît. They're coming for the children."

I froze. "Uhhh..."

He stooped and set the trumpet on the ground. Then he swept off his hat, and microbraids tumbled down to coil on his—*her?*—shoulders.

"You're a girl!" I said, shocked.

He—I mean *she*—smirked and tucked her hat into the back pocket of her pants. "She said you were a little slow on the uptake at times. Guess she was right. Now... I told you. They're coming for the children, including your newcomers.

They aim to take 'em. You gonna help clean up your mess, or will she need to find someone else?"

I shook my head, confused. "Who's 'she'? And who is 'they'? And who is—"

I didn't have time to finish. The strange girl let out a stream of exasperated words in a language I didn't understand and then stepped up close and dangled the SBP in front of me. "If you want this, follow me."

She turned and moved quickly toward the park's exit. I started after her, then remembered Granddad. I stopped and looked back at him. "The girl is gonna give me back my phone," I told him. "She just wants to show us something first, okay?"

He hesitated, then waved me on. "You go ahead without me, boy. Those clam strips might be making a comeback. The hotel is that direction anyway. Just ... hurry back, all right?"

I nodded, then took off. Granddad had become more trusting ever since I saved Nana. I just hoped his trust wasn't misplaced, because I had no idea what was going to happen next.

"Put some spice in your stride, boy—I might die!"

You know the worst thing about chasing after the girl who stole my phone? Listening to Anansi's color commentary as he critiqued my efforts. Seriously! You'd think he'd be a bit kinder to the person trying to rescue him from a stranger's clutches.

We'd raced up and down side streets and reentered the French Quarter. If trying to catch to up to the girl before had been difficult, now it seemed downright impossible. The crowds had grown in just the last thirty minutes, and, with the sun setting, it felt as if everybody in New Orleans—no, in the whole state of Louisiana—had decided to squeeze into these few city blocks.

And I was stuck trying to rescue an ungrateful trickster god who happened to be trapped in a magical phone that held the only clues to the whereabouts of the lost Alkean.

And people say I don't know how to have a good time.

"Tristan," Anansi said, his voice filtering through my ear-buds, which were apparently still connected to the phone. Alkean reception was incredible. "I've saved my place in books faster than you're saving me. I've saved dances for that special someone faster than you're saving me. I've saved—"

"I wish you'd save your breath and be quiet!" I snarled.

A woman wearing five Mardi Gras bead necklaces and a feather crown looked at me as if I was talking to her, then frowned and stalked away in a huff, like I'd offended her. *I* should've been the offended one—who only wears five bead necklaces at the same time? She should've had at least fifteen by now.

I continued to pursue the mysterious girl. It was frustrating—with every second that elapsed, Cotton was surely wreaking havoc somewhere out there. I had to end this, and fast.

We passed trinket shops and restaurants and bars swelling with customers. We passed closed museums and several ghost tours, and I wanted to shout at the tourists that the spirits were all around them...but I had to keep going. A giant church—the St. Louis Cathedral—towered overhead as we raced down the narrow street next to it and entered Jackson Square. As the girl dashed around people, they seemed to ignore her, whereas I had to shout "Excuse me!" every five seconds. It felt like I'd been running forever.

We crossed a wider street, and just when my lungs were about to turn in their two-week notice, she stopped in the middle of a giant field by the Mississippi River. As I hopped over the guide chains and approached her carefully, I saw a sign that read ARTILLERY PARK.

"You can hear them if you listen closely," she said, facing the river instead of me. She didn't even turn around when I moved within a few feet of her. The sounds of the Quarter faded behind us. A breeze came off the river, cooling the air.

"Who are you?" I asked.

"Maybe just try to grab the SBP?" Anansi whispered in my earbud, but I ignored him. Something was happening, something strange, and if there was one thing I had learned this past summer, it was to stop and pay attention to the out-of-the-ordinary. It might just save a life.

"My name is Seraphine." She said it with a bit of an accent. Her microbraids rustled as she shot me a look, and then she returned to staring out at the water.

I squinted to see what she was looking at and did a double take. There was a barge on the horizon. One of those big boats that carries cargo containers. This one looked to be completely full.

Seraphine glanced at me, then returned her gaze to the boat. She wore a look of frustration, as if she'd expected something more and had been disappointed. "She said you defended your friends without hesitation. If you care half as much about saving the children as you do about your phone, we might stand a chance."

I stepped closer, trying to piece together the mystery in the girl's words. "We?"

"You and me. That's what she said."

I took another step closer. "Seraphine, I'm not sure what—or who—told you all this, but I really need my phone back. It's...important."

"Because of the god inside, n'est-ce pas?"

"I... Yes. But how do you know about Anansi?"

Seraphine turned to smile at me. "She makes it her business to know all the children who enter the city, as well as the people with power. And you, Tristan Strong, happen to be both. When she told me you'd arrived, I just knew you—and Anansi—would be able to help. We must free my siblings. The creatures...they bring the children here for loading. They do it under the cover of the song of the spirits so she can't hear their cries."

"Loading?"

The strange New Orleans girl pointed across the water to the barge. "Onto that."

I shook my head. "I'm sorry. Who is taking children, and why? Have you called the police? The FBI?"

"They can't help. No, it has to be us."

I leaned forward and gently plucked the SBP from Seraphine's grasp. She didn't even notice, that's how hard she was concentrating on the river. I began to back away slowly as Anansi motioned for me to hurry up. "Welp, I'm sorry to be a disappointment, but I really should find my granddad before he cleans the entire Quarter out of fried clam strips. It was nice to meet you, Seraphine, but let's never do this—"

"But I thought you wanted to help your friends?"

I hesitated. "Excuse me?"

"Your friends. The one with the stones. The tiny angry one. And the cute girl with the bat."

Anansi froze on the SBP's screen. "Stones?"

"Cute girl...I mean, the girl with the bat?" I asked at the same time.

Seraphine nodded, then she fished around in her pocket,

pulled out a wad of paper, and tossed it to me. I caught it and blushed furiously when I saw that the paper had her phone number on it. The wad held something inside it, too—a stone. I quickly stuffed the note in my pocket, steeling myself for Anansi's teasing…but he'd gone silent. He was staring at the rock in my palm. When I looked at it closely, the breath slipped out of my lungs like they'd sprung a leak. Anansi took it even harder, slumping to the bottom of the screen and wrapping his two arms around all six legs.

It was a smooth, perfectly round stone. Black, flecked with silver and gold.

Junior had been here! And Ayanna and Gum Baby! But where were they now?

As if she'd heard the question, Seraphine pointed to the barge. "We don't have much time. She said your friends are walking into a trap. If we are going to act, it must be now, Tristan Strong."

Anansi met my eyes, all traces of the trickster gone, leaving only the hardened gaze of a god. Of a father. I sighed, then nodded and looked at Seraphine. Cotton could wait… For now.

"What do you need us to do?"

3
THE RETURN

FIVE MINUTES INTO THE RESCUE ATTEMPT, EVERYTHING DISSOLVED into chaos.

Minute one:

The barge was anchored out in the middle of the Mississippi River. Which... I mean, have you seen that river? It's like an eight-lane expressway filled with mud and fish. In comparison, morning rush hour on the Dan Ryan freeway just outside Chicago seemed like a gentle crosswalk. Then there was the wind whipping up waves, making the river look like an ocean cutting through land... Look, I know being afraid of heights is supposed to be my thing, but choppy waves are a close second.

Anyway. TMI.

Seraphine and I scoured the shoreline for a stealthy way to reach the vessel, but the only thing we could find was a small warped wooden dinghy with no oars or motor to propel it forward.

Minute two:

As we were climbing into said dinghy, Anansi hissed into my ear, "Someone's coming." Seraphine looked at me strangely when I dropped into a crouch on the river side of the boat, but she followed my lead when I relayed Anansi's message.

"Let us hope it isn't one of the river patrollers, or worse," the girl said grimly. She met my inquisitive expression with a shake of the head. "She said foul things have been roaming the waterways as of late."

"You keep saying 'she said,'" I whispered. "Who are you talking about? Your mother?"

Seraphine smothered a laugh. She tilted the hat on her head jauntily. "You are not the only one who rides with a god, mon cher."

Just then something rustled nearby. We tensed. I got Seraphine's attention and mimed an attack, and she nodded. We crouched lower and waited for whoever it was to get a bit closer. We'd have one chance—if we didn't take down our assailant quickly and quietly, the people on the barge would hear, and our one shot at surprise would be lost.

The rustling came nearer. And nearer. And...

"Now!" I shouted.

Seraphine and I leaped out at the same time. She went

high and I dove low, intending to wrap my arms around the person's legs while Seraphine quickly clamped a hand over their mouth. At least, that was the plan. Instead, something heavy whacked me across the shin, sending me tumbling head over heels in pain.

Dusk was throwing shadows on everything, so I couldn't get a good look at our attacker's face. I made a second rush at them, and again something swiped at me. This time I ducked, bobbing and weaving so I didn't get hit, and then tackled the person hard to the ground.

"Who are you and why are you following us?" I hissed. I was angry. Impatient. My friends could be in trouble on that floating death trap, and here I was fighting a stranger. I was seconds away from squeezing my fists and unleashing the destructive power of the akofena shadow gloves on them when I saw Seraphine's eyes widen. She stepped back.

"What are you doing?" I asked her.

She didn't respond. Instead, she simply released our captive, who looked at me with a familiar confused expression and a crumpled map in his hand.

"Is this part of the tour, too?" my cousin asked, his giant promotional pizza spatula in the dirt next to him.

I groaned. "Terrence, what are you doing here?"

The skinny nine-year-old wriggled out of my grasp and clutched his spatula to his chest. Gumbo stains covered his reunion T-shirt, and blades of grass were sticking out of his hair as he stood and looked around.

"You were supposed to give me a tour, remember?" Terrence said.

"How did you even find us?"

"We were on our way to get some beignets when I saw you run across the street. The line was out the door, so I decided to see what you were doing." He stared at Seraphine. "Who's this? Another cousin?"

I sighed. "No, she—"

"Your girlfriend?"

"No!"

Seraphine raised an eyebrow as Terrence nodded and said, "Another one who's outta your league, huh?"

I was just getting ready to launch myself at him again—and Terrence must have seen something in my eyes, because he yelped and scampered behind Seraphine—when a sharp cry pierced the night air. It came from the barge and carried across the river before it abruptly ended.

Someone was in pain.

"We do not have time for this," Seraphine said, her fists clenched. "We must figure a way across, and now."

I rubbed my hair in frustration, and then my eyes landed on Terrence. More specifically, on the pizza spatula he carried. It would be a perfect oar for the dinghy. We could paddle across, and no one would hear us coming. That is, if he'd let us have it....

"Hey, Terrence..." I began.

His eyes flicked from mine to his spatula and back again, and he shook his head. "Nope, nuh-uh, don't even *think* about it."

"We just need it for an hour or so, and we'll bring it back good as new."

"Do you know what's in that water?" Terrence said, pointing at a piece of trash bobbing along the shoreline. "Look! That's a diaper! And you want to put my brand-new spatula in there? And look! Look at them. What are they doing?"

He was pointing at a pair of raccoons near the diaper. From here it looked like the bigger animal was trying to put it on the smaller one, and the little raccoon was attempting an escape. I didn't blame it. I wouldn't want to wear a soggy diaper, either.

I tried again. "Terrence, please, we need it. It's important. A matter of life and death. People are relying on us, and if we can't help them, something horrible might happen. So please. I'll convince Granddad to buy you a new one. I promise."

Terrence stared wide-eyed between Seraphine and me, then across the water to the barge, then back at me. He licked his lips.

Another cry echoed in the night.

"Terrence!" I said.

"Fine," he said. I exhaled and was about to thank him when he raised a hand. "But only if I can come with you."

I hesitated. That didn't sound like a particularly good idea, but what other option did we have? Even now I could hear the barge engine revving up. In a few minutes it would move on, and then the children aboard, including Ayanna and Junior (and Gum Baby, I guess), would be trapped. I couldn't let that happen. "Fine. But stay in the boat and don't make a sound."

Seraphine shook her head. "Un moment, s'il vous plaît. Tristan, are you sure? There is little room, and—"

But Terrence had already dashed past her and was helping to push the dinghy into the water. He hopped inside and I followed. After a moment, Seraphine climbed in with a look of reservation, but I knew she wanted to get to the barge as much as I did. I didn't know what to expect once we got there, but I did know that I wasn't going to let anyone hurt my friends. Not if I could do anything about it.

I had the magic of Alke on my side. What could go wrong?

I learned two things right away.

First, paddling a leaky dinghy across the Mississippi with a single pizza spatula was—believe it or not—not easy. For every foot we moved forward, we moved three feet downriver. The three of us took turns struggling against the current. Even though the surface looked calm, it felt like we were making no progress at all.

The lights of the French Quarter illuminated the western bank. I could see St. Louis Cathedral rising into the night, lit from below by the festivities going on around it. Somewhere in there the rest of the Strong family was eating, laughing, and partying. I just hoped we'd be able to sneak back and rejoin them later without any fuss.

The eastern bank of the river was shrouded in darkness. That was the side we wanted to approach the barge from, so no one would see us coming. And as we tried to paddle upriver around the vessel, I learned a second, very important fact that probably would've been good to know before setting out on this adventure.

Barges are huge. Super huge! "That's a long platform," I whispered to myself.

"They're not called platforms," Terrence said excitedly, forgetting that he wasn't supposed to be speaking. "They're barges, and when they're all connected like that, they're called the *tow*."

"A toe?" I asked.

"Like you're towing something, not what pokes through the hole in your sock. Not that I have any holes." This last comment was directed at Seraphine, who nodded gracefully at the pointless remark.

*Any*way.

Barge *tows* are huge covered *platforms* made of individual barges that, when linked together, can almost reach the size of a football field. They're pushed from the rear by one or two tugboats, blocky vessels with their wheelhouses situated high in the air. This barge only had one tugboat, and it was an ugly-looking thing. Smoke poured out of its lower deck, and the smell of diesel, sulfur, and mildewy socks drifted from it. And the bridge! The captain's compartment loomed like an angry cyclops in the cloudless night, and as we slowly made progress around the bow to the stern, the masthead light seemed to follow us, staring at me with a blistering red eye.

The enormity of the task quickly became clear. We had to sneak aboard, find our friends, and sneak back off without getting caught.

Easy, right?

Right.

Luckily for us, the sides of the barges weren't very high. I steered us toward a section where some netting dangled over the edge. After the dinghy bumped up alongside it, I extended the paddle to Terrence, and when he grabbed it, I wouldn't let go until he met my eyes.

"Don't leave the boat," I whispered. "Hang tight here, and we'll be right back."

He didn't look happy, but he nodded. I watched him for a second, then turned and followed Seraphine up the netting. She was already on the deck in a crouch, peeking around a rusted red cargo container. As I squatted next to her, she glanced at me and frowned slightly. "You take a risk, Tristan Strong, bringing your family to your battles. Aren't you worried he will be caught in the crossfire?"

I reached for the adinkra bracelet on my right wrist. Dangling from it were my gifts from the gods. The Anansi symbol. The akofena from High John. The Gye Nyame charm. The Amagqirha's spirit bead from Isihlangu. They gave me strength, power, and right now, all the confidence I needed. My heart beat double time in my chest, and I could barely restrain myself from sprinting toward the tugboat and demanding the release of my friends.

"He'll be fine," I managed to say. "Let's go."

The individual barges were connected by thick rusty chains hooked onto giant metal pegs. I stared at one and shuddered, resolving not to look at them again if I didn't have to. They reminded me too much of the giant bossling iron monsters I had battled back in Alke. We hopped over them, skulking in the shadows of the containers as we moved to the next barge along the tow.

"What do you think's inside these?" I whispered.

"Normally?" Seraphine thought for a second. "I think grain, or chemicals. But..." Her voice trailed off, and then she turned and jogged to the rear of the container we were hiding behind. She stopped at the doors and started wresting the giant bolt pin from the lock.

"Hey, what are you doing?"

The pin squeaked loose, and Seraphine swung the giant door open. She nodded grimly, then jerked her head at the inside. "It is as I thought. Empty. The barges seemed to be riding high in the water, and it's because they carry nothing."

"Where are the children?" I asked. "And my friends?"

Seraphine looked around uneasily. "I do not like this, Tristan. She said the children would be here. She's never wrong."

As we moved to the next barge in the row, I kept turning my head like a periscope. A feeling of unease worked itself up my spine and into my brain, until all I could think about was the lack of anything we'd expected to see. It didn't make sense!

"Let's check the tugboat," I whispered. I led the way across the third barge, water splashing up between the gaps and tow chains clinking eerily in the dark, toward the boat idling at the rear. I thought it was my imagination, but as we got closer, the light seemed to shrink around us, until the world beyond the barge didn't exist. It was just the two of us creeping through the night, the sound of my breath carrying on the breeze.

We jumped from the final barge to the prow of the tugboat. The deck vibrated under our feet. Seraphine elbowed me and pointed upward without speaking. A light still flickered at the very top of the boat, up in the wheelhouse. We looked at each other, then at the door leading inside, and I took a step forward.

"Wait," Seraphine said in a low voice, grabbing my arm. "Listen."

"For what?"

"Shh…" She cocked an ear, then turned on a dime and began to sprint back toward the barge we'd just left. I followed, confused. The feeling that I was being watched intensified as we sped away from the tugboat, and I checked over my shoulder.

Just for a moment, it looked as if someone was standing in the bridge window.

But that was pushed from my mind as I finally heard what Seraphine had. Knocking was coming from one of the containers to our left. Someone was trapped inside!

I skidded to a stop in front of the container doors and began to help Seraphine yank the bolt pin free. It was partially rusted and somewhat bent, but after several attempts we finally managed to remove the iron rod. I tossed it behind me.

"Ow!"

I whirled around to see Terrence standing there, his pizza spatula cradled in one arm as his left hand vigorously rubbed his shoulder. "You hit me!" he accused.

I pointed at him. "You were supposed to stay in the dinghy!"

"Y'all were taking too long," he whined. "And I kept hearing weird noises. When can we go back, Tristan? I don't like this."

"In a second. We just—"

Seraphine finally got the door to the container unstuck, and it creaked open with a loud squeal that made everyone flinch. I took a step forward, eager to see who we had rescued. Ayanna? Junior, maybe? That would make Anansi happy. Maybe some of the children Seraphine and her boss were searching for would be inside as well. We all rushed in...

And stopped.

"Empty?" Terrence said. "You did all this for nothing?"

Seraphine took another step, then paused, lifting her shoe to study something.

"You okay?" I asked.

She shook her head. "Fine. Just stepped in something sticky."

I paused. "What did you say?"

"I just stepped in something sticky, almost like..."

I closed my eyes in pain as a shout echoed in the container, high-pitched and very, very loud.

"Well, look what the sap dragged in!"

Three things are certain in life. Death, taxes (from what I've heard), and Gum Baby appearing when she's least expected, not needed, and silence is preferred. Gum Baby didn't do silence. At all. In fact, I was pretty sure Gum Baby only had two volume options—loud and obnoxiously loud.

Still, I had to fight back a smile when the tiny terror, master of the sapback, and self-proclaimed heroine of Alke, Gum N. B. Baby, emerged from the shadows of the cargo container and stood glaring up at us with her hands on her hips. She wore her trademark black turtleneck, black pants, and tiny shoes that I always bit my tongue to keep from calling doll-like. Had she drawn her version of the Chuck Taylor emblem on them? Wow. Anyway. Her hair was in cornrows that swept diagonally across her head and ended in braids that alternated between red, black, and green beads, and green, yellow, and red beads.

"Well?" Gum Baby demanded. "You all get a good look? Memorized Gum Baby's style? Good. Gum Baby's tired of all y'all dragging down her vibe. Maybe she'll rub off on your fashion sense. Especially you, Bumbletongue. Surprised you ain't in a hoodie. Don't your suit jackets have hoods, too? Glad to see you switch it up now and then."

I rolled my eyes and stepped back. "It's good to see you, too, Gum Baby."

The little loudmouth scrambled up to stand on my shoulder as she peered suspiciously at my family reunion T-shirt. "The things Gum Baby has to put up with to get the job done. Gum Baby once had her own boat in Alke, and now she's back where she started, on a Bumbletongue steed. And the one time she could've used one of your raggedy pouches, you fail her—again! How the mighty have fallen." And yet, even as she complained, she nestled down and looked around. "Well? Introduce Gum Baby! Stop being rude, thistle-head."

Seraphine, her eyes twinkling, dropped into a curtsy. "She already told me of the mighty Gum Baby. Bonjour, mon ami. It is a pleasure to meet you. My name is Seraphine."

Terrence, eyes wide, just waved at the talking doll.

"That's my cousin, Terrence," I said.

Gum Baby eyed him, then sniffed and nodded. "Gum Baby gonna have her work cut out for her if she gotta look after *two* Bumbletongues. But maybe she can sap out the bad habits in this younger one. You beyond saving, big head. Gum Baby just gotta live with it. She failed you."

Terrence snickered, and I cleared my throat. "Can we get back to business, please? Gum Baby, what are you doing here? There were supposed to be children. . . . Where'd they go? And where's Ayanna and Junior?"

Gum Baby shrugged. "The name is Gum Baby, not Gum Babysitter. Wasn't no kids on this boat, and Gum Baby been waiting here for a week. So, as usual, Gum Baby don't know what you talking about. She's got her mission, and that's it."

I growled something that I don't think I should repeat, but before I could continue to argue, Seraphine addressed Gum Baby. "Pardonnez-moi, but you say you are here on a mission? What were you waiting for?"

Gum Baby swept her braids back behind her shoulder. "Weeeeeell, since you asked so nicely, Gum Baby's setting a trap for a ghostie."

"A ghostie?"

She nodded. "Gum Baby's been following it for some time. Gum Baby almost had it, but it escaped. Ayanna and Spider-Boy are back upriver." Gum Baby looked worried all of a sudden. "Maybe. Everyone got separated after the ghostie attacked."

Terrence, who was shuffling his feet nervously behind me, peeked around and worked up the nerve to ask a question. "What does this ghostie look like?"

Gum Baby flashed an evil grin. "No one's ever seen it completely, because it's covered in a dirty, tattered cloak. But it glides around like a bat, and it shrieks like Bumbletongue did that one time he thought a wasp was chasing him."

"That wasp was huge!" I snapped.

Terrence bit his lip. "Does...does this ghostie walk on all fours sometimes?"

Gum Baby tilted her head as she thought. "Now that you mention it...Gum Baby doesn't know. Gum Baby don't keep manuals on terrifying creatures. Although..." She broke off and slid down to the deck, where she sat with her chin on a fist.

"That's really specific," I said to Terrence, pulling my gaze away from the tiny terror. "Why would you ask that?"

He pointed behind us, toward the tugboat. At first I couldn't see anything but shadows...until I looked up and saw a long, lanky creature scuttling down from the top of the wheelhouse like a monstrous crab. A shrieking cry that scraped at my bones filled the night.

"Because it's right there!" Terrence shouted.

4
CATCH A FIRE

I WANTED TO FIGHT.

The anger that had been simmering within me as of late was trying to bubble up to the surface. It was as if rage were flowing through my arteries instead of blood, fire was filling my lungs instead of oxygen, and at any given moment the two were going to mix and I would explode in a fury. It terrified me.

Not the potential loss of control.

No, I was terrified of how excited I was about releasing that rage.

"Come on!" I shouted at the creature, squeezing my fists. Four silver-black boxing gloves, with silver fire rippling around them, appeared in midair, two on either side of me. I scrambled up the ladder of the nearest container—a long orange metal box with stickers slapped all over it—and stood on the ridged top. Everything faded away—the lights of New Orleans's French Quarter across the river, the tugboat behind me, the past, and the future. It was just me and my opponent, and I could feel my anger taking over.

This was a haint! One of Cotton's minions. Something to be defeated, to be pummeled, to unleash my pent-up frustration on. Whatever its intent, it was going down tonight.

The monster dropped to the other end of the container with a violent *thud*, jostling the nearby barges and shaking the whole network. Slowly, it stood upright, until it towered over me on two twisted limbs that were wrapped with strips of the same material its cloak was made out of. The hood was pulled down low, so I couldn't see its face, but sibilant whispers emerged from within, like a chorus of snakes hungry for my defeat.

Well, I wasn't going anywhere.

I opened my mouth to shout at it again, but another voice cut me off. "YEAH, CHUMP, YOU REMEMBER GUM BABY? ROUND TWO, THISTLE-HEAD. COME GET SOME! THIS MOVIE IS RATED G FOR *GUM BABY*, SO COME SEE THESE HANDS!"

Gum Baby stood on my shoulder, her hands filled with sap, a scowl on her face. And you know what? I wasn't even mad. For once I agreed with the tiny terror's aggression. Let the creature learn that it chose the wrong ones to fight today.

The haint leaned forward and shrieked that same wordless

scream that Seraphine and I had heard on the other side of the river. So it hadn't been a child in pain—it was a lure. My teeth squeaked as I ground them together. All right, I was here now, and I wasn't leaving without a fight.

Another shriek, and this time I screamed back at it, my own wordless expression of rage. Gum Baby shouted a high-pitched challenge, too, and together we were louder than the monster could ever hope to be. The haint dropped to all fours and scuttled forward. I didn't wait for it to arrive—I lunged, bringing the pain with me.

We clashed in a maelstrom of fists and sap and claws.

The monster attacked with all four limbs, whirling and spinning, stabbing and swiping with lethal intent. It took all my boxing training to dodge the blows. I silently thanked Granddad for all of those drills he'd put me through, from forbidding me to use my hands to block attacks to forcing me to bob and weave at the end of every training session when I was drained and exhausted. Right now, they were the only things saving my life.

But I was attacking, too. The shadow gloves flashed in and out, jabs and straights, hooks and uppercuts. Gum Baby flipped from my left shoulder to my right and back again, hurling sap balls and insults with equal intensity. I dodged a slicing strike, slipped a bull rush, and turned and fired three punches at the back of the haint.

Thud! Thud! Thud!

It stumbled, but before I could celebrate, the monster spun around and sent an attack whipping toward my chest. I tried to duck its limbs, but they crashed into my shoulder and I went tumbling, barely staying on the top of the container. Gum Baby leaped off me and fired a barrage of sap at the creature before flipping backward, but she was a tad slow. Another attack clipped her, sending the tiny heroine rolling toward me. I managed to grab her before she fell off the side, and we stood together. The haint shrieked again. I was breathing heavily, and it barely looked winded.

It took a step forward, then jerked up short. One corner of its cloak had become stuck to the container surface. Gum Baby's barrage had found its mark. I smiled. "Yeah, now what, buddy? Your move."

The haint turned to examine the sap trap as it tried to pull free. The cloak strained, then slowly, loudly, it began to tear.

R-I-I-I-P.

The smile faded from my face as the creature revealed itself.

"What is that?" Gum Baby asked. "I thought it was a ghostie?"

"Seraphine!" I called, taking a step back. But she wasn't the one who responded.

"I know what it is!" Terrence shouted. He'd climbed halfway up the ladder and now peered over the top of the container. "It's a coffle!"

I glanced at him, then stared back at the monster. It was shaking itself, as if it had just shed its skin and felt renewed. It *did* have a head, just like none I'd ever seen before. Two long, wooden, bone-like structures protruded from the opposite sides of a loop, forming what looked like the skull of a hammerhead shark. Its body was a chain, and its four limbs were thorny, viny branches. With a loud *crack*, the branches snapped in two, then in two again, and so on, until sixteen crab-like legs made of splintered wood clattered on the metal cargo container top.

"A what?" I called over my shoulder.

"A coffle! I saw it on the plantation tour.... You know, the one you missed?"

"Terrence!"

"Sorry! They were used to fasten slaves together when they were marched from the house to the fields and back."

"Um..." Seraphine said from below. She crouched in the narrow alley formed by the containers behind us. She appeared to be setting up something on the deck of the barge, but I couldn't make out what it was. "Can you spare us the history lesson until we've escaped?"

I licked my lips as I faced the twisted wood-and-iron creature. There was no way I could dodge that many limbs. I'd be skewered. The first rule of fighting monsters (I had two): Choose your battleground carefully. Too open and you can get overwhelmed on all sides and end up sinking beneath a

47

swarm of opponents. John Henry taught me that when he and I defended the Thicket in MidPass from iron monsters. I'd forgotten to do that when I faced the Kulture Vulture in the mud outside the City of Lakes, and I'd nearly paid the price. I was determined never to make that mistake again, and seeing Seraphine working below gave me an idea.

"Go back down!" I shouted to Terrence. "Get between the containers. We'll lose it on the barges!" At least I hoped we would. The creature looked too big to be able to maneuver easily between the narrow corridors. And maybe, if we were lucky, it would fall between the barges and get swept away by the Mississippi.

Hey, you have to speak your dreams into existence.

And if somehow we turned the tables and got the jump on the monster, the akofena shadow gloves had all the firepower I needed to even the odds, sixteen serrated wooden limbs or no.

"Move it!" I shouted, and Gum Baby, who'd been rolling a ball of sap twice as large as her usual projectiles in her hands, jumped off the container and scampered away. I leaped down to the deck of the barge, caught my balance, and took off down an aisle. I heard the coffle's footsteps (Limbsteps? Branchsteps?) as it raced along the container tops. I risked a glance back and immediately regretted it. It sped forward like a cross between a scorpion and a crab, its legs jutting out at sharp angles, the remainder of the shredded cloak flapping in its wake like tattered streamers. The dark, knotted limbs reminded me of something, and when I realized what it was, my breath caught in my throat.

The Shamble Man.

My last opponent, one I'd failed to beat on my own. Right now, the Shamble Man, aka Bear, was on my grandparents' farm, recovering from the poison he had absorbed by wearing King Cotton's mask. I'd only been able to defeat the enraged bear with the help of several goddesses—Lady Night, Keelboat Annie, and Mami Wata—all of whom were keeping an eye on him back in Alabama.

Whoever or whatever *this* monster was, the coffle, it was something new.

Fine. It had been a while since I'd a chance to hit something.

Except I'd forgotten the second rule of fighting monsters. (Remember I said I had two? It's okay if you forgot, too. Happens to the best of us.) It is: As a hero, you're responsible for the crew you brought with you to the fight.

"Tristan!"

And as I skidded to a stop, I remembered too late the one person who couldn't defend himself.

The coffle stood over Terrence and shrieked.

Terrence was huddled in a ball on the deck of the barge tow. Only the narrow confines of the space had prevented him from immediately becoming a Strong kebab. The coffle hovered above, several sharp legs questing for the nine-year-old while the rest of them kept its body balanced as it straddled two containers. The monster raised one limb, ready to stab downward, when a large disc of sap slammed into the right side of its head. I turned to see Gum Baby prepping another sticky Frisbee by rolling a giant ball of sap and jumping on it to flatten it down. She then picked up the projectile with both hands, spun in a circle like an Olympic discus thrower, and hurled it at the haint.

The coffle shrieked as the sap disc crashed through three of its legs and it reeled backward. Gum Baby flapped a hand at me. "Don't just stand there, *do* something!"

I shook my head to snap myself out of my frozen funk, then looked around for an object to throw as well.

"Tristan, help!"

Terrence was now trapped behind a thicket of sharp wooden legs. . . . How was I supposed to free him? If only I'd had High John's ax, or John Henry's hammer . . . But de Conquer hadn't been seen since we fled Alke, and the hammer was the whole reason Alke had blown apart. It had probably shattered into a million pieces that were floating through a million dimensions.

Just then Terrence met my eyes, his own streaming tears as a monster he could have only conjured in his nightmares terrorized him in real life. My indecisiveness hardened into

anger, then fury, and then rage. I screamed a wordless challenge and rushed the coffle before my brain could convince
me that it was a horrible idea. I didn't care. Let whatever
might come, come. Never let it be said Tristan Strong waited
for a fight. Tell them I took the fight to my opponents.

SMASH!

I crashed into several of the haint's legs with a shoulder
charge, then stepped back and dropped into a crouch. With a
squeeze of my fists, the shadow gloves rippled into existence.
Except this time I couldn't stop squeezing. I was just so . . .
angry! I clenched my fists so hard that my nails dug into my
palms and I thought I might start bleeding.

The two sets of boxing gloves trembled. Slowly they
moved closer together on either side of me, the top pair
descending to meet the ascending bottom pair. When they
finally touched, they merged in a flash of shadow and black
flame. Now there were only two gloves instead of four, but
the silver fire that rippled along the outside of them began
to change. They grew darker and darker until they were a
glittering black blaze. The gloves flared up on either side
of me, framing my vision. A tunnel of fire. Good. That's
how I felt.

"Keep punching," I said through gritted teeth, and sent a
right hook whistling at the coffle.

The shadow gloves battered seven limbs aside. Even more
important, the coffle's wooden legs began to burn with black

fire. The creature took several steps back, but I continued to swing. Left. Right. Hook. Straight. I wanted to make it pay for what it had done. What it was doing. I heard faint shouts, but the outside world was far away. It was just me and the coffle. And only one of us was going to walk away from this.

Left jab. Left uppercut.

Every punch was a statement. My hands were doing the talking for me, and every word they spoke was the answer to an unasked question.

Bam! That was for the terror that Cotton and his minions, like the coffle, had inflicted on others.

Bam! That was for the pain and the suffering.

Bam! That was for the missing children we still hadn't found.

Bam! And that was for making me afraid again. The only way to suppress my fear was to swamp it with anger, so I hit and hit and hit and—

"Tristan?"

Terrence's voice finally slipped through to my ears. I looked up just in time to see the twisted chain torso of the coffle collapse to the ground in a charred pile. I stood there, my chest heaving and my hands on my knees as I tried to gulp down air. After a few seconds I looked around for everyone else.

Terrence sat in the middle of a circle of smoking splinters.

Gum Baby stood next to Seraphine, and both of them were watching me warily. My cousin didn't look at me at all.

"What's the matter?" I asked. I stepped forward, then paused when they flinched.

"Tristan—" Seraphine began, but Gum Baby cut her off.

"Turn off the fires, Burning Boy!" she shouted. "You gonna light up this whole place!"

Burning Boy? I stared at her, then looked down, confused. Sure enough, I was on fire. The black flames from the shadow gloves now covered my hands and wrists, even though the gloves themselves had disappeared when I unclenched my fists. And the flames were slowly rising up my arms.

"What do I do?" I asked, panicking. I'd never been on fire before. Wasn't it supposed to hurt? I couldn't feel a thing, but I still flailed my arms, trying to extinguish the blaze. Unfortunately, all that did was send black sparks to the barge deck, where, to my horror, they coalesced, turning into an inferno that I could definitely feel this time. It was like once the flames left my body they became real, and they were more dangerous than any I'd seen before.

The blaze spread rapidly. Seraphine scooped up Gum Baby and began to retreat. Terrence followed, his eyes wide and his pizza spatula clutched tight to his chest. No one looked at me as they ran past. I jogged after them, still confused and panicking because the flames on my arms wouldn't extinguish. And every time I brushed against something—a barge tie, a container wall, anything!—it caught fire. At this rate, I wouldn't be able to go back to the city. What if I set New Orleans on fire? And I couldn't get into the dinghy—it was made of wood! Maybe I'd just float on the Mississippi forever, doomed to remain in the water in case I—

"Watch out!"

Seraphine's scream brought me up short, and I skidded to a stop behind to the others, careful to remain a few feet away so I didn't burn them. Not that it mattered, because directly in front of us, like an angry zombie phoenix risen from the ashes, the coffle reared its ugly head.

The monster emerged from the flames shrieking a battle cry. Nearly all of its legs were gone, and it trembled on the three remaining ones like a twisted tripod. Its chain torso smoked, and one side of its restraint-head had burned away. Bits of singed cloak floated off over the water like ash as it clattered forward, desperate to get to us.

Flames blocked our retreat.

And a monster blocked our escape.

I raised my fists, then hesitated as flames continued to ripple up toward my elbows. But I had to fight ... didn't I?

The coffle shrieked again and lunged forward ...

... only to be knocked down by a giant wave. Somehow, the water missed the rest of us completely. Once it receded, a slim Black woman with long locs that drifted in the air behind her stepped onto the barge. She raised her hands and a second blast of water sent the coffle careening off the barge and down into the depths of the Mississippi. The woman watched it drown, then turned to fix a fierce glare on me.

"You," Mami Wata said, "are in big trouble."

5
LECTURES AND WARNINGSSS

THE WORST LECTURE I EVER SAT THROUGH HAPPENED TWO DAYS after my best friend died. I'd decided to skip English class. I don't remember actually making the choice—it was more a gradual realization that I didn't want to move from the stall in the boys' bathroom I'd locked myself in. I guess I was angry at the world and whoever had decided to put someone as funny and understanding as Eddie on the planet just to take him away. That was before I'd started therapy, before Mr. Richardson had taught me how to work through the feeling that everything was spiraling out of control, before he showed me the "Angry Octopus" technique, and before I even knew of a place called Alke. Back then it was just me and my anger.

I thought I would explode if I left that stall. So I didn't.

When Mrs. Flowers, the assistant principal, found me after school nearly two hours later, she took me to her office, where my mother was waiting. I thought Mom was gonna be furious, but instead there was disappointment in her eyes, which was ten times as bad. To make matters worse, she pulled out her phone, called Dad, and put him on speaker. Everyone in the office heard the lecture on responsibility and grief he gave me. I was mortified.

That was THE WORST scolding I can remember.

Until now.

"What were you thinking?" Mami Wata asked me.

It was the next evening. I'd slept through the remainder of the previous night and most of the day and still felt exhausted. Letting out that much anger, fighting with the new shadow gloves—it had taken its toll. Thankfully, the flames had disappeared once I calmed down. Now the only things burning were the questions everyone had.

We were gathered in a long, elegantly furnished ship's cabin with plush couches, fancy throw pillows (which, despite what their name implied, you weren't supposed to touch, let alone throw), and a small marble bathtub in the corner filled with bright jewel-like fish. Skylights opened to the starry night, and more fish flashed in glass aquariums built into the walls. I sat in a tall, polished wooden chair with a soft velvet pillow covered in with golden embroidery. Seriously, it was the fanciest room I'd ever been in, and I'd visited the houses of Dad's heavyweight-champion friends.

Then again, how would you expect a goddess to travel? In a water taxi? Don't be silly.

No, we were all aboard the *River Queen*, a gorgeous paddle steamship with mermaid carvings on the side of the hull. On any other day, I'd be thrilled to travel around in luxury like this.

"I don't think the boy was thinking at all," said a disappointed voice from a chair across the room.

Like I said, we were all aboard the steamship. Almost all of us. Seraphine had slipped away in the chaos, saying she already had one god to report to. I never did find out who that god was, but I envied her ability to escape. The *River Queen* currently carried Gum Baby, John Henry, Nyame, and Mami Wata . . . as well as every single member of the Strong family reunion. Most of my cousins, aunts, and uncles were downstairs, where a DJ who looked suspiciously like a boar in a tracksuit and bucket hat was playing all the latest hits.

Apparently, after Nana and Granddad received a message from Mami Wata to meet her at the boat, they had rushed to the banks of the Mississippi River with all the relatives in tow. (You can't say my family won't ride for one of their own.) Somehow Mami Wata managed to convince my cousins and aunts and uncles that they'd won a night aboard a luxury river yacht, and now they were living their best life. I could hear happy chatter and laughter filtering through the windows.

But a few Strongs were in the suite with me. Terrence,

who hadn't relinquished his death grip on the pizza spatula despite everyone's best efforts, shivered on a couch in the corner. Granddad sat beside him, one arm thrown over my cousin's shoulder, watching the proceedings. But it was the third Strong who had just spoken, and I looked over to meet my nana's eyes. She wasn't scowling, but she was nowhere near happy.

My grandmother shifted in her seat, the knitting in her lap untouched, and held my gaze. "What you did was foolish and dangerous. Dozens of people could've been hurt, Tristan. *Dozens.* Including your own family and friends. Why would you do something so reckless?"

"Not to mention nearly getting yourself killed." Anansi's voice was quiet, and yet the trickster god's words reached every ear in the room. Granddad had propped up the phone on a seat nearby, and Anansi sat on an app icon in the middle of the screen, his head bowed as he studied his hands. "You can't hurl yourself into battle after battle as if you're invincible, boy. Value your life. And the lives of those that follow you. Don't throw their sacrifices away."

He didn't say it outright, but I knew he was talking about Junior. Something had changed between Anansi and me ever since his son had stayed behind to battle Bear, sacrificing himself to give me and others a chance to escape. The spider god had become more withdrawn. Quieter. Less tricky, and that was perhaps most worrisome of all.

"Anansi—" I began to say, but Gum Baby cut me off. To my surprise, she did it in my defense.

"Before you adults with your big selves get to yelling at Bumbletongue too much, none of y'all came to help Gum Baby." The sticky doll (don't tell her I called her that) sat in her own chair, her tiny legs kicking in the air as she leaned against on the seat cushion behind her. "Gum Baby was in that container for a week. A *week*! Nothing to do but listen to the ghostie moan and wail and hiss about being stuck on the barge while the others got to have fun. Gum Baby tried to start a bee log, but she couldn't find any logs in the container, and bees don't like the river. How she supposed to get followers if ain't no bees on the river?"

She stopped to take a breath and looked around. Everyone in the room stared at her, confused.

I sighed. What did it say about me that I'd understood everything she'd just said? "She tried to start a *blog*."

Granddad, who was taking all this in stride way better than I ever would've expected, cleared his throat. "You sayin' she was doing one of them internet video diaries?"

"No, that's a *vlog*," John Henry boomed from his spot on the floor, arms folded behind his head. "Vee-log. Gum Baby's talking about a *blog*, short for *web log*." He lifted his shoulders when I looked at him in surprise. "Had to find something to do while I got my feet back under me. Started digging around the web."

Nana wrinkled her brow. "Ain't a web log the thing those space warp captains do at the beginning of each episode?"

This was getting out of hand. "Nana," I said, "that's a captain's log, from *Star Trek*. But that's besides the point. Gum Baby, what did you mean when you said the coffle complained about 'others'? What others?"

Gum Baby shrugged. "Gum Baby ain't take notes. All she knows is the ghostie kept hissing about orders from the boss and saying it wasn't fair. But what wasn't fair was Gum Baby having to come up with five or six content posts before even launching her bee log. Gum Baby ain't a planner! She's more of an off-the-cuff, spontaneous entertainer. So maybe bee-logging ain't for Gum Baby. Maybe a late-night talk show?"

At some point you just have to turn away and let her ramble on her own. I looked at Anansi, who'd gone still at the mention of a boss, and when I scanned the room, every one of the Alkeans was looking at me. There was only one person the boss could be, and technically he wasn't a person, he was a haint. It was time to come clean.

"Cotton," I said aloud, and the room darkened briefly as the lights flickered.

"That thing from the mask?" Mami Wata asked.

"The haint inside the Maafa?" John Henry said at the same time.

Gum Baby stopped kicking and shuddered. Out of

everyone in the room—in fact, out of everyone from Alke and this world—Gum Baby was the only one besides me who'd actually laid eyes on the king of haints himself.

I looked around the suite. "Yes. To both questions. But even more importantly, he's here. In New Orleans."

Everyone started talking at once. John Henry wanted to form a search party, while Nyame demanded a meeting with the leaders of the city to plan what to do next. Granddad wanted to go back to the hotel and negotiate a discounted rate for haint hazard, while Nana just sat there and knitted thoughtfully. Finally Mami Wata had to make a sharp gesture with her hands, and the lights flared bright turquoise for a moment. Everybody fell silent.

"Tristan," Mami Wata said, moving closer. "How do you know Cotton is here?"

I swallowed.

The image of the haint strolling through the French Quarter lingered at the forefront of my mind. I wasn't worried about myself so much, but about everyone else. I mean, some of the Alkeans weren't back up to full health yet. John Henry was still recovering from nearly disappearing after Bear attacked him with his own hammer. And then there was Nana and Granddad, and my other relatives. I only had to look at Terrence, still shivering on the couch, to know that I couldn't risk any of them getting hurt.

"Tristan?" Mami Wata prodded.

I shook my head. "Like Gum Baby said, the coffle said 'the boss' was nearby. And I thought I saw him in the French Quarter today. If we move quickly, we can—"

"We?" Nana looked up from her knitting. "Ain't no *we*, baby. You're staying put."

"But Cotton—" I started to protest.

"Isn't what you need to be worried about," Granddad said. "Listen to your grandmother. You've done enough. Let others help sometimes, boy. You can't do it all."

Nyame, standing at the window, nodded suddenly and turned around and addressed the other gods and goddesses. "The sun's completely set. If we are to act, the time is now."

Wait a minute. "Act?" I asked.

"You aren't the only one tracking the haint," Mami Wata said. "We've been keeping an eye out for nearly a week now. And if he's here, you're not safe. So, from now on, you will be confined to quarters. I took the liberty of arranging it with your grandparents while you were sleeping."

"What?" I looked at Granddad and Nana. They nodded.

Nana leaned forward. "Tristan, honey, this is serious. Your grandfather and I have been talking—"

Granddad placed a hand on her arm, then sighed. "We've been talking, boy, and I hate to say it, but it might be . . . safer if you rode up north with Mami Wata while we stay in the city a little longer for the reunion. And she's gonna watch over your phone for a while, too."

"That's not fair!" I said, almost shouting. They were essentially grounding me!

Nana stood and walked over. She patted me on the shoulder and said, "Dear, life isn't fair. But I want you to keep yours as long as possible, so I'm gonna put you out of harm's way until this all blows over. Mami Wata said you could have one of the cabins on the *River Queen*. You'll be traveling in style."

Nana stroked my cheek as Granddad followed Nyame and John Henry out, one of his arms draped around Terrence's shoulders. Then she headed for the door herself. "A little bit of Alke goes a long way, so just stay on the boat and relax. Focus on dealing with that anger inside you. Ain't no good gonna come until you do."

With that, she was out the door as well, following the rest of the Strongs and Alkean gods to the dock. And with no children rescued, my friends still missing, and Cotton somewhere out there, I was left alone with the horrible feeling that I'd let everyone down.

Well, not totally alone.

"So how can Gum Baby get her own paddleboat?" The miniature messy marauder had scrambled up to one of the windows and was peering out at the steamship's giant paddle. It splashed and churned through the water as the vessel slowly beat against the strong current, just trying to stay in place.

Gum Baby continued to lay out reasons she deserved her own steamship and the extensive list of names she would give it (*Gumming Around the Mountain*, the HMS *Gum Baby*, and her personal favorite, *Sun's Out, Gum's Out*), but I couldn't focus.

Grounded! How could they ground me? I was only doing my job. You know, trying to catch a haint and save the free world as we knew it. Far be it from me to try to keep everyone safe. I shook my head and folded my arms across my chest. Grounded. *Pfft.* Fine, whatever. At least I wouldn't have to participate in the annual Strong family karaoke contest. In fact—

SPLASH!

When I looked up, the window was empty. "Gum Baby?" I called.

Nothing.

I got up and walked over, grumbling the whole time. "Seriously, if this is another one of your sap experiments gone wrong, like the sap balloons, or the sap traps you hid in my brand new Grape 5s that one time, I'm gonna tell Nyame who's been drinking his sun tea. And you *know* how possessive he gets about that."

I looked up into the rafters of the cabin. You never knew with Gum Baby. Sometimes she liked to drop down on me from the ceiling like a bull rider into the chute and shout *Go, Bumbly Steed!* while kicking her heels. No joke.

But she wasn't there.

"I'm not playing. Gum Baby?" I reached the window and leaned out cautiously, peering upward first. She could be on the deck above, ready to pounce on me. But the only thing I saw was the night sky, the moon partially hidden by a bank of clouds. I pursed my lips, then looked down and froze before slowly backing away, my pulse racing and my mouth dry.

A giant snake, black as the night outside, eyes bright yellow with emerald-green pupils, slithered through the window and into the suite. It moved in shallow curves, winding from side to side around the chairs and the room's support pillars. Its head was the size of my own, and even before all of its body was inside, it lifted its front several feet off the floor and stared me in the eyes.

"Sssalutationsss, mortal. Another of the Lady'sss straysss, hmm?" Its tongue flicked out every other word, tasting the air and creeping me out at the same time. Not because I haven't seen a snake do that before, but, you know, because *it was talking to me!* It had a drawl, too, I noticed. A low, humming twang with a lot of bass in the voice.

I retreated even farther into the room, looking for an escape.

"What'sss the matter, boy?" the snake said. "Cat sssnake got your tongue?"

My fists began to squeeze. I wanted to call forth the shadow gloves to defend myself, to punch the snake back out the window in a blaze of flames.

Flames.

The image of the black fire creeping up my arm flashed in front of my eyes, and my fingers uncurled. No. Terrence's look of terror after I'd pulverized the coffle still haunted me. And Cotton's words lingered in the back of my head. *You know this ain't over, right?*

The snake cocked its head as it swayed from side to side. "Wait...I know you. Yesss, you're the boy all the ssspiritsss are in such a tizzy about. The ssstoryteller. A modern-day bayou griot, they sssay. Trissstan, am I right?" My name lingered in the air as the snake slithered closer. "Well, then, ss-since the boss isssn't here, you'll have to deliver the messsage to her, ssstoryteller."

"A snake," I finally said. You'd think, after a summer of discovering a whole world filled with magic, folk heroes, and my own ability to interact with both, I'd be prepared for anything, but somehow I just never thought a giant snake was in the cards for me.

"Sssorry?"

"A snake," I repeated. "I'm talking to a snake. Is that... Am I supposed to be doing that?"

The giant reptile let out a long exasperated hiss and shook its head from side to side. "Sssee, thisss isss what I'm talking about. One of my cousssinsss makesss it to the big ssscreen and sssuddenly all talking sssnakesss are evil. I tried to tell him not all represssentation is good represssentation, you know?"

I nodded along, not sure what to do other than keep it talking.

"But I digresss.... You must passs the messsage to the bosss, understand?"

"What message?" My voice croaked. The snake nearly filled the room now, and it still wasn't completely inside yet. More and more of it coiled inside through the window, and a bead of sweat rolled down my forehead and dropped to the ground.

"Normally I'd follow protocol and ssspeak only to the bosss, but desssperate timesss and all that." The snake eyed me up and down. "Desssperate indeed."

"Hey!"

"Relax, boy, jussst a joke. Heroes are so tesssty thessse daysss. Not like before. But sssince you're here and Maman de l'Eau isssn't, sssit up and pay attention."

Maman de l'Eau? Oh, it meant *Mami Wata*.

"Boy!"

When a forty-foot-plus giant snake shouts at you, you sit up straight and salute. "Yesss! I mean, yes, what's the message?"

The snake flicked its tongue at me in annoyance. "The messsage is thisss: The watersss around Old Angola don't feel right anymore. There's a foulnesss in the currentsss, and the sssspiritsss in the area are growing ressstlesss. They're getting angry."

I shook my head, confused. "Angola? As in Africa? Is this about iron monsters again? And what do you mean the spirits are getting angry?"

"Lisssten, ssstoryteller! Now isss the time for hearing and not ssspeaking. Maman de l'Eau will undersssstand, but only if you tell her exactly what I sssay. Tell her the ssspiritsss are angry! Sssomething ssstirsss in Angola. Sssomething long ago buried. The water reeksss of fear and the fish avoid the deep, ssstill partsss of the river. Even the birdsss no longer fly overhead. Mark my wordsss, ssstoryteller, listen to the warning of Yemonja! All the godsss will fall if the evil in Angola risesss!"

The final hiss didn't fade but grew in volume until it filled the cabin and forced me to cover my ears. The giant snake lunged, and I just managed to hurl myself out of the way, banging my head on something sharp behind me. An explosion of lights bloomed in front of my eyes. A blur of scales zoomed overhead as the full length of the snake curled around the room, the tail lashing into couches and armchairs, before it shot out the window into the night. One moment the reptile seemed to fill the entire space, and the next the room was empty and black as my eyes fluttered shut.

Only the final part of its warning lingered, though I couldn't tell if it was an echo or just in my head.

All the godsss will fall if the evil in Angola risesss.

6

MORTAR OVER BONES

I KNEW I WAS DREAMING WHEN EDDIE SHOWED UP.

My dead best friend entered the cabin and sat in one of the chairs. He didn't look at me. Didn't speak. Still wore the same Malcolm X T-shirt and the same thick-framed glasses. I stood up and walked over, a giant lump in my throat. The last time I'd seen him, Eddie and I were in the bowels of the Maafa, the ancient sentient slave ship that had once terrorized Alke, and he'd said I could never speak to him again. And as I waved at him and tried to get his attention now, I guessed that was true, because he didn't once look in my direction.

At some point, while I was focused on Eddie, more people appeared in the room. They didn't walk through the door or climb through the window like the giant snake. They just . . . materialized. One minute it was just me; the next, every seat in the suite was occupied. By folks I knew.

An elder ancestor spirit from Isihlangu was in the front, a talking skull in his lap. Two small bears sat next to a wrinkled woman, and when she turned to hush one of them, I inhaled sharply. It was my great-aunt Denise, Nana's sister, who had died recently. In fact, everyone at the Strong reunion had just celebrated her life earlier in the week. I remembered her wide smile from the picture, and now she was turning it on...were those Bear's cubs?

A sharp caw sent me whirling around in shock. Old Familiar, the shadow crow of Alke, ruffled his wings in the back of the cabin, where the giant bird took up the entire wall. Unlike everyone else, who was ignoring me, Old Familiar cocked his head and stared at me before cawing again and stabbing his beak toward the person speaking in the front of the room. When I turned to look, I recognized the man.

High John the Conqueror.

He was in the middle of a lecture. Of course. Only I would dream about a lesson during my last few days of summer vacation.

"All right, everyone," he said. "Let's pick up where we left off. The buried narratives. Finding the stories within the story, the ones that exist in the white space. The blanks on the pages...what do they frame?"

Suddenly he turned to me, and though I could still hear him addressing the ghosts in the room, High John's voice crashed like a tidal wave into my skull.

"What do you see, boy?" he asked.

I shook my head. I didn't have an answer.

"What do you see?" he asked again. This time he turned to the window, staring out at the cityscape. In my dream it was still nighttime, but now I could see a bright light casting a glare into the suite.

"What do you see?" High John asked a third time, and then he turned back to his spectral students.

I glanced around. None of the spirits paid me any attention. I turned back to Eddie, who had a pen and notebook in hand and was scrawling away furiously. I grinned and peeked at his paper. Sure enough, he was doing what he'd done back when he was alive, when we'd shared six out of seven classes.

He was doodling.

Somehow, that bit of memory gave me confidence. I went over to the window. Outside, the French Quarter shone. Like, I couldn't make out individual buildings, or people, or anything. It was a single smear of yellow-orange light. Almost . . . almost golden.

I inhaled. The light was a beacon.

When I turned around, High John stared at me again as the rest of the class faded away. He smiled. "What do you see?"

Before I could answer, he walked off, disappearing through the wall.

Eddie was the only spirit remaining in the room. He slid

his notebook into his backpack and tucked his pen into his shirt pocket, like he'd always done at school, and then stood and walked past me.

"Eddie?" I knew he wouldn't answer, but I couldn't help it. He never acknowledged me, though.

CAW!

Old Familiar stretched his wings at the back of the room, turned his beak, and fixed one large golden eye on me. He cocked his head, as if asking a question and waiting on an answer.

I nodded. "I know what I have to do."

Old Familiar ruffled his feathers and hopped. With two flaps he was airborne, each wing touching a wall in the suite, and the giant shadow crow flew straight at me. I didn't move. I just shut my eyes.

When my eyes fluttered open, thunder boomed. I sat up and winced. The back of my head ached where it had slammed into the floor when I dodged the giant snake. But High John's words lingered, and I shoved myself upright. I ran over to the window and leaned out into the night. From here New Orleans appeared like it should on a summer evening. Vibrant. The French Quarter practically hummed with energy as the sounds of music and cheer reverberated across the water.

What do you see?

My adinkra bracelet hung on my right arm. I reached for it now, avoiding the akofena and instead grabbing the sky god's charm, Gye Nyame. With this gift I could see the stories that made up the world and the people in it. I began to close my eyes, but something weird happened.

The power activated on its own, before I summoned it. Like the akofena's fire back on the barge.

"What is going on?" I whispered. But when I raised my eyes, that mystery faded, because New Orleans lay written before me.

I saw stories—written in French and Spanish and Chitimacha and English—about the birth of jazz and the death of neighborhoods. I saw tales of the Fon and the Ewe and the Igbo, and legends of Vodun and Vodou and the spirits within. Languages I didn't recognize formed words that I did, all spiraling up Canal Street and Peters Street and Chartres Street, avenues paved with the history of the city.

But there were other stories, too, hidden behind that history. I could see them like faint pencil marks not quite erased. As I squinted, the words shivered and grew brighter, until eventually they outshone everything that had been scrawled on top of them.

I read about the slave ports that had dotted the Mississippi River.

I read about rice, and sugar, and the crops raised on plantations in the city.

I read about people treated as cargo.

I read about the glamorous buildings that had been built around the sale of men, women, girls, and boys like me. Some older, some younger. My eyes followed the flowing script of a Fon mother's lullaby as she was separated from her children in one of those buildings. I read the history and saw that the structure had been torn down decades before I was born, and now a glitzy hotel stood in its place. The hotel where some of the Strong family members were currently staying.

Mortar over bones.

Finally, I read about the barges that had hauled the shackled enslaved north, up the river, to a giant plantation. A free man's protests were scrawled in the grass of Artillery Park, where he'd been kidnapped and sold back into slavery. A family's prayers were carved into the pillars lining the docks along the Mississippi, where they'd been separated, never to see each other again. These were the hidden narratives High John had been talking about. This is what he had meant.

I blinked and the sky god's power faded away. My view returned to normal, and New Orleans reappeared as a modern city teeming with nightlife. I frowned. There was more to the construction of my world than I'd realized.

My eyes slid across the waterfront as I sighed. Cryptic instructions from gods and their messengers were going to be the death of me. I watched a tugboat push a barge up the river in the darkness, and my eyes narrowed. It was the same barge we'd fought the coffle on. The memory of the shadow gloves setting everything on fire stabbed through me again, and I took a deep breath.

What do you see?

All the godsss will fail if the evil in Angola risesss.

I froze. Cotton had come here for something. What if it had something to do with the snake's warning? And what if—

My vision blurred, then sharpened. I stumbled and managed to grab the windowsill before I fell. What was happening? The spirit bead? But I hadn't activated it.

As soon as I looked back out the window, the question answered itself.

The barge was crammed end to end with spirits. Boys and girls. Mothers and fathers. People of all ages and—by the look of the clothes they wore—from all different eras huddled together, and the reason stalked into view seconds later.

Coffles, several of them, towered over the spirits. Some stood in the middle of the barge like slave drivers while others skittered around the edges like overseers. Movement caught my eye and my chest tightened as I saw more spirits waiting on the riverbanks in the shadows, lines of them trapped between the coffles and the water.

They hauled the enslaved up north, to a giant plantation.

I turned to look for Gum Baby, who'd never reappeared. That was starting to worry me. I reached for the SBP in my pocket, then remembered it had been confiscated. I made a sour face. Being grounded really interfered with saving the world. But maybe it was for the best. What would they say? Gum Baby, Anansi, John Henry, or Granddad, or even Nana . . . What would their advice be if I tried to alert them? *Leave it to the adults! Don't rush in! Stay put and keep your head down!*

And you know what? For ten seconds I did exactly that.

Until *another* coffle crawled out of the river and began to scuttle through the shadows into the city. This one headed south. The others had gone north. They were cordoning off the French Quarter! Everyone inside it, including my relatives and the Alkean gods, would be trapped. Whatever Cotton was planning, I had to stop it—now.

7

WHEN THE HAINTS...
COME MARCHING IN

A SHROUD LAY OVER THE FRENCH QUARTER. NO ONE COULD SEE IT
but me. And as I sprinted up Canal Street and slipped through
the crowds on Bourbon Street, I wanted to keep it that way.
Music played and tourists danced. The smell of treats both
sweet and savory wafted up one street and down another.
Bright neon lights indicated bars I wasn't allowed to enter
while inside grown-ups laughed and shouted and ignored the
state of the world for a few minutes. In other words, everything seemed normal.

But I knew better.

Under the street music, I could hear a drumbeat. Low and
steady. The kind that played when Alkean magic was nearby.
The kind that warned me to keep my eyes open. I could see
a shimmer in the air throughout the Quarter, a sheen that

drifted over certain spots. Something was about to happen, and I only had a few minutes to find my family and my friends from Alke before everything exploded.

"Hey there, big man, where you going in such a hurry?"

That voice.

My feet stopped by themselves, and my heart skipped a beat. That voice haunted my dreams. Or my nightmares. I slowly turned around on the sidewalk, hoping against hope that it was my imagination. I was just hearing things . . . right?

A man sat at a small round table on an outdoor patio. He wore a plain white linen suit, white penny loafers, and his stringy white hair was neatly combed and swept down to hide the entire right side of his pale face. Thin black sunglasses perched on the end of his nose, and one sharp eye peered over them at me.

And yet everything about him was wrong. Evil oozed off him like heat haze above asphalt on a summer day. I took a step forward, my fists clenched and the need to summon the shadow gloves singing in my blood.

"Cotton," I squeezed out through gritted teeth.

The last time I'd seen the haint this close was in the bowels of the Maafa. Gum Baby had been by my side, and together we'd driven the orchestrator of the iron-monster terror into the bottom of the Burning Sea. And yet here he was, sipping an espresso as calm as you please.

"Ah, ah, ah," the disguised haint said as I closed in. He smiled, wide and humorless. "Better watch those hands. Wouldn't want to set this lovely historic area on fire, would we? No, I thought not. Not after you torched the barge and nearly burned your cousin." Cotton took a sip of thick black liquid—was that even coffee?—and set down the cup. "How is little Terrence, by the way? Still terrified of you?"

My fingers trembled. I wanted to leap across the table. That's what Cotton did to you. He got under your skin. Picked at weaknesses that hadn't scarred over yet and poked your most vulnerable places. Cotton was a bully, and everyone knows how aggravating bullies are. And his followers threatened the entire district we stood in. So I kept my cool. I had to figure out what he wanted, then find my family and escape.

"What do you want?" I finally managed to ask.

"Oh, you know." He sat back and let his fingers walk along the railing separating the two of us. His nails were long and sharp, and discolored on the undersides. They moved like the coffles, and I shuddered. "I want it all, baby boy. I want the stars and the moon. Shoot your shot, they say, and I'm shooting." He flashed his smile again. His teeth were pointed and stained, too.

"You sound like a cheesy fitness instructor," I said.

Cotton's smile faded. "Always with the jokes, boy. Well, tell me if you think this is funny."

He reached inside his jacket. I flinched, and he smirked at my fear. He pulled out a closed fist and then, finger by finger, revealed what he held and set it on the table. I stared at the object, my jaw dropping. It was a smooth, perfectly circular black stone with gold flecks. One of Junior's.

This was the second time someone had produced one of his throwing stones. Where *was* Junior? Did Anansi know his son might be in the vicinity? I almost let a grin cross my face as I imagined how the skinny son of Alke would react when I saved him.

But the urge to smile disappeared. This could be a trick. . . .

"Now I heard you know somebody who can sling these things like nobody's business," Cotton said. "Is that right?"

I didn't answer. My eyes remained fixated on the stone. Was Junior okay? Was Ayanna with him? Where were they?

"Well, it just so happens I met me a boy, right around your age as I think about it, and he could clip the wings off a fly with one of these things. I know because he showed me."

"Junior would never talk to someone like you!" I shouted. Several nearby pedestrians glanced at me, then moved away. I tried to swallow the rage that threatened to consume me again, and I forced my hands flat against my thighs.

"I know . . ." Cotton repeated, leaning in closer and lowering his voice, "because I *made* him show me."

The words lingered in the air between us for several seconds before the haint relaxed and spread both arms wide in a placating gesture. "Now, please, please, don't get all worked up. I haven't hurt the boy—yet. But that's only because I'm a kindhearted gentleman, and I need you to do me a favor."

"What?"

"I need your expertise, your ability to find magic in the world and tell its story. Do what you do best—tell me a tale. Tell me about them gods that traveled over here with you. Tell me the ins and outs of your world, who's in power, who's hungry for change. Tell me how to shoot to the top, and I'll be sure to take you with me. I got me a way, but it's too... too violent. Ain't no need for all that. You and me can knock this out easy." Cotton looked me square in the eyes, and all traces of humor evaporated as the soulless haint's glare burrowed deep into me. "You promise to do that for me, and I'll help you find your friends."

The world stilled around me. "You want me to snitch."

"Aw, don't call it that." Cotton leaned back in his chair and picked at his teeth. "You make it sound so dirty. People been trading information for advantage for centuries. Money is cool, but information is power. A tip here, a hint there... You and me can make moves all the way to the bank. The only thing I want you to do is tell me something good. Can I count on you, big man?"

He nudged the throwing stone toward me, one sharp finger tapping it slowly. And to be truthful, I considered it. For a brief second, I hesitated. I wanted to find my friends. They were in a strange new world because of me. I had a responsibility to show them how to move through a society where people could see them but couldn't perceive the magic that was in them, where people would dress them in their expectations and nothing more. The unfamiliar could get lost here, and once you dropped out of view in this world, it was *out of sight, out of mind.* The only people who could save you were the ones who knew you were there.

I knew my friends were near here. Ayanna. Junior. Thandiwe. I just had to find them.

But I saw how Cotton was handling that stone. Though he was offering it to me, his clawlike finger remained in control of it. And any offer Cotton made would be the same— it would allow him to get his hooks into me. The requests would be small at first—information here, a timeline there. But over time his demands would grow. I could see it in the haint's face. Greed lurked behind his sunglasses.

"No," I said.

The finger stopped tapping the stone. "Excuse me?"

Time slowed. Pedestrians streamed around me, laughing, nodding their heads to one of the many rhythms intersecting in the Quarter. Bourbon Street funneled them deeper inside, where they would try to find whatever it was they were looking for that evening. Food. Drinks. A good time. But I was looking for something, too, and I'd finally figured out that Cotton would never give it to me, not that easily. Which meant all he was doing right now was stalling.

I backed up. The haint stood. "What do you mean, no?" he snarled. "I'm giving you a lifeline, boy. Grab it before you drown. Grab it before I turn this world upside down and all of it dogpiles on your chest. Grab it now!"

I spun around, squeezing the spirit bead on my bracelet. The world went dim as I searched up and down the block for ghosts, spirits, and everything in between. Nothing. They were all gone. Taken to the barges.

I kicked myself mentally. I'd been so preoccupied with Cotton, just as he'd intended, that I'd lost sight of my primary goals—finding my family and alerting the gods.

When I turned back to Cotton, I stumbled backward in shock. The spirit bead revealed his true appearance, and the horrible image was seared into my brain. I let go of the bead, but the picture remained. Why were my powers so unpredictable all of a sudden? I didn't want to look at him, but I was afraid that if I looked away, he'd attack.

Vines crept in and out of his sleeves and the cuffs of his pants, and his eyes, no longer behind sunglasses, smoked at the corners. His hair was lank and matted, snarling on thorns that poked out of his face and neck. He grinned, and I turned away in revulsion at just how long his teeth really were. When I looked back, he was folding his napkin and dabbing at the corner of his mouth, but his gaze never left me. I watched him warily.

So when he lunged forward, I slipped to the side, leaving him grasping at air.

Cotton laughed. "I had to try once, boy. Can't blame a haint for that."

My fists clenched, and black flames began to ripple in the air. But Cotton didn't move. Instead, he pulled out a rusty pocket watch, checked the time, and sighed. "Time's up, boy," he said simply. "I gave you a chance. Now, we can have it out right here, or..."

I gritted my teeth as the flames grew. People were starting to look at me strangely, though others laughed and pointed, as if I was just a part of the Bourbon Street spectacle. "Or what?"

Screams cut into the night. At the far end of the street, just past some jugglers, a coffle sprang into the crowd.

"Or you can go and save a few worthless lives. Your choice."

Cotton turned and began to walk down the street in the opposite direction, slipping between gawking pedestrians as he whistled a tune. I started after him, but the crowd pressed toward me, eager to see what was happening. I forced my fists to unclench, trying to make the flames disappear. I couldn't let them touch anyone! It felt like it took forever, but the fire finally petered out and I dashed forward, hopping to keep an eye on Cotton. In order to reach him, I'd have to squeeze past a group of women linked arm in arm. . . . I might've made it if a familiar shriek hadn't split the air.

I could just see Cotton's hat lift as he saluted me. With a growl of frustration, I turned around and raced toward the screams.

8
THE KIDS ARE ALL RIGHT...
FOR NOW

IN BOXING, WE CALL MULTIPLE PUNCHES THROWN IN QUICK
succession a *combination*, or *combo* for short. Boxers use them
to string together attacks, target weaknesses, and overwhelm opponents. Combos are cool to watch, and when
you're in the ring and you pull one off successfully, it's pretty
sweet. The Walter Strong special, my granddad's favorite
combo, is the one-two punch—a quick jab followed by a
straight. He likes to say the other boxers never knew what
hit them.

We all could have learned a thing or two from the coffles.

The monsters attacked with lightning speed, from different angles, and never in the same pattern twice. Three
of them towered above the fleeing crowd. They slashed
and sliced, sending the tourists scattering throughout the
French Quarter. The night filled with screams as I fought

my way through the crowds. No one knew which direction to run—people dashed out of bars before clumping together in intersections of tight alleys and narrow streets. I managed to shimmy through a cluster of panicked college students before finally bursting into a clear space . . . only to realize a coffle stood there.

Because of course. The monster was between me and the riverfront. A few of the college students gawked at it and held up their phones, unsure whether it was an attraction or a threat, and I shook my head. Some people have no sense. But their impending horror-movie failure was the least of my concerns.

The twisted wooden creature shrieked, and the other two appeared at its side.

"Oh, great!" I shouted, throwing up my hands. As if the night couldn't get any worse.

The trio cut and slashed their way forward, and finally— finally!—the college students scattered. Two of the coffles dashed after them, on the left and right. They didn't allow anyone past, cutting off escape routes with vicious stabs of their front limbs, while the third coffle scuttled through the crowd with its pincer heads threatening to clamp around the necks of stragglers too slow to get out of its way. The coffles were working as a team. Looking for someone. And it appeared that they found him or her, because suddenly all three converged on something I couldn't see.

I had to take action.

"Hey!" I shouted at the coffles, sidestepping a man and woman who were racing past me. "HEY! Over here."

I waved both arms and then bent down to pick up a half-full cup someone had left on the curb. I hurled it at the nearest creature.

"That was my drink!" someone protested.

I rolled my eyes. "Sorry!"

The cup smacked the lead coffle upside the head, and the creature pivoted to look at me.

"That's right!" I shouted. "This way! I took down your brother or cousin or nephew-in-law earlier. You wanna test me, too? Come on! I'm right here."

I had to get the three of them to follow me. Maybe I could lead them away from the crowd and back to Artillery Park. Or to the plaza in front of the St. Louis Cathedral. I'd sprint as fast as I could back to Congo Square if I had to. Anyplace other than the packed streets of the Quarter.

There was only one problem—the monsters weren't paying me any attention.

The three coffles towered over a tiny duplex that was wedged between a souvenir shop and a walk-up gumbo stand. I snuck closer to get a better view, hiding behind a pickup truck parked across the street. The monsters were trying to use their sharp, splintered limbs to tear down a wooden barricade blocking the doorway to the lower apartment. Several kids leaned out the second-floor window, hurling rocks, bricks, and insults at the intruders.

"Your arms too short to box with the gods!"

"Better get your weight up!"

"I've lit matches bigger than you!"

I don't know if the coffles understood how badly they were being roasted, but they certainly didn't appreciate the kids raining down projectiles. The monsters screeched in triumph when one of the barricade's boards finally ripped free, and some of the insults stopped as a few of the kids looked concerned. I frowned. They couldn't have been much older than me—in fact, several looked to be younger, around Terrence's age.

SNAP!

A second board cracked, and the coffles began to slash through the gap. Screams came from inside. I glanced to my left—the creatures still weren't paying any attention to me, and I could probably sneak away now and go find my family and friends. But then I turned back to the cornered kids and swallowed hard. I couldn't just leave them....

I started to clench my fists, then hesitated. Could I risk using the shadow gloves? No, I...I couldn't. My previous rage still scared me, and Cotton's smirking laugh lingered in the back of my mind. I looked around, then grabbed a section of pipe lying in the gutter next to me. Sometimes you have to do things the old-fashioned way.

CRUNCH!

The first the coffles knew I was attacking them was when

the leftmost monster went down in a heap. The pipe wasn't as devastating as the shadow gloves, but it worked just fine on the creatures' spindly legs.

I swung again and again, trying to take out the coffle before it could rise. The monster wriggled and writhed on the ground, and I had to hop and dodge its flailing limbs or my legs would've been ripped to shreds.

"Hey, look!" The shout came from above my head. I couldn't check to see who it was, because a second coffle now stalked me, scuttling sideways around its still-writhing partner while a continuous, low keen came from its serrated mouth. It edged to my right, then moved even closer.

"Watch out!"

This time I *did* look, and thank goodness for that.

"Sweet peaches!" I said, diving beneath a swing from the third coffle, who'd crept up on my left and tried to ambush me. Now I had two monsters hemming me in, and try as I might, I couldn't escape. They didn't fall for my feints, and their multiple long legs could pin me to the ground if I got too close. I scrambled to my feet and licked my lips, trying to find a way out. I couldn't lose like this, not to a pair of wooden crab monsters.

The coffle on my left lunged. I parried the attack with the pipe, then ducked a swipe from the monster on my right. A burning sensation ripped across my forearm, causing me to yelp and drop my weapon. I tried to retrieve it with my other arm, but the third coffle had somehow managed to rise up, and it now staggered forward, just within reach. The monsters shrieked, and I took a deep, shuddering breath.

My wrists burst into silver flame.

I couldn't avoid it anymore. The tension in my shoulders and the fear in my chest and the overwhelming feeling that this was the end of Tristan Strong sent churning waves of anger rippling through me, and I began to ball my hands into fists.

"Hey, in here!"

A voice shouted at me from behind the broken slat barrier. Hands gripped my shirt and pulled me into the opening in the doorway just as one of the coffles slashed at the spot where I'd been standing. I stumbled into darkness. I turned, ready to swing at whoever—or whatever—had clutched at me, only to see a kid with her hands in the air. A young Black girl in a wheelchair, her hair in pigtails and her eyes wide.

"Sorry!" she said, backing up quickly. "But we need to get out of here. That barricade won't hold for long and— Hey, are you on fire?"

No sooner had the words left her mouth than the second-to-last board splintered beneath the stabbing attack of a coffle. I fell on my butt and scrambled backward. All I could see of the monsters were their legs as they patrolled back and forth in front of the entrance, too large to enter but still sending occasional slicing probes through the doorway.

The streetlamps cast shadows across the sidewalk outside. Screams echoed in the distance, but from what I could tell, this particular area was now free of tourists. At least my distraction maneuver had accomplished that much.

I shot up to my feet. The silver flames on my wrists had disappeared, thank goodness. But when I peered outside, something else stopped me in my tracks. Beyond the coffles, across the street, by the very pickup truck I'd hidden behind, stood a tall figure. I couldn't tell if it was a man or a woman, but it was definitely an adult, and they were clothed in all gray from head to toe. They wore what looked like a slasher-movie hockey mask over their face—also gray, with a solid red line drawn diagonally from the right eye to the left side of their chin. Their eyeholes were pools of black.

The girl in the wheelchair tugged on my arm. "Come on, this way!"

"Okay," I said, nodding. I moved to follow her. After a second I looked back out the door.

The masked figure in gray remained motionless, but I could feel their eyes following me into the dark.

The kid ("Jessica, but my friends call me Jess.") led me through a dark hallway, up a ramp, and through a second-floor door into an abandoned kitchen. She kept up a steady conversation as we moved through the shadows and stopped at the far wall.

"It's a good thing I found you. You looked like you were ready to give up. I've seen it before. Those things never quit. I had one chase me for thirty minutes before Memphis finally helped me."

"Memphis..." I repeated dully, my mind on figuring out how I was going to get back to the *River Queen* and warn my family and the gods.

"Yeah, Memphis. You'll see. They can help you."

"They?"

Jess nodded. "Memphis is nonbinary."

"Got it."

After some preparations, Jess slid aside a stained curtain hanging from a doorway to reveal a rooftop terrace. The building next door, separated by an alley, had a similar outdoor patio. The space between the two roofs was narrow enough that it could be spanned by a couple pieces of lumber. Jess rolled across them without any hesitation, spinning around after reaching the adjacent house and beckoning me to follow. I gulped and tried not to think about falling down to the alley that was probably covered in *delightful* offerings the tourists had so *thoughtfully* left behind.

I managed to tightrope-walk across without losing either my balance or my lunch, and Jess led me over a few more makeshift bridges before bringing me to an outdoor elevator that led to the top of a nondescript brick building. It was a store, currently closed, and we traveled up to the top to discover several homemade tents and multiple worn sleeping bags scattered across the roof. A lean-to shelter made of old plywood and a plastic tarp had been propped up against an HVAC ventilation fan. A few kids lay inside, but Jess waved me away from them and hurried over to the edge of the roof, where a pair of binoculars rested on a brick ledge that came up to my knees.

The whole time she'd been leading me, Jess had kept up a steady stream of one-sided conversation. I mean, she talked about everything. The coffles. The Quarter. The moon. It reminded me of my cousin Terrence and how once he latched on to a subject he wouldn't let it go until he'd exhausted all possible topics surrounding it. I chuckled, and then the humor died away. I hoped he was okay. I hoped *everyone* had made it out of danger safely. It was torture not having my phone with me. I'd gladly deal with a sulking Anansi if it meant I could have a few reassuring words from someone that everything was going to be fine.

"So, this is our lookout," Jess was saying. "It's how we spotted you."

I shook my thoughts away. "Lookout?"

"Yep. We try to keep an eye out for other kids and get to them before the monsters do."

"You mean the coffles?" I asked.

Jess picked up the binoculars and glanced at me with her eyebrows raised. "Is that what they're called? I'll have to tell

Memphis. We've been trying to figure out what they are for the last few weeks."

Her words hit me like a bucket of ice water. "Weeks? This has been going on for *weeks*? Why haven't I heard about it? Why hasn't anyone been talking about it?"

Jess shrugged. "You don't sound like you're from around here. Nobody ever talks about kids gone missing. Or if they do, it's a few words, a picture, and then on to the next headline."

I thought about the tourists at the restaurants, talking and eating as the news played in the background. And Seraphine had mentioned missing kids, too. Where was the uproar? The search parties? Could this somehow be connected to the coffles loading spirits onto the barges? And speaking of...

"So," I said, sort of in a daze, "what about the coffles? I saw some people recording them on their phones. Why isn't the internet blowing up about them?"

Jess sighed in frustration. "I don't know. Memphis was asking the same thing. In fact, the whole reason they went out today was to get pictures of the—you called them coffles?—so we can try to get them trending. Get more people to pay attention. But Memphis has been gone for over an hour now.... I was going to go look for them when the coffles saw me."

A sharp whistle rang from the streets below, cutting off whatever response I might've had. Jess brightened and grabbed the binoculars. "That's Memphis!" Another set of whistles rang out, and her face fell. "They're in trouble. Come on!"

We dashed to the opposite edge of the roof, where Jess leaned dangerously over the ledge, straining to look for something in the glare of the Quarter's bright lights. After a few seconds she stabbed downward with her finger. "There!"

A flashlight blinked, the beam shooting up into the night before it turned off. Jess mumbled to herself, keeping her finger raised as she tried to work something out, then she suddenly spun her wheelchair around and zoomed over to the elevator.

"Come on!" she shouted back at me. "We gotta help!"

I followed her. "Help what? And how? I need to get back to the river."

"I've never been that far," Jess said, rolling across one patio bridge and over to the next. "But Memphis can take you! If there's anyplace you need to go without anyone noticing, Memphis'll get you there. But we gotta help them first, or we ain't going anywhere. Ever."

I stifled a comment, then scrambled after her. All right, I'd save one more person. Then I'd get back to the boat before anyone noticed I'd been gone. Find Gum Baby. Let Mami Wata know about Cotton and the snake's warning. Maybe by now Nyame or John Henry or one of the other Alkeans would have news about Ayanna and Junior and Thandiwe.

The thought of being reunited with my friends burned bright in my head, and I latched on to it. Yeah, maybe there would be news.

Jess led me across patio after patio before we rushed up a ramp to another rooftop. The space was empty save for four piles of bricks, rocks, and a couple broken tree branches at each corner. She rolled to the northeast corner and let out a trio of piercing whistles. This time I caught the flashlight beam as it speared the night before turning off. Memphis was close, real close. Jess nodded to the pile of debris as she locked the brakes on her wheels. "Get ready. When I say so, help me push all this into the alley."

I peeked over the edge. "Are you sure?"

She didn't answer. Instead, she began to count down. "Three. Two. One. Push, push!"

She shoved against the massive pile, and, after a second of indecision, I joined her. Slowly, noisily, the bricks and rocks began to shift, before they tumbled over the edge in a deluge of dust and grit. An ear-piercing shriek cut the night, and my heart leaped into my throat. What had I done? Was someone injured? I remembered Granddad once telling me about a hotel that had collapsed in the Quarter and the devastation it had caused. I leaned over the ledge, horrified at what I might find, only to see several twitching wooden legs sticking out from the rubble.

A coffle. We'd taken out a coffle. The relief sweeping through my body made my knees tremble.

"There!"

Jess pointed down the alley where a kid with a cloak (a *cloak*?) was just turning a corner. We rushed to the other side of the roof, and Jess glided down a homemade ramp that led into the open second-floor window of an empty apartment. We went out the back door, across another patio ramp-bridge, and then into a house similar to the one where we'd started. Jess stopped me at the back door, peeking outside as she opened it just enough to allow in a sliver of light.

Suddenly she whipped it open all the way, and the kid dove inside. Jess shoved the door shut, then locked it and motioned for me to grab one end of a heavy wooden table. We managed to slide it in front of the door just in time.

Something jiggled the doorknob.

We held our breath as a shadow stepped into the light seeping through the crack under the door. The knob jiggled again, then once more. My heart thudded in my chest, and I was sure whoever it was would kick down the door and drag us all out. In that instant, hiding in the dark with two other kids I'd never met and shared nothing in common with other than the very real fear of being taken away, I knew that if I moved—if I even breathed—it was over.

After what seemed like an eternity, a voice spoke outside

the door. "Yes, ma'am. No sign of them. No, ma'am. Yes, ma'am. On my way."

The shadow disappeared, and the sound of footsteps faded.

We all exhaled. Jess and I exchanged a shaky smile, and then she hurried to help her friend.

"Memphis, are you— What are you doing?" she asked.

I turned to find a large kid, eyes narrowed, sticking a phone screen in my face. It was showing a news feed, and scrawled across the top in big bold letters was a headline that felt like a punch to the gut.

RIOTERS IN THE FRENCH QUARTER, it read. Underneath was a picture of me hurling a cup full of liquid, a look of raw anger on my face.

The hand dropped and the phone disappeared inside the cloak.

"Tristan Strong," Memphis said. "Bet it seems like everyone's been looking for you."

Memphis Jones stood a full head taller than anyone else in the room, and the bright royal-blue cloak they wore made them seem twice as wide. With golden-brown skin, hooded eyes that revealed nothing as they sized you up, and a curly ponytail with clean-shaven sides, their presence engulfed us all. Everyone seemed to take their cues from them, and the energy visibly picked up as Memphis walked around, checked on the younger children, and nodded while the others relayed tidbits of info.

There were a dozen of us or so back in what Jess called "the Hideout"—the rooftop refuge with the lean-to and the kids napping inside. Several beanbag chairs had been dragged into the middle of the roof, and someone produced mismatched novelty cups from the Quarter and passed around a cool jug of lemonade. If not for the events of the evening, it could have been a fun and relaxing get-together. Instead, it was a war party.

"I don't understand," I said for the fifth time. I held Memphis's phone in both hands, my elbows on my knees as I leaned forward and stared at my picture. "Where are the coffles? Did no one get a picture of them?"

Memphis winced and dropped into a chair across from me. We both waved good-bye to Jess as she began to lead a few of the younger kids down into the house, and then Memphis cradled their shoulder, moving it in slow circles while shaking their head. "You're asking the wrong question." Their voice was low, almost raspy, as if they were suffering from a cold. "The real question is, who took the photo?"

I shrugged. "Probably one of the college students drinking nearby."

"You sure? Look at the picture."

I studied the phone, and once again I wished I had the SBP with me. Anansi's advice would have been really useful at that moment. But I didn't, so I tried to think like he would. I zoomed in, rotated it, and pursed my lips. Then...

"Wait." I looked up. "They got a clear shot of my face. Which means whoever took the photo was in front of me... near the coffles."

Memphis nodded. "That person wasn't worried about the monsters.... They were worried about *you*. So," they said, reclining in the beanbag, "seems like you got a few enemies, Tristan Strong. Some look like you and me, and some look like they hopped straight out of a horror movie."

I narrowed my eyes. "For someone who just outran giant sentient prisoner restraints, you don't seem that fazed. Why?"

Memphis stared at me, their face screwed up in thought, hands fiddling with the ends of their cloak. "'The eye sees only what the mind is prepared to comprehend.'"

"What?"

"It's a quote I read once. Basically, people will try their hardest to ignore something that doesn't fit in with their reality." Memphis stood and beckoned me to follow. "Everybody in this place has seen some wild stuff. Scary stuff. Stuff that makes you angry, stuff that makes you cry. That monster—a coffle, you called it? It ain't nothin' but a Tuesday afternoon around here. But for those whose life fits neatly inside the rules, if they see it, they'll pretend they didn't."

"So... like sweeping it under a rug?" That was one of Nana's favorite expressions. It's when you hide something and pretend nothing happened. I tried it once. Literally. Used a broom to gather up a giant pile of dirt and leaves and swept it under one of her hallway rugs. I don't know what I did wrong, because as soon as Nana came into the hallway she saw the rug sticking up like a camel's hump. Adults need better sayings.

Memphis snorted. "Something like that."

We descended into the house, climbing over barricades of furniture and pushing aside an overturned desk to reveal a hidden door. Memphis put a hand on the doorknob, then paused.

"Look, I want you to know one thing. Those kids up there? They're family. I treat them like they're my blood. And I'm not gonna let anything put them in danger. I do what I do because no one else can, and it needs to be done. Kids like that, someone sees them on the street trying to hustle up food and they're liable to call the police on them, and that's the last thing they need. They need help, not a record. Once they get into the system, there's no getting out. That's why I do what I do."

"I understand," I said, but Memphis shook their head.

"Nah, I don't think you do. You know the risks. So do I. But those kids upstairs ain't like you or me. I can handle myself, but I was two seconds from being skewered and dragged off to who knows where. What's going to happen when I'm not here and one of them goes outside and the monsters attack? Or when them new folks, the ones with the masks, start yanking us off the streets? We need help, man. If you got a way to stop these things, you've got to show me how."

"The masks?" I echoed.

They didn't answer. Instead, their gaze fell to my adinkra bracelet.

My heart dropped. They were looking at my magic charms. I slowly shook my head. "I'm sorry, but..."

Memphis sucked their teeth and turned away.

"They're not something I can share like that," I said. "Believe me, if I could pass on the powers, I would."

"Yeah, I get it." Memphis studied the door for a second, then looked back at me. "We're on our own. I just heard you were different."

I folded my arms across my chest and stared at the shadows playing across the ceiling. "Sorry to disappoint you. Somebody told you wrong."

Memphis nodded and opened the door, flicking the light switch and then standing aside. "I guess she did."

I looked at them curiously, then peered inside the room, only to let out a strangled gasp as I took in the girl sitting in a chair. She was surveying several younger children who were sleeping on a pile of blankets on the floor. Her left leg had a bandage on it, her right arm cradled a gold-painted baseball bat, and there were several shards of what appeared to be the remains of a coffle in the corner of the room. The girl lifted her head and made a shushing gesture.

"You can have five minutes," Memphis said, folding their arms and leaning against the doorframe. "And then she's gotta rest. You should get some sleep, too. She said y'all needed to leave for the river ASAP, but you're gonna have to wait till dawn. Too dangerous to go before then."

I nodded, but words didn't come as I dropped to the ground next to the injured girl, her golden bangles twinkling in the dim light.

"About time you showed up," Ayanna whispered.

9

THE FERRYMAN'S WARNING

NOTHING MOVED IN THE FRENCH QUARTER. SHUTTERED WINDOWS and locked doors were the only witnesses to our passage as Memphis, Ayanna, and I descended from the rooftop refuge at dawn. We carefully removed the debris that blocked the entrance, then replaced it once we were outside, disguising the Hideout as an abandoned duplex. It felt wrong. I wanted to advertise the fact that there were children trying to survive inside. Where was the help? The GoFundMes and the shared PayPal accounts to give them a leg up? Could we Kickstart a system that would come to their rescue? As I'd been doing a lot lately, I bit back my frustration and pushed it deep down. I would carry their stories if no one else would. Besides, I had enough to worry about.

"You're sure my grandparents told us to go back?" I asked. My voice carried in the silent morning, and I winced at how loud it seemed.

Ayanna nodded, grimacing a little bit. "Yes."

"But they actually said that? Nana didn't want me to come find her?"

She sighed. "You keep asking me, and it's not going to change. Your grandmother specifically told me to tell you to take your hard-headed behind back to Mami Wata. I don't know how she knew you'd be here, but then again I don't know how your grandmother does a lot of things. Runs in the family I guess."

I muttered something rude under my breath and Ayanna elbowed me, and it felt good to sort of be back to normal. Well, except for the fact she was hurt, I hadn't warned or rescued anyone like I'd intended, and there were more vulnerable people in the world than I realized. Another successful mission. Not.

We stepped into the day and got smacked by the humidity, even at that early hour. Memphis swept ahead of us, their cloak trailing behind them as they stalked down the street. Putting our differences aside, I appreciated their offer to get us to the riverboat. I knew what leaving those younger children behind, even temporarily, must've felt like. Memphis had given them a home, someplace where they felt safe and secure, with others just like them.

I chewed my lip and stared at my adinkra bracelet. Memphis wanted me to share the power the Alkean gods had granted me. But how? And what if something went wrong?

No, the best way I could help was to find Cotton and put an end to his schemes. Stop him, stop the coffles, and stop the weird masked people. That's what I had to focus on.

Fog rolled through the alleys and side streets, a lone straggler from the previous night's festivities. It was the perfect cover, which we really needed since Ayanna's injured leg prevented her from moving too fast. She limped beside me as Memphis led us through alley after alley, her face growing more and more troubled as I caught her up on what had happened to me.

"A giant snake told you to warn Mami Wata, and you tried to, but King Cotton appeared at a restaurant?" Ayanna shook her head. "So in other words, just a normal Tristan Strong day."

I rolled my eyes. "Har-har, good one, high five. What about you? How did you end up with Memphis in New Orleans?"

"I got sloppy," she said, embarrassed. "Junior and I got split up about a week ago. We were trying to find Gum Baby, who—how do you deal with her?—had decided to chase after a monster that attacked us."

"I deal with her reluctantly," I muttered, and Ayanna elbowed me. "But we found her."

"Gum Baby?"

I nodded. "Locked in a barge container on the Mississippi. She said she'd been chasing a 'ghostie.' Turned out she meant a coffle."

Ayanna pursed her lips. "Right. Junior and I ran into a

trap. Specifically, we ran into two or three of those coffle creatures. I tried to hold them off so we could get away, but one of them got too close and almost took a chunk out of me. To escape, I had to jump into the river." Her face grew pale as she lost herself in the memory, and I placed a hand on her arm. She inhaled, then smiled and looked at me. "I was in the water for hours, or at least that's how it felt. Every time I tried to come ashore, those things were waiting for me. Finally I managed to climb aboard an empty barge. As soon as the coast was clear, I swam to shore. There I ran into Memphis trying to keep coffles off the younger kids, and then you showed up."

"She washed up onto the bank upriver," Memphis said without turning around.

"Near a dog park," Ayanna muttered.

Memphis laughed. "Three showers later, she still smelled like a labradoodle. But that ain't all. Show him what we found the other day."

Ayanna reached into her back pocket and pulled out a piece of gray plastic. She handed it to me and shuddered, as if she hated even the feel of it. I grabbed it, then paused. Pressed my lips tight together. I'd seen it before. Last night, on the person across the street from the Hideout.

It was a hockey mask with a red slash across it.

Just as Jess had promised, Memphis escorted us through the tiny streets and back alleys of the French Quarter without our so much as hearing another soul. We tiptoed toward the river as the rest of the city slept. If Memphis was still upset about my unwillingness to share my powers, they didn't show it. Instead, they whispered jokes and gave us an unofficial tour of the city, pointing out spots where odd jobs could be performed, where food could be acquired, and where a sidewalk grate might warm someone on a cold night.

When we reached the edge of the Mississippi, I got an idea. I still had Seraphine's contact information in my pocket, and I passed it to Memphis. "She's sort of like me," I said. Then, waving toward Ayanna, I corrected myself. "Like both of us. Seraphine's got friends in high places. She said one of them cares for the children no one else sees, so maybe she can help you. . . ."

Memphis seemed startled, then nodded. They clutched the slip of paper like it was an unexpected allowance. The phone number wasn't an adinkra. It didn't automatically ensure better days in the future, but it was something. I had to do something. Too many were doing nothing.

No one stopped us on our short trip to the *River Queen*. Ayanna and I borrowed another dinghy—this one with a motor—and managed to pilot our way across the still morning waters without incident. We scrambled aboard, sent the tiny boat back toward land, then tiptoed into the sleeping cabins.

There was an empty one across the hall from mine that Ayanna could settle into. For a second I tried to think up an excuse I could offer as an alibi for my disappearance, since it was now morning and I'd been gone for the whole night. But I'd brought back Ayanna. Whatever punishment Mami Wata wanted to add onto my grounding, it would be worth it. I sighed, then turned to find the others. Might as well get it over with. The sooner I got yelled at for leaving, the sooner I could let everyone know about Cotton, the coffles, and the snake's warning.

But just then Ayanna smiled at me and pulled me into a hug.

"What was that for?" I asked.

"For being you. Stubborn and thickheaded, and more than wrong on a few occasions..."

"Uh...thanks?"

"...but you're always there for your friends. And...well, thank you."

I shrugged, trying to think of something cool to say, but my opportunity was ruined by a loud voice.

"Why is Bumbletongue blushing?" Gum Baby asked as she trotted down the hall. She carried the SBP in both hands like I might carry a stack of books too tall for me to manage. Every time she took a step forward, she staggered to the right or the left, doing her best not to drop the phone. Where had she come from, and how had she gotten her sticky hands on it?

"I'm not blushing," I said, blushing furiously.

Gum Baby leaned in close, studied me, then shrugged. "Gum Baby can't help you until you're ready to help yourself."

"What?"

"Gum Baby knows what you want! It's clear. You and Ayanna, you have a special relationship. You want to carry her things, open doors for her, drive her around, wear a shiny hat and suit and—"

"That sounds like a chauffeur," I interrupted.

"Isn't that what you want to be?" Gum Baby looked back and forth between Ayanna (who wasn't helping *at all*, just smothering a laugh with the crook of her elbow) and me.

"No!" I shouted.

"Oh." Gum Baby looked me up and down again, then offered the SBP, a faint look of disapproval on her face. "You don't want to carry things?"

I growled something unintelligible and grabbed the phone. She sighed and turned back to Ayanna.

"Sure don't carry your *own* weight," she muttered, then patted Ayanna's good leg. "Gum Baby should've known, seeing how she had to drag his dusty suitcases into his room earlier. Some people. C'mon, Gum Baby needs to have a talk with you. Alone. No boys out loud."

"You mean *allowed*?" I called after her as they entered the other cabin.

"No, out loud!" Gum Baby said, starting to close the door.

I shook my head, then glanced down at the SBP. Anansi

was on the screen, but he hadn't said anything this whole time. The trickster god was studying the Maps app, trying to locate more alerts. I watched him for a minute or so, not wanting to break his concentration. I hadn't seen him smile in weeks, not since we'd returned from Alke and Junior went missing. I couldn't even remember the last time he'd tried to be sneaky.

It was concerning.

"Anansi, are you—"

"Busy," he grunted.

"What?"

"I'm busy. Trying to find our people." He didn't look at me as he enlarged a cross section of the Mississippi River and the cities along it, but I felt the accusation in his words.

"I'm trying, too," I said. "I found Ayanna!"

Anansi snorted. "Of course."

"What's that supposed to mean?"

He exited out of the Maps app and whirled around to face me. "It means you didn't *find* her—you stumbled upon her while kicking dust around out there. It means there are hundreds of others waiting to be rescued, but of course you find the girl who..." He trailed off and stomped up the side of the screen to a web in the corner.

"The girl who what?" I asked, getting angry now. "What're you trying to say?"

He didn't answer.

"Anansi?"

"Did you find any clues about Junior?" His voice was quiet, his arm slung over his eyes as the web hammock swayed back and forth.

I thought back to Cotton and the black-and-gold stone he had offered as proof. And what Ayanna had said about her and Junior getting separated. "Yes, but—"

"But there was something you felt was more important, right?"

There was no good answer to that question. I opened my mouth, closed it, then tried to pick my way through the verbal land mines. "Not *more* important, but if I didn't—"

"If you didn't do something, something only you were capable of doing... danger, calamity, catastrophe, right?" Anansi lifted his arm and looked at me. Exhaustion lined his face, and he waved an arm toward the stairs behind me. "Well, you're in luck, because you're needed once more. Mami Wata's waiting for you up on deck. Maybe freshen up before seeing her—show at least one god some respect."

I tried to explain one more time. "Anansi—"

"Just leave the phone in the room, boy. You're not supposed to have it, and I need to rest."

I sighed. The screen turned off and I stood there staring at my reflection in the Alkean glass. That could've gone better. I dropped the phone on the bed in my suite, waited one more second for a joke, a smile, a wink that never came, then quickly grabbed some new clothes and went to change. I'd come back and talk to Anansi later, right after I delivered the warning.

And maybe after all this was done, I could guard the mermaid carvings or something. Can't lose a friend if they're fastened to the wall.

The *River Queen* churned upriver as I climbed onto the deck. I stopped for a few seconds to watch the opposite bank go by in a blur. It was impressive, really. Not sure what I expected, seeing as the only other riverboat I'd ridden on had been Keelboat Annie's, but a vessel that moved like a Lamborghini wasn't at the top of the list.

Someone cleared their throat. Mami Wata was waiting for me with her arms crossed. She wore a navy dress that swirled around her ankles even when she wasn't moving. Silver earrings dangled from her ears, and her hair was piled in an elegant flourish atop her head, a blue-and-silver head wrap keeping it steady. The deck of the *River Queen* gleamed in the sun, banishing all shadows for the foreseeable future, but the goddess's furious expression could've spawned thunderclouds. I took a deep breath and walked up to her. Let the lecture come—it was what I deserved.

But she surprised me.

"We need your help" was all she said before turning and marching to the opposite end of the steamship, calling out commands to the vessel as she went. I followed, confused. She led me down a service ladder that barely skirted the massive paddle wheel and onto a platform that seemed to float just above the water. Occasionally the Mississippi would rise in a soft splash against the worn wood, as if saying hello. There, Mami Wata stood with her arms folded and eyes closed. Waiting, I realized. On me?

I shuffled my feet. "Um, I know I was supposed to be grounded and—"

Her hand rose sharply, cutting off my words. Mami Wata's eyes were closed and her face cocked to the side. She was listening to something, or so I thought. But when she spoke, I realized she was listening to *someone.*

"He's here," she said.

I looked around. "Who's here?"

She didn't answer. Instead, her hand fell in a helpless sort of gesture. "The boy means well, but he's stubborn. Are you sure you want to . . ." Her voice trailed off, and she remained still. Listening again, I guessed. I was at a loss and also concerned that I was eavesdropping. Maybe it was time for me to mosey on back up the ladder and finish being grounded.

"Okay," I said. "I'm just going to—"

Mami Wata's hand reached out and closed around my

wrist like a vise. Her eyes flashed and she nodded at the white-capped river behind the churning paddle. "He's ready to talk to you."

I glanced behind her, then cleared my throat. "Who?"

She sighed. "Use the powers given to you, Tristan. I can sense the request but not the content. You must speak with him. And quickly. We need to know what has transpired up ahead—I do not wish to enter the situation ill-informed."

I glanced from the river to her, and back to the river. Then it clicked. There was a spirit nearby. *That's* who she was talking to, and who apparently wanted to talk to me now. I grinned. "Oh! Of course."

She nodded and began to climb back up the ladder. "Remember, it must be quick."

"Okay, I will. Let me just . . ." I reached for the Isihlangu spirit bead.

"Can you hear me?" a trembling voice asked.

The words cut through the paddle's splashing and the *River Queen's* creaking. I paused. My fingers hadn't even touched the spirit bead yet. I licked my lips nervously, then glanced up.

A man stood on the deck of a small, dilapidated river ferry that was floating right next to us. The boat looked like the next swell of the Mississippi would split it into water-logged pieces of lumber. The man wore an old, beat-up boater hat and a pair of suspenders that were failing at the one job required of them.

And I could see right through him.

He took off his hat, squinted upriver, then turned back. "Can you hear me?" he repeated.

"Yes," I said after swallowing a couple times. Why did this keep happening to me? I wasn't touching the spirit bead, and yet I could see the ferryman clear as day. "Yes, I can hear you."

"Good," he said. "'Cause you don't have much time. Turn this boat around and get out of here. You don't know what you're doing. You don't walk up to a door and enter Angola. More likely than not, you end up on Angola land without even realizing it. The air just feels different. Angry. Old. It ain't like them steel-and-glass buildings in the comics or the movies, neither. No sir, the sun sits right on your neck as do your time down in Old Angola.

"Don't get me wrong, now, there was some bad men in there. Did some awful things. Terrible things. But you know what? Bad men are still men, you understand? Still men. You don't lock up a man for thirty years with nothing but his shadow and the kiss of cool concrete as his companions. You don't send a man out to pick cotton by hand, eighteen hours out of the day, no matter the weather. There's a lot of broken souls littered around Old Angola.

"So you be careful. The spirits is angry. Angry! They anchored to the place that leashed them and broke them, and it's gonna take more than a shiny promise to get them to move on."

The fear in his warning pierced through the questions I wanted to ask. He looked at his hat as if surprised to see it off his head, then wrung it like a rag as he stared nervously upriver again. What could frighten a spirit? He was already dead.... Nothing could hurt him. Right?

"So..." I tried to digest what he was saying. Angola? The country in Africa?

"Just turn around," he begged. "It won't let us go. We already stuck here, doing the best we can, and now it wants more and more and won't let us remember the little bit of our lives we got left. It's eating everything and won't let us go!"

Mami Wata's voice carried down to me. "Tristan! Should we keep going?"

The spirit trembled, repeating his last words over and over. "Won't let us go. Won't let us go..."

"Tristan?"

I began to tell her to turn the *River Queen* around when the spirit looked at me. "He won't let us go."

He?

"Who?" I asked. "Cotton? Is it a haint? Is he the one who's scaring you? Tell me where he is. I can take care of him." The words poured out of me, fierce and full of determination. But the spirit didn't notice. He and his ferry just faded away slowly as he repeated the warning over and over.

"Won't let us go..."

Mami Wata peered down over the edge at me. "Tristan, did you hear me?"

I stared at the spot where the ferryman had disappeared, then shook myself. His instruction to turn around couldn't have been clearer.

But Cotton.

"Keep going!" I finally shouted back up. Mami Wata's lips pressed together into a thin line, but she nodded and the paddle wheel groaned as it began to churn faster. I chewed the inside of my cheek, trying and failing to ignore the flutter of worry at the bottom of my stomach even as I turned toward the ladder. "We have to keep going."

I climbed to the top deck, still deep in thought. Why was the spirit so scared of a place called Angola? And why did the ferryman think I was someone it needed to warn? Did he have me confused with some relative? I mulled over the thought for a moment, then dismissed it. I could worry about that later. Right now I had to figure out what Cotton was up to in the area and put a stop to the haint's designs.

"Oof!"

I'd bumped into Mami Wata. "Sorry, I was distracted. Have you seen Ayanna? I brought her here and..."

My words slipped away. Mami Wata hadn't even acknowledged me. She stood near the edge of the *River Queen,* both hands gripping the wooden guardrail as her nails gouged the surface. The goddess's teeth were clenched and her eyes firmly shut as her whole body trembled with effort.

"Mami Wata?" I asked slowly. "What's wrong?"

Her eyes fluttered open, and I took a step back from the twin pools of swirling gray staring back at me, just as Ayanna shouted something from the front of the boat.

"Everything," Mami Wata said.

The steamship rounded the bend, and the tree-lined riverbank gave way to tangled weeds and brown grass. The sun sat heavily on my shoulders and forced me to squint to see what was up ahead. At first I struggled to identify it—a sprawling landscape with whitewashed buildings collected inside an industrial fence. But if the guards on horseback didn't give it away, the line of people chained together in the distance quickly brought me up to speed.

"A prison," I said faintly. "Angola is a prison."

10
ANGOLA

WHAT WOULD COTTON WANT FROM A PRISON?

"Tristan?"

Ayanna moved up beside me. She held the SBP in her right hand, extended so the screen faced Angola. "Anansi said he felt something and wanted to come up and look," she said. "Do you think the prison guards will try to stop us? Are we allowed to get this close?"

The *River Queen* felt whatever it was, too. Several of the wooden mermaid carvings above the waterline glared or grimaced and shifted to the opposite side of the steamship, as if shielding themselves from the aura permeating everything.

"I think..." I said after studying the prison for a few moments, "the guards assume we're something else. 'The eye sees only what the mind is prepared to comprehend.' Just a ferry passing through."

"You might be right, my boy," Anansi said. "We should keep it that way."

I looked down at the phone. Ayanna handed it over, and I flipped it to see Anansi chewing on his lip. "There's something real dangerous in these parts. It's making all six of my legs itch. I think the farther we get from this place, the better. What do you think, Wata?"

Mami Wata had moved up alongside us, and though her eyes had gone back to their normal color, the tension hadn't drained out of her body. She studied the prison, then nodded. "I agree. We cannot stay here. The water, it... it cries."

I clenched my fists, then forced myself to uncurl each finger one at a time, until I was sure I could speak without my voice trembling. "No. Both the snake and the ferryman mentioned Angola. Cotton has to be here."

"Leave Cotton to your elders, boy," Anansi snapped. He took a deep breath, then tried again. "We've delayed the search for the missing Alkeans long enough. And something in the area is interfering with the phone's alerts. We have to move on."

I looked at Mami Wata. She nodded. "If we linger here, I fear we'll draw the wrong attention. The current is fighting me most strongly, as if desperate to hold us in place."

Ayanna placed a hand on my shoulder. When I looked at her, her apologetic expression sent my already low morale even lower. "Maybe they're right."

"Gum Baby ain't scared," the tiny doll muttered as she climbed up into my hoodie. "But she's a team player, so if y'all wanna leave..."

Everyone looked at me. I turned and stared out over the water. Were they right? Could I have misheard the snake? Could the warning have been a red herring placed by Cotton to keep us off the trail of his real objectives? I just didn't know anymore.

"Fine," I said. "I don't see anything, so maybe..."

Wait....Was that it?

"Tristan?" Ayanna called my name and gave me a little shove. "You all right? You spaced out there for a minute."

"I can't see anything," I repeated.

"Yes, we know."

"No, I don't think you do." I turned to Mami Wata. "You *feel* something, don't you? You said it was the currents trying to keep you in place. Wouldn't currents try to wash us back downriver?"

Mami Wata frowned. "Yes, but—"

I whirled around, forgetting that Gum Baby was still in my hood and nearly tipping her out. Ignoring her threats, I focused on the river ahead of us. I closed my eyes and squeezed the Isihlangu spirit bead. Then I opened them again.

My breath whooshed out of my lungs as if someone had just sucker punched me.

"Tristan?"

It couldn't be. It wasn't possible.

"Tristan!" Ayanna was next to me, grabbing me by the shoulders. Gum Baby smacked me across the face a couple of times to snap me out of the daze, but the real jolt was what loomed high in the sky around the prison.

Water splashed onto my face. Mami Wata stood over me, another wave of river water dangling threateningly in midair. The goddess eyed me. "What is it?"

My mouth opened and closed. How could I help the others see it?

The eye sees only what the mind is prepared to comprehend.

That was it. I had to show everyone what I saw, as if they were looking through my eyes. Maybe I could do it with the spirit bead. I grabbed Ayanna's hand, stuffed Gum Baby back into my hood, and took Mami Wata's hand as well.

"What—" Ayanna began.

"Trust me," I said.

She wrinkled her brow but didn't say anything more. I took a deep breath and closed my eyes. I needed to link us. Form a connection between the four of us (yes, I was including Gum Baby) that held tighter than any chain or coffle ever could. I thought of Alke and the magic we all possessed, granted by the land that was destroyed but we all still carried in our hearts.

See what I see, I implored.

I opened my eyes.

Ayanna gasped, her hand squeezing mine in shock. Mami Wata frowned in concentration as she surveyed what lay across the river. And Gum Baby?

"Now, Gum Baby knows that violates all sorts of zoning regulations." The little doll stood on my shoulder with her hands on her hips, a pair of fake eyeglasses having appeared suddenly on the top of her head. "Gum Baby needs to start issuing some citations."

A monstrous, nearly see-through house was superimposed over the prison.

Its columns propped up a warped, slanted roof, and swirling gray pools of smoke replaced the windows. A sagging second-floor balcony nearly obscured the main entrance, where bloodred brick stairs led to double doors of splintered bone, like the tongue of some wild, ravenous beast running along its teeth.

As I realized what this meant, I felt sick to my stomach. Beyond angry. Helpless. All at the same time. The house I was seeing was Old Angola, a long-gone plantation. Angola the prison had been built on the very same spot.

This is what Mami Wata's snake had been trying to warn me about. And the spirit of the ferry. Both had said that the dead were furious.

The spectral plantation was still haunting the land, devouring any and all nearby spirits. Bright trails of smoke coiled out of every door and window, every crack and seam. They wiggled through the air like tentacles, some questing for prey, others dragging victims inside. I couldn't hear the spirits' screams, but the looks on the faces of those who disappeared into the maw of the house would be seared into my brain forever.

And, I saw too late, several long tendrils had wrapped themselves around the *River Queen*.

Trapped.

The single word flitted through the inside of my head like a bird in a cage. We were stuck in the middle of the Mississippi, at the shallowest section of the bend in the river, with a spectral plantation latched on to us like a kraken wrapped around a ship at sea.

Mami Wata strode to the front of the *River Queen*, both arms outstretched as she summoned every ounce of power from the water to propel us forward. The giant paddle groaned as it scraped the bottom of the riverbed, while the wooden mermaid carvings leaned as if trying to tow the boat free.

None of it worked.

"It's too shallow!" Mami Wata shouted as she moved past us and descended to the lower deck. "I'm going to see how badly damaged the paddle is."

That left me and Ayanna alone.

Well, not quite.

"Hey!" A sap ball bounced off my ear. I growled something rude under my breath as Gum Baby slid down from my shoulder. "Y'all trip buddies now?"

It was only then that I realized that Ayanna and I were still holding hands. Gum Baby dropped into a toddler squat and raised one charcoal-drawn eyebrow at me. I blushed and Ayanna rolled her eyes as we stood there awkwardly.

"Anyway," I said, a bit too loudly, "this has got to be what the snake warned me about."

"Mmhmm," Gum Baby said.

"Hush and take Ayanna's other hand," I told her. "I have more to show you. See how the plantation fields overlay the exact dimensions of the prison fields?"

Ayanna nodded. "And look at the guards."

The prison's sentries, still riding horses, trotted slowly along the fields where the living human prisoners labored. But with the help of the Isihlangu bead, we also saw grotesque spirit creatures connected to the ghostly plantation by translucent braided ropes, as if they were marionettes and the house was the puppet master. The creatures reminded me of centaurs, except with six legs instead of four, and two bulky arms that hung nearly to the ground. They walked the same paths as the human guards, and the similarity in how they watched their charges began to creep me out.

But what did all this have to do with Cotton? Had he awoken the spirit plantation as he had the Maafa, the evil sentient slave ship from Alke? Was he trapped inside it? If so, good riddance.

The *River Queen* groaned, then shuddered and began to move—sideways.

"What was that?" I asked, running to the edge.

"Tristan, look out!" Ayanna shoved me down, and we both went tumbling as a massive spirit tentacle swept overhead. "It's pulling us to shore! We'll be stranded and— Mami Wata!"

The goddess stood in the middle of the water, waves surging around her as several tentacles tried to encircle her. They lashed at her, dove beneath her, and even tried to coil around her like a python squeezing its prey. Her arms trembled with the effort of raising wave after wave to fend off the attacks.

Gum Baby was running along the second-floor guardrails, firing sap ball after sap ball at the tentacles and complaining when her missiles went straight through them.

"Unfair!"

"How in the world?!"

"Y'all cheating!"

I scrambled to my feet and sprinted to the other side of the ship. Furrows of sand bunched up as the bottom of the boat began to get stranded on the riverbank.

Ayanna appeared at my side, pointing up the shore some thirty yards away. "Oh no."

"What?" I looked in that direction, then froze. "Sweet peaches."

A section of the prison—a squat one-story building separate from everything else—appeared to be merging with several of the tentacles from the spirit plantation. Trails of gray and black smoke wound between the cinder blocks, which glowed briefly before the entire thing began to shudder like an earthquake had just hit. Giant gray bricks fell from the structure, dislodged by whatever force was shaking the land.

I'd never witnessed evil come to life before. The fetterlings and bone ships back in Alke were already terrorizing MidPass when I fell through the sky. The Maafa had also existed prior to my arrival. By the time Bear, under the venomous influence of King Cotton's mask, had kidnapped Mami Wata and was holding her captive in the burned-out remains of the Thicket, the Tree of Power had already been poisoned by the remains of iron monsters. I'd always thought evil wasn't created—it respawned.

So to see the plantation's tentacles—the ones not currently dragging spirits into the darkness behind its doors—wrap around part of the prison, pull it apart, and reconstruct it into something even more horrific made fear take root in my chest, where it couldn't be dislodged.

Colossal cinder-block legs formed, thicker than tree trunks.

Metal bars twisted around stone to make a giant rib cage.

Two iron grilles turned into eyes, and a thick, bolt-studded metal door served as its mouth.

And, perhaps most terrifying, a copper-red discharge leaked from the cinder blocks around the eyes, making it look like the creature wept blood. As the tentacles finished their assembly and withdrew, the monster shook itself to life with a roar that sounded like an eternity of car crashes, and it turned to fix its gaze on me. I couldn't help myself—I stepped back, afraid.

"Ah, I see you're admiring my latest creation."

The voice, slick and smug, came from across the river. My fists clenched instinctively. Ayanna inhaled sharply. "Is that—?"

"Old Lint Ball himself," Gum Baby said, her voice tight with anger.

Cotton stood on the dilapidated porch of the plantation. He wore old-fashioned riding pants, high black boots, and a beige dinner jacket over a white linen shirt. His hair was swept back, and I could see a hat in his hands.

"He looks...normal," Ayanna said.

"If he gets closer, we'll use the spirit sight," I whispered. "Don't let him fool you."

"He ain't foolin' nobody!" Gum Baby shouted. "Gum Baby put him away once—she can do it again." She began to leap down from the boat, but I caught her and shook my head.

"Wait....Something isn't right."

Cotton laughed. I didn't know how he could hear us, or how I could hear him as if he was standing right next to me.

The haint hopped down off the porch and began strolling toward us through the high grass. As he walked, tentacles from the house writhed and swirled on either side of him, an eldritch escort. Watching them made my stomach twist. He and the plantation were the architects of so much pain. Combined, what further evil could they accomplish? My eyes flicked to the cinder-block giant watching me from the prison grounds. I guessed I was about to find out.

Cotton stopped just beyond the crest of the riverbank, his hands in his pockets and a wicked grin on his face. Seconds later, a sap ball went whizzing across the water, aimed directly at the haint's head. Just before it reached him, a tentacle snaked out from behind him and slapped the projectile aside. Cotton rolled his eyes.

"Come now, can't we be civil?" he asked.

"What—" I began to ask.

"Let me be civil upside your head again, Lint Face!" Gum Baby hurled another sap ball, and she was preparing a sap balloon when Ayanna restrained her and tried to calm her down.

Cotton's smile faded as he stared at Gum Baby. She'd been the one to trap the haint and send him to the bottom of the Burning Sea. From the look of pure loathing on his face, he hadn't forgotten.

"You can't hide forever!" I called out to him. "I've got a nice blue haint bottle with your name on it. Had my nana pick one out."

Ayanna wore a strange, confused expression. Gum Baby eyed me warily. Mami Wata was still fighting off tentacles, splashing them against the far bank while avoiding the clutches of others. Her energy was flagging, however, and I wasn't the only one who noticed. Cotton grinned as he began to pace leisurely back and forth along the crest of the riverbank.

"Tristan, my boy, what makes you think I'm hiding from you? I'm *grateful* to you! You're the one who brought me to this world."

"Liar!" I shouted.

Cotton raised his hands. "Now why would I lie about this? You freed me and some of my good friends, and you took us to Alke. Then you brought Alke here. Well, I'd like to repay the favor. I've got some business to attend to up north, but I can't leave here without extending some good old-fashioned Southern hospitality. Let me introduce you to one of my new friends. Show 'em, darling."

This last statement was directed at the plantation house. It shuddered, and then hundreds, maybe thousands, of new tentacles erupted from every crack and crevice. They shot into the air, writhing like worms on hot pavement. Then, to my disgust, they came down as one . . .

. . . straight into the metal mouth of the stationary cinder-block creature. The monster roared as it was infused with the spirit of the plantation. Once the prison creature had sucked in most of the house's hazy smoke, it took a step forward.

"Um," Ayanna said, "Tristan?"

Cotton started laughing. The monster took another stride, then another, and Cotton walked toward it. The creature bent over and offered him a crumbling cinder-block hand. Cotton stepped onto it and the monster lifted him up.

Only the faintest trace of the house lingered now—nothing more than wisps of smoke. The plantation had been consumed, and the creature that had ingested it looked angry enough to destroy everything in its path.

That meant us.

"Tristan?" Ayanna called. "We need to help Mami Wata! She's tiring."

The prison monster stomped up to us, Cotton now riding on its neck. The haint leaned over with both hands under his chin, his elbows propped on the creature's head.

"Tristan, meet Old Angola, my ticket out of here. Old Angola, Tristan."

"You can't run forever, Cotton!" I shouted.

He smirked. "Go ahead and try to chase me. Unless you don't want the death of a goddess on your hands. But then again, everyone around you is always dying. . . . Maybe you're like me and you don't care."

"Tristan, come here!" Ayanna shouted. She hopped over the side of the *River Queen* and began to wade to where Mami Wata was staggering in the river shallows.

"Poor Tristan," Cotton said with a shrug. He started to

whistle as the prison monster—Old Angola—began to stomp upriver. "Always a step behind. Don't worry, though! I'll find your friends and make sure to tell them..."

He turned, and, just before his evil steed disappeared around the bend ahead, I once again saw the horrific true form of the haint underneath the disguise. Complete with his burning hatred and desire for power.

"...I'll tell them you send your regards."

11

HAINT NO RIVER WIDE ENOUGH

I USED TO PLAY THE SUPERPOWER GAME WITH EDDIE WHEN WE were bored. You know, the one where you take turns selecting a highly specific, sometimes silly act and claim it as your ultimate ability.

For example, Eddie used to say his superpower was being able to scoop out the perfect amount of peanut butter when he was making a sandwich. Regardless of whether he was using a spoon or a knife, or the PB was crunchy or creamy. "I am a FORCE!" he used to shout when making a snack after school.

Me? My superpower isn't as filling, but it's definitely useful. I can tell when a person is going to lose it. Get furious, explode in a rage, blow a gasket... I know all the signs. Our neighbors back in Chicago loved me, because I could predict when their toddler was about to throw a tantrum, and I'd always head him off.

Eddie used to think it was funny. We'd go to the corner

store and he'd point to a group of people and ask me who was going to start an argument first. He marveled that my pick was always right, and he would jot down notes for his future graphic-novel scripts. He thought it was some kind of psychological trick I'd learned from a comic book. I let him believe that. I didn't have the heart to tell him the real source of my predictive powers.

It was easy to tell who was angry. I saw the same signs every morning when I looked in the mirror.

Now, as Ayanna left Mami Wata's cabin, I knew she was upset. I watched her go down the hall and into another room without saying a word.

"You going after her?" Anansi asked from his seat in the middle of the SBP's screen.

"Should I?" I asked.

We'd just managed to get the *River Queen* moving again after several hours of repairs. Leaks had popped up belowdecks, and the paddle wheel had been knocked off-kilter. Maybe I could go double-check that the steamship was okay. Triple-check if needed.

But Anansi gave me an *Of course* look. "Absolutely. Can't work out a two-person problem by your lonesome."

"I don't know. . . ."

"Look, either you go talk to her or I will the next time I see her, and I'll tell her all about those little speeches you got saved on here."

My heart skipped a beat. "You wouldn't."

The ghost of a smile crossed the trickster god's lips, the first I'd seen since we'd arrived from Alke.

"Those were private!"

"Should've read the terms and conditions, my boy. Terms and conditions."

I pushed off the pillar I'd been leaning against. "I'm gonna tell Nyame to reboot you when I see him again. Turn you into a walkie-talkie." With that, I shoved the phone deep into my pocket and followed Ayanna.

She'd entered the meeting room where I'd been grounded, and when I walked in, she was staring at a bundle of rolled-up documents. She didn't acknowledge me. Instead, she unfurled a giant map, trying to hold down the ends as she studied it.

I pulled out the SBP and dropped it on the top left corner. "Here, let me help," I said.

Ayanna nodded, still not speaking.

I sighed. "How's Mami Wata doing?"

Ayanna bit her lip. "Okay. She's doing okay. Tired. Holding off all those angry spirits, on top of keeping the *River Queen* running, drained her." She closed her eyes. "She's just . . . tired."

Mami Wata wasn't the only one. I could see that exhaustion had settled on the former pilot's shoulders like a cloak.

"Ayanna," I began, "I—"

"I had a friend once," she interrupted. "A close friend."

Oh. *Oh.*

"We went through pilot training together, built our rafts together. He was the best I'd ever seen. But when the iron monsters came, something changed in him. He got angry. So angry, all the time. And look, we all were upset, but he . . . It was like he couldn't stand even the thought of them. He began to hunt them down. And it got so bad that eventually the iron monsters figured it out. Whenever he was inside the Thicket, fetterlings would gather outside it like moths to a flame. They wouldn't screech or attack—they just stood there, silent and creepy."

Ayanna leaned on the table, her head bowed. "One day he couldn't take it anymore. He wanted to go out and kill them, and I didn't, and we argued about it. He flew into a rage, took his raft, and left. We heard fighting and went out after him, but by then it was too late. The fetterlings used his anger against him, and I lost a friend. The Thicket lost a great pilot."

Ayanna fell silent and I took a deep breath. I knew what it felt like to lose a friend, and to feel at fault, as if I could've done something that might have prevented his absence. It ate at you. Like a wolf on the inside, chewing away at your heart.

"Ayanna, I'm not—"

But she cut me off again. "Cotton is doing the same thing, Tristan. The same thing! He's baiting you. Making you so angry you can't think! And then you go off after him without considering your safety or the safety of others." She finally looked at me. Her eyes were red and angry. "And people get hurt."

I didn't know how to respond. She wasn't wrong. Mami Wata was now weakened because I had fallen into Cotton's trap. Terrence was scarred—if not physically, then mentally—because I hadn't been able to control the akofena's fire.

I thought about Cotton astride Old Angola, and the chaos and carnage the haint could leave in his wake. Just the idea of it forced my fingers to clench into fists, and I had to flatten my hands on the giant table. I needed to stop him...but how could I without risking my friends' lives?

The *River Queen* shuddered, jarring me out of my head. "Okay," I said. "I'll try to stay in control from now on. Promise."

Ayanna watched me, unsure. I raised my right hand and stood at attention, then crossed my heart with my left hand. "Promise," I repeated.

The boat shook again and I sighed. "And if you take over the steering from Gum Baby, I promise not to throw her overboard."

That drew a smile, and some of the tension drained from the room. Ayanna shook her head. "Leaving her alone in the pilothouse is another strike against you. Honestly, you're one bad move away from a mutiny."

I pointed at the map. "So let's figure out the next move together. You can pilot this thing, right?"

"Boy, I can pilot whatever I choose. I'm fine—you clean your own house." She folded her arms and glared at me in mock severity. "You tell me where we're going, and I'll get us there. Got it?"

"Yes, ma'am," I barked, throwing a salute that almost knocked me out. We grinned, and just for a moment, for one second out of what seemed like an eternity of suffering, things felt good.

Gum Baby muttered slightly frightening threats when we relieved her of duty, but I distracted her by handing her a mini banjo I'd found in a tiny display in one of the suites. "Just no 'Ballad of the Gummy,'" I said, inwardly cringing at the prospect.

Gum Baby scampered out onto the roof-deck and proceeded to pluck some notes with serious aggression. Why was everything so angry with her? And how she got that tiny instrument to make such a loud racket, I'll never know.

There was nothing but wide-open river ahead for miles, so I let her play a concert for a horrified Anansi while I strolled over to the other side of the boat. I sat down, dangled my legs over the edge, and stared off into nothing. Sometimes you just have to turn off your brain.

Fields of green and brown grew across the river. We chugged past them all, the bright blue sky and the warmth of the sun nearly enough to fool me into thinking this was a normal trip. The last leg of a summer vacation. Hopefully Granddad and Nana had made it back to the farm okay. I knew Ayanna had seen them, but—

WHUMP!

The SBP landed on the deck a few feet behind me and slid toward the edge of the boat. I stopped the phone before it could tumble off. Anansi sneered in the middle of the screen.

"You can get mad all you want—that was the wrong chord!" he called back to Gum Baby.

A sap ball hit the screen.

I sighed and wiped the SBP clean with my shirt. Glad to see we were all getting along.

"Did you talk to Ayanna?" Anansi asked.

"Yeah," I said, my attention back on the fields across the river. More farms. Were some of them former plantations?

"Went that well, huh? No matter. You two will work it out."

"There's nothing to work out," I snapped.

"Of course. Keep telling yourself that. Just like there's nothing going on with your powers and your *inability* to control them. Right?" Anansi shook his head and then jumped up, grabbed the bottom of the Contacts app, and started doing pull-ups.

"What are you doing?" I asked after a few seconds of watching.

"What does it look like I'm doing? Did you see Old Angola? I'm getting into shape. Been lazing about for too long." He climbed up between the Contacts app and the Diaspor-app, propping himself on both arms as he started a set of tricep dips. Every time he exhaled, a tired emoji appeared and floated to the top of the screen. Anansi paused after ten reps. "Being cooped up in this digital time-out has slowed my instincts. You do your boxing training even if you don't have a match coming up, right?"

"Yeah..."

"Same thing applies for me. And for you, it's twice as important."

"Why?"

"Because that haint has put a target on your back, boy! Listen, I know I told you before to let the grown folks worry about him, but after that mess back downriver, everybody needs to step up. You most of all. You're also the one the spirits are talking to, and you're the one Alke is relying on to rebuild it! Don't you see? You can't sit back and expect it all to work out."

I threw up my hands. This was getting too confusing. "So I can't sit out the fight, but if I fight, I put other people at risk!" The memory of black flames engulfing the barge rose before me, and I tried to blink it away.

"No one said don't fight—it's about staying in control. That's what training does. Ask for help when you need it, but remember, people, spirits, and even gods are counting on you to fix this. So fix it!"

He stared at me for several seconds with a stern expression until another loud banjo pluck forced him to cringe. "Send me back over there, and you think about what I said, will you?"

I slid the phone across the deck, my thoughts a mess. Everybody seemed to want me to do something different, and their advice and instructions were pulling me in opposite directions. I felt like a giant rubber band. What scared me was what would happen when I finally snapped.

Anansi started shouting at Gum Baby before he'd even reached her. The tiny doll just played louder.

"Don't come over here starting something, Web Butt," she warned.

"I need to start wearing earplugs, the way you're playing. Did you even tune that thing?"

"Gum Baby's gonna tune your face with some sweet chin music if you keep talking."

I ignored their argument and turned back to the fields across the river. Anansi's words echoed in my mind as I watched the wind bend the grass. He was right, of course, but something about his pep talk worried me. It was almost like he was questioning my commitment to Alke and the folks still missing. His son was included in that group, after all. A new note had been lurking in his voice—doubt.

Anansi was starting to lose faith in his Anansesem.

Shame washed over me. The Anansi adinkra was the first one I'd received, sent to me from beyond the grave by my best friend. Was I no longer worthy of it? I stared at my hands and the bracelet on my wrist. No. I couldn't accept that. I could do better. I could *be* better. If I needed to learn control, I would practice. Starting right then.

The music and the argument and everything else faded away as I closed my eyes and clenched my— No, not the shadow gloves. Not yet. I would try the spirit bead. When I opened my eyes, the world took on a foggy look, as if I were peering through a steamy shower door, and all of a sudden I wished I'd done this sooner.

Spirits were fleeing downriver.

Ghosts of Black folk from generations past ran alongside the riverbank. Mothers. Fathers. Children. They clutched their belongings and each other. They kept glancing back fearfully, as if they were being chased, but I couldn't see anything behind them. The river curved just up ahead. Had Cotton stopped near here to let his pet giant gobble up more spirits? If so, I'd be ready for him this time.

One of the spirits—an older girl with two younger children

in tow—noticed me watching. She frantically waved her arms for me to follow them as they ran behind the others, who disappeared after thirty feet or so. The girl stopped for a moment and pleaded to me with her eyes. It was like she wanted to protect me, to take me with her...to where, I didn't know, but someplace other than where the *River Queen* was headed. We stared at each other, me confused and her terrified.

"Tristan!" Gum Baby's shout startled me, and I jerked around. She was pointing straight ahead. "You need to see this!"

"Okay," I said, scrambling to my feet. When I glanced back at the bank, the spirit girl was gone, but the look on her face stuck with me.

What was she so afraid of?

Chaos awaited us. Just around the bend, a large sandbar split the Mississippi in two. Three riverboats—smaller steamers with only one paddle and boxy, windowless cabins—looked like they'd collided and run aground on the sandy island. One of the boats, white with a single red stripe painted along the hull, had overturned. The two other boats were gray and listless, though they didn't look like they'd sustained damage. The area was silent, and the sun beamed down on us as we drifted to a stop and took in the accident scene.

"Where is everyone?" Ayanna asked. "The passengers. Did they . . . ?"

She didn't finish, but I knew what she was going to say. "I don't know," I said. "We should stop and see if they need help."

Gum Baby stomped toward us, her tiny banjo slung over her back. "Sapsolutely not, Bumbletongue. Ain't got time for your heroics. Gum Baby knows a trap when she sees one. Shoot, Gum Baby invented this trap. It's the old Tricky Sticky."

We all stared at her.

"The what?" I asked.

"You heard me. The Tricky Sticky. Find your mark, pretend you're stuck, then *SAP-SAP*, you go upside their head before they know what hit 'em."

Anansi opened his mouth, then closed it. Ayanna shook her head. I took a deep breath, getting ready to argue, then paused and cocked an ear.

"Did you hear that?" I asked.

"Help!"

A faint cry was coming from the overturned boat.

I dove off the side of the *River Queen* in an instant. Concerned shouts came from the deck, but I pushed away from Mami Wata's boat and swam to the sandbar. The overturned steamer looked none the worse for wear, other than, you know, being upside down.

I knocked on the hull. "Hello? Anyone in there?"

Whispers floated on the wind. I looked around me, confused. One of the beached gray boats looked a bit closer than it had before. I frowned.

"Boy! Help me, quick!"

I turned to see a sharp, severe-looking woman lying on the sand. She had bobbed silver hair and was wearing a white pantsuit. Her skin was gray and nearly translucent, so see-through it reminded me of old milk beginning to separate. One of her legs appeared to be trapped beneath the overturned boat, and her sand-covered face had tear tracks running down it.

"Help me, quickly now!" She held out a hand with the practiced ease of someone who expected to be obeyed. She was stuck but didn't look too put out about it, despite her pleas for help.

"Where are you?" Ayanna's shout cut across the water.

I started to turn, but the woman flapped her hand at me.

"Come now, boy, what are you waiting for? My other leg to suffer the same fate?"

I shook my head and grabbed her hand. I winced at how cold it was. Must've been from being dumped in the water.

"Sorry, Miss..."

"*Mrs.* Mrs. Roller. But I suppose you can just call me Patty," the woman said. "Everybody else does."

"Mrs. Roller, I mean Patty, shouldn't I try to shift the boat so you can—"

"Nonsense. Just pull me. Big strong boy like you, I'll be free in no time." Patty smiled, a thin-lipped quirk of the mouth that didn't look happy at all. Then again, she was probably hurt. I tugged, and she scooted forward and got to her feet. Easily.

"Thank you, Tristan. I never could've freed myself without your help," Patty said, holding on to my arm with one hand and brushing sand off her face with the other.

Alarm bells rang in my head. "How did you know my name?"

She froze.

My eyes went to the spot where she'd just been lying. Under the overturned ship I could now see a shallow trench. She hadn't been stuck at all.

"Tristan, the boats!" called Ayanna. "Look out!"

This time I did turn around. The other two gray vessels— the ones I thought were beached on the sandbar—had miraculously launched themselves and now cut off my retreat to the *River Queen*. When I turned back around, Patty still gripped me, and her face was free of sand . . . but the tear tracks, like stained ink, remained.

The spirits running away . . .

Mrs. Patty Roller . . .

Pattyroller.

Patroller.

Slave Patrol.

Patty's fingers began to burn like cold iron against my skin as she leaned in close.

"We've been waiting for you, Tristan Strong."

12
HAINT BLUE

RUN.

The word boomed inside my skull. Patty Roller's hand encircled my wrist like a handcuff as she chuckled. Her two patrol-boat escorts crowded in even closer as she spoke in a casual tone that still dripped with menace.

"Let's see now. I believe I saw a news report about a riot you started." Patty shook her head and adopted a forlorn expression. "So much violence and mayhem. Upsetting the good, respectable people in such a manner. It is my sworn duty to bring children such as you to a new, well-structured environment. A place where you can be taught appropriate behavior."

"I don't need your lessons," I said, gritting my teeth and trying to break away from the cold bite of her grip.

"You all need to be taught a lesson!" Patty shouted.

I recoiled. For a second there...No, it couldn't be. I couldn't have seen what I thought I did.

Patty took my silence for submission. She nodded, straightened her hair, and cleared her throat. The tear tracks on her face faded slightly as she calmed down.

"That's better. You'll learn faster when you're docile."

Docile?

"Now come along. There are more of your kind to gather, not to mention the wretched ghosts traipsing up and down these banks. Like gnats, they are. I'd rather collect children than those spectral nuisances any day."

As she began to pull me over to one of the gray patrol boats, I thought about what Patty had just revealed.

"So you're the one taking the missing children..." I said slowly, though my thoughts were running a mile a minute. "For what?"

"Why, education, my dear." Patty smiled, and I shuddered and looked away. "Children these days are *lacking* good, strict discipline in their learning." Her other hand shot out and gripped my chin, forcing me to stare at her face and acknowledge what I'd noticed before, what had set my heart pounding as I stood trapped on that sandbar.

Patty Roller's sharp teeth glistened as she smiled, and her permanent tear tracks flared when I managed to press the spirit bead on my adinkra bracelet between my wrist and upper thigh.

I blinked, and Patty Roller's eyes smoked at the corners. She was a haint.

"Now, then," she said.

CRAAAAACK

The patrol boat to my left disintegrated into splinters as the *River Queen* rammed her way forward.

"Tristan!" Ayanna shouted. "Run!"

In the chaos and confusion, Patty's grip on me loosened for just an instant. I jerked free and took off across the sand.

Run.

Run like the spirits I'd seen earlier, driven by the fear of being captured, of being dragged back to an environment and routine and mentality that stripped them of humanity even in death.

Run like the kids in the streets of New Orleans, trying to escape the pitfalls the system had created for them. The same kids Patty Roller was scooping up left and right, apparently in an effort to try to "reeducate" them.

The mere idea was wild, and if I wasn't running for my life and freedom, I would've stopped and laughed. People were always trying to teach us the "proper" things, when the facts we needed to learn weren't included in any history books.

Like how an education was an education, until it wasn't.

Like how half of New Orleans had been built on the bloody red stories of slavery.

Like how coffles were for harnessing teams of animals...
or slaves.

Like how a prison had been built on the site of a plantation.

Like how the faint outline of a Black man stood at the far
end of the sandbar....

Wait, what?

The man, clearly a spirit, wore a faded blue collared shirt
tucked into blue pants, and a hat tilted jauntily on his head.
He looked to be about my dad's age. As I sprinted his way,
he turned and walked toward the edge of the water, where
he disappeared.

"What...is...happening?" I gasped out. I risked a look
over my shoulder. The mermaid carvings on the starboard
side of the *River Queen* had grabbed the second patrol boat
and were in the process of battering it to smithereens. But
Patty Roller's steamboat had righted itself and now chugged
after me with her at the helm. It didn't have as much power
as Mami Wata's flagship, but it was still gaining on me, and
I was running out of sandbar.

Suddenly the spirit appeared again, this time across the
river. He beckoned for me to follow. I reached the end of the
sand, glanced back at Patty Roller leaning over the rail of her
boat as she hollered at me, and waded into the water. Luckily
it wasn't too deep, as the sandbar must have obstructed the
water on the opposite side, but still...Could I ever have an

adventure where I wouldn't get wet? I needed to start wearing Crocs at all times, just in case.

I reached the bank, and three new spirits appeared. Like the first, they were Black men in the same blue outfit. Two of them looked to be in their twenties, and one was just a little older than me. They smiled at me in welcome.

"You all need to get out of here!" I shouted as I began to sprint upriver. "Go! Before they catch you!"

The spirits disappeared, then reappeared twenty feet in front of me and farther from the river.

"Didn't you hear me?" I called. "They're coming for me and you!"

Patty Roller was catching up. I could understand her shouts now.

"You ungrateful little stain on society, get over here! I will hunt you down, you hear? I will not rest until you receive the proper care and tutelage that someone like you deserves."

Yeah, I had no doubts about what sort of *care* I'd get from her. Her tone was similar to Cotton's. Did all haints talk with a superiority complex wedged up their butts, or were these two related somehow?

The three spirits in blue stood on the riverbank by a pile of wood. They motioned for me to join them, and I shook my head in despair. Did they not understand the danger?

"You all have to—" I started.

I slowed as I got closer and saw that the wooden debris was actually an old sign. A marker indicating the city limits. Apparently we weren't far from... I kicked aside a wooden spar and read the name written in faded white paint.

"Vicksburg, Mississippi..." I looked at the three spirits, who beamed at me. "Birthplace of the United States Colored Troops."

Ah, so they were soldiers. The spirits turned and walked up the hill beyond the sign, and again they beckoned me to follow. I did, since it got me a bit farther away from Patty Roller, who'd slowed down to try to see where I'd gone. At the top of the hill, we joined the original soldier, the older one who'd appeared on the sandbar. He pointed down into a valley where the outskirts of a city could be seen.

"Vicksburg?" I asked.

He nodded.

"And I should go there... why?"

The soldier gestured to a manmade tributary that forked from the Mississippi and led straight into town. He then pointed at Patty Roller's boat and pretended to shoo it away.

"We'll be safe there?" I asked.

Another nod.

I hesitated. Vicksburg looked far away, a long distance from the *River Queen*, which was slowing down as if beginning to tire. The mermaids had lost their grip on the other patrol boat, and Patty Roller's red-striped vessel was still chugging forward. She'd catch me if I stayed on the main river, which curved sharply until it almost doubled back on itself. But if I followed the spirits and took this detour, I could reunite with my friends later on. . . .

"Okay," I said. "I'm with you. Let's go."

The spirits smiled approvingly. The youngest soldier pumped his arms in a familiar gesture.

Run.

13
IF ONE OF US AIN'T FREE...

THERE ARE A FEW THINGS I SHOULD HAVE BEEN AWARE OF BEFORE following a group of spirits on a breakneck race to escape capture. Nothing too out of the ordinary, but I figure a PSA here will save future Anansesem (we started a movement, not a moment) the embarrassment of doing what I did.

First, spirits don't tire. They don't suffer from exhaustion, sleep deprivation, nightmares that keep them from resting and recovering, or even the occasional mid-sentence yawn that encourages adults to send them to bed early. Nope. None of that. They do what they have to, no pauses, no interruptions. Kinda inspiring . . . unless you're the one trying to keep up with them.

"How . . . much . . . farther?" I gasped out as we cut across a field and started loping down a wide paved road. They didn't answer, and I grumbled but continued running, trying to keep an eye out for oncoming cars and the gravel they'd kick up.

See, that's the second warning about fleeing with spirits I could've used ahead of time. Those spectral sprinters didn't have to worry about hazards or obstacles the way I did. A huge semi bearing down on us? They didn't care, ran right through it. Me?

"Gaaaaaah!!!" I shouted as I dove off the asphalt and tumbled down the embankment on the side of the road. The truck, hauling the trunks of recently cut trees and showering pieces of bark down on me, roared past. I stood shakily and dusted myself off. I took a step—

SQUELCH

My foot sank up to my ankle in thick black mud. The small river gurgled past, laughing at me all the way.

"That's it!" I shouted. "I'm done! No more running."

I pulled out my foot, grimaced at the smelly mud that was caking my Chucks, and glared up at the four spirits who had materialized in a semicircle around me. The soldiers weren't looking at me, however. They stared at the river and a sign on the opposite bank.

"Vicksburg Historical Society Future Site of USS *Cairo* Memorial Plaque," I read aloud. I looked at the closest soldier, a man about Granddad's age. He had a graying mustache and scars running along one side of his face. He noticed my gaze and smiled.

"Our story. Freedom," he said.

"So you *can* talk," I said. "'Bout time."

A horn blared downriver. Patty Roller's boat! It had navigated the smaller river mouth and was now chugging toward us in the distance. I whirled around to address the soldiers. "Okay, we have to keep going. Where to, huh? Where do we run now?"

The older man shook his head and pointed at the river. "Our story. Freedom."

"There's nothing there!" I threw up my hands in frustration. "Nothing! We're going to get caught if we stay here! Now what? What am I supposed to do now?"

As desperation warred with despair inside me, I felt paralyzed by indecision. A haint bent on capturing me and children like me was minutes away from accomplishing her goal, and I was seconds away from giving up.

The older spirit continued pointing. His three companions were wading into the middle of the water, slowly disappearing. I squinted. No . . . there was something under the water. Something long and wide.

I inhaled sharply.

The spirit smiled again, this time with a trace of pride in his eyes. He pointed at my right wrist, then at himself, then at the river. "Our story," he said again. "Freedom."

I nodded. I thought I understood . . . but could I do it? I'd never tried anything like this with the adinkra bracelet, and after the catastrophe on the barge tow in New Orleans, I hesitated.

But what choice did I have?

The old soldier hefted his belongings on his back, and as he did, I noticed rust stains on his shirt cuffs and the bottoms of his pant legs. From iron shackles. The spirit followed his comrades into the river and disappeared. I was alone...but I had a job to do.

Anansesem. The carrier of stories, the recorder of stories, the reteller of stories. I'd been shirking my duties. And if Patty Roller had her way, if Cotton got what he wanted, the stories I carried and the ones I hadn't recorded yet would be lost forever.

Not today, fam.

"Let me tell you a story," I whispered as I grabbed the Isihlangu spirit bead...and the Gye Nyame adinkra.

Two charms of power at the same time.

My vision went black...

...and when it returned, the story of the soldiers blasted through the water and unspooled in front of me. Fiery words seared my eyes and burned their painful way into my mind.

And I read.

Thunder crashed and lightning shot past my face. Had I been caught in a storm? My ears rang, and I couldn't see more than a foot in front of me.

"John, you okay? We gotta go."

The voice came from nearby, but I couldn't see who spoke.

Everything was blurry...and yet, if I focused, everything was as clear as if I were watching a movie. I was still on the riverbank, and there were others around me. This wasn't my usual Anansesem magic. I was *inside* the story!

"John!"

"Right here!" I called. Except my name wasn't John, and it wasn't my voice. It was someone else's, even though it came from my mouth. This was too weird.

A man appeared out of the fog. He beckoned to me, and I recognized him as the oldest soldier, though now he didn't have on his uniform, just some tattered pants and a cotton shirt. The scars on his face were fresh, and there was a desperate anger in his eyes.

"We gotta go, now, while the storm makes it hard for them to track us."

I—we?—nodded and began to follow him. We knew him. Trusted him. Our father? No, our uncle. He led us through the fog as the storm raged around us.

"Where are we going?" we asked.

"Heard them Union boys are up around Vicksburg," he answered, never breaking stride. "Folks said they carrying freedom with them. We get to them, join up, and maybe we can get the rest of the family north, too."

Vicksburg. For an instant my thoughts separated from John's, and I saw the town as it had looked from the hilltop. The supermarkets, the gas stations, the casinos. Then our thoughts merged again, and Vicksburg appeared as it had in his time. The forts, the siege works, the cannons. Our uncle led us across muddy tracks and fields filled with lines of white tents.

The fog returned, wiping everything away, though I still heard the voice of our uncle guiding us forward.

"Hurry up, son. You in the USCT now, ain't got no time for slouching."

We looked down. Now we were wearing the uniform I'd seen the spirits in earlier. The USCT. I remembered Terrence talking a mile a minute about one of the museums he'd visited down in New Orleans.

And Black people fought in the Civil War! he'd said. *Artillery, infantry ... They even served on gunboats along the Mississippi, like the USS* Cairo. *The United States Colored Troops. The USCT.*

That's right. So, John and his uncle had fought in the Civil War. I wrestled with that idea for a few moments as we ran through the spirit's memory. What if your choices were either to remain enslaved or to risk trying to escape and avoid capture just to end up fighting on a battlefield where you might die? *Freedom.* That's what the old soldier, John's uncle, kept saying to me. It meant having control over your own life, your own education, your own words and actions. Some people died for want of it. Some people died having never obtained it. And some fought a war for it.

"John!"

The shout came out of the fog, and we looked up to see a dock with a weird-looking boat tied to it. Like a steamship that had been covered in armor. It was completely enclosed, save for openings where cannon barrels poked out. John's uncle stood in front of us, his hat in his hands and resolve in his eyes. His uniform seemed older, more worn and patched up. So did ours.

More time had passed, I realized.

"I said no. This ain't for you—you get up to Fort Pillow and find your friends, you hear me? If what I heard is true . . . Well, you just go find them. Leave this to me."

He turned toward the boat—the word *ironclad* popped into our head—and we moved to follow him aboard.

"No!" he shouted, just as cannons boomed and a flurry of activity erupted in the fog around us. "Go! We've got this."

"I can help you!" we screamed.

John's uncle disappeared into the ironclad. I could just barely read the lettering on the side before the fog swallowed it up.

USS CAIRO

"Here they come!" someone shouted.

The ironclad chugged away from the dock, steam and smoke billowing out behind it as it moved downriver. Dozens of cannons fired from the ship, aimed at something I couldn't see.

Suddenly a violent tug pulled me into the fog—I had the

sensation of being dragged at a breakneck pace. And then I was in darkness, a sliver of light in front of my eyes as I held something heavy in my arms. I was looking out a window... no, a viewport. The floor tilted beneath my feet. I was on a boat. The ironclad—I was aboard the USS *Cairo*. This time I was in a different person's story. I saw a young man on the bank—John, the spirit I'd just shared the previous memory with. Now that I could get a good look at his face, my jaw dropped.

"Freedom." The old spirit spoke from my mouth. "Go get your freedom, boy."

I had one second to see a determined expression settle on John's face before he turned and ran. It was just as well, because as soon as he disappeared over the hill, on his way to wherever Fort Pillow was, the USS *Cairo* exploded.

The last thing the man had seen was his nephew.

The last thing I saw before I was kicked out of the man's memory was a friend of mine, wearing a younger guise than the one he'd worn in Alke.

It was High John the Conqueror.

Too many things whirled around in my head. The soldiers of the USCT fighting for the Union. High John the Conqueror, first enslaved and now a god.

Cannons fired, and a giant splash echoed through the evening. I blinked, then jerked myself back to reality. The ghost of the USS *Cairo*, in its fully intact form, floated on the water in front of me. Downriver, Patty Roller's ship had stopped to do battle with the *River Queen*, which had managed to catch up to her. Patty Roller's vessel and one of the smaller patrol boats now flanked Mami Wata's riverboat on the left and right. Even worse, tentacles—like the kind that had emerged from Old Angola—had reached out from the patrol boat and were slowly strangling the steamship.

"Orders, young man?"

I looked at the USS *Cairo*, wreathed in purple-and-orange fire, with its cannons of gold. The spirit of John's uncle stared at me expectantly.

"Me?" I asked.

The old man smiled. "You fighting for freedom, right? For your friends? Just like my nephew. I've seen power before, son, and I'll tell you the same thing I told him. It ain't just your freedom you gotta fight for, it's *everyone's* freedom. If one of us ain't free, none of us free."

The battle downriver raged on as the sun crept closer and closer to the horizon. Night was coming. I licked my lips as the power of the gods danced through me. It was one thing to be able to see spirits, another to be able to see the stories that made up the world. But it was something else entirely to be an active participant in those stories. I couldn't describe the experience other than to say it felt like my skin was made of lightning and my words were thunder.

"So," the old soldier said. "Orders?"

I took a deep breath. If someone wasn't free, no one was free. My friends. The children Patty Roller had snatched. The spirits Cotton's prison monster had eaten. I had to free them all. And it started here.

I pointed at the smaller patrol boat with its octopus arms. "Fire!" I shouted.

The USS *Cairo* belched flame and light as its cannons, made of the spinning golden names of the four Black soldiers who served aboard, attacked.

The patrol boat disappeared in a cloud of smoke and ruin.

The *River Queen*, now facing only one opponent, pulled away and steamed forward. Patty Roller's boat, its red stripe glistening in the light, followed. I could just make out the haint standing at the prow. Her face twisted into a sneer as we locked eyes.

"Fire!" I shouted a second time.

The cannons aboard the USS *Cairo* boomed again, just as the mermaid carvings lining the side of the *River Queen* screamed in unison and sent a mighty surge of water back toward Patty Roller.

The haint shrieked as the combined attack blasted her boat backward, the force carrying her downriver and out of sight.

14

THE GODS MUST BE CRANKY

"I THINK I FIGURED OUT WHAT COTTON IS DOING WITH HIS GIANT, ugly fortress of horror," I said.

We were in the throne room of the *River Queen*. Me, Anansi, Gum Baby, and a weary Mami Wata. The goddess sat on her wooden throne as three tiny mermaid carvings on the headrest plaited her hair. She looked drained beyond measure, even more than she had after Angola.

When Ayanna had picked me up from the banks of the Yazoo River near Vicksburg, she'd told me that Mami Wata had put all her reserve energy into fighting off the patrol boats, and it nearly wasn't enough. Ayanna was navigating the steamship now, and we currently chugged upriver, back on the Mississippi and moving at a good clip. But maintaining that speed was all Mami Wata could manage at the moment. Patty Roller had taken a serious toll on her. I hoped that John Henry and Nyame would rejoin us soon. They were still off pursuing Cotton, but I was starting to get the impression that we needed all the backup we could get. If it hadn't been for the USS *Cairo*, and my combining the adinkras and commanding the power of the spirits, the battle would've been lost. I still couldn't believe any of it had really happened.

Now, with her eyes half-closed, Mami Wata listened as I tried to relay everything I'd learned. "Tell me," she said softly as she leaned back in her throne.

Ayanna had draped a blanket over my shoulders, and I pulled it tight as I began to pace around the room. "I don't have all the pieces of the puzzle yet, but we know Cotton chose the haunted plantation of Old Angola for a reason." I swallowed and forged ahead. "He combined the evil power still in that house with the prison of today and created a monster."

"What does that have to do with the spirits?" Anansi asked. There was a challenge in his voice, but I didn't shy away from meeting his eyes as Gum Baby cradled the SBP.

"He's hunting them," I answered.

"Wait, wait, wait." Gum Baby bounced down from the chair she was sitting on, propped the SBP on it, and stomped forward. "Let Gum Baby get this straight. Old Thorny Butt is hunting spirits? Why? What is wrong with people? First old fake-tears lady is capturing children, and now we gotta rescue Gum Baby's ancestors, too?"

Mami Wata pursed her lips. "The two serve the same

purpose, I'm sure of it, but as yet I can't guess what Cotton's goal is."

I hesitated to respond. Not because I thought I might be wrong, but because I might be right, and if I was, the answer scared me. It scared me a lot.

"Tristan?" the goddess asked. "What is it?"

I took a deep breath. "When I was out on the river, I grabbed two of the adinkra charms at once, and I *saw* through two different spirits' eyes. I saw their experiences. That's what helped you—the spirits' untold stories."

Silence gathered in the throne room before Anansi sighed. "Is that all?"

Mami Wata leaned forward. "Yes, but why would the haint want spirits?"

I started pacing. "Cotton's raiding places where Black people suffered in large groups. Think about it—the French Quarter, where Africans landed and were sold as slaves. The plantation, the prison. And if I'm right, I know where he's going to be next."

The goddess raised an eyebrow.

"Fort Pillow."

Anansi frowned. "Why there?"

"It was the site of one of the biggest massacres of Black soldiers in the entire Civil War. People fighting for their freedom were cut down by Confederate soldiers without remorse."

"Which means hundreds of spirits…" Mami Wata said. She leaned over and tapped one of the mermaids on her throne. "Ask Ayanna to come down, please." She reclined again, and it looked like it was taking all her energy to do so. When Ayanna walked in a few seconds later, the goddess's voice was barely above a whisper. "Can we reach Fort Pillow from the river?"

Ayanna moved toward the map and traced her finger along the route. "Yes. It's just off the main river, in a place called Tennessee. We're about to cross the border now, so we're making good time." She looked worried, as if the speed we were traveling was too much for Mami Wata to sustain. Just how much of the goddess was in her steamship? I wanted to catch Cotton, but not at the expense of one of our own.

"It looks like that fort is"—Ayanna squinted—"just north of a major city called Memphis. Maybe we can rest there and—"

Anansi perked up, interrupting her. "Memphis? Did you say Memphis?"

Ayanna nodded at him, and the spider god hopped to his (six) feet, becoming more animated as he paced up one side of the phone's screen, walked upside down along the top, then came down the other side. "Okay. Okay, that's perfect. I've been getting alerts coming in every hour, and they're all located in Memphis. Junior *has* to be there. If we can get there before Patty Roller or Cotton or anyone else, we can rescue him!"

"And the others," Ayanna added. "Like Thandiwe, and Chestnutt, and—"

"Yes, them too, I suppose. Now we'll have to leave right away, and Wata, you'll have to put more juice in the wheel. There's no time to waste."

Ayanna looked skeptical. Gum Baby had climbed up the back of Mami Wata's throne and was giving the mermaids advice about how to braid hair.

I stepped forward and held up a hand. "Wait. Look at her, Anansi. She's barely recovered from the last battle. She needs to rest."

"Rest?! There's no time—"

"We will find Junior!" I shouted. "But we have to be smart about it. We can let Mami Wata cruise along the river and meet her on the other side of Memphis. If we take a taxi—"

"A taxi?! You want to take a taxi into battle?"

I tried to maintain some sense of calm. "It's not a battle. Not yet. We need to know more about Cotton's plans before we—"

"Cotton's plans?" Anansi scoffed. "His plans are to create chaos."

"And we have to figure out how he intends to accomplish that. He's harvesting spirits, but what's he going to do with them all? Why does he keep going? It doesn't make sense."

"What doesn't make sense is how that haint has purchased real estate in your head. You're making mistakes left and right. Charging into fights you can't win. Ignoring the very people you're supposed to protect!"

"So I've made mistakes!" I shouted. "I'm trying!"

"Then try *harder*!" he roared.

Everyone in the room stared at the two of us. Anansi glowered at me, his eyes bloodshot and his voice raw. What was with him? Why couldn't he see that I cared about finding Junior just as much as he did?

"Anansi," I said in a calmer tone, "we *will* rescue the other Alkeans. But we also have to stop Cotton before he causes more mayhem. We can't be divided at a time like this."

"The only thing that's divided," the trickster god said quietly, "is your attention. It's because of your lack of focus that we're in this mess. You know, at first I thought you were just growing accustomed to the task of leadership. Now I'm beginning to think you never had that quality in you. I should have done this a long time ago."

His words landed like slaps to my face. "What are you talking about?"

But it was Mami Wata who answered, her eyes closed. "Anansi... has requested that your title of Anansesem be revoked and that his time under your supervision be considered complete." When she opened her eyes, I could see more than exhaustion in them. I also saw regret, and apology. "I sent word to Nyame, but until he returns, the decision will have to wait. If the sky god rules in Anansi's favor, then the

Story Box will be removed from your possession, and Anansi will be reinvested into his proper form."

Her words robbed me of everything keeping my legs upright. If it weren't for Ayanna's hand, I would've fallen when Mami Wata spoke her next sentences.

"You are hereby put on temporary probation and will remain in your room, where you will be grounded until further notice. For the time being, I will take charge of the Story Box."

15

REAL HEROES TAKE TAXIS

NO LONGER AN ANANSESEM.

Even if I was only on probation and could somehow convince Nyame and the other gods that this was all one huge mistake, the very idea of spending any length of time away from the SBP seemed unbearable. Stories had become my life. My purpose! Even now I wanted nothing more than to slip out into the night and find this realm's High John. Or seek out more spirits and ask them to tell me about their accomplishments. How many phenomenal people had history forgotten? I needed to know. The world needed to know! That was the job of an Anansesem. My job. At least it *was*.

No chance of that happening now.

I sat alone in a chair in one of the *River Queen*'s many guest cabins. Stream beds had been carved into the wooden floor and then covered with glass so water could trickle across the room, while the walls displayed flickering scenes of storms raging across different environments, like deserts and mountain rain forests. I even thought I saw Nyanza, the City of Lakes, which had been Mami Wata's home back in Alke. Surprisingly, watching the violent storms calmed me down. I guess I appreciated anything that seemed more chaotic than my life at the moment.

Someone knocked on the door. When I didn't answer, they barged in anyway.

"Wow, Bumbletongue, you're so rude. Gum Baby was coming to console you, but you're just too good for that, huh?" The tiny doll stood in front of me, hands on her hips. She shook her head. "Well? What are you doing just sitting there? Is your butt cold?"

"What do you want me to do?" I muttered.

"Stop feeling sorry for yourself and help Gum Baby save the day! Or does she have to do all the work around here?" Gum Baby rolled a tiny ball of sap in her hands and raised it threateningly.

I shook my head in disgust. "Didn't you hear them? I'm on probation."

"Gum Baby don't hear too well—it's all the sap." She pretended to dig in her ear.

"Well, it's true. What am I supposed to do now? Wait and let Cotton take over the world? Let him and his haint crew—and, by the way, we don't know how many other members there are—bring panic and pain to everyone around him?"

Gum Baby had dropped into a crouch and was staring at the miniature rivers in the floor. "Hm? Oh, were you talking to Gum Baby? Sorry, she thought you were doing that one thing you always do. Now, what is it called? Oh yeah, whining. You done whining?"

"Hey, that's not—"

Gum Baby did throw a sap ball at me this time. "No, Tristan Talk Time is done. Gum Baby has the floor." She pointed at the ground. "See, she even wrote her name on the glass—Gum Baby's floor. Now listen up, whiney-heinie. So what if you're on probation. You can't be a hero without a phone? Stop relying on objects to accomplish your objective, my gummy."

I opened my mouth to protest, then paused. Did...Did she actually have a point? Sweet peaches, she did.

"You're right," I said.

Gum Baby cupped her ear. "What's that? Gum Baby told you she's hard of hearing. Give Gum Baby her flowers like you mean it."

I rolled my eyes. "*N-E*-ways, I guess I really don't need the SBP."

"Now you're talking. Stop relying on material things. That's the mantra of the gummy. Follow the Gum-true path and stick to it." Gum Baby trotted over to the window and scrambled up to the sill. "Has Gum Baby ever led you astray?"

I sighed, refusing to answer that. "Okay, let me think. I

need to wait until we get just outside the city, then sneak off the boat and catch a ride to Memphis. We find Junior and the others, then we go take down Cotton before he can reach Fort Pillow." I clapped once. "We can do this."

Gum Baby raised the window, then clapped her hands as well, spraying sap everywhere. "Gum Squaaaaaaaad!"

I wiped my eyes clean and glared at her.

She shrugged. "Not Gum Baby's fault you don't wash the sleep out your eyes in the morning. Now let's go before you chicken out."

"Not yet. We need to wait until—" Something in the tiny terror's expression stopped me, and I looked at her suspiciously. "Hold up, where are we?"

"Ayanna convinced Anansi to help us get to Memphis faster. She said the sooner we got here, the sooner we could get an answer from His Grumpiness Nyame. That made ole Web Butt hustle. Should've seen him working with the mermaids."

Sneaky. I nodded. "Okay, first things first, we need to find a way to call a cab," I said. "Maybe there's a public—"

Gum Baby grinned, then reached into her sap-pack—I mean *backpack*—and pulled out a purple-and-gold flip phone. "Gum Baby got that covered."

"Where in the world did you get a phone?" I asked, horrified. Something about Gum Baby having enhanced powers of communication felt like a disruption in the natural order of things. "And I thought you said no material—"

She tossed me the phone before backflipping out the window, shouting as she fell. "Gum Baby stay making moooooooves!"

I stared at the phone, then peered out the window. One of the *River Queen*'s lifeboats rocked on the water beneath me. Ayanna sat in it with her baseball bat in her lap and an oar in each hand as Gum Baby clambered up into the seat opposite her.

"Well?" Ayanna said. "You coming, flyboy?"

I grinned. There's nothing like friends who have your back.

"Just one thing," she said, freezing the smile on my face as a sly grin crossed her own. "This rickety rowboat won't last if you jump down into it. So, um, you're going to have to get wet."

The taxi driver took us from the dock all the way to midtown Memphis. He stopped in what looked like a war zone.

"Sorry, folks," he said. "I can't get any closer than this. Something is blocking the road up ahead."

He couldn't see what the trouble was. I looked at the two friends with me in the back seat and could tell they couldn't see it, either.

"That's fine," I said, eager to get my soaking-wet self out of the tiny hatchback. "We'll hop out here. Thanks for the—"

"Whoa, whoa, whoa, there, buddy," the taxi driver said, turning around in his seat. The old Black man had a bushy mustache that wriggled across his face like a caterpillar. "Y'all might be kids, but that was a grown-folks' fare. Y'all need to get together and come up with some money."

"Oh, right," I said. "Forgot for a minute." I couldn't tell him what had distracted me, because he wouldn't have believed it.

Fortunately, Nana and Granddad had given me some spending money for New Orleans before they grounded me. I started digging in my shorts for my wallet as Ayanna leaned over and whispered, "Tristan, what are you doing? If the road is blocked, have him drive us around it."

Gum Baby nudged my legs from her hiding spot down below the seat, but I ignored her and continued to scrounge in my pockets. Where *was* that wallet? "Trust me," I said to Ayanna. "We want to get out here."

The taxi driver was watching me in the rearview mirror, and I didn't think he'd appreciate it if he heard me say that I just saw a group of spirits fleeing from what looked to be the Memphis Zoo. So, in response to Ayanna, I just pointed at my adinkra bracelet, then out the window.

Gum Baby tapped me again and I glared down at her. "What?" I whisper-shouted.

The sticky menace held up a credit card and my jaw dropped open. How in the world had she . . .

"Gum Baby keeps it for emergencies, just like her phone." She patted my leg and settled down on my shoe. "Don't worry,

Bumbletongue, Gum Baby will teach you financial literacy once this is all over. She won't even charge for it."

The taxi driver looked at me suspiciously as he accepted the slightly sticky card with the name GUM N. B. BABY on the front. But it worked just fine and he handed it back. "Y'all be careful now. It's a mess up ahead. Also, I heard them talking on the news about missing children. Go straight home, you hear?"

"Yessir," I said. "Just have to go see my uncle real quick. Thank you!"

As the taxi pulled away, Ayanna stared at me like I'd sprouted wings behind my ears. "What uncle?"

I pointed to the sky above the zoo. The park and the streets around it had been cordoned off due to structural damage. And from the cinder blocks I saw strewn about, I knew which giant monster had caused the destruction. I waited, waited some more, and then stabbed my finger upward again.

"That uncle," I said, as a giant bird the color of ink and shadows dove out of the clouds. A man was on its back, and they disappeared into the trees inside the zoo.

High John and his spirit crow, Old Familiar.

16

THE OLD TRICKY STICKY

THE ZOO WAS A DISASTER.

"Hoo boy," Gum Baby said. "Somebody got their butt *whooped.*"

The entrance, a giant tan structure that sloped down on both ends and had colorful pictures of animals painted all over the surface, was in ruins. A bent metal sign called it the AVENUE OF ANIMALS. It looked like the elephants had escaped and tap-danced up one side the avenue and break-danced down the other. Rubble lay in piles all over the courtyard in front, and something had twisted the metal turnstiles like used paper clips. Flowers and shrubbery had been torn up by their roots and strewn everywhere.

"Who could've done this?" Ayanna whispered.

I didn't answer, but I suspected it wasn't a *who*, but a *what*.

As we walked through the damaged entrance and followed the trail of ruin deeper into the zoo, Gum Baby shook her head and let out a low whistle. "Gum Baby ain't seen destruction like this since..." She paused to think, then nodded. "Probably since the last time Bumbletongue had to save the world."

"Hey!" I said.

Somehow, the little terror had finessed her way into riding on my shoulder ("Clearly, Gum Baby's the best lookout.") and she was snapping pictures of the damage as we crept past Cat Country, where the lions and tigers—and, bear with me, were those black panthers?—were kept. Gum Baby zoomed in on one of the enclosures, then sighed.

"Gum Baby used to know a giant cat. Never knew if it was a lion or a tiger, but Captain Bigtooth was a dear friend."

I rolled my eyes. "How could you not know what kind of cat it was? Did it have stripes, a mane, what?"

"Gum Baby don't question identities, Bumbletongue—that's rude!"

Ayanna flapped a hand at us as she peered down the path at the next exhibit. "Will you two be quiet? There's something going on up ahead."

"What is it?"

"Who wants a piece of Gum Baby?"

Ayanna didn't answer. Instead, she tiptoed off the path and moved quickly across a patch of grass into the shadow of a large building. I followed, Gum Baby watching our backs from her perch on my shoulder, and we all huddled next to the rear corner of the structure and slowly peeked around.

The back of the building had been destroyed. Glass skylights, partially shattered, dangled over the gaping hole, and a giant sign was wedged in the branches of a tree.

"Tropical Bird House," I read aloud.

"Shhh," Ayanna hissed, pointing. Lumps lay in rows on the grass nearby, but I couldn't tell what they were. Gum Baby jabbed me in the side of the neck (um, ow?) and turned my head back toward the giant hole in the building. Shadowy figures moved around the darkness inside. They whispered to each other, calling out instructions, and we shrank down as two of them walked outside lugging another one of those weird lumps.

"Are those—" Gum Baby whispered.

"Birds?" Ayanna finished. "I hope they're not dead. . . ."

I didn't answer, because at that moment, the figures holding the lumps entered a circle of light cast by one of several bent lampposts. The figures were humans—adults—and they wore shapeless gray cloaks and plastic masks. Running diagonally across each mask, in thick splotchy paint, was a wide red line.

"Come on," the one nearest to us said, "get it into the light. Is this it? Is this the one? It's pretty big, right? He said it'd be really big."

"I don't know..." the second one said. "It's tough when they're struggling like this. But... I've seen bigger birds. Ostriches, for example. This is... Isn't this a stork or something?"

"I don't know, I'm not an aviation expert."

I bit back the urge to shout at them that *aviation* meant planes, not birds. I'm glad I restrained myself, because their next sentence would've punched the words back down my throat and sent them to live in the pit of my stomach.

"Well, that bird has got be in here somewhere—some sort of shadow crow, they said. It came this way, and we checked every other place."

Shadow crow? Oh, no! They were after Old Familiar! But what was he doing in a zoo in the middle of Memphis? And why were these two bedsheet-wearing examples of cosplay gone wrong trying to find him? I doubted the reason was for anything good, and that meant only one thing.

We had to stop them.

"Uh-oh."

I turned to see Ayanna and Gum Baby exchange a knowing look, and I sat back on my heels and frowned. "What?"

"We know that expression," Ayanna said. "You just decided to do something dangerous without thinking of the consequences, for you or the people with you."

"Well—"

"And," Gum Baby interrupted, "Captain Disasterix probably hasn't thought about what happens *if* his plan succeeds. If you can even call it a plan. It only got one step. Step one: 'Save me, Gum Baby!' That ain't a plan, that's a prayer."

"Amen," Ayanna said, and the two grinned at each other.

"Can we please focus on saving Old Familiar?" I said through gritted teeth. "If we find him, we'll find High John, who can help us stop Cotton."

"Boy, fix your face," Gum Baby said, throwing a tiny ball of sap at me. "Gum Baby, as a matter of fact, actually has a plan. Just follow her lead."

"Wait!"

But the little menace was down my side and sprinting forward before anyone could stop her. Ayanna and I held our breath as she skirted the shadows, somersaulted over one or two birds—I think they were flamingos, but with all of them covered with blankets, I couldn't be sure—and landed *directly* between the two birdnappers.

"Is she tying their shoes together?" Ayanna asked.

I closed my eyes and inhaled deeply. "No, she's sapping them together. And now she's leaving something on the ground behind— Sweet peaches, I think she's setting up a Tricky Sticky."

Ayanna pointed. "Look, she wants us to come over."

Sure enough, Gum Baby was beckoning for us to join her, and I shook my head in resignation. "I think I know what happens next. Shall we?" I extended my arm as if the two of us were heading for an evening stroll.

Ayanna smothered a laugh but linked her arm with mine. "Why not?"

Together, we stepped into the light. I started whistling, and Ayanna began twirling one coil of hair that had escaped her head wrap. If it weren't for the chaos and destruction around us, it would have been really nice.

"Oi!" One of the masked figures, a man by the sound of it, ruined the mood. He turned and pointed. "What are you two doing—"

"Harold, watch out!" The other adult, a woman, grabbed him by the arm. "What do you want?" she called to us. "You're not allowed to be in here."

I exchanged a look with Ayanna, then turned back to them. "But...you're not, either."

"Did you break in? Harold, call the police."

I stared at what they were carrying—a bird bound in rope and blankets—then surveyed the destruction all around us, and finally took in their outfits. "So, let me get this straight..." I said slowly. "You're going to call the police...on *us?*"

Gum Baby had snuck away and was dancing impatiently in the shadows behind the dynamic duo, but I wanted to understand what gave the two masked adults the idea that they wouldn't get in trouble, too.

Then Harold spoke. "Heyyy...I recognize this guy. It's

that boy who started the riots down South somewhere. Remember, Darla? On the news? The one we wrote to the newspaper about?"

The lady—Darla—thought for a second. "The sit-ins?"

"No, the other one."

"The bus boycott?"

"Mmm, I don't think that's it."

"The kneeling?"

I interrupted. "You know, none of those were riots. Not sure you realized that."

They both glared at me. "Of course they were!" Harold snapped.

Darla's hand flew to her mouth. "Oh my gosh, I *do* recognize him. His face was all over the news. Harold, quick, call nine-one-one!"

The man's phone was out so fast I thought he had magic powers as well. He glanced at the birds, then at the destroyed aviary, and I knew what he was thinking as soon as a wicked gleam entered his eye.

He was going to try to pin this destruction on *me*!

I lunged forward. "Wait, don't—"

Harold took a step back, and just then the Tricky Sticky engaged. The man tripped as his feet became tangled with his partner's, and the two of them landed on the ground just as the Frisbee-size sap trap exploded in a sheet of sticky stuff that enveloped everything within a square yard. I was actually impressed at the control. Neither Ayanna nor I got hit, and neither did any of the birds. But the two weird adults in masks wriggled around on the ground, unable to speak as their mouths were covered in sap.

Gum Baby dusted off her hands. "Gum Baby might as well stay here with the monkeys, because she's a natural guerilla."

While Ayanna and Denmark Messy discussed what should be done with our captives, I took a cautious step toward the hole in the aviary's rear wall. Could Old Familiar really be in there? Where was High John?

Whatever the case, I wouldn't get my answers out here. I took another step inside, then another, easing my way into the darkness. I couldn't see a thing. Now, I'm not a scaredy-cat, as evidenced by my previous adventures and the certificate I printed off of a phobia website (seriously, you can find a certification for anything these days). But something about the gloom in the aviary chilled me to the core. Maybe it was the absolute silence that greeted me. No chirps, tweets, or hoots. Maybe it was the thought that whatever had smashed a hole in this building was still nearby. Could animals . . . like gorillas . . . have escaped from other enclosures? All of a sudden I couldn't rid myself of the image of a giant silverback rushing at me, and my chest grew tight. That was it—I had to get out. I turned to rejoin Ayanna and Gum Baby . . . and spotted Harold and Darla wriggling free.

"Hey!" I shouted.

But Harold had gotten an arm unstuck and was jabbing at his cell phone. "Hello? Hello? Earl, it's Harold again. Yes, I know this is the fifth time tonight, but I'm for real this time. We've got us a real live criminal!"

I was just cupping my hands around my mouth to tell the others to run when a noise sounded to my left.

I froze. "Hello?"

Rustling. Creaking. But no response.

"Old Familiar?" I turned and squinted into the darkness. "Is that you?"

I inched back inside. There *was* something in there, hiding in the rear. I had just made out a silhouette when it exploded into motion.

CAW!

A beak the size of a folding chair rushed toward my chest, ready to skewer me.

Old Familiar burst into the night, and without thinking (yeah, yeah, go ahead and say it, *Tristan never thinks before he acts*, har-har-har) I grabbed the giant crow's hackles, the feathers around his neck. Within seconds I was airborne, hanging on to the bird for dear life. Someone screamed so loud my ears popped, and it wasn't until I stopped to inhale that I realized it was me. Old Familiar shot up into the night, but it wasn't a smooth journey. The crow herked and jerked left and right, flying at weird angles like he was zigzagging while doing a loop de loop, barely avoiding a stand of trees with an animal-themed playground beneath it.

"Old Familiar!" I shouted. "Hey, it's me! Tristan."

The crow cawed and tried to climb higher, then squawked and plummeted a dozen feet before regaining altitude. My heart, meanwhile, was probably still falling. Did I ever mention that I have a slight problem with heights? No? Hmm. Well, maybe you weren't paying attention, just like Old Familiar wasn't paying attention to my pleading shouts for him to slow down.

"Take it easy!" I said, finally managing to climb on top of his back. "Don't you recognize me?"

The bird responded by diving again, flapping awkwardly as he tried to dislodge me.

Or was he?

Every so often, Old Familiar would turn his head, peer at me with his giant black eye, let out a harsh caw, then attempt to flap. At first, I thought his actions were meaningless. After a while, though, I paid attention to them. And I noticed his right wing. It was crooked, and every time the crow tried to straighten it to gain some stability, the wing gave out on him and we fell through the air again.

Old Familiar croaked and looked back at me once more.

"Do you need my help?"

Caw!

"Okay, tell me what to do."

(Look, I know this situation sounds unbelievable, what with me taking directions from a giant crow that *National Geographic* would throw a fit about, and you're well within your rights to look at me with a healthy dose of skepticism, but if you're going to get off the bandwagon, you gotta do it now, because this story only gets wilder.)

Old Familiar managed to get himself lined up, and then he looked back at me again.

I nodded. "Ready when you are!" I shouted.

That's when I noticed our destination. We were heading directly for the partially destroyed aviary, and Old Familiar showed no signs of stopping. Instead, the crow gathered speed.

"Um," I said.

We flew over the trail of destruction at the zoo entrance, over the huddled, sticky forms of Harold and Darla, and over Ayanna and Gum Baby. The latter two were jumping up and down, waving their arms in warning as if I couldn't tell the bird and I were on a collision course with a concussion.

"What are you doing?" I shouted. "Pull up—we're going to crash!"

Old Familiar continued to guide his rapid descent (a kind way of saying *clumsy fall*) toward the gaping hole in the building. I gripped a handful of feathers and tried to guess how many bones I'd break if I jumped off when we were low enough to the ground. Probably at *least* ten. Maybe even twenty. But I'd survive . . . right?

A single cry interrupted my plans. *CAW!*

I gritted my teeth and hauled on the bird's good wing in an attempt to slow it down. For a brief, terrifying moment, nothing happened. Then every feather on Old Familiar's back rustled at the same time . . . against the wind. Shining and black, they stood on end like arm hairs, and I felt a tingling moving up my hands as I continued to hold on. This was power! Magic!

The aviary loomed ahead. Ayanna and Gum Baby shouted warnings, but it was too late. Old Familiar let out a harsh cry as we plunged through broken brick wall and into the dark. Air howled past my face as rubble crashed down behind us. I squeezed my eyes shut, convinced we were going to ram into a bird enclosure at top speed and it would be *Bye-bye, Tristan Strong, you had a good run.*

But we kept flying.

And flying.

I opened one eye. That couldn't be right. The aviary wasn't that long—how were we still flying? Then I opened both eyes, because I couldn't believe what I was seeing.

The zoo collapsed underneath us as we passed over it. No. It *unbuilt* itself. Brick separated from brick, nails popped out of pieces of lumber that floated and stacked themselves into piles. We flew on. The fences around the animal enclosures coiled their wires and removed their posts. The food court dissolved into heaps of plaster, the water drained from the fountains, and cement exploded into powder that sorted itself into bags.

We were outside of time. The last time this had happened, High John was showing me the destruction of the Thicket in MidPass. But why was his spirit crow doing it on his own now?

Old Familiar cawed and looked at me. I pulled the wing again, trying to steer him back to Ayanna, Gum Baby, and the present. But we left the zoo—or the lot that would become the zoo—and entered the city proper. Neighborhoods disappeared before my eyes. Houses, apartment buildings, commercial businesses—everywhere I looked, the city was undoing itself. We circled above it like the complete opposite of a vulture as we watched Memphis return to its roots. The world grayed as if a filter had been dropped over it, and I blinked several times until I confirmed my eyes weren't the problem.

Finally, after ten minutes, Old Familiar descended to the ground, awkwardly but at least upright. I was safe. But where were we? We'd landed in a cluster of houses, but I'd never seen any like these before. They were small, constructed of wood and nothing else. Seven or eight had been placed in a circle with a communal garden in the middle.

Originally painted white, the houses were now scorched black.

"Where are we?" I whispered to Old Familiar.

He cawed and ruffled his feathers but otherwise didn't move. I slid off his back, keeping one hand on him just in case I had to make a quick getaway. "Hellooo?" I called out. "Anybody here?"

No one answered.

I whispered to Old Familiar. "I don't know why you brought me here, wherever and whenever we are, but I hope you know your way back."

Caw!

"Yeah, well, whoever lived here is long gone. Hopefully they got out okay. This is a ghost tow—"

I broke off just as a young man in a soldier's uniform walked up the hill, saw the burned-out shell of a neighborhood, and froze.

I froze, too.

Not because he could see me. No, it was because I recognized him. It was John, the boy who had escaped slavery and joined the USCT. The ghost who had looked like High John.

John started running, passing right by me and Old Familiar as he sprinted to the torched homes. A painful wail tore its way out of his throat as John dropped to his knees and pounded the ground. Tears streamed down his face. I looked away and swallowed the sudden lump in my throat.

"Old Familiar, that you?"

It was a different voice, and it made me turn around so

fast I got whiplash. I knew that voice. Had argued with that voice. Suddenly, Old Familiar's actions made sense. The giant bird had been told to bring me to . . . wherever we were. And the man—no, the god—who had sent him appeared in the broken window of one of the burned-out homes.

"Tristan Strong," High John the Conqueror said weakly. He coughed. "Might be I'm in need of your help." And with that, the god collapsed.

17

GODS IN GRAYSCALE

GODS CAN'T DIE. GODS CAN'T DIE.

The thought repeated itself over and over as I leaped onto the burned shack's sagging porch. The door shattered when I shoved it open. Dust and the smell of smoke filled the air, and I choked as it filled my lungs.

Gods can't die. Gods can't die.

But I was wrong, wasn't I? Stories defined the gods and gave them their power, and if their stories were erased, the people they served forgot about them and they faded away. John Henry, one of the strongest gods I knew, had nearly died after Bear attacked him with his own hammer. The big man eventually pulled through—barely—and as I stumbled through the hollowed ruin of a home, I desperately prayed High John would do the same.

"High John?" I shouted.

"Here," he said from his position in the corner of the

house. He wore a long cloak that was ripped and gashed in several spots, black pants, a cream shirt, and his traditional pouch around his neck. He sat in a pile of debris, one hand clutching his chest. I approached slowly, confused and cautious and fearing the worst.

"What happened?" I asked, crouching by his side. "Who did this to you?"

High John let out a pain-filled chuckle. "Your haint friend. Caught me and Old Familiar by surprise. Barely escaped with my life. I'm a bit winded, but I'll be fine. Just had to high-tail it out of there before things got any worse and I lost my opportunity to talk to you."

"Me?"

High John nodded, then winced. I reached for his cloak to see if I could help and he slapped my hands away. "Leave it, Tristan. There's no time. Help me up."

This feeling of me arriving too late to save a hurt friend was all too familiar. I lent him my shoulder, and High John levered himself to his feet and beckoned me to follow. "Come on, I need to show you something."

"I saw you," I said as we hobbled to the door. "Outside. Younger and less flashy, and apparently dead, but it was definitely you. And that wasn't the first time I saw you, either. How is it you're a ghost but you're also here?"

High John tried to smile but it came out more like a grimace. "You saw him, huh? Boy been doggin' my steps ever since I set foot in this world. Sometimes it felt like I was chasin' *him*."

"But how can he be here if...you know, you're here?"

"You mean if I'm alive?" High John asked drily. "Well, I reckon big John Henry told you 'bout it once. How the dreams and stories of this world helped power Alke and everyone in it."

I nodded. When I first arrived in Alke, John Henry had explained the connection between that world and my own. In Alke, the power of stories was what the iron monsters, Cotton, the Maafa, and even Anansi desired above all. The ability to control the narrative and shape how the future of the world would look. In the wrong hands, the power was dangerous.

"Well, let me ask you this," High John said as we exited the shack and moved across the porch. "You ever hear of somethin' called the John tales?"

I shook my head. "No, but don't you think we should get you some help, or maybe—"

High John cut me off with an impatient chop of his hand. "You gotta listen, Tristan. I'm tellin' you, there ain't much time. I've done a lot of research into this."

"Why?" I bit my lip after the question slipped out, but High John didn't seem upset.

"Because I wanted to understand how the stories in this world gave me my strength. Like the ones your Nana passed to you and others. People died for them. So when you brought us all over here and I found myself standin' in the middle of a store as big as one of Nyame's palaces, and it was stuffed wall to wall with books and maps and all the stories a god could dream of, I figured maybe, if I learned about my stories over here, I'd get even stronger." He fell silent, thinking.

"Did you?" I asked. "Did you grow stronger?"

High John sighed. "Tristan, you have no idea. I found old John tales and young John tales. John the trickster and John the tricked. Free John and Slave John. So many stories. I traveled across this country, me and Old Familiar, lookin' for more. You don't understand, boy—every time I read one of my stories, I could feel the power in them. So I took them. Reclaimed them."

We walked to the hard-packed space between the other homes in the destroyed neighborhood. A scrawny sapling—oak, or maple—grew out of the dirt. Old Familiar watched us, his one broken wing dangling awkwardly from his body.

"I don't understand," I said. "You read the stories and grew powerful?"

High John shook his head impatiently. "No, I *consumed* them. Took them from the world. I thought I was being smart—no one can destroy your stories if they're inside you."

He stared at the burned homes around us, seeing them while not really seeing them. "But libraries and books aren't the only place to find stories. No, sir. And you should know that—remember the first time we met?"

I nodded. Inside the great mountain fortress of Isihlangu, I'd argued with High John over possession of the Story Box. It's where I met Thandiwe and the elders who helped govern the Ridgefolk. And those elders happened to be spirits.

"Wait..." I said, my mind racing. "Spirits are a story source, too...."

High John grinned. "Now he's catchin' on. Think about it. All the spirits you've run into had stories they wanted to tell. Tasks incomplete. Injustices..."

He trailed off. I waited for several seconds as he closed his eyes. When he opened them, he looked off to the right. "Thandiwe! Remind me to tell Tristan about the children. It's...it's the children."

"High John?" I said, gently shaking him.

The god blinked, then his eyes focused and he frowned. "Losin' myself..." he muttered. "Where'd I fade out?"

"Are you—"

"I'm fine!" he snapped. "No time for that. Where'd I leave off?"

"You were talking about spirits and their stories," I said. "But you just mentioned Thandiwe, and...something about children? Do you know where she is?"

He flapped a hand at me. "Later. You have to understand

what I'm tellin' you. The haint knows that a spirit's story is incredibly powerful. All they need is someone to talk to."

I bit my lip. High John's mind seemed to be at war with itself. Still, he had a point. Eddie had been a spirit when he'd warned me about Anansi's tricks. Bear's two cubs had been spirits trying to tell me that their father was the Shamble Man. Spirit stories could reveal truth.

"Now, I ain't got the talents and powers you do," High John said, "but I did have something else: a spirit crow. With Old Familiar's help, I started hearing the John tales from spirits scattered across the land. That's when I ran into him."

He pointed at the John spirit still crying on his knees in front of the burned homes. "He ain't the oldest John tale, or even the most popular. But Old Familiar found him as we were searchin' for more spirits and their stories. Bird-brain actually mistook him for me." High John reclined his head and took a deep breath. Then another. It wasn't until I shifted positions to try to support him better that he looked up. When he saw me, his eyes lit up.

"Tristan! Old Familiar finally found you. Come on, boy, we need to talk."

I stopped. "But . . . we've been talking."

High John frowned at me. "We have?"

I nodded and watched as he peered around in confusion, then softly hit his thigh with his left fist, his right still clutching his chest. "Losin' my hold," he muttered.

Once, when I was eight, my parents took me with them to visit a friend of the family, an older woman who used to be a professor at the university where Mom worked. She seemed nice, the old professor, but she kept repeating herself, restarting conversations they'd already had, and telling Mom where to drop off assignments. Each time she did it, I could see the pain it caused my mother. Later, on the car ride home, Mom and Dad had explained to me what Alzheimer's disease is, and how it affects the brains of some adults as they get older. The thought of losing my memories had haunted me for weeks, and I'd obsessively filled notebooks with every experience I'd ever had and then stashed them in secure places around the house. That habit had prompted Mom to start buying me journals, and it was one of the reasons Eddie's mom gave me his journal with our English project in it after he died.

High John sighed and looked off into the distance. "Where was I?" he whispered.

I pointed at the John spirit. High John nodded. "He's a part of me. His story is one of the ones that gave me power in Alke. And heaven knows, I ain't got much of that left. . . . But you have to see. You have to see what that haint Cotton is doing. He's eatin' history, Tristan." High John continued to limp over to Old Familiar. He stroked the crow's feathers, then gestured for me to join him on the bird's back. "Come, let me show you."

"Shouldn't you be resting?"

"Here, grab hold," he said, ignoring my question. High John placed my hand over Old Familiar's good wing, then closed his eyes and took a deep breath. Then another. After several seconds, he opened his eyes and shook his head. "Too weak," he muttered. "You're gonna have to do it."

I gawked. "Excuse me?"

"You're gonna have to step outside of time again, Tristan."

I started to back away, but he kept hold of my wrist. "Look, I can barely step outside of my apartment without causing some catastrophe," I said. "One time I tripped and crashed through the door of the apartment across the hall. Do you know how embarrassing it is to have to explain to your parents that the neighbors called the police because you're clumsy? No, I don't think so." I was babbling, and High John wore a smirk.

"You ain't got a choice." He placed my hand over my heart, made sure I had a good fistful of my own hoodie, and then put his own uninjured hand on my shoulder. "How you gonna get back home?"

He was right. If High John couldn't send us back out of this grayscale version of Memphis, it would be up to me. I'd only arrived here because Old Familiar knew where to go. Now I had to lead us back. Great. One more responsibility on my shoulders. Pretty soon I'd need a checklist. Was this how grown-ups felt? No wonder they stomped around with frowny faces all the time.

"You don't have the practice of it," High John continued, "so Old Familiar's gonna be your guide. Just make sure you have a firm hold on him, focus on the place you tryin' to see, and the old featherbag will do the rest."

I hesitated. "What about you?"

"Oh, I'm not goin' with you, boy. I'm gonna sit here for a spell."

"You're not—"

"No, and before you start complainin', I was high-steppin' outside of time when I was your age."

"Great," I muttered. "And I bet you had to walk ten miles through the snow, uphill both ways, when you did it."

"What'd you say?"

"Nothing, nothing." I sighed. "Fine. Where—or when, I don't know—am I going?"

High John's face grew dark. "You'll know it when you see it."

I threw up my hands in disgust.

Seven pristine homes, white paint, blue trim, a communal garden in the center of them all. I was right back where I'd started. Did this whole stepping-outside-of-time thing need a boost? New batteries? Did I have to unplug Old Familiar and plug him back in? What was going on?

"High John," I said, turning around, "I don't think it—"

The Alkean god wasn't there. It was just me and Old

Familiar on the hilltop overlooking town. And, as I examined my surroundings, I realized that while I was right back *where* I'd started, I wasn't back *when* I started. There was no fire damage, no smoke-filled air. The sapling was no more than a sprout. This was before the catastrophe had struck the neighborhood.

But where was everybody?

Caw!

I turned around just as Old Familiar flapped awkwardly into the air. "Hey!" I shouted, but the shadow crow was already flying to a stand of trees in the distance. I contemplated going after him—that bird was my ticket out of here—but decided against it. I'd stepped outside of time to this spot for a reason. The house where I'd found High John was the closest to me. He'd wanted me to learn something from this trip, so maybe I had to start in there.

One day I would write a tell-all memoir about gods and their lack of clear directions. Just once I'd love for someone to hand me a to-do list for heroes. *Complete items one through five and you too can save the day.* Good grief.

The wooden stairs were solid and painted blue. The door was still intact, and the brass handle gleamed in the sun. I knocked, waited, then rolled my eyes at my mistake and stepped right through the wood. Being a temporary ghost has its advantages.

The burned single-room shack I remembered was now a

cozy home divided into rooms with hanging sheets. I wasn't really sure what I was supposed to be looking for, and I didn't want to invade anyone's privacy, so I kept mostly to the doorway and peeked around. An old woodstove blazed merrily, two wooden chairs on either side. A bed had been shoved into one corner, and in the other was a long wooden table holding carvings in different stages of completion. Pictures had been hung on the wall, and something grabbed my eye, so I stepped closer to examine them.

In the first, an older Black man and woman stood proudly with their hands around a young boy who held a wooden carving of a deer. It was pretty good, actually, and the kid beamed with pleasure as he held up his creation. I smiled. It reminded me of Terrence with his pizza spatula. My smile faded.

I moved to the next picture, exhaling and trying to get the image of fire out of my head, and paused. I knew the person in this picture. The young man wore a crisp blue army uniform and a military-issued hat, and he stood beneath the sign that read USCHA OF MEMPHIS. It was John, the spirit. This was his home? No, his parents' home. No wonder his spirit had been so upset earlier at seeing it burned down.

I moved away and sighed. I still didn't know what I was supposed to be looking for. After giving the home one more quick glance, I shrugged and—

Wait, was that a scream?

The sound had been so faint, I might've imagined it. Still, I'd been here too long. It was time to find Old Familiar and get back to the real world. I—

There it was again! Definitely a scream. Someone was in trouble! I placed the carving back on the table and took a step toward the door—

CRASH!

—only to dive backward and land heavily on my back when someone kicked open the door and threw a burning bottle and rag inside. Flames exploded out of broken glass and spread everywhere. More shouts and screams.

"Get the next one!"

"Don't leave any standing."

"Get 'em out of here!"

It took me a second to realize that the shouts weren't aimed at me, and that the glass and flames—as dangerous as they looked—couldn't hurt me. *You're a ghost in this time, remember?* I told myself. Still, I cautiously stepped out the door, wary of more flaming bottles aimed in my general direction. Spirit or not, I didn't want to test my luck.

It was chaos.

A nightmare.

Flames shot fifteen feet into the air. Every house in the small neighborhood was on fire. I couldn't see anyone, but the screams... I knew the screams would haunt me for the rest of my life. So many. Old, young, I heard them all.

I turned to run down the hill. I don't know what I was planning to do. I couldn't speak to anyone in this world. But I couldn't stand still, either. People were hurting.

It didn't matter.

Below me, the rest of the town burned. There was no escape for any of the occupants. Even though I knew that this had already happened a long time ago, a tear rolled down my cheek as the screams kept coming, and that laughter, that vicious and cruel laughter floated over everything.

That's when I understood what High John had wanted me to witness. It hurt that I'd had to watch someone's home and community burn down to learn it.

A rush of air blew past me, and I looked back to see Old Familiar swooping in through the flames. The shadow crow cawed at me, then cocked his head as if asking was I ready. I nodded, wiped unspilled tears from the corners of my eyes, and reached out to touch his feathers. I closed my eyes tight and tried to shut out the flames. I stepped forward....

When I reentered the gray world of the spirits, High John's eyes were closed and he lay slumped against the ground.

"High John!" I shouted. My stomach flipped and my breath grew short. I feared the worst.

The god stirred. "Hng. Who's yellin' like they ain't got no sense? Tristan? Boy, you got to turn that volume off ten. I'm liable to have ringin' ears for the rest of my life now."

I squatted down next to him. "I know. I know why you sent me there."

The humor faded from High John's eyes. He looked away, over to where the remains of the house—the John spirit's house—stood. He sighed and, after a few moments, spoke in a pain-filled whisper. "Memphis Race Riots of 1866. Nearly all of South Memphis was destroyed, boy. Black-owned homes, businesses, restaurants. People were killed. Abused. Beaten. And yet no one was ever brought to justice. That's what I learned from that spirit. No one was ever brought to justice."

I gulped. "And the spirits are doomed to relive that over and over? Looking for loved ones who never answer, or trying to put out flames that'll never die?"

High John nodded.

I stood and started pacing, trying to connect the dots. Spirits as sources of stories. Cotton. The auction houses of New Orleans. Old Angola, the horrific plantation in Louisiana. The slave barges of the Mississippi. And now the riots of Memphis. "That's why Cotton is feeding spirits to that Old Angola monster. He's trying to harness the power of their stories by consuming them."

"I've seen what happens to the spirits," High John whispered, "when the haint is done feedin' them to that walking fortress. They're torn apart, Tristan. Like smoke driftin' away on a breeze. And the Breakers..." He trailed off, his eyes closing.

I leaned over him and tried to shake him gently. "High John?"

He looked at me, then blinked. "Tristan, you made it! Old Familiar got you here in one piece, huh?"

No. No, no, no. "High John," I said desperately. "You said something about Breakers. What are Breakers, and what do they have to do with Cotton? We don't have much time!"

But his eyes were fluttering shut again. I grabbed his arm, and he managed to look at me. Frustration clouded his face and he gripped my hand. "Listen, boy, I'm fadin' here. Fadin' fast. You gotta find Thandiwe. Hear me? She knows what to do."

"But—"

"No, just listen. Ask . . ." He paused to take a deep breath. "Ask Old Familiar to help you. Ask him! He's a smart old bird, he'll get you where you need to go. I just need . . . I just need to rest." And with that last set of instructions, High John the Conqueror closed his eyes and let his head droop against the grass.

Behind him, the spirit with his face cried.

18
SPIRIT UTILITY VEHICLE

GODS CAN'T DIE.

Gods sure are heavy, though.

The streets were empty as I trudged down the hill to the tree where Old Familiar waited. Dim light from the not-quite-risen morning sun filtered through the spaces between buildings and under highway overpasses. The sapling I'd seen in the spirit memory was now a green giant in the middle of the city. Its branches stretched all the way across the street, and its roots had buckled several squares of sidewalk. I'd seen that back in Chicago, but now I actually stared at the phenomenon as I carried High John down toward the tree. Tendrils of roots peeked through cracks in the concrete. Imagine that. Surviving a devastating riot, and decades upon decades of the city changing and hardening around you, and still having the strength to break through the obstacles keeping you from growing.

Gods can't die.

I hefted High John, checked to see if he was still breathing, and continued. If I could just get him to Old Familiar, maybe the bird could help. The shadow crow had carried Ayanna after she was injured by brand flies, transporting her to the Mmoatia of Alke, who had performed their healing magic. Had any of the whistling fairies made it over to this world? I wondered. Anansi would know. I struggled to keep High John balanced in a firefighter's carry while I reached for the SBP, only for my hand to fall back to my side.

Right. The phone had been confiscated.

The burning in my chest started up again. The anger . . . it, it, it . . . it just boiled inside of me with nowhere to go. I heard the start of a drumbeat. I tried to take a deep breath, then a second. I needed to calm down, or else. . . .

A whisper of air brushed past me. "Stop following me," I said.

After a few seconds I stopped and turned around. The young man's spirit—I'd started calling him Spirit John in my head—walked a few paces behind me, determination on his face. I couldn't look at him. He reminded me too much of the god in my arms, and how I couldn't control the adinkra powers anymore—they just came and went as they pleased. "Just stop following me," I muttered again.

The spirit didn't listen.

I looked down. Was High John moving? I thought he was.

I tried to quicken my steps and finally reached the bottom of the hill. Just a few more feet, and then Old Familiar would know what to do.

Gods can't die.

I knew a lot of the John tales. I could find some. Stories were power, and High John just needed a bit more. The adinkra weren't enough. We could use Gum Baby's phone to call Anansi and Mami Wata, and they'd help. Or I could go to the hospital. They had to have something that could bring a god back, right? Tylenol, maybe?

Gods can't die.

Old Familiar stared at me with his head cocked as I approached. His beak, longer than my arm, gently touched High John's chest, and the shadow crow ruffled his feathers in distress. He hopped away, then threw his head back to let out the loudest caw I'd ever heard him make. It rang through the morning quiet, echoing off buildings that silently bore witness.

I laid High John gently at the base of the tree trunk and tried to prop him up like he was taking a nap against it. He looked peaceful, and I swallowed.

"High John!" I called out, shaking him. "High John! We're here. Come on, you can't be— High John!" The god stirred, and a sob of relief tore out of my chest. "OH . . . oh, you're still alive. Man, I . . . Look, we're here. Old Familiar is right here. Now you two can go get you some help. I—"

High John turned his head so that his eyes met mine. His sad smile cut off my words. "Tristan," he whispered. "Take this."

His right hand fell away from his chest, the fingers uncurling to reveal the root bag.

"No," I said, shaking my head. Teardrops fell onto my hand as I pushed the bag away. "No."

"Take it. Old Familiar needs you. He's lost here. This ole bag got some power left in it still. You wear it, and I promise I'll be with you. Now take it. Take it!"

He started to try to get up and I finally took the bag, if only to get him to rest. High John nodded, then sighed and sank back against the tree. He glanced over at Spirit John, who was standing with his hands shoved into his uniform pants pockets, and the two exchanged a nod. Something was communicated there, something I couldn't decipher, but the spirit turned and began walking up the street.

"All right, Tristan, I need you to do me a favor." High John had his eyes closed and his face twisted in pain. "Go ahead with Old Familiar. Find Thandiwe . . . the kids. Go on now. I'm just gonna close my eyes for . . . a second."

I knew an adult's dismissal of a kid when I heard one. They did it all the time when they wanted to talk among themselves about something they thought we weren't ready to hear. I looked at Old Familiar. The crow flapped his wings, even the injured one, and hopped between us.

"Is he...?" I couldn't bring myself to ask the question. It clumped up in my throat, and I swallowed several times and then changed what I'd been about to say. "I mean, will he be okay?"

The crow stared at me.

"Right," I muttered. "I'm going."

I followed after Spirit John, who'd stopped at the corner across the street. Cars were beginning to rattle along the overpass as Memphis started a new day. I glared at the highway. Didn't they know a god was dying here? How could... How could the world just go on?

I thought about Eddie then. Even now, several months after the accident, I still felt the pain of the loss. Grief never went away, but we were expected to keep going, to get over it. But you didn't get *over* grief. You put it inside your heart with all the other baggage you'd collected while existing, and you tried to get *along* with it. But who would grieve High John in this world? How, if his story and his friends were scattered and fading?

Some Anansesem I'd turned out to be. I guess Anansi and Mami Wata had been right to put me on probation.

Spirit John watched me as I approached, and when I stopped in front of him, my words just started tumbling out. "I don't know what I'm supposed to do next. Where am I supposed to go? Cotton is out there, other haints are out there, and now the missing children are a part of this, too?

I can't do this. I just can't. I failed, didn't I? The akofena, Anansi, being a hero. You all chose the wrong boy. I'm sorry."

A loud clap of thunder shook the sky. I looked up, confused. It was a clear day, with not a thundercloud in sight. I turned to check on High John and Old Familiar back at the tree, but an SUV driving down the street blocked my view of them. When the car passed, I gasped. The god and his bird were gone! And the tree...

The giant walnut tree had grown several dozen feet. The ground beneath it where High John had lain was now covered in calla lilies, flowers with petals so dark they looked like shadows. And if you turned your head just right, at a certain angle, you could almost see the outline of a god napping beneath their leaves. A shrine to a folk hero in the middle of the city.

I don't know how long I stood there crying.

Each sob brought a different memory. High John appearing in the middle of Isihlangu. High John pulling me outside of time, us soaring on Old Familiar's back. His magic ax chopping up the hullbeast that had threatened the mountain fortress. His root pouch helping a poisoned Ayanna until the Mmoatia could heal her. His beef with Nyame. His love of Alke.

High John was Eddie's favorite hero. I hoped the two of them were together now, swapping stories.

The SUV pulled to a stop in front of me. All black, from

the paint to the tinted windows to the rims on the tires. It moved silently, like one of those electric vehicles Nana coveted. At first I thought it was an unmarked police car, but then I spotted the hood ornament.

A crow with its wings outstretched.

"No way," I said, wiping away the tears.

The passenger door in front of me lifted up from the bottom and away, like the wing of a bird, and the silver-and-black interior gleamed. A silver *O* and *F* had been stitched into the back of the driver's headrest.

"Old...Familiar?" I asked slowly.

The headlights flashed and the horn honked. It sounded suspiciously like the harsh call of a crow. Spirit John slipped past me and got inside, then looked at me expectantly. I hesitated, then climbed in after him. The front dash had a giant screen bigger than most TVs, and on it was a map with a route displayed between a crow icon and two smaller icons.

"Are those Ayanna and Gum Baby?" I asked. "Okay. Let's go pick them up. And then—"

Another icon appeared. Another face, all the way on the opposite side of Memphis. I nodded, then inhaled. Thandiwe. High John had wanted to me to find her. Said she needed help. That was step one, then. After that, Cotton and the other haints would follow. "Yes. Let's go."

As the SUV pulled off (Old Familiar apparently had a self-driving license), I looked out the rear windshield, staring at the tree and the flowers until we turned the corner. Then I squeezed the root bag I still clutched in my hand and slipped it around my neck.

Gods can't die…as long as you remember them.

I don't recall when Ayanna got into the SUV. I don't remember Gum Baby curling up next to me, or Old Familiar driving us through Memphis morning-rush-hour traffic, or even the phone conversation I apparently had with Nana, who somehow had Gum Baby's number.

You know what I do remember?

The sounds of thunder and roaring ocean waves when I first witnessed High John the Conqueror stepping out of time.

"Tristan? We're here," said Ayanna.

I sat up and looked around. The SUV idled outside a dingy brown warehouse on a long city block full of dingy brown warehouses. A garage door had a very realistic mural of a vicious Rottweiler on it, along with the words KEEP OUT in bright red, and the side door was covered in BEWARE OF DOG signs. All in all, I didn't feel very welcome.

"Where exactly is *here*?" I asked.

Gum Baby climbed into the front seat and squinted at the display. "Orange Mound? Where's that? See? Gum Baby knew she should've drove. But noooo, all of a sudden y'all worried about drivers being able to reach the brakes. THAT'S WHAT SAP IS FOR, AYANNA."

Ayanna gently bonked the little doll on the head with her bat, and the two exchanged silly faces. My lips creased into a small smile. I knew they were doing it to keep from crying over High John.

I looked at Spirit John, still sitting silently in the third row. Ayanna and Gum Baby were oblivious to his presence.

"Okay," I said to those two, opening the rear passenger door and sliding out. "Let's go meet this contact."

"Are you sure this is what you're supposed to do?" Ayanna asked.

I shrugged. "It's what . . . I think so."

She got out after me, her golden-tipped bat strapped to her back, followed by Gum Baby, who immediately climbed up into my hood and started recording our approach with her phone.

"What are you doing?" I asked.

"Gum Baby documents everything for her fans, Bumbletongue. Told you to get on social media. My last stream got over five hundred views."

I paused just outside the warehouse's side door. "Five hundred? That's pretty impressive. What were you streaming?"

Gum Baby didn't answer, and as I reached for the doorknob and she aimed the phone at me, realization struck. I craned my neck to glare at her.

"You didn't!"

"Relax, Bumbletongue, Gum Baby believes in getting permission before she records."

I stared at her suspiciously. That sounded like there was another shoe waiting to drop.

Gum Baby stuck a blob of sap on my shoulder and mounted the phone so her hands could be free. "And that's why Gum Baby asked your grandmother to tell her stories about you when you were younger. Gum Baby's making a documentary, see. She's an orca historian."

I grabbed the doorknob and chuckled. "You mean an *oral* historian. Fun fact, orcas are dolphins. So..."

Unfortunately, just as I began to twist the knob, someone inside yanked the door open and I went tumbling into darkness, landing hard on a metal surface that cut my palms. And if that didn't completely derail our attempts at stealth, Gum Baby's shout, which echoed around the warehouse interior, took care of the rest.

"DOLPHINS NEED TO TELL STORIES, TOO, PROFESSOR BUMBLETONGUE!"

A light switched on. Five hooded figures with their faces shrouded in shadow loomed over me and Gum Baby, who'd somehow managed to land on her feet. Four more appeared outside, behind Ayanna, and forced her inside. The door slammed shut.

The good news? No sign of a Rottweiler.

I didn't have time to get up before another hooded figure—taller and carrying a large object on their shoulder—approached. They dropped into a crouch in front of me.

"If it isn't Mr. Mississippi Fire himself," they said.

I cocked my head. I knew that voice.

"Thandiwe?"

She pulled her hood back to reveal red-and-teary eyes. Then the princess of Isihlangu held out her hand to help me up.

"Tell me how he died."

19

THE ROLLING THUNDER

WE WALKED IN THE SILENCE OF SURVIVORS.

That's a type of quiet I can't stand. It'll show up at funerals, where people won't speak or will talk in hushed tones so they don't disturb you, when all you want is for someone to disturb and distract you. Or it'll show up when you walk by the bedroom of someone who will never sleep there again, or maybe in the middle of the night, when you wake up and remember that you will never see a certain person on your way to school, to work, to church. That silence ate away at me. It was unnatural, and I hated it. I'd suffered through that silence once. No way was I going to do it again.

"You know," I said, "High John is the one who helped me get over my fear of heights."

We were walking through a wide corridor that—according to the signs hanging on the walls every few dozen feet—used to be designated for forklifts carrying spare railroad parts.

Or a bunch of Bigfoots wearing space armor. It was hard to tell, partly because of how old the place was, and also because of all the tags.

The hallway leading to Thandiwe's hideout was covered in graffiti. Hundreds of tags in every color you could imagine. I pointed out a snazzy rainbow one as we walked—Thandiwe and Ayanna in front, me and Gum Baby (on my shoulder, where else?) behind them, and Spirit John bringing up the rear.

The Isihlangu princess had grown since I'd last seen her. She wore gray leggings with black beads stitched down the sides and a long silver tunic with excerpts from different books printed on the front. There was a skateboard strapped to her back, and it took me a while, but I eventually recognized it as her forebear, the shield she had carried back in Alke. It had transformed like Ayanna's staff had. I didn't see her kierie, the club-like weapon the people of Isihlangu wielded, but I guessed that would've raised a few questions in this world. Unless it too had turned into a baseball bat. I was looking around suspiciously for something like a club when the princess turned to me and raised both eyebrows.

"You?" Thandiwe said, the skepticism heavy in her tone. "The screaming thief of Alke, not afraid of heights anymore?"

"I said I got over them, not that I'm completely unafraid. There's a difference."

Ayanna bit back a laugh as Gum Baby grabbed the collar of my hoodie and pretended to scream.

"NO! NOOOOO! Bumbletongue is too annoying to die! Ooohhh, if only he'd listened to that incredibly brave and fearless orca historian, Gum Babyyy."

I rolled my eyes as the three of them cracked up. "Say what you want, but that time we all flew on Old Familiar, racing the Maafa back to the Golden Crescent, I barely thought about heights or falling."

"Yeah, we knew what you were thinking about," Gum Baby muttered, flinging a ball of sap at Ayanna.

My face turned twelve shades of red as Thandiwe burst into laughter again. She threw her arm around Ayanna's shoulder, who stuck her tongue out at Gum Baby before glancing at me and looking away.

"Well, High John didn't bring *me* a crush," said Thandiwe. "But he did bring me along when he started looking for his stories."

I perked up. "The John tales?"

Thandiwe nodded. "He told you about them?"

I looked behind me, and Spirit John met my eyes. He wouldn't stop following me, and I'd given up trying to get him to speak. I was getting used to him. What was one more ghost haunting my footsteps?

"Something like that," I finally responded.

"Well, we started in Alke, and then after..." said Thandiwe. "Well, after everything happened, we landed here. Something in the area called to him, and we started investigating. He kept saying the spirits around here were upset, and he needed to find out why. But one day we stumbled on some runaway kids and took them in. They wouldn't talk about where they'd been, or maybe they *couldn't* talk about it. They weren't making sense. Something about a talking horse that was chasing children."

Ayanna and I exchanged worried glances. Was this another one of Cotton's tricks?

Gum Baby grumbled as her tiny fingers flew across her phone's keyboard. "Now Gum Baby gotta face rodeo rejects? Enough with things talking when they shouldn't."

Just as I opened my mouth to point out the irony, Ayanna dropped back and elbowed me in my ribs.

"Don't you dare," she whispered.

I shut my mouth. Everything I was going to say went out the window anyway when Ayanna hooked her arm in mine.

"It's too dark to see in here," she whispered in explanation.

Cool. Cool, cool, cool. Just be cool. Just be—

"Stop mumbling, Big Head. You ain't cool," Gum Baby grumbled as she continued to text on her phone. "Kids these days. Always trying to be cool."

"ANYWAY," I said, "before he... Well, High John told me to find you, Thandiwe. He said something about the children."

Thandiwe stopped at a wide door and whirled around. "He did? What was it?"

I shook my head. "That's just it—he never told me."

The princess of the Ridgefolk twisted her face in confusion, then pulled a key from her pocket and unlocked the door. It slid open like a barn door, and bright light and peals of laughter spilled out. Thandiwe smiled at our shocked expressions.

"What?" she said. "I'm a princess, remember? I have to stay in style." She walked inside and we followed, stepping onto a catwalk that looked over a massive indoor skate park.

Yes.

A skate park.

There were vert ramps and rails winding around mini ramps, quarter-pipes and half-pipes—I even saw a bowl all the way in the back. Everything had been painted in bright colors, from sky blue to neon pink, and—maybe most important of all—kids of all ages skated around having fun.

"Mrs. Z, the owner of this place, said she'd planned on making it a safe space for the vulnerable. Children, especially. As long as we agreed to help them, she let High John and me stay for free and even threw in a few meals when she learned we were searching for others lost like us. Once word got out that we weren't turning away runaways or orphans or kids just needing somewhere to go after school, I guess we got pretty popular." Thandiwe smiled sadly and looked back at me. "High John said it's what you would've done."

I swallowed. Someone shouted at that very moment, and we all looked down to where a young Black girl in denim overalls sat on the warehouse floor holding her knee.

"Sorry," Thandiwe said, "give me a second." She pulled the skateboard off her back, ran a few steps, then dropped it and jumped on top. She rode down the giant ramp, kick-flipped up to the rail, and used it to grind all the way over to where the little girl sat.

I scoffed. "I can do that."

A ball of sap bounced off my head. "Why you always lying?" Gum Baby demanded.

The rest of us reached the floor of the converted warehouse a few minutes later, via the stairs. Thandiwe had comforted the injured skater and was walking her to a lounge on the far side of the space when the little girl stopped and looked at me strangely.

"Who are the new people? They look funny."

Thandiwe patted her shoulder. "Now, Chayse, we talked about that."

"Sorry," the little girl muttered.

I grinned. "Don't worry about it. I guess Gum Baby does look a little funny."

Another sap ball stung my head, and this time it was accompanied by a whispered threat. "Gum Baby's gonna sap your lips together when you go to sleep. See if you can talk slick then."

Chayse was shaking her head. "No, I like her. She's cute."

Gum Baby sniffed and examined her nails, which— Did she even have nails?

"Gum Baby got the drip, what can she say?"

But Chayse pointed behind me. "Him. He's the one that looks funny, sorryIjusthadtosayit."

I frowned. Him? I turned to find Spirit John still following me, his hands in his pockets.

"You can see him?"

Chayse nodded, and Ayanna, Thandiwe, and I stared at each other.

"Wait," Ayanna said, "who is she pointing at?"

"Spirit John," I said slowly. "A ghost. Which means she can see spirits . . . without an adinkra. And if she can do that, that means—"

"She could be at risk," Thandiwe finished.

We all stared at each other, the implications becoming more horrific the longer we thought about them. If Chayse could see spirits, she had a little magic in her. Cotton would want that, either to use to find more spirits, or to take for himself. Was this why all the children were being taken?

I balled up a fist. "I think we need to call an assembly."

All the children in the skate park—around thirty of them, ranging in age from seven and seventeen—gathered around the edge of the bowl. Before we joined them, Thandiwe explained to us how the giant structure came to be.

"Apparently, kids used to skate in abandoned swimming pools. But some adults started complaining, so Mrs. Z had this built."

From the ground, it looked like a collection of two-by-fours and prayers, but when we climbed up a ladder on the back side, a decent bowl awaited. A few kids were skating around inside it, some wearing Rollerblades and some using boards like Thandiwe's. A Black girl in a hijab demonstrated lip tricks ("Stop making smooching sounds, Gum Baby!") where she skated up the side of the bowl, paused with the front edge of the skateboard resting on the edge, then rode back down. Everyone else stood or sat and watched, whooping in encouragement after every trick.

Then Thandiwe skated down, and the kids went wild. The princess met the girl with the hijab in the middle and the two of them high-fived. After that, Thandiwe had the bowl to herself.

And she put on a show.

She rolled up one side, grabbed the nose of her board with her left hand and did a handstand with her right. She rolled up the other side, spinning in midair and landing perfectly. The kids pounded the bowl with their hands and feet and cheered. Ayanna and I screamed right alongside them. It was incredible!

Finally Thandiwe rolled into the center of the bowl, kick-flipped, and came to a stop. She held up both hands and waited for the cheering to stop.

"Who are we?" she shouted.

"ROLLING THUNDER!" everyone shouted back.

"Who are we?"

"ROLLING THUNDER!" Gum Baby shouted in my ear as everyone stomped the bowl.

It did sound just like thunder. I cocked an eyebrow questioningly at Ayanna.

She shrugged. "I don't know, maybe it's a morale-boosting thing."

Someone sat down on the other side of me. It was the girl in the hijab. "You got it!" she said cheerfully. "Rolling Thunder, the best skate squad in all of Tennessee. Hey, I'm Hanifa."

"Ayanna, Gum Baby, and I'm Tristan," I said, gesturing to each of us. I thought about introducing Spirit John but instead chose to wait. We'd find out shortly whether she could see him.

Hanifa nodded at us, then slid her skateboard behind her and pulled her legs to her chest. "A lot of the younger kids were feeling left out, especially the ones still learning to skate. So T"—she pointed at Thandiwe—"came up with the name Rolling Thunder so we could all belong to something."

"Like a family?" I asked.

Hanifa nodded and grew serious. "Some of the kids have homes. Family they go back to after hanging out here after school. But a lot of us don't, and the city is rough. We had to move around constantly, from shelters to hotels to a friend's place. Thandiwe and Mr. H were helping us find permanent living arrangements...."

It took me a minute to figure out that "Mr. H" was High John.

"But now that he's gone..." Hanifa fell silent for a few seconds, then sighed. "I guess we'll have to move on again."

I chewed on that as Thandiwe began to speak from below. I'd never given much thought to kids being homeless. Dad worked with a group shelter back in Chicago, but here, seeing it firsthand and realizing that some of the kids were no older than my cousin Terrence, made me wonder how something like that could happen....

And now Cotton and Patty Roller were snatching kids like the Rolling Thunder squad because they might have magic in them. It wasn't fair.

"Tristan," Ayanna said, nudging me. She nodded into the bowl, where Thandiwe was beckoning me. "It's time."

I nodded, then hopped off the lip of the bowl and slid down inside. We'd decided to address everyone at once— there were too many kids to check them one by one. But now, as I stared up at all the faces, it felt like I was standing in front of a school assembly. For a brief moment it was kind of scary. But as I met each pair of eyes, some black, some brown, some green, and some blue, set in faces ranging from brown to tan to nearly chalk white, I saw the same expression staring back at me. A familiar one.

Anger.

I straightened. I knew anger. Expressed and controlled, anger could be a powerful fuel for change. If suppressed or left unchecked, it could be disastrous.

And there had already been too many disasters for my liking.

"Okay!" I shouted, jumping high into the air and stomping the ground with both feet when I landed. "Everybody clench the muscles in your body as tight as you can. Ball up your fists, grit your teeth, and squeeze!"

Some kids did it, while others looked at me as if I'd sprouted horns.

"That's it, good job, keep going! Pretend"—I opened my eyes and waggled my eyebrows as I whisper-shouted—"like you're holding in a fart."

That did it. Everyone burst out laughing, including a few of the older kids. Ayanna rolled her eyes while Thandiwe face-palmed and shook her head.

"What you just did," I said as the laughter began to subside, "was relax. And you're going to need to do that for what I'm going to show you next—magic."

Murmurs circled the bowl. One of the older kids, a Black

boy with three parts in his curly top fade, stood with his arms folded. "You talking about card tricks and stuff?"

"No," I said. I took a deep breath. "I'm talking about magic. Magic from stories and the power in them."

The boy scoffed. "Yeah, right. Ain't no wizards 'round here. That's movie stuff. Why are we even listening to you?"

"Hey!" Thandiwe said, but I held up a hand to cut her off.

"No, he's not wrong. Why are y'all listening to me? I'm just a kid, a stranger at that. Am I right?"

There were a few skeptical nods. Ayanna looked worried, but I smiled at her. I knew it would come to this, and of all the powers granted to me by the Alkean gods, this was one I knew I could control.

"Let me tell you a story," I said, closing my eyes and squeezing the Gye Nyame adinkra. When I opened them, every surface of the warehouse shimmered in a haze of gold. Sentence fragments inched along the wood of the bowl, while poetry stanzas swirled among the rafters. Love stories. Tragedies. It was the history of the warehouse and the city of Memphis as told by the lives of the workers who called it home.

"Look at his eyes!"

"Holy cow!"

"Is that for real?"

"That's wild!"

The last comment came from the boy with the curly top

fade. I looked at him, and the sheer amazement on his face let me know he now believed. "What's your name?" I asked.

"It . . . Dexter," he said.

I nodded. "Dexter, what if I told you that everyone in this room might have some magic in them? Would you believe me?"

He shook his head, then paused, a guilty look on his face. "I mean, how? Why us? Nothing makes me special."

I grinned. "I'm afraid you're wrong, because I'm looking right at it."

He looked confused, but I'd noticed it right away. Each of the kids had a story fragment nestled in their chest, right above their heart. A piece of the story of Alke lived on in each of them. The Diaspor-app didn't have to tell if they were Alkean or not. As of this moment, to me, they all were. *We* all were.

"But how do we know?" Dexter asked.

I turned and beckoned, and Spirit John walked through the wall of the bowl. Everyone gasped, and a few kids screamed. When Gum Baby flipped out of my hoodie and landed in front of me, everyone cheered. And when Ayanna slid down to join us and held her glowing bat aloft, the golden face on it scowling at everyone, the entire warehouse rang with applause. I couldn't help it—my grin stretched from ear to ear. It felt like we were superheroes, and for the first time in a while, a little bit of tension eased out of my shoulders.

"HELLOOO!"

The loud voice echoed through the commotion and everyone grew quiet just in time to hear an exasperated question whip through the air. My shoulders tensed up again.

"Now, who is doing all that hooting and hollering?"

20
ERZULIE

"GRANNY Z!" GUM BABY SHOUTED. "LONG TIME NO SEE!"

Granny Z? The woman who stared down at us from the top of the bowl didn't look like a grandmother at all. Not that there's one way all grandmothers should look, you get me, but still—I couldn't quite put my finger on why the tiny Black woman with the twinkling eyes seemed so odd.

When she joined us in the center and I could get a better view, I thought maybe it was the purple-and-green nylon jogging suit she wore, complete with a pair of Grape 5s that looked fresh out of the box.

Or maybe it was her haircut, close-cropped and curly, with a matching purple lightning streak zigzagging across her scalp.

Or—and I think this was it—it could've been how Gum Baby practically leaped into the air to dap her up.

The old woman cackled as she and Gum Baby performed an elaborate handshake that left sap everywhere and me shaking my head. "GB, I got your texts!" said Granny Z. "Been putting that phone I gave you to work, I see."

Ayanna and I exchanged confused glances, but just then Thandiwe stepped up and gave the newcomer a hug.

"Hey, Mrs. Z, how was your trip?" she asked.

The woman surveyed the area, let her eyes linger on me, and then turned to the rest of the kids hanging around the bowl and made shooing gestures.

"Y'all go 'head and scoot," she said. "Big ole ears trying to hustle up some talk. Go on now! Otherwise that food I set up by the door gonna get cold."

That did it. Within seconds the entire bowl was clear of everyone but the five of us. Six, if you include ghosts, and at this point who doesn't? The sound of whooping excitement echoed throughout the warehouse as the Rolling Thunder fell onto the buffet.

"Now, then." Granny Z turned toward us, fixed a stern gaze on me, and folded her arms. "What you scaring my children for? Gum Baby, I thought you was keeping an eye on this one?"

The tiny terror had the nerve to glare at me. "Gum Baby never agreed to be a babysitter. Bumbletongue is hardheaded. Working Gum Baby's last nerve. And the second-to-last one. Two nerves!"

I held up both my hands. "Wait, how do you two know each other?"

"See? Ain't nobody got time to repeat themselves."

Granny Z sighed. "Now, now, GB. Why don't y'all go get some food, too, so I can talk privately to Mr. Mississippi Fire here."

I frowned as Thandiwe gave the old woman a kiss on the cheek. "Why does everyone keep mentioning that?" I complained.

Ayanna squeezed my arm and scooped up Gum Baby. "Stop whining, flyboy, and deal with it."

Gum Baby stuck out her tongue at me as the three of them left, and a pang hit me in the chest at the sight of the trio laughing and joking together. I couldn't help but feel that we were missing someone. Junior should've been here with us. I'd promised to find him, and so far I'd failed.

Then Ayanna looked over her shoulder at me, brushed back her curls, and smiled, as if she knew I was feeling sorry for myself, and my pang of sorrow turned to something else. Something confusing.

"Nah-uh," Granny Z said sharply, and I turned to see her wagging a finger at Spirit John, who was trying to follow the others to the food. The ghost boy took on a shocked expression, and Granny Z tutted. "Don't make that face at me. I need to talk with you, too."

I empathized with the spirit's look of terror.

"And you . . ." She was talking to me now. "Gum Baby helps me keep an eye on strange things, especially when it comes to my children, and I got some words for you."

Screams of laughter rang in the air, and I raised an eyebrow. "These are all your children?"

"All children are my children," she said matter-of-factly. "That's what she told me, and that's how I move through the world."

"She?" Not this again!

"Oh, by the grace of Bon Dieu, does no one explain things around here? Gum Baby!" Granny Z stomped her feet.

"Gum Baby ain't no babysitter!" came a shout.

The older woman beckoned us to come with her, and Spirit John and I trudged behind her out of the bowl and over to a dark office in the back of the warehouse, the only room I could see inside the renovated building. She produced a key from inside her jogging-suit jacket, opened the door, and led us inside. A desk with a wide-screen all-in-one computer on top sat in the middle of the room, with a pair of chairs on either side. I sat in one and raised an eyebrow as Spirit John sat in the other beside me. I couldn't help but see High John in his face, and it pained me to look at him for too long.

Granny Z stood behind the desk. "What do you know of the loa?"

"Low-uh?" I repeated.

"*Loa*, boy. *L-O-A*. The mystères. The links between the High God and his people on earth, served by the mambos, their priestesses. Like my Seraphine."

I began to shake my head in confusion but stopped. "Wait. I...I met a girl down in New Orleans whose name was Seraphine."

Granny Z smiled. "One of my brightest. I trained her myself. We serve the same loa, Erzulie Dantor."

"Erzulie..." I repeated slowly.

Granny Z nodded. "A family of loa that, among other things, are the mothers and protectors of those unable to protect themselves. Those who honor and revere Erzulie Dantor, like Seraphine and myself, have a duty to watch over the innocent. That's why I say all children are my children, and a child in need is a child the world has failed. And we are failing, Tristan Strong!" She slammed the palm of her hand on the desk. "You, me, Seraphine...we are losing the battle for our children. Evil is gathering in this city right now, and I can barely protect the little ones in here."

Guilt crept around my shoulders. "I know, but if I can just capture Cotton—"

"You're ignoring the people right in front of you just because you got something personal brewing between you and that haint. Boy, don't you see you're playing right into his hands?"

"I'm helping as much as I can," I protested.

Granny Z pointed at Spirit John. "So why, boy-who-sees-spirits, boy-who-holds-fire, boy-who-reads-the-story-of-the-land-and-carries-it-to-the-ears-of-those-starved-for-it, haven't you helped the child who's been following you like a bleating lamb?"

I looked over at him and then immediately looked away. My mouth opened and closed like a fish trapped in a bowl too small for it, because that's how the office made me feel at that moment.

"I don't know," I finally admitted.

"Well, I do." Granny Z came around the desk and leaned against it. "It's because you're scared."

"I'm not—"

"Boy, if I say you're scared, you scared. Ain't nobody worried about your bravery or your image. You scared of failing a friend. Again."

High John lying against the tree beneath the overpass.

I shook the image out of my head. Granny Z reached out, took my hand, and squeezed it. I opened my mouth to disagree again, and instead, other words tumbled out. "I tried, honestly I did. I tried and tried and tried. But every time I even think about using the shadow gloves, I get so angry I'm afraid I'll burn down everything in sight."

Granny Z nodded. "That's because you letting that anger control you, and not the other way 'round. You think you're the only one who gets mad? Boy, you read the story of this country, didn't you? You saw the spirits, the suffering, the violence . . . and you think *you* get upset?"

Granny Z's voice deepened. Her fingers trembled on the desk, and the computer rattled. Her eyes closed, and I could *feel* her fury building behind every word.

"Goddesses have been traveling to these shores on the prayers of the defenseless for centuries. We cry when they cry. Suffer as they suffer. Moan as they moan. My children are kicked, beaten, harassed, stolen, abused, abandoned, forgotten, and stripped of their rights every single day. And it's a sad fact that their abusers are always gonna be afraid that their own sins will be revisited upon them. And fear makes grown folks act like children. So yes, Erzulie Dantor knows *angry*. The Erzulie will always be angry as long as her children are unprotected. But I can control my anger, *use* my anger. The question for you, Tristan Strong, is why are you angry?"

A boom of thunder crashed around my ears.

"I . . ." The words wouldn't come out.

"Why are you angry?"

BOOM!

"I don't know!" I cried, shoving my face into my hands.

"WHY. ARE. YOU. ANGRY?"

"Because no one else is!" I shouted, standing up so fast the office chair tumbled backward. Spirit John stared at me curiously. "No one else is upset that children have gone missing! No one else is upset that the story of America has been written in blood! And no one cares that a haunted slave plantation-turned-prison-turned-giant is headed up the Mississippi under the control of a haint made of pure evil! I'm angry because the world keeps telling me I shouldn't be angry."

I broke off, panting from exertion. Granny Z's eyes fluttered open, and the tension seemed to drain from the room. She smiled at me weakly.

"Well, then . . . what you gonna do about it?"

BOOM!

That one wasn't thunder. That was something outside banging on the door. Something big.

"What in the—?" Granny Z said, turning around.

Out in the warehouse, someone screamed.

21
THE REDLINERS

I RACED OUT OF THE OFFICE AND INTO PANDEMONIUM. PANIC LACED the air as children ran everywhere, scrambling up vert ramps and hiding beneath the bowl's scaffolding. I fought my way through the crowd running in the other direction (yeah, yeah, but, you know...heroes) and skidded to a stop near the front entrance.

The door to the warehouse had been knocked off its hinges. A dozen or so masked grown-ups marched inside carrying torches and chanting, and my jaw tightened as I recognized the outfits they were wearing.

Gray cloaks. Plastic masks with a red slash. One of them held a bullhorn. It screeched when they turned it on and began to address the confused kids.

"ATTENTION, TRESPASSERS! YOU DO NOT BELONG HERE. THE POLICE HAVE BEEN CALLED. I REPEAT, THE POLICE HAVE BEEN CALLED."

I groaned as I recognized the voice. It was the same man from the zoo, the one who had tried to blame the mess they'd caused on me. Harold. Sure enough, Darla, his partner in crime, appeared next to him holding a torch in one hand and a sign in the other (which seemed very unsafe to me), and she shook both of them at the Rolling Thunder squad.

"This warehouse is not zoned for playground activities!" she shouted.

"Tristan? Tristan, where are you?"

I turned at the sound of Ayanna's voice. She spotted me, and she and Thandiwe raced toward me, Gum Baby on the pilot's shoulder. Her call must have drawn the attention of the masked HOA rejects, because Harold pointed at me.

"Hey, you! I know you—you're that kid from the zoo. Look, Darla! Darla? Oh, there you are. . . . Look, it's that boy from the zoo, the one we tried to pin—I mean, the one who trashed the place and ran! YOU! I'm making a citizen's arrest. Darla, did you see that? I made a—"

"Now, what in the world y'all think you doing?"

Granny Z rolled through the crowd on someone's longboard and came to a stop between the two groups. Children cowering on one side, grown-ups hiding their faces on the other.

Granny Z stepped on the tail edge of the skateboard and caught the nose as it shot up into the air. "The last time a group of masked folk came up in my place with torches and demands, I had to hide my babies under the floorboards."

Harold and Darla nearly fell over themselves in protest.

"Nonsense!" said Harold. "We would never!"

"That is abhorrent and a blight on our history," said Darla. "A shame and a disgrace."

"There isn't a racist bone in our bodies, right, you all? Not one."

"We, the Redliners, are the most tolerant and welcoming group you could find!"

"And empathetic."

Darla nodded as Harold stretched out both hands and said, "We just don't think you belong here."

I sighed as Darla tapped Harold on the shoulder and tried to whisper, unaware that the bullhorn was still on and everyone could hear her.

"Harold, dear, you're saying the quiet part out loud again."

"Oh," the bumbling bigot said, lowering the bullhorn and switching it off. "I am, aren't I? She'll never let me be the leader again."

I exhaled as I stared at the red line on his mask. I knew where I'd seen that before—on Patty Roller's boats that had chased us up the Mississippi. And that meant...

Hoofbeats clopped in the hallway, and I began to shout at everyone to run, escape, find a new hiding place. But it was too late.

Patty Roller rode into the warehouse atop the worst creature I'd ever seen. Worse than iron monsters and hull beasts and even Bear as the Shamble Man. A horse with dying lilies covering his rail-thin frame stomped mud-covered hooves on the floor and then reared to a stop when Patty tugged on his reins. Only a few strings of matted stringy hair served as the mane on his skeletal neck.

The horse swiveled his head to stare at me. His eyes were wilted roses the color of dried blood. The flowers opened and closed as his voice hissed like a dozen snakes threatening me at once.

"So this is the boy." The horse neighed and stamped his hooves. "All this fuss for naught but a morsel. Surprised at you, Roller."

The air flickered as the creature spoke, and I saw a second image of mounted terror superimposed on him: a different horse and rider—one of the torch-bearing marauders I'd seen when I was outside of time in Spirit John's neighborhood.

I gripped my head with both hands.

"Tristan?" Ayanna whispered. "What's wrong?"

I took a steadying breath and straightened. This wasn't the time for the spirit bead to flare. Not right now.

Luckily, Patty hadn't noticed. She was staring around the room of children, a strange look playing across her face. Like...disgust mixed with ambition. Avarice. Greed. And just like that, I was absolutely certain this was the group snatching children. Patty Roller, her masked gang of grown hallway monitors, and this...creature.

"Now, now, Twennymiles, my friend," Patty said, tucking

a wayward lily back against the creature's neck . . . what little of it remained. "Work before pleasure."

The horse trotted forward, leering at the children who shrank away. "Work, pleasure. Same coin," he said.

Thandiwe had been inching toward the left, and Ayanna's fingers were creeping to the baseball bat strapped to her back. I couldn't see Gum Baby anywhere.

"You all got to the count of two to get off my property," Granny Z snapped. "And then Imma show you what we did to them other hooded folk. One . . ."

"Now!" Patty Roller shouted, and the masked people exploded into action. At the same time, she lunged forward, reaching down from the back of Twennymiles and snatching at the crowd of children.

There were screams.

The hordes of masked intruders surged forward just as the lights went out, leaving their burning torches to illuminate the dark. It was bedlam.

Someone grabbed my arm. I whirled around, trying to free myself, until I heard Gum Baby shout in my ear.

"Quit Tristaning and go! Gum Baby saw that fake tear lady and her scary steed heading out the front."

I took off with Gum Baby on my shoulder, narrowing avoiding a man in a mask as I raced down the hallway to the door. We burst outside just in time to see the two haints disappearing around the corner, their captive with them.

Ayanna and Thandiwe ran out seconds later.

"Granny Z says...go....She's...got this," Thandiwe gasped.

I nodded and whistled. "Old Familiar!" I shouted.

An alarm chirped (cawed?) twice, and the SUV peeled out of its parking space and slid to a stop in front of us. We hopped inside—Spirit John had already materialized in the third row—and I knocked on the roof. "Follow that horse!"

Everyone grabbed a seat or handhold as Old Familiar took off, and I bit my lip in frustration.

Why are you angry? Granny Z's question came back to me.

I'd seen the child Patty had taken.

It was Chayse.

Once upon a time, a boy in a magical SUV chased two evil ghosts down the freeway.

Yeah, it sounds like a wild story to me, too. Well, it gets even wilder. See, I know you've probably seen car chases before. Maybe in your favorite action movie that's on its thirtieth sequel. Or in a video game that you pleaded with your parents to buy despite the wee bit of violence during that one scene, which was fine, really, you were mature enough to handle it, and besides, Dad always watched wrestling on Friday nights during dinner, so who was setting a bad example?

Sorry, that got a little personal.

Anyway.

The point is, you know what a car chase is. This wasn't your average one. Not when spirits and haints were involved.

Twennymiles ran like he'd stolen something. Which he had—or at least he and Patty Roller had. She clutched Chayse tightly with one arm as Twennymiles covered huge chunks of ground in a single stride.

Ayanna and I sat in the second row of the SUV. I was directly behind the empty driver's seat and watched the steering wheel swivel left and right as Old Familiar navigated around slower-moving traffic. Gum Baby pressed her face against the window on the passenger side, where she rode on Ayanna's lap. "Why ain't nobody honking at that horse? Is Gum Baby the only one concerned?"

"I don't think anyone sees it," I said. We passed a minivan loaded down for a vacation. The family inside seemed oblivious to both the woman with glittering tears flying off her face and the dead-flower horse, though one kid in the back did squint at Old Familiar as we zoomed past.

The eye sees only what the mind is prepared to comprehend.

Suddenly, Twennymiles gathered his legs beneath him and leaped forward, disappearing in a flash.

Thandiwe, sitting in the third row with Spirit John, gripped the back of my seat and leaned between Ayanna and me. "Where did they go? Did we lose them?"

"Gum Baby knew she should've drove!" The doll glared

at the silver initials stitched on the back of the driver's-seat headrest and grumbled. "Next time Gum Baby calls shotgun, it'll be a warning."

I ignored her. My senses were tingling—all of them at once. I felt a pull, a familiar tug, and I grabbed a handhold above the door. "Everybody hold on! I think we're stepping—"

A flash. A rumble. Drums. The sea.

"—outside ourselves," I finished.

We were driving on a river in the sky. Not alongside it, but actually *on* it! It reminded me of the floating rivers of Alke, in the City of Lakes. Beneath us was rolling green countryside. This was High John's magic at work. I squeezed the pouch around my neck.... It felt warm in my hands and gave me a teeny bit of comfort. But how could the haints travel like this as well? Twennymiles galloped a dozen yards in front of us, Patty Roller riding low on his back while gripping Chayse. Another flash, and they disappeared.

We followed, emerging back into the real world. Except—

"Where did the expressway go?" I asked.

Old Familiar now roared up an old country road, a curvy one-lane state road with no buildings, no city lights, and no Memphis anywhere nearby. A shape loomed out of the darkness—a route marker with a picture of the state of Tennessee above it and a two-digit number below.

"Gum Baby," I said, "let me see your phone."

She stared at me suspiciously but handed it over, muttering

something about me not being responsible. I sighed and tapped the highway route into her phone.

"According to this, we've traveled nineteen...no, twenty miles outside of Memphis."

Thandiwe snorted. "Guess we know how the horse got its name."

A memory tickled the back of my mind. "'And the devil was angry that he'd been tricked and climbed on his horse, named Twennymiles, and chased after them.'"

Everyone stared at me. "Was that a part of a story?" Thandiwe asked.

I nodded. "Nana told it to me once."

"Maybe...Maybe it's time to call in Mami Wata and John Henry," Ayanna said. She bit her lip as I started to protest and then cut me off. "I know you're trying to protect them from...whatever it is Cotton used to..." She glanced at Thandiwe, whose face tightened. "What he used to defeat High John, but this is getting serious, Tristan. We can't do this on our own."

I was going to argue, but a shout from Gum Baby stopped me.

"Horsey haint ahoy!"

We looked out the front windshield to see Twennymiles leaping into the air and disappearing. Old Familiar followed.

Flash. Drums. The sea.

We were on a set of train tracks deep underground.

Flash.

We were barreling through a neighborhood of lush lawns and mansions.

Flash.

We tore through a field with sunflowers stretching overhead and the smell of damp earth filling the air.

Flash.

Giant buildings with faded signs crowded us on both sides.

SHOES SHOES SHOES! read one.

GENTLY EDITED TEXTBOOKS! said another.

SANITIZED BIOGRAPHIES OF APPROVED HEROES! said a third.

Gum Baby climbed onto the dashboard and pressed her face against the windshield. "Gum Baby got a bad feeling about this place."

Thandiwe nodded. "Same here. Where is everyone? The stores are open, but..." Her voice trailed off, and I finished the thought.

"They're empty. This looks like an outlet mall. We used to go to one outside Chicago called Gurnee Mills. You could find a big selection of shoes and pots and stuff—at least that's why we'd go. This one, though... I've never heard of a store for discounted textbooks."

Old Familiar screeched to a halt. I leaned forward, searching the darkness.

"What's the matter? Did you lose them?" I asked.

The headlights turned off, and the SUV slowly reversed.

"Hey, we have to keep going forward! They took Chayse into one of these stores, I bet!"

But the car kept reversing. I muttered underneath my breath and opened the door.

"Tristan," Ayanna called, "what are you doing?"

"You all want to find the missing children, so that's what I'm going to do."

"Yeah, but . . ." She looked around. "This doesn't feel right. They could be anywhere."

Old Familiar slowed as I leaned out the door, then stopped so I wouldn't hurt myself. The horn cawed softly, but I ignored him. No way were those haints going to get away with kidnapping Chayse. It was my job to stop them, right? That's what Seraphine and Granny Z and Thandiwe and everyone kept telling me. I had a responsibility. Well, this was me being responsible.

"Stay here, then," I said. "I'll do it by myself."

Ayanna leaned back, hurt, and I turned away and began jogging toward the large building in front of us, the one with the brightest lights. A faded rectangular spot stretched over the front door, and I saw the sign that used to hang there lying overturned in a patch of weeds.

"Wait!" came a shout from behind me. Ayanna, with Gum Baby on her shoulder and her bat in hand, and Thandiwe, with her longboard strapped to her back, ran up to me. Apparently Spirit John had decided to sit this one out, which was fine with me.

"You're Tristaning again," Ayanna said. She grabbed my arm and linked it with hers. Thandiwe did the same on the other side. "And friends don't let friends go Tristaning alone."

I smiled. "Whatever," I said, feigning annoyance.

A flash of light and the sound of a camera shutter went off behind us, and we all turned to see Gum Baby—who'd hopped down and snapped a picture of us—now typing furiously into her phone. When she saw all of us glaring at her, she put a hand on her hip.

"What? Don't look at Gum Baby like that. Y'all wanna follow Bumbletongue into the spooky death store, go right ahead. Gum Baby is with the bird-mobile on this one."

Old Familiar had parked at the far end of the old worn parking lot, the SUV's hazard lights blinking in warning.

"It's fine," I said, trying to comfort everyone. "This might not even be the right spot. We'll peek in, see if we can find them, and if we don't, we'll duck out and keep looking."

"Oh, Gum Baby thinks you found the right spot for sure." The tiny doll trotted in front of us, crawled beneath the sign, and flipped it over. We all stared at the letters that appeared to have been painted with something I didn't want to look at too closely.

"'Patty Roller's Wig Emporium,'" I read. "'Prices...to die for.'"

The front doors hissed open.

We all stared at each other. Finally, with a gulp, I took a step forward and my friends followed. Even Gum Baby, though she muttered about it being a bad idea the whole time. And as we walked into the outlet store, I was beginning to agree with her. I couldn't shake the feeling that the doors—which hissed shut behind us—were the mouth of something horrific ready to swallow us whole.

22
PATTY ROLLER'S WIG EMPORIUM

NOTHING MOVED INSIDE.

Have you ever visited an outlet strip mall? Giant stores lure customers with the promise of amazing discounts, the deal to end all deals. Shelves are stocked with products you've never heard of, or weird stuff you've seen advertised on TV—all two-a.m. hangover purchases, as my dad called them. I'm not sure what a hangover is, but if it made me buy an automatic toenail clipper that looked like two machetes taped together, I wanted no part of it.

But inside Patty Roller's Wig Emporium, the products weren't weird or unnecessary. They were just . . . wrong.

Four aisles awaited—metal shelves that towered to the ceiling and stretched off into the gloom. I couldn't see what lay at the end of them. Giant posters dangled at the front of the aisles, each with a different style of wig pictured on it. I squinted. A couple looked like the kind of thing Patty Roller would wear.

An intercom crackled in the darkness, and a prerecorded message began to play.

"Welcome to the Wig Emporium, your one-stop shop for fitting into human society!"

Human society?

"Here you'll find a wig to suit your everyday needs. Have a history lesson you need to embellish? Try our no-nonsense Lecture Wig."

A small spotlight illuminated the poster at the far end, which showed a gray bun wig with horn-rimmed glasses attached to the sides.

"Gentrifying a community for eventual displacement? Try our special, the Currency Combover." The next poster to the right lit up, showing thinning brown hair parted neatly down the side.

As the speaker continued to play, I motioned to my friends to huddle up, and I pointed toward the aisles. "Okay, let's split up. Each of us take a row and check to make sure Patty or Twennymiles aren't hiding there. You find something, you shout, okay?"

Ayanna and Thandiwe exchanged glances. Gum Baby folded her arms and shook her head. "Gum Baby don't split nothing. She don't split checks, split ends, or split up search parties. That's how you get got, Bumbletongue, and Gum Baby don't. Get. Got."

I rolled my eyes. "Come on, y'all. Ayanna?"

She squeezed her bat between her hands. "I'm with Gum Baby this time, Tristan. We should stick together."

I shook my head. "And what if Patty escapes? This might be our only chance at catching her." I turned to Thandiwe. "You're with me, right?"

The princess of Isihlangu took her longboard off her back. With a tug on the wheels, it expanded into a wide oval, and straps appeared on the underside. Thandiwe slipped her left arm into it, wearing it like a shield. Then she pulled on the right front wheel—and kept pulling—until a long staff appeared and separated from the shield. She fastened the three remaining wheels to the end of the staff, so it looked like a club with multiple heads. Pretty cool trick.

"I think we should stick together," she said. "But if you do insist on splitting up, stay alert."

She handed me the converted club and I stared at it. "Is this a kierie?" The preferred weapon of Isihlangu's warriors was formidable. I'd seen Thandiwe batter iron monsters into smithereens with one.

The princess smiled. "What? You can take the girl out of the mountain, but you can't take the mountain out of the girl. Not in this neighborhood."

I snorted. "I wouldn't dream of it. Okay, y'all ready?"

"No," said Thandiwe.

"Gum Baby is doing this under PROTEST!"

Ayanna blew out a puff of frustration. "Fine," she snapped. "Just... be safe."

"When am I anything but?" I asked.

The look all three of them gave me forced me to clear my throat and move toward the aisle all the way on the right. "Anyway... you see anything, you shout. Got me? Shout."

With that, the four of us crept down our assigned aisles. But it wasn't until I'd stepped into mine that I realized the store's speakers were still playing their intro message.

"Finally, if you are a meddlesome insect who insists on selfishly interfering with our plans to better society—"

I stopped moving and stared at the wall above me, where a dusty speaker covered in cobwebs and black mold had been mounted next to a security camera. The cam swiveled until I could see the red dot pointed right at me.

"—we have the perfect wig for you. So come on in. Let's get you fitted."

I gulped and continued on. Patty Roller *was* here. And she was watching us. For a second I thought about calling out to the others, but that would alert the haint to the fact that I was onto her, and she might run again. No. Better to pretend I was unaware. Then we could turn the tables on her. But where was she hiding? And was Twennymiles with her?

I tiptoed along and tried not to stare at the gray faces on the wig packages on the shelves next to me. The eyes in the product shots seemed hollow, and the Snow White bob inside every package reminded me too much of Patty Roller.

All sounds were dampened. My footsteps echoed in the dark, my breath huffed, and the wind outside tried to beat down the doors, but that was it. I couldn't even hear Gum Baby complaining. I really hoped that was a sign that everyone was being stealthy and not . . . something worse.

Another camera swiveled ahead. *"Today's sales include fifty percent off our History Erasure wig, and a buy-one-get-one-free special on all wigs designed to trap self-proclaimed heroes."*

Something crinkled behind me.

I froze, then peeked over my shoulder. Nothing. But when I started to sneak forward, there it was again, the sound of something crinkling. Like when you try to open a bag of chips quietly so no one tells you to wait for dinner (not that I've ever done it, but you know exactly what I'm talking about). I paused again, then kept going. More crinkling. Whatever was happening, there was more than one person doing it. I almost shouted for the others when I noticed a sign on the wall—SECURITY OFFICE—and an arrow pointing to a door up ahead.

Of course! The cameras following my movements . . . Patty Roller had to be in the security office. I moved quicker now, still keeping an ear out for whoever—or whatever—was behind me, but I had her now.

The office door was cracked open, and the flickering silver-blue light of a TV or computer monitor spilled into the aisle. I readied Thandiwe's kierie, took a deep breath, then shoved the door open and dashed inside.

"Where is Chayse?" I shouted... to an empty room.

A desk sat in the middle of the space, facing a wall of security monitors. On the desk was a telephone—the kind that can control PA systems—with the receiver off the hook. A smartphone had been taped to the mouthpiece.

"Ahh, there he is," said a voice. It came from the cell phone and echoed through the store. *"Tristan Strong. Come to save the day, little boy? Come to play hero? Such a brave little man. Smart, too. Look how he sacrifices three friends to save a child he barely knows... and still fails."*

Sacrifices?

Movement caught my eye. The monitors. I moved closer, then inhaled sharply as I watched Gum Baby, Thandiwe, and Ayanna on three different screens. They moved down their aisles, looking this way and that... while something followed them. Shadows. The shapes were too quick and too many for me to be able to tell what they were exactly, but they scaled the tall shelves and moved along the tops.

"Yes, welcome to Patty Roller's Wig Emporium," the voice said,

and I could hear the smirk in the haint's voice as I turned and raced out of the office. *"Where lives are changed . . . forever."*

I sprinted toward the end of the aisle. "It's a trap!" I shouted. "Get out!"

"Tristan?" Ayanna called. "What do you—"

Her voice cut off, and fear filled my muscles.

"NO!" I screamed. I ran like I'd never run before. The breath ripped out of my chest and my lungs screamed for air, but still I ran. I slid to a stop before rounding the corner at the end of the aisle, and my foot kicked something. It crinkled. I looked down to see one of the cellophane bags that the Emporium's wigs came in. The bag was open, but the product shot remained inside, and I squinted at it. Something seemed different about it. Hadn't there been a— My eyes went wide. The gray expressionless face, the one that had given me the heebie-jeebies, was gone.

The shadows!

A scream snapped me out of my shock, and I sprinted around the corner. There was an open space near the rear of the store, and the roll-up door for deliveries was partway open. I continued running and then, at the last moment, dropped into a baseball slide and shot beneath the gap, landing on my butt outside.

Nothing.

"What in the—" I got up, spun around, and recoiled in horror.

Hundreds of gray shadows peeled themselves from the exterior wall of the store. They had no facial features except eyeholes—empty spaces that revealed the world behind them. The beings walked on two legs and had long arms that flailed like those wacky inflatable tubes outside car dealerships. But these weren't funny. The arms ended in whiplike fingers that twisted in the wind. The fingers cracked like gunshots as they curled and uncurled, and their claws sent up sparks when they scraped the ground.

High John, with a trio of gashes in his cloak, appeared in my mind.

Could these be the Breakers he'd tried to warn me about? Their fingers definitely looked like they could break someone. I swallowed, fear suddenly making my movements sluggish. If they could tear through a god, what chance did I have?

I backed up, squeezing the kierie tightly. The weapon would be useless against so many. I needed to use the akofena, the shadow gloves. I began to clench my fists . . . then stopped. What if the building caught on fire? My friends were still inside. No, it had to be the kierie.

"Tristan!" Ayanna's voice came from the right. A door opened and she poked her head out. "Tristan?"

One of the gray shadow creatures in front of me began to shiver. A mouth appeared where there had been nothing before, and it was wider than any mouth I'd ever seen. It screamed . . . and it sounded just like Ayanna!

The shadows lunged toward me at once, and I swung the kierie with all my strength. It connected with a few, and several of the Breakers popped into clouds of noxious smoke, but others swarmed forward. Sharp claws raked my back, and I screamed in pain.

"HEY, PICK ON A HERO YOUR OWN SIZE!"

Gum Baby flipped out of nowhere, her hands moving in a blur as sap rocketed through the air. Breakers exploded into smoke five at a time. I limped forward to help her, but she disappeared in a crowd of foes. I tried fighting my way free, but there were too many. We were being overwhelmed.

Suddenly Gum Baby yelped in pain. I flinched. I'd never heard the tiny doll make that sound, and it terrified me.

"Get off Gum Baby!" she screamed. "Tristan!"

"Where are you?" I shouted. A Breaker lunged at me and I dodged, slipping to the right and sweeping it aside. "Gum Baby!"

"Tristan!"

My fear turned to anger. I bulled my way forward, swinging the kierie left and right. "Where are you?"

A screech rent the air. "They're hurting Gum—"

Her voice cut off. I froze. No. No, no, no!

A harsh caw filled the air, and tires squealed as Old Familiar drove around the corner of the building. Thandiwe surfed next to it on her forebear, sparks shooting into the night as she held on to the driver's-side window. The two slammed into the crowd of Breakers, scattering them like leaves. Ayanna slid over the hood and attacked from the other side of the SUV, her bat glowing red-hot. The Breakers fled beneath the combined attack, into the shadows, where they disappeared.

But the damage had been done. A tiny figure lay on the ground at my feet, unmoving, and I sank to my knees. My hands trembled as I reached out, expecting a snarky complaint and a ball of sap at any moment. But... there was nothing.

Nothing except a lifeless wooden doll.

23

THE GODS HATE REDLINERS

NO ONE SPOKE TO ME.

Old Familiar drove us several hours north via back roads and two-lane highways. Ayanna sat in the seat next to me, Gum Baby cradled in her lap, and stared out the window for the whole trip. Thandiwe sat in the front passenger seat. Every now and then she'd look back at us, open her mouth, then close it and turn around. Spirit John hadn't moved from the third row. We rode like that for an eternity.

Finally we parked near a small dock in the middle of nowhere. The sun was just beginning to peek above the horizon, and the Mississippi River gurgled past, brown and mysterious. There the gods convened—three of them, at least. Nyame and Keelboat Annie had traveled with Mami Wata on the *River Queen* to meet us. Apparently Nyame and Annie had been out west looking for more lost Alkeans. Annie, dwarfing everyone, wore a pair of denim shorts and a wrestling T-shirt, her big hair pulled back into her trade-mark puff. Nyame, on the other hand, wore Lakers warm-ups with Kareem Abdul-Jabbar's picture on the back of the jacket ("Sky hook for the sky god," he said.). A pair of gold-rimmed sunglasses was pushed up onto his head and always seemed to catch the sun.

Nobody glanced my way as they all walked into Mami Wata's meeting room and shut the door behind them, leaving me out. Served me right. I'd been so focused on tracking down Patty Roller that I'd never even considered the fact that the haint could be leading us into a trap. Because of that, my tiny friend was . . .

The door to the meeting room opened.

"—like they stripped the magic right out of her."

Nyame's voice carried as Ayanna stepped into the corridor. She nearly stumbled when she met my eyes. I couldn't read the expression on her face, but she turned and walked in the opposite direction.

My heart sank even further. I wanted to run after her to tell her that I'd tried, that I missed Gum Baby, too. I took a step toward her.

"Tristan?" Mami Wata called me from inside. "Come in, please."

I stopped in my tracks and watched Ayanna disappear into another cabin. After a deep breath, I turned and stepped into the meeting room. Keelboat Annie leaned against the window on the far side, while Nyame sat in a chair with his fingers laced behind his head. Mami Wata was on her throne, and I was glad to see that she looked less tired today, but her expression could've been chiseled out of stone.

"You disobeyed your instructions," the river goddess said with no preamble. "From now on you are confined to quarters, and under no circumstances are you to leave without the prior approval of one of us three." She rubbed her temples and shook her head. "By Alke's brooks, we *will* get you home safe and sound."

I fiddled with my adinkra bracelet. "But what about Cotton? And Patty Roller and Twennymiles and the Breakers? Do we know where they are? What if—"

Mami Wata cut me off with a raised finger. "You. Were. Grounded. For your safety and everyone else's. And instead of telling us about the Memphis clues, you went and snuck off, putting your life in peril."

Keelboat Annie cleared her throat. "Tristan, there's no sign of your escaped haint or his walking prison anywhere. We looked while you were out. I done checked all the rivers, along with Wata, and ole man Nyame over there's been scouring the skies. Cotton must be laid up somewhere."

"We're still looking," Nyame said, "but until then..." The sky god lifted his hands as if to say *It's above me.* But like... he was the sky god. You shouldn't be allowed to say *It's above me* when your domain is the sky.

"Leave this to us," Mami Wata said.

She took a deep breath, and for a moment I saw pain etched on her face, like lines in the sand of a riverbank. It was hard to remember that others felt the loss of High John and Gum Baby just as much as I did.

But it was frustrating!

It seemed like we weren't doing anything about anything, just shouting and yelling and going back to our daily struggle of existing. I could feel anger lurking in the tips of my fingers and in between my shoulder blades. I took a deep breath. Then another. I looked down at my shoes and told myself, *Stay calm, Tristan. Stay calm.*

"I know—we know—it's been hard," Nyame said. "High John was our friend, too. One of our champions. And Gum Baby was . . . She was special. To all of us. We will mourn them, and they will—"

"They're not dead," I said.

Silence fell over the room. Then Nyame asked, "Excuse me?"

"They're not dead." I didn't look up from my shoes. "Gods can't die. Not if you carry their stories in your heart and on your tongue. Right?" Now I did raise my head, and the god and goddesses had that expression adults wear when something they've said comes back to bite them in the butt. It would've been funny, but for once I didn't want them to be wrong. I wanted them to agree with me.

"And I'm an Anansesem until you all take it from me, so if I carry High John's story to Chicago with me and tell my teachers, tell my friends, tell anyone who'll listen, he can't be dead. That's what y'all told me. Gods can't die. And Gum Baby, maybe she wasn't a goddess, but she walked the walk that gods are supposed to, so I'm including her in this, too. And gods can't die. Right? Gods can't die! Gods, no, LISTEN—" I backed up as Keelboat Annie walked over. "Gods can't die and they are NOT DEAD! They aren't dead. They..."

Keelboat Annie enveloped me in her arms and shushed me as anger roared through my limbs. It wasn't fair. None of this was fair.

Someone cleared their throat behind her. "Tristan..." Nyame began. "About you being Anansesem..."

The engines shuddered, then stopped. The *River Queen* fell silent, and we all looked at each other. I stepped back from Keelboat Annie, embarrassed at the wet spot my tears had left on her shirt. She tousled my hair, and then we all turned as Ayanna burst into the room.

"You have to see this!" she said, out of breath.

Trouble floated ahead of the *River Queen*.

When I saw who it was, however, I groaned and face-palmed at the same time. Face-groaned. What did I do to deserve this? Keelboat Annie glanced at me as she retied her ponytail and gripped the fractured keel pole she'd turned into a weapon. No, really. She wielded it like a quarterstaff, even though it was almost wider than me!

"Friends of yours?" she asked.

I let a long exhale slip between my fingers before I stood up straight and glared over the rail. "I need friends like them like I need a cramp in my side. They call themselves Redliners, and they've been messing up everything for days now."

A half dozen boats floated in a line and blocked the river. They resembled the ones that had escorted Patty Roller before the ghost of the USS *Cairo* blew them to smithereens. Gray, with a red stripe along the hull. I mentally kicked myself for not making the connection before.

"HALLOOO THE STEAMSHIP!" Harold shouted across the water.

How could I tell it was Harold? Easy. He was using that same dirty, dented megaphone, and his mask barely covered his face. Was he wearing sunglasses beneath it? And there was Darla next to him, arms folded across her chest.

Mami Wata marched to the bow of the *River Queen*. Her stare could wither stone, and I could see Harold shrink beneath it as the river goddess's shout echoed across the water. "Why do you block our way?"

"WELL, YOU SEE—AND YOU'LL HAVE TO FORGIVE ME, BECAUSE I HAVE NOTHING AGAINST YOU AND YOUR KIND, WHAT WITH THE HAIR AND ALL…"

I could feel Mami Wata's glare intensifying to gale-force winds. I was surprised the Redliners weren't blown completely out of the water.

"...BUT I'M AFRAID YOU CAN'T COME THIS WAY. WE'VE GOT TO KEEP THE DEPARTURE ON SCHEDULE, AND IF YOU MESS IT UP, WE'LL ALL BE IN TROUBLE. SO NO DICE, I'M AFRAID." Harold dropped the bullhorn and shrugged apologetically.

"And why," Mami Wata said, her voice low and cold, "do you think we'll be any trouble?"

"Oh, right! Because of who you are."

"Excuse me?"

Harold squirmed. "Not you, exactly. I'm sure you're fine. You remind me of a coworker, actually, and she's never any trouble. Barely talks to me, as a matter of fact. Can you imagine that?"

"Yeah," I muttered, "can you imagine?"

"So no, it's not you," the Redliner said. "It's the boy."

I froze. Keelboat Annie noticed and moved to the right a bit so I was shielded from his view. Nyame walked up beside Mami Wata and stood with his fists on his hips. Harold gave him a small wave.

"Hey there, sir. Nice shirt. Basketball? Love it. But, as I was saying, the boy. Is he aboard? I hate to ask, but could you bring him out and turn him over to us? We have a citizen's arrest outstanding, you see. It's not an official thing, but once we bring him to the police, I'm sure it will be. Got to protect our spaces, right?"

Darla's whisper echoed through the bullhorn. "Harold. The quiet part? You said it out loud again."

"Oh, sorry, dear. Ha-ha, I keep doing that, don't I? Don't tell the boss, okay? She said I'd be demoted the next time."

As they talked, I backed up. There was no telling what trouble those two and their gang of kid-snatchers would cause. And while I was sure the trio of Mami Wata, Keelboat Annie, and Nyame would easily take care of them should a fight break out, the other Redliners were pointing cameras at the *River Queen*, which let me know that, whatever the outcome, Harold and Darla would make sure the evidence worked in their favor. No, the best thing I could do was leave. But how?

I slipped down the stairs and grabbed my bag from the meeting room. Then it was a mad dash to the aft of the boat. I only hoped there was a lifeboat or dinghy I could use to escape, like last time. A few of the carved mermaids raised their eyebrows at me as I climbed over the guardrail and peered at the hull below.

No lifeboats.

Now what was I supposed to do? Jump in with a life vest? Maybe if got a running start I wouldn't have to swim as far and...

"Going somewhere?"

I looked back to see Ayanna on the deck behind me. She was unamused. I glanced around again, giving the area one final check, then sighed and climbed back over the railing. "I can't be here," I said. "You all will just get lumped into trouble along with me."

"And so you're just taking off without saying good-bye?"

"I don't want anyone else getting hurt—or worse—because of me."

"You don't get to decide when and where your friends have your back," Ayanna said angrily. "That's. Not. How. Friend. Ship. Works." She jabbed a finger into my chest with each syllable. "Friends are there for you, period, full stop. Do you understand?"

I opened my mouth to respond.

"No, be quiet and listen for once," she said. I closed my mouth as she continued. When Ayanna got going, her eyebrows scrunched up and her curls tumbled all over the place, no matter what hair tie or clip she tried to use. More importantly, I knew she was right. But what was I supposed to do? How can you need someone by your side and also want them far away so they're shielded from harm?

"Tristan?"

I blinked. Ayanna had a strange look on her face. Was she blushing?

"You're just staring at me," she said.

"Sorry," I blurted. "I agree."

"With what?"

I thought about it, then sighed and shrugged. "Everything you just said. If we're going to do this, if we're going to find Cotton and Patty Roller and put a stop to their plans, we're going to do it together. No more splitting up. No more silly heroics."

Ayanna shook her head. "Be heroic all you want. Just remember we're fighting, too. We're a team. Right?"

"Right."

Some of the tension drained from her shoulders and a small smile crossed her face. I smiled back at her, and I can't lie, it felt good to know someone would have my back no matter how wild the adventures got. Warm and bubbly and like I was floating.

Someone snickered nearby. Thandiwe stood on the stairs with a sly look on her face. "Why don't you two just hurry up and say it?"

My face flushed. "Say what?" I asked, my voice cracking a bit.

The princess covered up another grin. "Never mind."

Ayanna shot Thandiwe a look I couldn't decipher, then turned, her expression all business again. "Ignore her. But if you're serious about leaving, I think I know a way we can do it. You might not like it, though."

"*Pffft.*" I folded my arms. "Try me."

"Okaaay . . . but don't say I didn't warn you."

Wait, warn me?

The tip of Ayanna's bat began to glow, and the wood trembled in her hand. It shook left and right, then lifted into the air. The round barrel began to flatten and stretch, widening until it was the size of a couch. My jaw dropped.

It was a brand-new flying raft.

"GAAAHHH!"

My weight shifted, and I could feel myself starting to slide off as the raft zipped just above the ground, twisting around a stand of trees. I couldn't wait to see the internet buzz about my doom. *Boy Flattened into a Pancake in Bizarre Raft Accident Outside St. Louis.*

Deep inhale. "GAAAHHH!"

I lay flat on my back, spread-eagled, my fingers desperately trying to find purchase in the wood. What I wouldn't have given to have Gum Baby sitting on my chest right then and pretending everything was fine. I would put up with a million of her Bumbletongue insults just to endure her precoffinary measures one more time. Even in the terror that gripped my stomach as Ayanna's new raft swirled and dipped, I felt the sadness.

And beneath the sadness, doubt whispered.

All you bring is disappointment.

Finally, after what seemed like hours but which Thandiwe informed me had only been ten minutes or so, Ayanna slowed down and checked behind us. She'd taken a route that shielded us from view as we fled the *River Queen,* backtracking along the Mississippi before cutting through an abandoned farm and going north along the eastern side of the river. Now we floated just above a patch of wildflowers in a meadow near a freeway.

"So . . . what next?" Thandiwe broke the silence between the three of us.

The edges of my vision flickered. I turned my head to see Spirit John sitting on the raft beside me. Because of course. I rolled onto my side to look at the flowers instead.

Gum Baby should be here, too.

Ayanna glanced at me, as if waiting for me to take charge, but I continued to stare at the flowers as I now clutched my backpack to my chest. A pair of butterflies fluttered from petal to petal. It reminded me of the Thicket back in Alke, and the first time I'd brought a story to life. A cloud of butterflies had reenacted the time Gum Baby had broken into my grandparents' house. It was the moment when everyone realized I was an Anansesem.

No longer an Anansesem.

"We need to find the Rolling Thunder," Thandiwe said. "They trusted me, and I let them down. Who knows where they are right now, and how scared—" Emotion cut off her words.

Ayanna patted her arm. "We will. And when we do, we'll make Cotton and Patty Roller pay."

"How?" I asked quietly.

They both turned toward me, and Ayanna stared at me in confusion. "What do you mean?"

"How will we make them pay? Nothing we've done so far has worked. They've got everyone twisted to their side. The Redliners, the police, the news . . . I'm glad I don't have the SBP, because I'd be scared to see what people on the internet are saying about us right now."

"So we should just give up, then?" Thandiwe demanded.

"Of course not. I just . . . I don't know." I gripped the backpack tight, and Ayanna watched me.

"What's in there?" she asked suddenly. "You're clutching it like it contains all your worldly possessions."

I hesitated. Then, with trembling fingers, I unzipped the bag. Inside, her eyes closed and lying incredibly still, was Gum Baby. "I couldn't leave her," I explained. "Not with the Redliners threatening everything. And . . . I'm so used to having her nearby. On my shoulder. It hurt to leave her behind."

The two girls exchanged glances again, then scooted closer to me. I closed my eyes as they hugged me. So much pain. So much suffering. For what? First the spirits, then High John, now Gum Baby. Was I doomed to be constantly in mourning? Did I have to keep prayers on standby? Sorrow at the ready? The hits just kept coming, and I couldn't even dodge them. One after the other, they just came rolling along, like Anansi's Train of Despair.

My fingers stilled.

I done checked all the rivers, along with Wata, and ole man Nyame over there's been scouring the skies. Cotton must be laid up somewhere.

We've got to keep the departure on schedule.

Like they stripped the magic right out of her.

I let out a long, shaky exhalation. Ayanna and Thandiwe stood up and peered at me in confusion as my fists tightened and released. Tightened and released. Finally, after several seconds of trying to maintain calm, I looked at them both. The sun set behind the raft in golden rays. We were running out of time.

"I think I know how Cotton is transporting Old Angola," I said. "And I think I know where he'll be next."

Ayanna brightened and reached for her rudder to control the raft. "Can you guide us there?"

I shook my head. "No. But *he* can."

And I touched Spirit John.

24
THE HIDDEN CITY

WITH THE CONNECTION I'D MADE WITH SPIRIT JOHN, HE BECAME
more solid. Even Ayanna and Thandiwe could see him now.
This is what he said, through me:

My name was John. Not Johnny or Jonathan, not Hey,
Boy or—well, you know what they called me. I was just plain
John, and I wasn't born a slave. Remember that. I wasn't
born a slave.

("I think he wants us to remember that.")

"Hush, Thandiwe.")

Now, it ain't important that, midway through a trip from
my family's pecan farm in Tallulah to a market in Vicksburg,
mounted men calling themselves patrollers forced me and my
brother to prove we weren't slaves.

("You had to prove you weren't a slave?")

It also ain't important that they ripped up those papers
and locked us in chains anyway, or that the law the patrollers

claimed we'd broken wasn't fair. It was the law, right? Over the next three years me and my brother broke several laws, including trying to escape from our plantation prison, trying to trick the man who demanded we call him Boss, and even just talking about anything close to freedom. Especially that last one. Might've been a hundred laws telling us what we could and couldn't talk about, when it was allowed, and who we could talk about it with, too. *If the mouth is moving, work is stopping*—that's what the man who wanted to be called Boss said. But the talking and the not-talking, that ain't important. No, the important thing is *how* we could talk.

("I'm confused."

"I think I actually understand."

"You do? Ayanna, don't lie."

"*Shh.*")

Now some Sundays, his lordship and most honorable, the man who wanted to be called Boss, graciously allowed the people who actually worked the fields to rest. To recover. To rejuvenate. Planting, tilling, and harvesting that cotton, rice, and sugar drained the body and the soul. So us workers would make a little music. Sing some songs. Tell a few stories. Sometimes the man who wanted to be called Boss drifted by and listened in. He never heard anything alarming and would nod in a way that made it seem like he knew exactly what he was hearing. Songs and stories.

But you and I know different.

("Is he talking to Tristan now?"

"I think so.... Now *shhh*, I'm trying to listen!")

You and I know the might of a song. Of a story. The meaning tucked inside the words and the melody. Stories are power. The power to laugh at a system that treats you like property, at a man who claims to own other men, women, and children, and to laugh without getting caught.

("Wait.... He's talking about the John tales!")

The power to send messages, messages that lead to freedom. *Swing low, sweet chariot, coming forth to carry you home.* That's what is important. That is what you should remember. Because I did. I wasn't born a slave, and I didn't die a slave—the power in the stories made sure of it.

"Tristan?"

I opened my eyes. Thandiwe and Ayanna stared at me carefully, both of them with their hands raised. "Yes?"

"Let go of the rudder," Ayanna said slowly.

I looked down. My left hand gripped the raft's steering bar so tightly my knuckles were turning white. I frowned and unpeeled my fingers from the wood. When I glanced back up, the two girls had relaxed a bit, but they still seemed tense.

"What happened?" I asked.

Ayanna took the control and nudged me aside. "While you were telling John's story, you started flying us into the middle of nowhere."

"I what?"

A finger tapped me on the shoulder. Thandiwe. She pointed down. I looked over the edge of the raft, then winced and wished I hadn't.

We were hundreds of feet up in the air. A weed-covered field sprawled beneath us, with old rusted train tracks—six, no, seven sets, all lined up next to each other as they curved away into the distance. Evening had arrived. Under the glow of flickering streetlights, I saw that I'd apparently flown us to an abandoned railyard.

"I thought you said you knew how Cotton was moving the haunted plantation?" Thandiwe frowned as she looked between me and Spirit John. "How does this help us?"

Ayanna was right—we *were* in the middle of nowhere. Even Gum Baby's phone had trouble finding us on the basic Maps app. I wished—for the umpteenth time—for the SBP. Regardless of the tension between Anansi and me, we could've used his help about now. I rubbed my face, trying to will the exhaustion away. Maybe I was wrong. Maybe Spirit John couldn't guide us, and I was just clutching at straws. Maybe—

"Um, what is he doing?" Ayanna looked more than a bit concerned.

"Who, me?" I asked. "I'm not doing anything."

"Not you," she said. She pointed at Spirit John.

I'd forgotten the ghost and I were still connected. It had become so common for me to be the only one who saw him.

Usually he followed me and appeared at random, hands in his pockets and a tiny smile on his face. Now, however, he stared over the edge of the raft with an intensity that was almost scary. Like something was down there. Something dangerous.

"I don't see anything," I said, peeking over the edge again with a loud gulp.

"I thought you said High John helped you get rid of your fear of heights," Thandiwe said.

"Baby steps," I muttered. The princess laughed, and I turned away in a huff, only to raise my eyebrows as Gum Baby's phone chirped. It had finally downloaded a map with higher resolution. I frowned.

"This says we're in a place called National City. Never heard of it."

"Let me see." Ayanna leaned over to stare at the screen. "Population zero? No one lives here?"

Thandiwe looked over the edge again. "I could've told you that. It's a ghost town."

My head swiveled at her words and locked on to Spirit John. *A ghost town.*

"What if . . ." I began to say, then licked my lips and tried again. "What if the reason the gods couldn't find Cotton or you"—I looked at Thandiwe—"or the children who are being snatched off the streets is because they aren't hiding in this world?"

The two girls looked at each other. "What?" they said at the same time.

This sounded wild in my head, so I knew the two of them would look at me like I'd sprouted an extra nose when I said it out loud. "What if Cotton's hiding... *with* the spirits?"

I reached out, took both their hands, and closed my eyes.

When I opened them, the world was on fire.

No, that wasn't quite right. Beneath us, a city *built* itself out of fire, like a fuse in reverse, sparking in the night and leaving a trail of silver flame in its wake. It was an architectural Big Bang, but instead of creating the universe, it gave birth to National City.

I couldn't keep my jaw from dropping. And from the way Ayanna and Thandiwe gripped my hands, like they were my anchors to reality, I knew they were just as amazed as I was.

I mean, I could see houses twinkling north of us, and stores and parks to the south. The train tracks shone bright gold in the darkness, but they disappeared beneath a giant building—a train station?—that dwarfed the entire area. It was huge! Not so much tall as wide, and surrounded by fences on all sides. Tall gray metal panels separating pockets of this spirit city from everything else. Tiny pinpricks of light moved around inside the fences.

"Tristan?" Thandiwe squeezed my hand.

"Hmm?" There was something weird about all those tiny dots of light. Like, they seemed familiar.

"Tristan, what is that?"

"What is what?"

"Look!"

I dragged my attention away from the dots of light—it was really hard, like pulling yourself away from your favorite book mid-sentence, even though you already know what's going to happen. Because I thought I knew what those dots of light were. I knew *who* they were. But my brain refused to believe what my eyes were telling it.

Can't wait to tell Memphis that *one*, I thought.

And then I looked at what Thandiwe was pointing at.

"That!" she said.

"We have to help," Ayanna said quietly. I glanced at her. I didn't know whether she was talking about what I'd seen beneath us or the mayhem Thandiwe had pointed out.

Either way, she was right.

At the far end of National City, a crowd of spirits streamed across a bridge that led into a small town. From this distance I could almost pretend they were racing and the noise I heard was cheering. Almost.

Spirit John moved up alongside me. The older boy's face was tight with anger and fear. From the way my teeth were clenched, I knew his expression mirrored my own.

Another persecution.

A deafening roar shattered the air. My body twisted in pain.

"Tristan!"

I realized my mistake when I saw Ayanna's lower torso nearly fade away. I'd started to let go of her hand! If they were going to stay in this spirit realm and see what I saw, they had to hold on to me.

"What was that sound?" Ayanna asked. Her voice was trembling.

"That," I said, "was Cotton's monster. Look!" I pointed with my chin.

Trees shook on the opposite side of the train station, and Old Angola burst out of its hiding spot in the woods. My knees nearly gave out. It was even larger than before! It stood almost as tall as the station, and more of those steel doors had grown in its chest. It was impossible to miss. But I didn't see Cotton riding on it. Had he left his spirit-eating monster here to roam in this dog run for monsters?

I shook my head. None of that mattered. Regardless, Old Angola would devour everything in its path! I had to figure out a way to stop it.

"Um, what is happening down there?"

Thandiwe's question pulled my attention from Old Angola to the fenced areas below us. The dots of light (come on, brain, you know who they are, why can't you admit it?) were lined up and being funneled into the train station. One of the giant doors had opened, and I caught a glimpse of iron and steam before the door shut again.

A screeching whistle blew inside the building, and Old Angola roared in answer. The spirits screamed and began to run the other way, while the dots of light (*You can say it*—children. *They're children with pieces of Alke's stories inside them. That's what the lights are, Tristan.*) disappeared into the station.

"Tristan, we need to do something!" Ayanna shouted above the noise.

I hesitated. What could we do? Distract the monster until the spirits could get away? Or try and save the . . . children being herded inside?

"Tristan?" Thandiwe was staring at the kids. The look on her face rippled between horror, anger, and frustration. Ayanna had tears in her eyes. We had to act. But . . . the girls could only help if I kept them anchored in this spirit world, I realized. If I let go, they disappeared.

Fine. I wouldn't let go.

"We have to head off the spirits first!" I shouted. "If Old Angola eats them, it'll grow even more powerful." I looked at Thandiwe, whose hand trembled in mine, but she nodded. "We'll come back for the children. I promise."

Another promise made. Could I keep this one?

No, I couldn't think like that. I turned my back to Ayanna and told her to put her hand on my right shoulder. Then I placed Thandiwe's hand on my left shoulder. I looped the straps of my backpack, with Gum Baby inside, over their extended arms, and for a brief second it felt like we were all together again, flying off to fight monsters. Movement caught my eye. I looked behind me, and Spirit John stood tall, his face troubled. But the boy nodded at me and then reached out and placed his hand on my back as well.

There. Still connected to the people I cared about.

Now if only I could keep them all safe.

"Watch out, watch out, watch out!"

"There! Go, go, go!"

"Get out of the way!"

With the flying raft, we battled the prison monster in the middle of the train tracks. And by *battle* I mean we tried to annoy it to death. Another one of my superpowers! It stood between us and the giant station. We stood between it and the spirits fleeing the race-riots-on-repeat on the bridge. I could hear the victims' screams. Feel their terror. Just like I could feel the evil seeping from Cotton's twisted creation. And where was that haint? I had a nagging thought in the back of my mind. He wouldn't leave his monster unattended. Cotton relished control. Maybe he—

"Watch it!"

Ayanna sent the raft through a cluster of spirits and between the legs of Old Angola. I ground my teeth. *Focus, Tristan. Cotton can wait—his monster is the priority.* The haunted plantation prison-turned-giant bellowed a challenge, then slammed down a massive fist made of cinder blocks and haintacles (that's haint-tentacles, keep up with me, now) that barely missed us. Ayanna, one hand still clinging to me, put the raft into a tight 180-degree spin, pointed it upward, and sent us ripping across the monster's face. Several of the doors on its chest swung open as it lunged forward (OMG, what *was* that inside?), and Ayanna put on a burst of speed.

"That got its attention!" I shouted.

We swerved as Ayanna dodged the other fist, then twisted into a corkscrew spiral when several haintacles lashed out at us. We flew down and across the train tracks, barely skidding above the ground. My hoodie flapped behind me like a cape, and I nearly shouted at Gum Baby to hold on as we swerved and dipped. Old Angola lumbered after us, then pounded the ground with both fists and retreated. We were trying to lure the monster away from the spirits fleeing the violence, but it seemed unwilling to move too far from the train station.

Hmm, I thought.

Ayanna peeled away from the monster and headed toward the terrified spirits. Their pain stabbed my heart. We couldn't see the hate-filled people who had pursued them in life. But the spirits were doomed to repeat the most traumatic moments of their existence over and over and over again.

Ayanna must've realized the same thing at the same time. Her hand squeezed my shoulder. I put mine over hers.

"What can we do for them?" she asked.

What can you *do for them?* is what I heard. And I didn't want to let her down, but still...

I knew she felt my hesitation, because the raft slowed. "Tristan?"

"I...could try and read their stories....Find out what happened to them."

"There's hundreds of them!" Thandiwe yelled. She had her forebear in shield mode, and her makeshift kierie batted haintacles aside left and right. "We don't have time for one-on-one sessions."

I grabbed the adinkra bracelet with my right hand. "I can try to read them all at once."

"What?!"

"Have you even done that before?" Ayanna and Thandiwe shouted at the same time.

I tried to put on a confident grin and nodded. "Yep. High John showed me how." I didn't mention that it didn't work right the first time. Or that there'd only been a fraction of this number of spirits then. This was how I could prove to the gods that I was still an Anansesem, and, at the same time, release the spirits from the cycle of violence they were trapped in.

I only had to stay in control.

Another whistle shrieked twice inside the train station.

"Is a train about to depart?" I asked, turning to look, only to duck as something whipped over my head.

"Watch out!" Thandiwe cried as she avoided another haintacle and sent it twisting away with a backhanded swipe from her kierie. How she managed that while still keeping a death grip on my left shoulder, I'll never know.

I took a deep breath. Showtime. I gripped Nyame's adinkra but didn't close my eyes. Instead, I stared at a single point—the bridge. Focused on it. Didn't blink, didn't look away. Even when Ayanna sent the raft soaring upward, I maintained eye contact. My eyes began to tear, then blur, and right before I was going to have to rub them and start over again, a glint of gold appeared. Slowly, letter by letter, like an invisible hand performing calligraphy with ink made of starlight, words replaced the outline of the bridge.

I'd done it! High John would've flashed his wide grin and clapped me on the back if he was here . . . but he wasn't.

Spirit John moved beside me, as if sensing my thoughts. He kept one hand on my arm and stared at me until I nodded. Right. There were still more people to save.

Don't hurt my baby! If I can just get over this bridge, they won't hurt my baby.

The first spirit we flew past had her story cradled in her arms, written in a soft orange cursive that peeked out of a blanket like a swaddled ray of sunshine. I murmured her story, committing it to memory.

The next (*Please let them boys be at home, please, please, please . . .*) carried his words in a bag, and they knocked together like old-fashioned soda bottles.

"This is going to take too long," I muttered. I let my eyes scan the spirits running across the bridge as Ayanna brought us to a floating halt on the National City side. It felt like someone was stretching my vision wider so I could see more. I needed to see more.

I moved here to get away from the lynchings!

Where are they, where are they?

Mama, Mama, Mama, Mama, Mama. Ma—

Still not enough. I needed more stories. Even though reading each heartbreaking tale was like taking a surprise punch to the ribs over and over and over again, I kept going. I had to.

They grabbin' folks. I can't do this. Where's Dina? We need to get in the car and go, I don't care where. Oh God, we gotta go. . . .

Run, run, run, run . . .

Daddy?

More. MORE! Read more, Tristan! I could feel sparks of anger in my hands as I read fragment after fragment of spirits reliving the riots that had trapped them here. But I forced myself to keep going. I could control it. Use Mr. Richardson's Angry Octopus and all that.

Somewhere, from miles away, I heard Ayanna calling to

me. I wanted to let her know it'd be fine, I was okay, I just had to read more stories faster, but my lips weren't moving. I could only read.

Gotta get away. I ain't got nothin' left but the air in my lungs, and they ain't takin'—

Lord help me, I can't run no more. I can't run no more.

My granddad built this house, and I'm not leaving it for nobody.

"Tristan!"

Ayanna's fingers dug into my right shoulder as Thandiwe shook my left. I blinked. The air shimmered in front of me. I looked down, and my heart plummeted.

My arms were burning with the black fire of the akofena.

"No," I whispered.

Old Angola's roar split the night. The monster had finally found something tantalizing enough to lure it away from the train station it was guarding.

Me.

The black flames crept up my arm. To my shoulders. Toward the hands of my friends who were trusting me to keep them anchored in this spirit world....

I had to keep them safe.

Old Angola was only a dozen yards away when I turned to look at Ayanna. She saw something in my eyes and opened her mouth to protest, her hands trying to hold on to me. But I shrugged out of her grip...

...and tipped forward to fall into one of Old Angola's open steel doors.

The last thing I saw was Ayanna's face—twisted into a scream—fading as she returned to the real world and darkness swallowed me.

25
ALIKE IS A STORY

FIND THE PULSE OF THE STORY. LET THE RHYTHM BEAT LIKE A heart, and hold on to that pulse once you got it. Don't change it, no matter what anybody else says. Even if they call you a liar or selfish, or say you lucky to be here, or tell you to go somewhere else if you so unhappy, you don't let it go. Then speak those words. Tell the story.

Punishment: noun. Infliction of a penalty as retribution for an offense.

I've been punished before. Got detention for disrupting class. Was suspended for fighting. I'm not proud of how I acted those days after Eddie died and before Mr. Richardson started helping me through counseling. The school had rules, and I broke them—that was an offense. And I guess fighting doesn't help kids learn, does it? So I could understand that.

What crime did I commit? I didn't do anything! I was walking, laughing, joking, standing, sitting, driving, running, existing, and now I'm here! Dark and alone, nothing but me and shadows, me and this concrete, me and a slice of sunshine one hour a day.

The voice broke through my foggy dreams. A whisper, or maybe a mutter. It came from somewhere to my left. I was lying facedown on a cold floor, my cheek pressed up against what felt like steel. I rolled over and tried to open my eyes.

But my eyes were already open. It was just pitch-dark in . . . wherever I was.

Fine.

I reached for my adinkra bracelet. Maybe I'd been knocked unconscious and the Isihlangu spirit bead had worn off. I could reactivate it, or maybe even use Gye Nyame, the sky god's charm. Either one would reveal my predicament and help me find a way out of here. Simple as—

My wrist was bare.

For two seconds—one Mississippi, two Mississippi—I couldn't comprehend what had happened. I continued to squeeze my right wrist with my left hand, as if the act would summon the bracelet and everything would be fine. Instead, the only thing it brought was the first tendril of panic snaking up my spine.

What should I do? What *could* I do? I had no powers anymore! The last thing I remembered was falling off the raft, severing Ayanna and Thandiwe's connection to the invisible world of spirits and stories. And Old Angola had attacked . . . Had I been captured? Where was I? Where was Cotton? I vaguely remembered falling through a doorway. The image of the steel doors mounted on the prison monster's chest flashed into my mind. But there were no haintacles wrapped around me, no roars or thundering footsteps. Just a subtle rocking back and forth.

I reached behind me, searching for my backpack and the comfort of Gum Baby. Silent or not, her weight on me gave me strength I never would've admitted to her when she was . . .

When she was . . .

My fingers met with air. I wasn't wearing the backpack. No. NO!

My hands shot out, searching, colliding with a wall to my left and a wall to my right. The same in front and behind. No backpack. Just four walls, all squeezing in on me, silent and brutal. Trapped. I was trapped in a box, locked in the dark and alone.

Metal screeched and a sliver of light appeared a few feet in front of my eyes—a slot had opened in the door, revealing a barred window. A harsh white glare stabbed my pupils, and I blinked several times. Then I rushed forward, desperate for a breath of fresh air and a glimpse outside. Maybe I could . . .

But no, there was no door handle. No way for me to escape the box I was locked inside. I couldn't help but think of Spirit John's story, of being imprisoned in a tiny space as punishment for talking about freedom and his right to humanity.

I pounded the door and shouted, "Hey! Can anybody hear me? HEY!"

Nothing. Only the sound of my ragged breathing and a strange rumbling in the floor. But then, from outside my view, I heard someone chuckle—smug and dismissive.

"Now what did I tell you, my boy? Didn't I say you'd come to me? Boy, you fell into my arms like you was running home."

A face moved in front of the bars, its features cast in shadow, but I recognized the profile. And I knew the voice.

"I tell you, Tristan," Cotton said, "we're going to bring light to this country, my boy, mark my words. And you did your part!"

Cotton held up a fist. My bracelet dangled from his fingers, and he shook it at me.

"You're a hero," he said. "Because of you, me and Old Angola here ain't gotta rustle up any more spirits. You collected 'em for me! All it took"—the humor dropped from his tone—"was the power of the gods. Job well done."

I climbed to my feet even though every part of me, from my hands to my feet to the muscles in my jaw, wanted to stay on the floor.

"You're not going to get away with this," I growled. My voice shook with anger.

"Who's gonna check me?" Cotton laughed. "Your gods? Boy, let me tell you a thing or three—them gods of yours are in for a rude awakening, they rightly are. This world don't give an owl's hoot if someone can fly. It'll pluck the wings from their backs and put them in their place. But it ain't gotta be like that for you. Hop on my team and we'll be running this place by morning."

I shook my head. "You're a liar." My voice trembled, but I wasn't going to let the haint see me rattled, even if the only thing holding me up was that little bit of light coming through the slot. "I would rather sit in the dark than watch you play god. You're nothing like them. And when I get out of here, I'm going to put you back in your place—a lovely blue glass bottle dangling from a tree."

Cotton snarled and lunged. His clawed hands slipped through the bars on the window and snagged my collar, dragging me forward until my face pressed against the cold steel.

"Then stay in here and rot, boy. Meanwhile, I'll be taking over this country, city by city. I was gonna rest here awhile, let Old Angola plant himself so he can feed . . . but you know what I'm thinking now? I'm thinking we got all the power we need from that ole trinket of yours, so we can travel a bit and settle down wherever I feel like. Wherever I can have the most *fun*."

My heart skipped a beat. "No . . ." I whispered.

Cotton watched my face and leered. "Oh yeah, my boy. We're going to have a blast. Your friends and family and your tired little gods will make a good snack for my little baby prison." The haint straightened and backed up. His head tilted. "Now that he's had a taste, of course. That High John and . . . Gum Baby . . . mmm-mm."

My fist slammed forward, but Cotton was too fast. He danced away and I ended up with nothing but bruised knuckles from the bars.

A whistle shrieked and Cotton retreated out of sight, calling back to me as he departed. "I'll leave you a little light so you can see it all, my boy. Witness the transformation. This world ain't gonna know what hit it!"

And with that, the haint disappeared, whistling a tune that grated on my ears, and leaving me with one thought thundering in my skull.

We're doomed.

Black is a rainbow.

As light from the outside world flickered through the slot in the door, as shadows shifted around me, and as advice from elders and ancestors echoed in my ears, those four words Nana had paid an artist to put on the back of the Strong family reunion T-shirts floated to the forefront of my mind.

I thought I understood them now. On the wall next to the corner I had slumped down into, I saw the faces of loved ones who had helped me become the person I was today. My parents. My grandparents. Uncles, aunts, cousins (even Terrence). Eddie. Thandiwe. John Henry, Miss Sarah and Miss Rose, Nyame. Keelboat Annie and Mr. Richardson.

High John the Conqueror. Gum Baby. Ayanna. A kaleidoscope of brown, dark like the shadows I cowered in, as bright as sunlight peeking through morning clouds, and infinite variations in between.

Black is a rainbow that arches overhead for all to see. But the beginning of our rainbow, even though we know it is there and we talk about it, has been hidden from us. The story of our bloody arrival has been buried and sanitized. Why did it take magical powers to read about it? And where does the rainbow end? What's the point of looking for it if our pot of gold is burned up whenever we try to claim it?

Black is a rainbow, like the swirling colors on an oil slick viewed at just the right angle. The pain is there, but so is the beauty. I had to hold on to that.

I muttered those four words to myself over and over. They were all I had left.

Time passed. I don't know how much. The light remained constant, as did the rocking of the train. (Yes, I'd finally figured out that Cotton was riding the rails, with me in tow.) We could've been traveling for minutes, or maybe hours. I think I fell asleep at one point, dozing right there in my squat, my back pressed against the wall and my head on my knees.

The light from the window in the door rippled. I looked up and blinked. Was it my imagination or was the room getting brighter? No. Not the room. The light—it split into a thousand tiny little beams, as if someone outside was holding a prism in front of the bars. The beams shifted and curved while growing brighter, until—

I let out a sharp gasp. "You . . . But how?"

No answer came. It never did. Instead, Spirit John stood in the tiny cramped cell with me. He smiled and jerked his chin as if to say *Come on.*

I remained where I was, baffled beyond belief. "How are you even here? How can I see you?" This was impossible. I had no adinkra. No spirit bead from Isihlangu. No powers. No magic. Right? I reached for the root bag High John had given me, tucked under my shirt. Cotton must've ignored it. But that wouldn't let me see spirits. I didn't understand.

Spirit John cocked his head. The older boy wore a look as if he knew something I didn't. He shoved his hands into his pockets and jerked his chin at me again.

Nothing made sense. I waved my right hand through the air, just making sure I could see myself, that this wasn't a dream. I patted my legs, pinched my cheeks, and rubbed my stomach, staring at my body to confirm I was really present.

And that's when I saw it.

"Sweet peaches," I whispered.

There, imprinted on my chest like a spiraling onyx-and-silver tattoo, was a thread of Alke. A strand of the magical land's story. It coiled above my heart and gleamed with a shine too bright to be anything but magic.

Suddenly the unpredictability of my powers made sense. I'd been calling upon the magic of Alke through the adinkra. But this fragment of magic—the same I'd seen inside the members of the Rolling Thunder and the children kidnapped in National City—had been coming to my aid as well. It was like turning on the tap and having Niagara Falls rush out of your faucet. If you weren't expecting it and didn't have a way to contain it, what do you think would happen? Chaos, that's what.

When I looked closer, I saw that my fragment, unlike the others I'd seen, wasn't just one thread. Instead, different colors had been braided together. The silver of Isihlangu, the gold from the Golden Crescent, sapphire blue from Nyanza, and more. Each region of Alke, woven together.

"Black is a rainbow," I said.

Spirit John's grin grew even wider.

I stood and stretched, ignoring the tight space meant to keep me small. It had been designed to stifle and crush, to grind down whoever entered. No doorknob? No problem. I raised my fists, clenched them, and squeezed. I imagined the strength of two worlds coursing through my blood—one of flesh, one of stories.

I didn't need to look down to see the flaming boxing gloves of the akofena. The heat in my burning fists was proof enough.

CLANG! CLANG! CLANG! My fists hammered against the metal.

CRASH!

The heavy steel door exploded outward. It slid across the swaying floor and disappeared, three giant dents and all. I stepped outside my prison cell, fists still on fire. Took a look around.

We were on the last car of the train, an open-sided cargo container that was scuffed and beaten and covered in graffiti. Gray lightning streamed past us on either side. Occasionally I caught a glimpse of a building, or trees, or even a lake as we traveled over a bridge, but otherwise it felt like we were traveling outside of time.

"A spirit train," I muttered. "No wonder we could never find Cotton. I wonder where we are now?"

Then I shook my head. That didn't matter. We'd stop where we'd stop. It was what—and who—was on the train that mattered to me. Where was Cotton? I wanted to smoke him, and the black fire crackling on my fists proved it. I turned toward the front of the train and looked at Spirit John. The boy's grin was positively feral now, as if he relished the fight to come. I didn't blame him one bit.

"Let's go start a riot," I said.

26

THE BOYS ARE BACK IN TOWN

HERE'S WHAT I KNOW—ANGER UNCONTROLLED IS CHAOTIC AT BEST.
At worst? It's a time bomb. But anger leashed, anger harnessed, anger shaped and molded and given purpose? It can be a tool. A hammer for building up. An ax for chopping down. A fire for starting over.

As Spirit John and I moved from car to car, the black fire rippling up my arms and flickering around the six shadow gloves surrounding me, my anger grew with each step. With every beat of my heart. This time, however, I didn't let it rage out of control. I didn't let it get the best of me. I put it to work.

"Another one?" I asked. Grunted, really.

Spirit John nodded.

We stood in a converted passenger car, the last one before a dining car. This wasn't packed full of Amtrak luxury, however. All signs of comfort had been ripped out. That left a dark, narrow passageway with gray doors on either side. Rusted brown locks had been fastened on each, sealing the occupants inside. We'd already opened nearly two dozen compartments, freeing kids of various ages. Every one had the magic of Alke within them, untouched. I still didn't know what Cotton's ultimate plans were, but I didn't need to. I just had to stop him once and for all.

When we were at the second-to-last door, I glanced at Spirit John. "Let them know I'm coming," I said.

Spirit John walked through the door. I waited outside, counted to three, and backed up when I heard startled shouts come from inside. The ghost boy reappeared and nodded to me again. I took a deep breath and dropped into a boxer's crouch. Then, in an explosion of movement, I stepped forward, twisted my hips, and clipped the lock with a giant hook. The scorched metal shattered and shot away into the dark, and I was able to slide the newly unlocked door open.

Four children—three toddlers and a boy maybe a year younger than me—huddled in the corner. Threads of Alke coiled from each of them, and the story of their capture drifted slowly around them in wild, sloppy script. The handwriting of fear.

Somewhere in the back of my mind I marveled at the way all of Alke's magic was manifesting inside me at once. Could the same thing happen for these children if they were shown how to control it?

Spirit John stepped into the compartment behind me but then faded through the wall, I guess so as not to scare the kids any more than they already were. But...I don't know, maybe exit through the door instead?

The older boy in the group wore a pair of glasses and a T-shirt with the names of authors on it. For one long and excruciating heartbeat I thought it was Eddie. The resemblance... Before I could stop myself, I held out a hand, ready to dap him up. He just stared at it, and I cleared my throat.

"We're here to free you," I said gently.

The boy didn't move. Instead, he looked toward the wall where Spirit John had disappeared. "Was that a...a..."

"A spirit," I said. "Yes."

"Ghost!" one of the smaller toddlers said, a girl with a fuzzy bun on top of her head and a thumb in her mouth. She spoke around it one more time for emphasis. "Ghost!"

I squatted in front of her. "He's a *spirit*," I said. "An ancestor, here to help. He and I are partners."

Another of the toddlers, a boy with thick curls and a button nose, frowned. "Aunt-cestor?"

"Like Auntie Jendayi," the girl said. She nodded at me as if we were on the same page. I nodded back while stifling a grin.

"What are your names?" I asked.

They all looked toward the older boy. He hesitated, then cleared his throat. "Kweku. That's Marcus, Ruby, and Baby Lewis."

The curly-headed boy, Baby Lewis, smiled. "I'm named after John Lewis!"

Ruby looked puzzled. "Your arms are on fire," she said to me. "You should stop and drop." She thought about it, then added, "And roll."

Kweku stood up and moved in front of the toddlers, who were trying to count the akofena shadow gloves. "Are the . . . things gone?" he asked me. "The ones with the claws?"

Breakers! Were there some on this train? We hadn't run into any in the other passenger cars. I swallowed a lump of fear, remembering how they'd swarmed me outside Patty Roller's Wig Emporium. Gum Baby was the only reason I was still alive.

If the Breakers were somewhere up front with Cotton, Gum Baby was probably there, too. I had to get her back—who knew what Cotton or his minions would do with her? She had saved me, and now it was time to return the favor.

I stood and looked Kweku in the eye. "I'm not sure. That's why you need to take the little ones and move to the back of the train. Quickly. There are other kids there—tell them all to hide until I say it's okay to come out. We're taking over this train."

"I can help fight!" Kweku said eagerly.

I shook my head. "The best thing you can do is keep the others safe. That's your job, and I'm trusting you to do it. Can you?"

The boy swallowed his disappointment and nodded. I held out a fist, and this time we did dap up. He gathered the toddlers together—sort of like herding kittens—and began to move them quickly toward the rear of the train. I watched them leave, then turned and looked at Spirit John, who'd reappeared at my shoulder.

"Let's go," I said.

The final door had several locks on it, and that gave me pause. The Redliners really didn't want whoever was inside to escape. Good. The more I could mess up their plans, the better. Let them stress—they were gatekeepers, and we were smashing our way through their barricades. Starting with this door.

The shadow gloves incinerated the locks. I slid the door aside, then peered into the gloom.

A familiar face looked back, and I nearly fell flat on my behind in surprise.

"Tristan?"

I took a deep breath to douse the akofena flames and

reached out into the darkness. A thin brown hand grabbed my own, and I pulled the skinny boy to his feet. He didn't let go as he stared at me, then he limped forward to give me a hug.

"Thank you," Junior said.

Junior had always been thin, but now he was all bones and a shadow. Who knew how long he'd been in that cell? His eyes were wide and red, as if he hadn't slept in forever.

"I thought I'd never get out of there," he whispered. "Some nights I thought . . . I thought Cotton was right. That no one was coming for me. That my father—"

"Anansi never stopped looking for you," I interrupted, jabbing a finger into Junior's shoulder. "Never. It's all he thought about, day in and day out. If he were here, he'd tell you that himself. Cotton likes to hurt people where they're most sensitive. But he's going to get his. If it's the last thing I do."

"*We* do," Junior said, correcting me. He held out a hand to shake. "If it's the last thing *we* do." I grinned and grabbed it, and we stood together, two sons of Alke. You get me?

Spirit John appeared at the opposite end of the car, beckoning urgently. I nodded at Junior. "Let's get started."

The three of us stepped cautiously into the dining car. No one was inside. Just tables and booths bolted to the wall on one side and a small bar on the other. Plates and dishes were scattered everywhere. Claw marks gouged the walls, floor, and ceiling. Breakers.

But it was the last table, near the door to the next car, that grabbed my attention. A backpack sat on top—black with silver straps. *My* backpack. I was running toward it before I realized my feet had moved. I lifted it, unzipped it, and a strangled sob escaped me.

Gum Baby was still inside. Unmoving, but untouched.

I looked through all the other pockets. No sign of the adinkra bracelet. Cotton must still have it. *We got all the power we need from that ole trinket of yours....*

My fingers angrily squeezed the straps of the backpack as I slipped it over my hoodie. Something clattered to the floor, and I stooped to pick it up. Gum Baby's phone! Now I could get word back to the others. I flipped it open, hoping that magical Alkean reception would work here, pressed the key for the *River Queen*, and waited.

"Gum Baby?" a familiar voice asked hesitantly. I sank against the table in relief.

"Ayanna, it's Tristan," I said. "You all made it back okay?"

"Tristan!" Her voice grew distant as she shouted to someone in the background. "It's Tristan! Tristan, I'm putting you on speakerphone. Um...wait. Mami Wata, how do I put a mermaid on speakerphone? Press what? Tristan, can you hear us?"

"Yeah," I said. The smile on my face had to be stretching from ear to ear.

"I'm so glad you're okay," Ayanna said. "When you fell you disappeared, and we spent *hours* looking for you. Don't ever do that again! I will strap you to my raft and fly you to the moon if you scare me like that a second time. You hear me?" Her voice trembled a bit, and I swallowed whatever snarky comment I was going to make .

"Yes, ma'am."

"Good! Better be the last time you stress me out, boy. Got me all worried."

"That means you've been thinking about me," I said, still grinning like a doofus, before my brain caught up with me and I realized I'd said that out loud.

Junior let out a small laugh, and I felt my cheeks bloom with heat.

No, no, no, that wasn't supposed to be an outside thought—that was an inside *thought!*

My heart thumped like a rabbit trapped in a box. Silence stretched on the other end, and I thought about hanging up and staying on the spirit train for the rest of my life. It wouldn't be that bad an existence. A few Breakers would be nothing compared to the sweaty-palmed, hot-necked embarrassment I currently felt. I could live under the very table I stood in front of, surviving off floor food and whatever was behind the bar. Hermits are cool these days.

"Whatever thoughts are in my head," Ayanna finally said, "are between me and the bigheaded boy who comes back safe. Do you understand?"

I let out a breath I hadn't realized I'd been holding (yeah, yeah, I know, everybody does it once) and slowly, doofusly, the smile returned to my face. "Yes, ma'am. I understand."

"Good."

A new voice—louder, deeper, and definitely NOT Ayanna's—interrupted. "If y'all reckon y'all finished, maybe we could think about saving this here world? But only if y'all finished."

Wait, nope, the hermit life was back on the table. Under the table. Never forget you're on speakerphone, folks.

Ayanna must've felt the same way, because I could hear embarrassment coloring her voice when she spoke again. "Tristan, that's—"

"John Henry," I said, sinking down into a toddler crouch. "I figured."

"Well, everyone's here. John Henry, Mami Wata, Nyame, Thandiwe, and Keelboat Annie. Miss Sarah and Miss Rose are on their way with reinforcements."

"Reinforcements?"

"I'll explain later. I don't quite understand it myself."

"And Anansi?" I asked, glancing at Junior. The boy stiffened. I still hoped to convince the trickster god that I was worthy of the Anansesem title, and maybe his son could help persuade him. But the long pause at the other end of the phone didn't bode well. Sure enough . . .

"Anansi isn't here." That was Nyame speaking. "It's . . . complicated."

Grown-up-to-kid translation: We're uncomfortable talking about it.

Mami Wata spoke next. "Tristan, where are you? Ayanna came back and said you'd been fighting a monster. Are you safe?"

I hesitated, staring at a trio of gouge marks on the floor in front of me. "Safe enough, I guess. But there are kids on this train, a bunch of them."

"Kids!" That was Annie's voice.

"Yes, and I found Junior."

The cheer on the other end was so loud, I had to pull the phone away from my ear. This time it was Junior's turn to blush, and I grinned and threw a mock punch at his shoulder. There was a collective sigh of relief, and then Mami Wata broke in. "Do you know where the train is headed?" she asked. "We're moving fast, and once the *Queen* gets going there isn't any stopping her, not while I'm on board. But we need a destination."

I shook my head in frustration, even though they couldn't see me. "No. Spirit John and I were trying to figure that out when we found Junior and . . . well, that's when I called you all."

"Spirit John?"

"I'll explain later," I heard Ayanna whisper.

I took a deep breath. There was one more thing I had to confess. It pained me to do it, but I knew they'd find out at some point. I had to rip off the bandage and get it over with.

"There's something else. Cotton...he has the adinkra bracelet."

Silence. Then:

"He WHAT?!"

"Oh, Tristan. How?!"

"This is bad. THIS IS BAD!"

Everyone started talking at once. A choir of criticism. I held the phone away from my ear and winced. It went about as well as I'd expected. I stood up and turned to Junior, only to see him standing at the far door, a look of confusion on his face as he stared into the next car on the train.

I covered the phone with one hand. "What is it? Breakers?"

He didn't answer, just stood there, confused, as if unable to process what he was seeing. Everyone on the other end of the phone was still arguing about what to do next, so I walked over to the door and peered through. I had to see this for my—

The phone slipped through my fingers and fell to the floor.

"Tristan?" I heard Ayanna say. "Tristan, what was that? Are you okay?"

I knelt and groped for the phone while keeping my eyes

on the window in the door. It was impossible. And yet, everything suddenly made a sickening amount of sense. Cotton had basically told me where he was going, but I didn't connect the dots until just then.

"Tristan!"

I slowly moved the phone to my ear. "Ayanna."

"Are you—"

"Ayanna," I said, slowly and calmly, "I know where the train is heading."

"You do? Hold on." She shushed everyone in the background. "Where?"

I licked my lips. The next car wasn't a former passenger car, nor a cargo car, but something I'd seen nearly every day growing up. I'd ridden in one on numerous occasions. By myself. With Eddie. With my parents. Some days it was how I got to school, and other days it was how I got to the gym where Dad and I went for training.

It was an L-train car. And if the spirit train was now disguised as an L, that meant Cotton was headed toward...

"Chicago," I said.

27

BREAKER, BREAKER

THE INSTANT WE STEPPED INTO THE L TRAIN, I REALIZED MY mistake.

For the newbies, an L, short for *elevated*, is the opposite of a subway. Instead of traveling underground, L trains ride on tracks high above the streets, rumbling through and around Chicago day and night.

"Next stop, Oak Park," came the automated announcement over the train's public address system.

And, as on all public transportation, there are rules. *Watch your step. Let other passengers off before you get on. Bags don't need to sit in a seat. Don't ride in the trash car when taking the tram into Isihlangu.* You know, the basics. But the one rule I'd forgotten? It went like this:

Always look around to see who else is in the train car with you.

Mom drilled that into my head as soon as I was old enough to take the L by myself. I'd hop on the Green Line and ride

320

to Eddie's apartment across town. *Always be aware of your sur-roundings*, Mom had said. But this time I'd been so distracted with the spirit train's transformation that I hadn't noticed who was waiting for me in the single bucket seat near the middle of the car.

A Redliner sat there, a newspaper in their gloved hands.

"*Next stop, East Garfield Park,*" droned the automated system.

I paused. Maybe the Redliner hadn't noticed us. I didn't want to draw any attention before I was sure all the kids had made it safely off the train. Gingerly, I began to retreat, motioning for Junior to do likewise as we tiptoed out the way we'd come.

A chorus of whispers brushed past my ear.

The hairs on the back of my neck stood on end as I turned to find a Breaker wedged into corner of the ceiling above the door, like an oversize spider waiting for flies to land in its web. And, in case you haven't figured it out, we were the flies. The splotchy gray creature's impossibly wide mouth was open, revealing only coal-black darkness.

And then it shrieked.

"Wuzzuh?" The Redliner jerked upright, fumbling with a cord around their neck. I caught a glimpse of a graying beard before his mask dropped back into place and he stood and pointed at me. "You! You can't be here."

I backed away from the Breaker, which peeled itself off

the ceiling like molasses dripping out of a jar, its whip-fingers and club-arms grabbing handrails and poles as it maneuvered its way over the seats after me. It moved slowly. Lazily. And yet I knew at any second it could put on a terrifying burst of speed and attack.

It shrieked again. Seconds later, an answering shriek came from the car ahead.

Dang.

The Redliner blew three shrill blasts on a whistle and stood in the middle of the aisle, both arms outstretched. "You are not allowed in this space," he said loudly. "Go away. You can't be here. You are not allowed in this space."

He continued to repeat himself as if he were chanting the Mantra of Gentrification, +10 advantage to removing *undesirables*. It would've been funny—and sad, let's not forget sad—if it weren't for the Breaker skittering toward me. And then there was the small matter of a second Breaker in the next car.

A speaker crackled above me. "Tomothy, what's going on?"

I recognized the voice on the PA—it was Harold. How could one man always manage to show up at exactly the wrong time? It was like he had a field guide to bigotry.

I scowled and activated the akofena gloves. The Breaker was scuttling back and forth, trying to determine the best way to get at me. The flames of the shadow gloves blazed merrily, but I knew they wouldn't keep the monster at bay forever.

"Next stop, Shedd Aquarium."

Tomothy the Redliner didn't move. He just waited for the automated train stop announcement to finish, then shouted, "Got a couple escapees down here, Harold. What do you want me to do?"

"Did you blow your whistle?"

"Yep."

"And did you recite the Discouragement Chant?"

"You betcha."

"And they're still there? Interesting."

Tomothy scratched his head. "One of 'em's a bit weird, if I'm being honest, Harold. All on fire and whatnot."

"What knot?"

"Yep, whatnot. And on fire."

Harold mumbled something off-mic, then came back on full of excitement. "Darla says don't let him past—it's that same troublemaker, the one we've been searching for. Make a citizen's arrest, Tomothy!"

"Now?" Tomothy looked at me, then back at the speaker. "But he's on fire. And one of the Boss Lady's creatures is about to start nibbling on him."

"Next stop, Chinatown."

I stiffened. Chinatown was only one stop away from my apartment. I couldn't let the spirit train reach my neighborhood. Not when it was carrying all these Breakers and the Redliners. Unfortunately, both were converging on me at this moment. I licked my lips. Maybe I could dash past Tomothy and figure out a way to stop the train from a different car. I'd just tensed, ready to sprint for the far side of the car, when the door we'd come through hissed open. Baby Lewis stood there, his eyes big and ready to cry.

"Mr. Tristan? I can't find Kweku," he said.

The Breaker turned around.

I could see the events unfolding before they happened, and I was moving before I could talk myself out of it. The shadow gloves disappeared as I dropped and slid beneath the Breaker's gangly limbs, then hopped to my feet, scooped up Baby Lewis, and took off through the door into the dining car, Junior right on my heels.

More whistle blasts. More shrieks.

Baby Lewis squeaked in fear as the door behind us crashed open. My legs kept pumping as I held him close. "Don't look back!" I shouted.

The door to the car in front of us was open, and for a second I was relieved that I wouldn't have to waste precious seconds fiddling with it. The three of us ran through, and then I skidded to a stop, put down Baby Lewis, and gave him a little shove. "Go! Keep running. Get to the next car and lock the door behind you."

Junior managed to slide shut the door to the dining car. Then he tried to close off the car we were in. But no matter how hard he heaved on the door, it wouldn't budge.

"Next stop, Thirty-fifth-Bronzeville."

This was it. Home.

More shrieks filled the air as a horde of Breakers flooded the dining car. I tried to help Junior yank on our car's door. He'd lost a lot of strength after being stuck in a cell for so long. But the latch wouldn't work. Though the dining car door was closed, I knew the Breakers would soon bust through and swarm us. Dozens upon dozens of the gray monsters were in there, flailing their arms and beating the ground.

The PA system crackled again and, after a burst of static, Harold's voice came through a speaker in the corner. "Give it up, young men. It's over. Kindly return to your cells—I mean, your rooms—and don't make this harder on yourselves."

I gritted my teeth and let go of the door. I dared a quick glance behind me and saw Baby Lewis running through the next car. There was no one else in sight...but he'd left the door ajar.

"Do you see the Boss Lady's little friends?" Harold asked, dragging my attention back to the predicament in front of me. He sighed loudly. "Revolting, aren't they? But we have to work with whoever's available."

"You'd rather work with monsters than children?" I asked the disembodied voice.

"Of course not!" he said indignantly. "I'd rather do no such thing. But you've proven to be a thorn in the Boss Lady's side, Mr. Strong. And that's why this has to end here."

In the dining car, the Breakers crawled over each other, the tables, and even along the ceiling on their way to us. I started to back up, then stopped. If I let them through, there'd be no stopping the creatures from reaching the kids in the rear of the train.

"Junior," I said quietly. "Close the door."

"Yeah. On it." He started to jog away, then stopped. "Aren't you coming?"

I shook my head. "Go through and lock it from the other side. I'll hold them here."

"But—"

"Just lock it!" I yelled, cutting off his protest just as the PA system crackled again.

"Do you know what these hideous creatures are?" Harold asked.

I didn't answer. My attention didn't waver from one of the larger monsters, with whip-fingers as long as jump ropes. It crept forward, its head tilting in fits and spurts to the left, then back to the right.

"Tristan, come on…" Junior pleaded from the door behind me.

I ignored him. A deafening rush of whispers crowded my ears and I ground my teeth. There was nothing else to do. I lifted my fists and the shadow gloves roared to life, black flames licking up my arms.

"Breakers, my dear boy, were specialists," said Harold.

"Back when your people joyously worked for free in exchange for housing—"

"That was slavery!" I shouted.

"—you'd get malcontents like yourself. Ungrateful. Spoiled. Stubborn. Well, there were people you could be sent to. Talented, enterprising folks who believed that if you spared the rod, you spoiled the slave. Breakers would strip that pesky spirit from you in no time flat. You'd learn to appreciate what you had!"

"Strip . . . the spirit?" High John's prone form slid through my mind. Then Gum Baby's limp body in my backpack. Was that how . . . ?

"Gone!" Harold said cheerfully. "And the same will happen to you if you don't get back where you belong, Mr. Strong. Off to your room!"

The door to the dining car slid open and the large Breaker crept over the gangway connection to my car. I never took my eyes off it. This monstrosity was what had severed a god from his power, ripped the life from a brazen and fearless doll, and terrorized innocent children. Its claw-tipped fingers scraped the floor as it whispered gibberish at me. Horrifying gibberish that made my knees want to buckle, but still gibberish. Its mouth opened wide, then wider and wider still, and it let out a horrifying shriek that threatened to shatter every window in the car.

How could we win against Cotton if he had allies like this?

It was impossible. I already knew what would happen next. The Breakers would overwhelm me, rip any Alkean magic they found from my body, then discard me like an unwanted rag doll. Because to them, and to Cotton, Patty Roller, and the Redliners, anyone different from them who had power of any sort—power of determination, of voice, of unity, and yes, of magic—and didn't immediately roll over and obey their wishes was an Other. And Others couldn't be suffered to exist, let alone thrive, because then what would happen?

(The answer is nothing. Absolutely nothing. You know that, and I know that. But maybe Granny Z had said it best back at the skate park. *It's a sad fact that their abusers are always gonna be afraid that their own sins will be revisited upon them. And fear makes grown folks act like children.*)

So now the children had to act like adults. Such foolishness, man, I tell you. There was a train car full of frightened kids behind me and a mob of monsters in front of me, and the only adults on board hid behind masks and offered thoughts and prayers. That left Junior and myself. Two boys. Three, if you counted Spirit John. I really just wanted to go home. And now I had the chance. But leaving now would mean abandoning the vulnerable, and if I did that, I'd be no better than any Redliner or haint.

Strongs may argue. Strongs might bicker, fuss, and fight like all families do from time to time. But you know what we don't do? Give up.

Strongs.

Keep.

Punching.

The akofena shadow gloves shimmered as black flames roared around them and up my arms. I slammed my right fist into the opposite palm. Once. Twice. I dropped into the boxer's crouch perfected by Walter Strong and grinned at the Breakers.

"What are you doing?" Harold called over the PA system. "Surely you're giving up, right? Boy? Mr. Strong? Hellooo..."

I didn't answer him, because I was done speaking. Time to let my fists do the talking.

The large Breaker shrieked, an ear-piercing signal, and the rest of the gray monsters rushed forward. Whip-claws lashed out, a dozen—no, two dozen at a time, their pointed tips descending through the air like cleavers.

Snik, snik, snik

Too many to dodge or duck at once. Slip? No, cross-body block!

My arms crossed in front of me, left over right, at the last moment.

Snik, snik, snik

Their attacks were heavy but harmless, bouncing off the shadow gloves. Several Breakers fell back, squealing in pain as black fire crept up their whip-claws. More took their place. Again they attacked.

Snik, snik, snik

Once more they were repelled, but the force of their blows was driving me backward. I couldn't retreat far—the door to the next car was behind me. The car with Junior and the rest of the kids. I couldn't let the Breakers get past me. I dug in and inched forward up the aisle.

Snik, snik, snik

The power of the Breakers' blows grew stronger. More monsters were joining in the attack, squeezing together and sending out their whip-claws with no pause in between.

Snik, snik, snik

They rained blows on me, snarled at me, shrieked at me, roared at me, sent wave after wave after wave of pure hatred and malevolence, and it was all I could do to keep my arms raised and defend myself, because I was so tired, incredibly tired, of defending myself, but it wasn't just me I was defending, now was it? And every time I wanted to drop, say I was too tired, quit, give up, just let them win, I thought of Baby Lewis, of Chayse, of Kweku, of the Rolling Thunder, of every kid in every city of every country who didn't have someone to defend them when they needed it most and I kept. On. Standing.

Even when it hurt to keep my arms raised.

Even when I wanted to cry.

Even when the spirit train shuddered.

Even when I wanted to sink to one knee beneath the onslaught.

Even when the shadow gloves began to flicker like a nearly extinguished torch.

Even when the Breakers shrieked and the train screeched.

Even when silence came and I couldn't tell—through the fog of exhaustion and pain—if I was still conscious, and even when I feared I'd passed out . . . or worse.

Even when two giant brown hands gripped my arms and, despite the remaining flames, pulled me forward, lifted me, hugged me.

"I'm still standing," I whispered.

"I know," said John Henry. "I know."

"Cotton—" I tried to say, but the giant god cut me off, and his expression was grim.

"Tristan, I reckon we've got ourselves a bit of a problem."

Right. There was always one more fight.

John Henry glanced behind him, and I looked past him to see a huge hole he'd made in the side of the train car. "Look here, Tristan," he said. "Maybe you should . . . hang on back with the others. Make sure them kids is okay, you know what I mean?"

I stared at him. That was pretty much the same thing I'd told Kweku when I thought it'd be too dangerous for him. So yeah . . . I knew exactly what he meant. And I didn't like it one bit.

I ducked under his arms, ignoring his protests, and jumped through the hole. Dropped down to the elevated platform, holding on tight to the backpack with Gum Baby still inside. Keelboat Annie stood down the track a ways, five cars ahead. Her keel pole was stuck into the wheels at the front of the train, jamming them. That must've been the shuddering I'd felt.

Twenty or so Redliners were fleeing on the ground below, their cloaks between their legs like the tails of scolded dogs. I watched them run east, toward Lake Michigan.

"Don't worry, Tristan," Keelboat Annie shouted. "Soon as this here pole stops playin', we'll be after them, don't you fret."

But it wasn't the Redliners I was worried about—it was the giant structure they were running toward. I could just make it out in the distance.

No, not a structure.

A monster.

Because, in the shallows of Lake Michigan, near the beach where Dad and Mom would take us, where me and all my friends used to play together in the sand, Old Angola reared its ugly head.

And the spirit prison had grown.

28

CHICAGO OVER EVERYTHING

LET ME TELL YOU ABOUT MY NEIGHBORHOOD. BRONZEVILLE, IN Chicago. Last year my social studies teacher, Mrs. Tracy, gave us an assignment to research the areas we lived in. She was always trying to get us to learn more about the histories around us, and at first I thought it was silly. A street is a street, right?

Wrong.

Let's see what you know.

Did you know that Chicago was once a major trading post for Indigenous peoples, and different tribes traveled along trade routes that eventually became the avenues we ride on today?

Did you know that Chicago was one of several relocation destinations during the infamous Trail of Tears, when those same Indigenous peoples were ejected from their homes across the country by government order?

Did you know that Chicago is one of several midwestern cities, like Detroit and Milwaukee, that received Black people migrating from the South beginning in the early 1900s, looking for jobs, opportunity, a beginning, a restart?

Did you know any of that? I didn't. And do you know what all those people, those Chicagoans, had in common? The journey, the burdens they carried, and the communities they built when their tired feet and weary souls finally stopped. Those communities still exist today. Communities like Bronzeville, where Alvin Strong and Jessica Strong lived and raised their son, me.

Home.

I lived a few blocks away from the Thirty-Fifth Street station. If I took a left turn instead of a right, I'd be able to see the awning of my apartment building. I was so close and yet so far. Because I couldn't go home now, not with the city in so much trouble. I mean, this was where I lived! Where my friends, neighbors, and even strangers planted roots, where we grew. There was the corner store where Eddie and I snagged Flamin' Hots before huddling at my kitchen table and arguing over comic books. There was the bus stop where I waited before the sun rose. There was the barbershop, G's, where I got my hair cut and learned all the neighborhood gossip. This was home!

And Old Angola loomed over it all.

The air shimmered as the powers of Gye Nyame kicked

in, even without the adinkra, just as I'd expected. It seemed like every time I arrived in a new city, the magic of Alke wanted to show me the stories that rippled through it. New Orleans. Vicksburg. Memphis. National City. Now Chicago. And this time the golden threads decided to really show off.

Bronzeville's story was written in the streets, and each step I took sent words racing away from my feet. Bright curling script told of the hopes and dreams of the Black population that had swelled to bursting after the Great Migration. Fragments of song swirled off to frame the former location of the Regal Theater, where the city gathered to watch Black musicians tear down the house.

Rose-gold headlines marched off to queue up in front of the offices of the *Chicago Defender*, the Black newspaper that had played a big part in getting many Black families to the city in the first place, sending newspapers south on trains with tales of opportunity.

The story of my community was written in the footsteps of those who had lived here before me. And now the clawed hand of a haint threatened to erase it all.

"Tristan!"

I didn't know I was walking toward the lakefront until I heard someone shouting my name. Ayanna sprinted after me, and Junior limped close behind. Thandiwe lent him her shoulder, and Spirit John brought up the rear. We were hurting, broken. But we weren't defeated. Not while we still breathed.

"Are you okay?" Ayanna asked, her eyes searching me for signs of injury.

I nodded, even as Junior thumped me on the shoulder and glared. "Grandstander." Then his eyes softened. "Thanks," he said. "No one's ever really stood up for me like that."

I punched him back. (Hey, it's how we communicate!) "Next time you can be the human punching bag."

"Good. I don't know exactly what you did, but I bet it was stubborn and hardheaded."

I bowed. "Guilty as charged."

"Ha-ha," Ayanna said. "Nyame said the Breakers are heading east, to the lake." She looked worried as she stared past me to where Old Angola lurched in the distance.

Junior studied me. "You know your eyes are golden?" he asked. "Did you ever think about wearing sunglasses for that? It's kinda weird."

I sighed. "It's from Nyame's power, and... You know what? I'm so glad you're back."

"And you're still sort of on fire," he went on. "Tiny flames, just there, on your eyebrows. Is that normal?"

Before I could put him in a headlock, a bellow shook the area. Spouts of steam erupted near the shore, and we all watched grimly as Old Angola continued to grow. It had been the size of a train station before, and now it was as tall as a ten-story apartment building.

I took a few steps forward, then looked back to see the four others following me.

"Well?" Ayanna asked. "What're you waiting on?"

"Weren't you going to try and stop me? Talk me out of rushing in?"

"Would you listen?" Thandiwe asked.

"No."

Ayanna raised her hands as if to say *Well, there you have it.* "I'm done arguing with your big head. I'm saving my energy. Growing as a person."

I shook my head. "There was an insult in there somewhere."

"I'm gonna put in another if you don't get going. Wasting all this time."

I took another step, then turned. "Thank you," I said quietly.

Junior looked back and forth between Ayanna and me and finally asked Thandiwe, "Are they...?" He waggled his eyebrows so hard he looked absolutely ridiculous. The princess winked at him, and Junior nodded. "Got it. About time."

"Hey!" I shouted, but Ayanna grabbed me by the arm and started marching me toward the lake.

"Let's go, superhero."

Chicago never did know how to act in the summer. That's one of the reasons I love it. On a normal day in the middle of August, the lakefront would be packed. I remember Dad trying to get us out the apartment at like five in the morning just so we could get a parking spot and claim our little oasis in the sand. By noon *everyone* would be out there—teens in cars with music pumping from their speakers, college students getting in one last break before they returned to whatever super studying college kids did, and even grown folks trying to catch a breath in between the pressures of humidity and life. Everybody was looking to have a good time, screaming and shouting and laughing.

Today there was only screaming and shouting, and they weren't happy sounds.

People lined the sidewalks and crowded the balconies and fire escapes along Oakland Avenue. Phones were out and recording, and as we—a squad of four kids and a spirit—headed down the street toward the green-soaked entrance to the Thirty-Fifth Street pedestrian bridge, I desperately wished Anansi was with us, too. He would know the right thing to say. Break the tension with a joke, maybe, or give us a word of warning. But he was still missing. I glanced at Junior, who limped along gamely, his hand on his sling pack, a smile quirked on his lips. He looked so much like his father right then.

A giggle broke through my thoughts. We all looked at Ayanna, who waved her hand in apology before a fresh peal of laughter escaped her lips.

"Walking toward monsters tickles you?" I asked. We slipped around a knot of children pointing at Old Angola, but with wonder, not terror. A group of adults—their parents, maybe—clustered nearby in front of a barbecue take-out joint, whispering and looking around nervously.

Ayanna shook her head. "No, it's just . . . you're always fighting your big final boss fight on a beach. And you're always complaining about getting wet, so I thought you might want to duck into there and get prepared." She giggled again as she pointed to a little pop-up store that had taken over an empty building. That happened a lot—sometimes it'd be an art gallery, or a fashion show, and other times it was a music-video shoot. This time it was a . . .

"'Beach bargains,'" I read aloud. A mannequin in neon-blue flippers, tie-dyed swim trunks, arm floats, and a mask and snorkel posed in the store window. I looked at Ayanna, who was doing her best to contain a fresh spurt of chuckling. "You want me to go to war with haints and monsters with arm floats."

Ayanna doubled over and burst into guffaws. After a second, Thandiwe chuckled, Junior grinned, and I shook my head and smiled. Ayanna leaned against Thandiwe, who patted her back sympathetically as she gulped down air. Within a few moments she stood upright and wiped tears from her eyes. It looked like she was going to be fine until Junior squinted and said, "Maybe Breakers hate swim noodles."

The image of Junior chasing after one of the gray monsters with a red Styrofoam pool toy forced a snicker to escape from my lips, and then we were all cracking up.

A couple walked by quickly, staring at us and sucking their teeth. "Poor things," I heard the woman mutter. "They're terrified."

I finally started walking again, and everyone joined me. Our smiles faded as we moved closer to the bridge. "Do you think this is the final battle?" I asked.

Ayanna looked at me. "What do you mean?"

"I mean, is this it? If... *when* we beat Cotton, will that be the end? Or is something else going to come looking for a fight? Isn't that how it works? There's always another fight."

No one answered, and I stopped as we reached the last cross street before the entrance to the pedestrian bridge. A line of trees, part of the park surrounding the beach, blocked the waterline, but Old Angola towered over everything. From here I could make out the additions to it, even without the spirit vision. More steel doors dotted its frame, like soul-stripping freckles. But a drawbridge, partially raised, now protruded from one of the monster's legs. A dark gated entrance waited at the end of the rotted wooden access way. I swallowed. The edges of the darkness shimmered, like heat coming up from concrete.

Click

Just then my spirit vision engaged. I guess because I'd stared at the weird energy leaking from the entrance for too long. That's what that shimmering was—energy. But now

I could see even more spectral details, like the haintacles swarming up and down the lake, flailing and thrashing.

I took a deep breath. "Final battle or not, if any of you—"

"STOP RIGHT THERE!"

A miffed voice shouted at us from across the street. I groaned as a familiar Redliner holding a bullhorn marched down the sidewalk opposite us. Harold. Darla and others followed him, but it was a much smaller group than the one that had attacked Granny Z's skate-park refuge. They brandished signs with silly slogans like DO YOU BELONG? and 2, 4, 6, 8, EVERYONE DISCRIMINATES. Harold held up his bullhorn, flinched at its squeal, then pointed at me. "THAT'S FAR ENOUGH."

I threw up my hands. "Don't you have a job or something?"

"DON'T YOU?" he shouted.

"No! I'm twelve!"

Harold laughed. "DO I LOOK LIKE A DOOFUS?"

We all side-eyed each other.

"HEY! THAT'S NOT FUNNY! DON'T MAKE ME PERFORM ANOTHER CITIZEN'S ARREST."

Thandiwe stepped forward, her kierie pointed at them. "Why are you so concerned with where people go? Don't you realize you're working for a monster?"

"First of all," Darla said, her hands on her hips, "we're not working for anyone. This is a volunteer group, and we're protecting our safety."

"By making everyone else unsafe?" Junior called. "Yeah, right."

A crowd of onlookers was starting to form. I saw some faces I knew—kids from the Rolling Thunder, kids from my neighborhood, people who worked around the block.

"Tristan, look," Ayanna whispered in warning.

Gray shadows flitted in the trees beyond the bridge. Breakers!

I approached Harold and Darla. It was time to end this.

"We're done letting you tell us where we can and can't be. I'm going to that beach, and my friends are coming along with me."

Darla snatched the bullhorn from Harold and stabbed a finger at me. "YOU WILL DO NO SUCH THING. THERE WILL BE NONE OF THAT . . . THAT . . . *BEHAVIOR* ON OUR LAKEFRONT."

"You don't even live here!"

"THAT'S NOT THE POINT!" she shouted. "YOU WILL SCARE AWAY THE PEACEFUL CITIZENS WHO JUST WANT TO ENJOY THEMSELVES."

My jaw dropped open. There was a monster growing ten feet wider and taller every minute right behind them!

A hand settled on my arm. "It's not worth it," Ayanna said.

"But . . ." I sighed. "They're so annoying."

The crowd behind us started getting angry, and they were on our side. Store owners and neighborhood folks began to flood the street, yelling and shaking fists, flip-flops, and even a grill spatula at the Redliners.

"Y'all leave them kids alone!"

"Who do you think you are, coming up in our neighborhood saying who can go where?"

"And wearing masks. Scared to show your face, Joe?"

"Kids, y'all go ahead and have fun."

I started walking forward, and Ayanna, Thandiwe, Junior, and Spirit John followed. Harold and Darla and the smattering of other Redliners held their line as we approached, brandishing their signs like bats, but when the entire community moved with us, their resolve broke and the masked cowards scampered back across the bridge. The trees rustled as the Breakers followed them.

The two groups may have been deterred, but they weren't defeated. Not yet. I planned on taking care of that real soon. First, though, there was something else I had to do.

I stopped just in front of the bridge and turned to Spirit John. The ghostly boy had a determined look on his face, but it changed to surprise when I shook my head at him.

"This is as far as you go," I said. "If Cotton or Old Angola get ahold of you, you're done for. That monster will devour you, and I'm not gonna lose you again."

The spirit looked toward the beach, then back at me, clearly frustrated.

"I know," I said. "But remember what your uncle told you?

This isn't your fight. Let me—let *us*—fight for you. We've got this."

I wasn't sure this would work, but I took off High John's root pouch and looped it over Spirit John's head. When it touched him, while I still held on to the cord, the pouch rippled and turned semitransparent. I let go and it appeared on his neck in a matching ghostly hue. Like it was where it belonged.

"If something happens to us—" I started to say, but Spirit John held up a fist, cutting me off. I dapped him up (*that* was a weird sensation) and he smiled sadly. Then he nodded at the bridge as if to say *Go on*.

"Yeah," I said. I took a few steps, then looked back. The last I saw of Spirit John, he had his face turned up to the sky and his hands in his pockets. A flash of light rippled in the air, and he was gone.

I caught up with my friends and we crossed the bridge, our shoes slapping against the pavement. We cut through a park, dodging benches and the spectators who were gawking at Old Angola or the retreating Redliners or both. Finally we reached Oakwood Beach, and there I stopped so suddenly that the other three collided into my back, sending us all sprawling into the sand.

"Ow! What'd you do that for?" Junior complained.

I didn't answer.

"Seriously, you need to work on your communication skills," he said.

I got to my feet, still silent. I could feel Junior glaring at me, but my eyes were elsewhere.

"See? Right now, you're not even apologizing. It's that sort of—"

Thandiwe clamped a hand over his mouth and pointed to the scene in front of us.

Old Angola stood ten times as tall as it had back in Louisiana, and five times as wide. Rows and rows of steel doors lined its cinder-block structure, with no way to access them from the outside. I shuddered, thinking about how the haunted prison plantation captured its victims. The haintacles were dormant now, but at any moment they could lash out. And all that paled in comparison to what was unfolding in the shallows.

Patty Roller and Twennymiles stood surrounded by a collection of Redliners and Breakers. Both haints glared at me as the Breakers' shrieks cut through the thunder of the waves beating the shore. No one moved, though, even as I took a cautious step forward.

Because they were waiting for someone else.

Cotton descended from Old Angola's lowered drawbridge like a conquering tyrant surveying his newly won territory. He was barefoot, and thorny vines covered his legs and arms.

A simple white button-down shirt with rolled-up sleeves and linen pants completed his look . . . except for the haintacles that extended from the prison monster and wound around his waist. His eyes smoked and flashed red, while his arms bulged as Old Angola pumped him full of power. The haint stepped onto the beach, spread his arms wide, and shouted so that everyone on the beach could hear.

"Tristan Strong! Welcome." He smiled and extended the back of his hand to me. "Come greet your king."

29
BEACHFRONT BREAKER HUNT

HE WAS NOTHING BUT A

Plain black boy.

Someone had painted part of a poem on a line of boulders that stretched along the shore. I knew that poem. It was by Gwendolyn Brooks, and my ELA teacher last year, Mrs. Drummond, had taught it and others from a book called *A Street in Bronzeville*. Yeah, that's right, like my neighborhood. Mrs. Drummond spoke about the poems the same way she talked about the city of Chicago—with reverence. She wasn't just my teacher, she was also a poet who'd written several books of her own, and she loved the idea of the stories inside our cities. The narratives they told. History etched into the bones our communities were built on.

History.

Hidden stories.

And what was a hidden story but a job for an Anansesem?

Cotton strolled up the sand until he stood a few yards away from me. He looked amused as the four of us lined up to face him. "What's this?" he asked. "A welcome party? Shoot, Tristan, you didn't have to go that far."

My fingers trembled. It was his mocking tone that infuriated me. And the cocky smile, one side of his face writhing as he bared too-sharp teeth. And the way he had so little regard for whoever he hurt, whoever he trampled, whoever he dismissed on his way to acquire more power. My jaw clenched, and every muscle in my body turned into granite. Loud roaring filled my ears, like the waves on the shore but angrier, and I could feel my skin growing hot, as if any second now I would burst into—

A hand settled on my wrist. It was cool, calming. Ayanna moved next to me and—ignoring Cotton—tapped my chest with her other hand. *Control.*

I took a deep breath and nodded to let her know I understood. Losing my grip on my anger wouldn't help us. I had to control it. I looked at Cotton while pointing at Old Angola. "You're finished. It's over."

Cotton—did a flash of anger cross his face when I didn't erupt in fury?—chuckled. "Finished? Boy, I ain't even got started yet. And you ain't got enough years under your belt to be telling me anything. Come on, big guy. What is this supposed to be, really? A show of strength? Tristan, I *am*

348

strength! Look! I done brought a piece of home for you to enjoy, and you shove it back in my face like that? That ain't right, son."

A crowd was beginning to form along the beach and on the bridge. A lot of the kids from the neighborhood were getting a closer look at what had landed in their backyard.

"What do you mean 'a piece of home'?" I asked. I had to figure out Cotton's plan. There was something I wasn't seeing, a trick up his thorny sleeves.

All traces of amusement disappeared from the haint's face. "Home, Tristan. The seat of power. Where you and I can rule this country from! Think about it ... your power and mine, combined. We can shape this world the way we see fit."

"I would never join you," I spat. "In anything."

"Aw, come on, don't be like that. We're similar, you and I."

"I'm nothing like you!"

"Look at you—anger just boiling outta your pores. Itchin' to make a change. Well, so am I!"

I ground my teeth, and only Ayanna's hand on my arm kept me from flipping out right then and there. "No, you don't want power. You want power *over* others. You want control *over* the rest of the world. You want worship, and you don't care who you destroy to get it. You're nothing but a greedy ghost of a bully, and it's time you got locked up in your bottle again."

Cotton laughed. Actually laughed, clutching his belly and throwing his head back so far his hat nearly fell off. "And what's that gonna do? Somebody will just break it open, someone who don't care about what little rituals was brought over by your people to catch my people. Naw, my boy, I'm here to stay. And you? I told you before, the world don't care about you! Running 'round trying to save everything, do everything, be everything to everyone, and all you got is some dead friends and a doll! Looking for some stories. You think the world cares about your stories? From what I heard tell, you ain't even a Anansesem anymore, and Anansi abandoned you. So why do you care about a few dusty old tales that don't impress nobody?"

I flinched. Thandiwe inhaled and Junior whirled to face me.

"Is that true?" he asked.

I hesitated, then nodded.

Cotton laughed again. "See? Your gods don't have faith in you, and your friends shouldn't either, since all you do is get them caught or killed. You bury that little doll yet? You all alone, boy." His face twisted into an angry scowl as he stomped back and forth in front of us. A swell of noise rose behind me. I risked a glance back to see more people gathering.

Cotton stopped and glared at them. "You still running

'round trying to save a world that left you behind. A world that don't care if you go missing! You see any of these folks rushing down here to help? They don't care! Just a bunch of vultures here for the show."

"That's a lie!" I said. *Right?*

"Then why haven't you heard of any of the history you done dug up? Hmm? Because nobody cares, that's why! Bury it and build over it, that's the move."

"You don't know what you're talking about!" I shouted.

But his words ate at me. The slave trading in New Orleans. The plantation that was turned into a prison. The riots in Memphis and National City. Was it true no one cared? Why didn't everyone shout about these stories in school, or turn victories into holidays, or put them on T-shirts and sing about them in songs or make movies about them? Was that history not important enough?

Ayanna let go of my arm and stepped forward. Her eyes narrowed as she stared at Cotton. She looked him up and down, her lips pursed.

Cotton eyed her back. "You got a question, darling?"

She sniffed. "More of a comment." She turned to me. "He's stalling."

Cotton stiffened.

I frowned, then looked around. Hundreds of people were gathered on the lakefront now. A few adults, but mostly teens and children. Kids from the community who were curious, kids from the spirit train who'd followed us. A whole beach crowded with young people.

I froze.

Where were the Breakers?

I spun around and shoved Ayanna aside just as Cotton lunged forward, just as screams ripped through the crowd of kids behind us, and just as hundreds of haintacles erupted from every steel door on Old Angola.

The beach exploded into chaos. Children ran screaming left and right as Cotton stalked us across the sand. He didn't run, didn't even seem to be in a hurry as he chewed up chunks of ground with his long strides. He was propelled by the haintacles wrapped around his waist, and he laughed uproariously as the rest of the prison plantation's appendages terrorized everyone else.

And don't get it twisted—we tried to fight back. Junior, aka Stone Thrower, zipped gold-flecked rocks at Cotton's head, one after the other, but the haintacles just batted them away. Ayanna danced in and out with her bat twirling in a golden blur, while Thandiwe dipped and spun with her makeshift kierie and forebear shield.

Cotton chuckled as the two didn't even come close to hitting him. "Now, now, little ladies, don't mess up your hair."

And me? I tried to call upon the akofena shadow gloves, but there were too many people around. Every time the black flames flickered to life, I either had to extinguish them or risk burning a child who was running past in terror. So I swallowed my anger as best I could and ushered children to the exits as we fled the haint.

"Go, go!" I shouted to a group of nine- or ten-year-olds huddling behind a giant sandcastle. I pulled them up and pushed them toward one of the beach access points farthest away from Old Angola. The plantation prison lashed the water and churned the sand like the twisted offspring of a haunted house and a kraken.

WHUMPH!

The sandcastle disintegrated as Cotton crashed through it, his eyes wild with hate and the writhing haintacles driving him forward at lightning speed.

"Get over here, boy," he spat as he clawed for my hands. I remembered how his thorns had once latched on to me, and I threw myself backward . . . leaving Junior in front.

Cotton snarled in anticipation. "Fine, I'll just take another one of your friends!"

The ground trembled.

Sand rattled and bounced around. The sandcastle, now just an unrecognizable mound, flattened completely. Even the lake seemed to withdraw as a long shadow fell across the beachfront and a giant hand reached down to block Cotton's path.

"I reckon it might be time for you to leave our children

alone. Seems you need a playmate your own size." That rumbling voice. It thrummed, quiet and powerful, but there was a hint of anger lurking inside, too. A promise of retribution, of a bent back straightening, of a proud chin rising, of a people's strength surging.

John Henry stepped in between us and Cotton.

"Come on, then, and tussle with grown folk."

The big man and the haint stared at each other across the sand. John Henry's arms were crossed over his chest, his feet planted solidly in the sand, and from where I scrambled up it looked like he was anchored to the earth itself, a giant carved out of stone.

Cotton sneered. The corners of his eyes smoldered and the haintacles thrashed. "Another story god, fresh for harvesting. Fatted calf and whatnot."

I grabbed Junior and pulled him out of harm's way. He looked shell-shocked and exhausted. "You okay?"

He nodded. "Still a bit weak...from being stuck in that cell...I guess. Don't...want to go back."

His breath was coming in hitches, like when you run a race and get a cramp in your side. He jerked his head toward the standoff. "What do we do?"

I bit my lip. "Let's get the rest of the kids off the beach and to safety."

Ayanna and Thandiwe ran over to us, both panting. Thandiwe was clutching her left arm, but she refused our attempts to examine her. Instead, she pointed at John Henry.

"We've got to do something. He's going to get hurt!"

"He can handle hims—" Ayanna started to say, but Thandiwe shook her head and looked at me, her eyes wide as if begging me to understand something.

"No, he *can't*. It's going to happen all over again, and then that haint will grow even stronger."

It took a second before realization struck. "You mean like High John."

She nodded. "Where are the Breakers?" she asked breathlessly.

"I don't know, and that worries me. Come on."

We started to search the beach, but Junior jerked suddenly, and I thought he'd had a spasm of pain. "Look!" he cried.

John Henry had unfolded his arms, while Cotton sank into a crouch, like some sort of feral beast—a jackal and snake combined into one. For several seconds nothing happened. The world went still. The clouds paused, the waves froze, and the breeze disappeared, as if everything in sight were holding its collective breath.

And then it exhaled.

Cotton snarled as a haintacle shot out, intent on lassoing

the big man's neck. But John Henry just plucked the wriggling ghost appendage out of the air and squeezed it with one hand. Another haintacle shot out, and another, but again John Henry snagged them. He gripped them, lifted one foot, and then exploded into motion, charging Cotton like a linebacker and planting a shoulder squarely in the haint's chest. Cotton flew back a dozen yards—through the air!—before landing and skipping across the sand like a stone across a pond.

We opened our mouths to cheer, but Cotton was up again before we could make a sound. He stamped his feet while shrieking like a wild animal in pain, then charged. More haintacles joined him, rushing forward to lash at John Henry. The big man batted them aside, but still more attacked. They snaked in and out and around one another, twisting and turning to find an opening. John Henry dodged the first wave, snagged several in the second, but missed a few that slithered around his legs and tried to upend him. He roared a challenge. Both of his hands squeezed, rotated, and pulled. Cotton's sneer faded into disbelief as John Henry began to haul in the haintacles like ship's ropes and drag Old Angola toward him. One step. Two.

Loud groans filled the air. The plantation prison trembled in the shallows as clouds of dust billowed from its seams. Could he do it? Could John Henry really pull—

Cotton slammed into the folk hero's knees. John Henry's legs buckled, and for a brief moment, he teetered off-balance.

More haintacles shot out, ready to wrap around him and drag him away.

"Too many," I whispered.

"What?" Junior looked at me.

"There's too many. John Henry will be—"

Twin shadows streaked across the beach, followed by a flare of scorching light. Vortex winds blasted sand everywhere, and the haintacles recoiled. The screaming, whistling sound of something flying at high speed through the air pierced our ears.

"The Flying Ladies!" Ayanna shouted. "And—"

Black wings unfolded. Golden eyes glared.

Miss Sarah, Miss Rose, and Nyame landed next to John Henry.

"Um..." Thandiwe pointed toward the trees near the beach entrance, where clouds of fog began wafting out from between the leaves. I narrowed my eyes. This was familiar. More and more fog filled the air until we couldn't see the trees at all. Booming laughter rolled through the air.

The *River Queen* emerged from the fog, the mermaid carvings screaming war cries as the vessel chugged down the sand on a carpet of mist. Mami Wata stood at the prow. Her hair billowed behind her, and both of her arms stretched out on either side. Keelboat Annie stood next to her, and it was her laugh that continued to shake the air. The *River Queen* skidded into the shallows as the mermaids glared at Cotton and

Old Angola, while Annie and Mami Wata leaped over the side to join the other gods on the beach.

"Kids, get on the boat, now!" Mami Wata shouted.

"But—" I said.

"NOW!" Annie and Mami Wata and Miss Sarah and Miss Rose and Nyame all shouted simultaneously.

Well, if they were going to be rude about it . . .

"They're all here!" Ayanna said as we climbed into the *River Queen*. She looked at me with relief in her eyes. "Together, they might have a chance."

I wanted to believe that. I truly did. But Old Angola kept growing, cinder block by moldy cinder block. More and more haintacles continued to pop out of its seams. And Cotton didn't seem fazed at all as the Alkean gods gathered around him in a semicircle. In fact, he seemed to relish the sight.

"Oh, it's a party!" he said, cackling as he stood with his hands on his hips. "Y'all jumped-up joketales think you can take down the king? Come on, then! One at a time, all at once, don't matter to me one bit."

"Why is he so confident?" I asked myself.

Junior must've thought I was talking to him, because he shrugged. "Does it matter? He can't beat them. Not on his own."

I watched Cotton retreat a bit, moving closer to the shallows. All the gods followed him, trying to keep him boxed in. Smart, except . . .

Not on his own.

Cotton retreated farther.

They're all here.

"It's a trap..." I said slowly.

Everyone turned to look at me. Thandiwe, Ayanna, and Junior looked at me as if I'd suddenly started speaking pig latin. And look, if I planned on becoming an expert in any language, it would be pig latin. But at the moment I had to warn everyone.

"It's a trap!" I shouted.

"Tristan?" Ayanna said.

I started to run toward the edge of the steamboat, but Junior was leaning on me, so I could only hobble. "Cotton wants them all together. The Breakers are nearby, just waiting to ambush them like they did High John. JOHN HENRY!" I shouted, trying to get their attention. "IT'S A TRAP!"

But it was too late.

The shallows exploded in a spray as Twennymiles surged out, Patty Roller on his back. Behind him—both in the water and emerging from Old Angola's main entrance—raced hundreds of Breakers. The gray monsters shrieked as they followed the two haints to their next targets: the gods of Alke.

30

A NEW CHALLENGER HAS ENTERED

GODS AND MONSTERS FOUGHT ON THE SHORES OF LAKE MICHIGAN.

They all moved so fast, I could hardly keep track of the action, even from our vantage point on the *River Queen*. John Henry tangled with haintacles in his arms while fending off sneak attacks from others. Keelboat Annie bellowed challenges as she came to his aid, swinging her massive keel pole. Miss Sarah and Miss Rose whirled in twin cyclones of feathers and fury, whipping across the beach as they grappled with Breakers. Nyame and Mami Wata fought as a team as well, the goddess raising wave after wave to crash down on the beach, the sky god sending flares of light that stabbed through the water droplets in spears of red, blue, and yellow.

Have you ever been whupped by a rainbow? It looked like it hurt.

And yet it didn't seem that it was going to be enough. Old Angola continued to disgorge Breakers, shrieking and slavering mindless beasts intent on ripping the magic and spirit from us all. Patty Roller stirred the ones around her into a furious horde, Twennymiles carrying her around the battlefield in giant leaps.

And then there was Cotton.

The haint was unstoppable. Too quick, too strong. Old Angola poured more and more power into him, the haintacles wriggling beneath his shirt and slinking around his arms and legs until it was impossible to tell where haint ended and the plantation prison began. His laughter cut through the air like a rusty machete.

"Ha-haaaaaa," he cackled, spinning beneath one of John Henry's attacks as he threw sand into the giant folk hero's eyes. "Is that all you got, big guy? All y'all fighting and you haven't made up a lick of ground. Tire yourselves out, my babies. My Breakers will harvest all that strength and feed it to my pet."

Old Angola shivered and rumbled in the shallows as if agreeing with the haint. I couldn't take my eyes off it, even as the battle raged beneath us. My friends shouted warnings and pointed at different sections of the beach, but my gaze stayed fixed on the monstrosity that was growing ever larger and would eventually swallow us all, imprisoning us with nothing but cement and shadows for company.

"Watch it!" Ayanna screamed as a haintacle tried to yank Miss Rose out of the air.

A Breaker leaped at Keelboat Annie's unprotected back...

...only to fall to the sand in a heap under a barrage of stones. Annie turned, saw that the threat had been dealt with, and waved her keel pole gratefully at Junior before returning to deal with another batch of shrieking gray monsters.

But I glimpsed all this out of the corner of my eye. Something was happening behind Old Angola. A disturbance on the horizon. It looked...familiar.

"Tristan, watch out!"

Junior yanked on my hoodie, sending me sprawling to the deck just in time to avoid a flailing Breaker as it hurtled overhead. He grabbed my arm and helped me back up. "Now isn't the time to be daydreaming!" he shouted. "The gods're in trouble."

I stared at him. Junior limped back to the railing next to Ayanna and Thandiwe, all three of them leaning over to see better. Old Angola rumbled again, and the entire beach shook. The *River Queen* shifted slightly, and Junior slammed his hands against the wood and turned.

"That's it," he said. "I'm going to help. I can't just stand here and do nothing."

Thandiwe nodded and hefted her shield. "Me too."

The two headed toward the ladder and Ayanna started to follow. "Come on, Tristan," she said as she passed me.

I licked my lips, peered at the horizon to make sure I

wasn't seeing things, and looked back at my friends. I could feel the weight of Gum Baby in my backpack as I shook my head. "No."

They all stopped and whirled around in shock. I winced at their looks of betrayal, hurt, and even anger, but I didn't budge.

"No?" Junior repeated.

"No."

"What do you mean, no?" Junior poked me in the chest. "You're the one who dragged us on this road."

"I know," I said softly.

"Whole time fussing and yelling about we need to get after Cotton, and now we're here you're too scared to fight?"

"That's not it!"

Ayanna looked back and forth between us. "Tristan, we need you. Don't do this."

I shook my head. "No. This isn't how we win."

Junior threw up his hands. "Not fighting is how we lose!"

"I'm not saying we shouldn't fight—I'm saying we're fighting the wrong thing!" I nodded at Old Angola. "*That's* what we need to stop. Even if we manage to beat Cotton, that thing will still be there feasting on everyone who's too tired to continue. Look!"

I pointed to the beach. John Henry and Annie were back-to-back, surrounded by haintacles that tried to batter down the two pillars of strength. Miss Sarah and Miss Rose no longer flew as fast or as high. Even Nyame's gleaming rays seemed duller now.

"They're losing," I said softly.

"All the more reason to help them," Ayanna said. She grabbed my arm. "We can make a difference."

"Maybe," I agreed, and I put my hand over hers while looking at Thandiwe and Junior. "But hear me out. No, listen! Someone once told me that it wasn't my job to get sucked into every skirmish in the war against evil, but to fight the battle that will turn the tide. Old Angola is that battle. We can chase Cotton all over the beach, all over the country, all over the world, but if we don't stop the monster that's giving him power, we're right back at square one! So that's where I'm going."

Junior glared at me. "Who told you that mess?"

I swung one leg over the railing to the ladder and began climbing down to the sand. "Somebody I should've been listening to for a while now."

Thandiwe looked over the edge at me, then at the raging battle. "But how are you going to get there undetected?"

"No one's going to be looking at me. They'll be distracted."

"By who?" Junior scoffed.

"Them," I said, and I turned and pointed toward the lake, behind the monstrous plantation prison, where the smudge on the sky had grown bigger and darker, taking the shape of a bird. A giant bird, on whose back I'd flown before.

Old Familiar.

The giant shadow crow soared toward us, no longer injured, his wingspan still as wide as a jet's. Three familiar figures stood in a line on his back. For a moment I thought there were four, but it must've been a trick of my eyes, a cloud of feathers or something. I didn't get a chance to linger on the thought, because the person in front yelled to me as the crow landed.

"Sorry it took me so long!" the man said. "Had to convince some friends to fight." He rubbed his head ruefully. "With me, not against me."

The other two figures jumped down, and I smiled at the familiar duo being back together again.

Bear and Brer.

And—

"Dad?" Junior whispered.

Anansi had entered the fray.

The spider, the rabbit, and the bear stood together and faced down the haint.

Everyone was focused on the newcomers. Even my friends. Junior stared at his father with a fierce gaze that alternated between pride and anger. Thandiwe and Ayanna studied the sudden lull in the fighting, whispering to each other about strategy and planning a surprise raft attack.

And me?

I dropped to the sand with a quiet *whumph,* then took off. They didn't need to come with me. Too many of my friends had already gotten hurt doing that. And this next part was probably going to be the most ridiculous, wild, reckless, and dangerous thing I'd ever done.

I headed for Old Angola.

No one paid me any attention. Why would they? Two of the best-known folk heroes and a West African god had joined the other deities of a destroyed world. Together they stood in direct challenge to a haint who wanted their power.

Bear's fur—brown and graying at the tips—was still patchy in spots where he'd worn the iron-monster armor back in Alke. He didn't carry a weapon, but his claws were as long as knives, and he held his massive paws away from his body, ready to strike. Judging from the low growl rumbling deep in his chest, it sounded like Bear was seconds away from doing so. He had a score to settle with Cotton, who had poisoned his mind with hatred.

I didn't know what to make of Brer—I'd never technically met him. Anansi had impersonated him back in Alke. Apparently, he'd mimicked the battle-scarred rabbit's mannerisms perfectly, even fooling his longtime friends, but I had no frame of reference. This Brer had a wild look in his eye—dangerous, reckless. I liked him already.

And then there was the trickster god himself. He'd appeared in his completely human form, without spider legs, and gone were his graphic T-shirt and carefree attitude. This Anansi wore a tailored navy suit, a white button-up shirt with no tie, pants that stopped just above the ankle, and shiny black loafers with golden buckles. His hands were in his pockets as he strolled to the middle of the battlefield, seeming completely oblivious to the Breakers and haintacles gathering around. Brer and Bear followed, and all eyes were on the trio.

I waded into the shallows, trying to make as little noise as possible. Old Angola lurked just ahead, looking even more disgusting and depressing than before. It shuddered, and another rusted steel door appeared halfway up its side. The door clanged open, and a haintacle slithered out.

I froze.

The snakelike tip wavered in the air. For a brief moment, it swayed in my direction. Was my mission over before it had even started?

One second passed. Then another. I held my breath.

The haintacle shivered, like a rattlesnake's tail on mute, and wriggled down the side of the prison toward me. I bit my lip, hesitant to bring out the shadow gloves. They would be like a flare, letting everyone know where I was. Still the haintacle moved closer. If I did nothing, it would wrap me up and drag me behind that door, never to be seen again. I wanted to get inside, but not like that. It moved closer. And closer. And—

"WHERE'S THAT RAGGEDY EXCUSE FOR A GHOST?"

Anansi's voice boomed over the beach. The haintacle paused, twisted away from me, then shot out to join the others. I let out a sigh of relief. For once I was thankful for the trickster god's big mouth.

Cotton, haintacles now sprouting from his back like poison roots, shouldered his way through the horde of Breakers spread out across the sand. He sneered. "Now, ain't that something? Looks like the petting zoo has arrived. And here I am fresh outta carrots. Guess I'll just have to—"

The haint paused in confusion. Anansi had never stopped. Instead, he continued to walk past Cotton as if the haint wasn't even there. The Breakers, following Cotton's lead, looked around but parted to allow Anansi to keep on walking. We all watched him head directly for Patty Roller, who was still sitting atop Twennymiles. The trickster god stared up at her, and I could hear his words from where I hid twenty yards away.

"You're the one who took my son," he said.

Patty Roller sniffed and refused to meet his eyes. "Your *son* needs better manners. Teaching to learn his place. Once this infernal magic is stripped from their feeble frames, the education will commence for him and the others. After we do away with your meddling."

To my surprise, Anansi nodded. "Funny thing is, I agree. I haven't been the best teacher. Not to him, not to anyone. But I'll be a five-legged arachnid before I let you scar another kid."

Patty Roller leaned over and laughed. "And who, pray tell, will stop me? You?"

Anansi kept looking at her, but his voice grew louder. "Everybody's got their role to play."

Was he talking to me? I couldn't help but feel that way. It was all the encouragement I needed. The ramp leading into Old Angola was *right there*. I was so close, and all the Breakers were on the beach. The haintacles were busy, too, either reinforcing Cotton or wriggling around the other Alkean forces.

"Unfortunately, I won't have the honor of showing you the error of your ways," Anansi continued. There was something in his voice, a playful note that made me pause with one foot on the ramp and look back. "That privilege goes to an old friend."

And Old Familiar let out a harsh caw that rang to the sky. I squinted. There *had been* someone else on his back. She'd been sitting. Not hiding, but preparing. And now she slid down off the shadow crow and dropped to the sand, wearing her purple-and-green jogging suit and holding a cane in one hand. I winced. I didn't envy Patty Roller.

"Here she is!" Granny Z shouted. She marched across the sand, shaking her cane at Patty Roller and Twennymiles. "Here she is! You see? The no-good, child-stealing, lying, cheating, fake-crying duchess of destruction. Erzulie, you see? Here she is!"

Patty Roller scoffed. "Who is this old—"

And then she stopped. Patty Roller opened her mouth, closed it, and opened it again. Nothing came out. She couldn't speak! The ground beneath her began to shake. Twennymiles tried to rear, but the horse's hooves had become stuck in the sand. No, they were sinking!

"The Erzulie been watching," Granny Z said, her cane pointing at the haints like a judge's gavel. Even Cotton looked wary of her, and the Breakers and haintacles cleared a circle around the doomed duo. I shook my head. Cotton didn't care about anyone, even those on his own side.

"The Erzulie been watching! Erzulie Dantor says the children are under *her* protection. No one harms them and sleeps soundly. No one threatens them and lives peacefully." Granny Z spun in a slow circle, daring anyone to challenge her claims. Nobody did. "She says no one brings suffering to *her* children and walks the streets without fear."

Sand crept up Twennymiles's legs and swept around Patty

Roller in fierce blasts. It scoured and scuffed them, ripping away the wilted flowers in a storm of dead petals. Again the ground rumbled, and more sand showered Patty Roller, knocking her hair—a wig?—askew and sending her reeling. She tried to scream, clawing at her throat, but not a peep could be heard.

"The Erzulie been watching!"

Patty Roller and Twennymiles disappeared behind the miniature sandstorm.

"The Erzulie been watching!"

I turned and ran up the ramp. Everyone had their role—it was time for me to perform mine.

"The Erzulie been watching!"

The ground settled; the howling stopped. I reached the gaping hole that led deep into the plantation prison, then peeked behind me.

A pile of white flowers lay on the ground where Patty Roller and Twennymiles had stood. On top of it, mussed and disheveled, rested a silver wig. I grinned, then plunged into the darkness as the battle once again erupted behind me.

31

SHE DON'T MISS

THE HALLS OF OLD ANGOLA WANTED TO EAT ME.

I'm not joking. They told me themselves. Now, I know what you're thinking—I'd been under a lot of stress, maybe I was hearing things, maybe I bumped my head and was still out on the beach somewhere. But trust me.

"Another one, another one, into the dark they must come."

See?

And the voice came from everywhere, as if there were speakers in the slimy walls. The floor rose and fell as I walked through the shadows. I tried not to think about how it felt like I was inside a living creature. Something that breathed. Something that didn't want me poking around inside it.

Doors appeared, followed me down the halls, and then disappeared when I turned to look at them. Shadows rippled along the floor. And what's worse, corridors appeared where at first there'd been only walls. It was like a maze that rear-ranged itself as soon as you blinked.

"Eat it, grind it, make us grow, make us grow."

I tried to ignore the hissing whispers and kept moving. One foot in front of the other. Although I didn't know where I was supposed to go. If I was being honest with myself, I actually hadn't thought I'd make it this far. But now I needed to figure out how to stop Old Angola and to cut off the power it was funneling to Cotton.

But how do you stop a monster that is also a building?

I continued walking. The walls trembled again. Some-where ahead in the distance, the sound of brick grinding against brick echoed, and a cloud of dust shot out of a cor-ridor that suddenly appeared a few feet in front of me. I jumped back, but when nothing snarling or slimy sprung out at me, I peeked inside.

"Bring them, drain them, make me grow, make me grow."

I clenched my jaw. "You're not scaring me," I called into the night, even though that's exactly what Old Angola was doing. I just refused to admit it. "I'm going to shut you down if it's the last thing I do."

I really, *really* hoped it wouldn't be the last thing I ever did.

CLANG!

A door slammed shut behind me, and I nearly jumped out of my skin. I whirled around, fists raised, but no one was there. Instead, the cement brick walls began to re-form and reshape themselves, and the door slid backward into the dark. I gulped. This was getting creepy.

"Where is it?"

I turned. The whisper had come from the newly spawned corridor. I was doing my best to ignore the words now, as I was sure Old Angola wanted nothing more than for me to spend all my energy fretting over ghostly threats and to waste away while getting completely lost. No, I had to focus.

"Where is it?"

But there was something about that whisper. Something familiar.

No, ignore it, I told myself. *It's another trap.* I passed the corridor, determined to keep moving. Outside, my friends were fighting for their lives. For the lives of the city, the country, the world—*two* worlds! Alke lived inside the hearts of the children. If we didn't win this battle, I would've failed twice.

"Take it, break it, build up our bones."

"Where is it?"

I froze. There were two distinct whispers. Two different voices. The first was the prison plantation. I could hear the hunger in its words—the desire to consume, to devour, to destroy the strength, will, and spirit of those who were imprisoned inside. I sensed its need to grow, to use that which it had stolen to get even larger, hungrier, and more evil.

But the second whisper... It was different.

Smaller.

Desperate.

Despite every alarm bell that rang inside my head, I turned and walked down that new corridor.

"Where is it?"

I knew that voice. I'd heard it saying those exact words, in fact. It had happened a month earlier, though it felt like a year, after everything we'd been through. If not for that voice I wouldn't be here, wouldn't have traveled to Alke...

...wouldn't have met the gods and goddesses, heroes and heroines. Wouldn't have met Junior or Thandiwe. Wouldn't have met Ayanna.

The corridor ended at a wide central atrium-like space with no ceiling, just a weird tree trunk growing from a pit in the middle. The tree was giving off a purple light that speckled the walls and doors. From here I could see hundreds of doors—on this level, on the level above that, and above that, on and on up into the sky. Too many to count.

"Where is it?"

It sounded like the whisper had come from the base of the tree. I stepped out of the corridor into the purple light... only to stumble backward as the trunk split into about twenty different sections.

"Sweet peaches," I muttered.

That wasn't a tree.

It was a giant cluster of haintacles.

As I watched, one of the wriggling appendages curled downward, wiped the floor of the pit, and then reached up to the top of the atrium. I edged closer and squinted. The group of haintacles lifted cement cinder blocks, plastered them against the inner walls, and returned for more. They were building Old Angola from the inside!

"Where is it?"

I swallowed, slowly moving toward the pit, already knowing what I was going to see, even as another haintacle appeared to swipe something from the floor. It made sense, actually, now that I knew what it was. What better way to build a spirit prison than with the stickiest adhesive known to humankind?

I sat down on the edge of the pit, pulled my backpack off my shoulders, and cradled it in my lap. The doll inside didn't move. Couldn't move. Not without the energy that had been stripped from her, the spirit that had been stolen by the Breakers and delivered to Old Angola.

The tiny spirit that I now saw walking in circles around the pit.

"Hey, Gum Baby," I whispered.

Funny how, when the time to speak had passed, there was so much I wanted to say.

Gum Baby's spirit trudged around the cluster of haintacles. She disappeared from view, then returned, a constant confused and dejected expression on her face. Translucent sap dropped behind her as she walked—even as a ghost she was sticky. Seeing her like this, all sad and defeated, felt wrong.

A haintacle descended and swabbed the floor behind Gum Baby. With the ghost sap smeared on it, the snakelike arm lifted itself toward the highest row of cinder blocks. Something snapped inside me. How dare they use her like that?

"Hey!" I shouted, sliding off the edge to land in the pit. I ran up to the haintacle cluster and kicked one of them. "HEY!"

But they ignored me. Maybe one heartbroken boy wasn't tempting enough to distract them from building a haunted plantation prison. I kicked the haintacle one more time, but in my anger I only clipped it with my heel. I lost my balance and tumbled. Gum Baby's wooden body fell out of my hands and skidded away. I slammed my fist into the floor. Then did it again. It was all so unfair! How could terrible things continue to happen to decent people?

I didn't realize I was still pounding the floor until my knuckles began to ache. A deep, noiseless sob shuddered through me, and I just wanted to lie there and never get up. What was the point?

The spirit of Gum Baby trudged around the pit again. She passed by her body without giving it a second glance. Spirit sap fell onto it, and I saw one of the haintacles begin to descend out the corner of my eye. Panic filled me. What if it took the wooden doll with it when it came to collect more sap? I scrambled to my feet and ran across the pit, snatching up the doll just as the giant evil appendage rumbled by.

Something crinkled inside Gum Baby's clothes.

I frowned. That was weird. I looked around, then backed into a small depression in the wall of the pit and crouched down to investigate. After a few seconds of searching the miniature black turtleneck and pants, I found the issue. A wadded-up collection of tiny papers had been stuffed inside the cuff of her right pant leg. I pulled them out and read the title aloud.

"'The True Life Story of Gum Baby the Great.'" A grin crossed my face as I read the subtitle. "'Not to Be Read by Any Bumbletongues.'"

"'Seriously, this means you, Tristan.'"

"'Last warning, Tristan!!! Do not read!!!'"

I looked down at the doll in my lap and shook my head. The rest of the pages were blank—she'd never gotten around to writing her story. I smiled, then folded the papers and leaned my head back against the pit wall. Maybe she'd never gotten around to it, but that didn't mean I couldn't tell my own version of the story right now.

I cleared my throat. "Gum Baby the Great was the *strongest* hero across two worlds. She led an Anansesem to a realm that needed him, and rescued that realm from the evil threat he brought into it. She fought for her friends, never gave up, and never complained about it." I thought for a second, then added clarification. "She didn't complain *too much*. But she just wanted to go on adventures, and she deserved her flowers."

Something about her sap attack needed to come next. I opened my mouth, then paused.

The spirit of Gum Baby had stopped walking...and was looking at me. No, not at me—at the doll in my lap.

I stood up and licked my lips. "Can...can you hear me?"

The spirit didn't say anything. I sighed. It had been worth a shot. Maybe this was what happened sometimes. I slumped back against the wall and lifted one of Gum Baby's wooden hands.

"Gum Baby's sap attack was the most..." My voice trailed off.

The spirit had raised her hand as well. Was she reacting to the story? Maybe she *could* hear me.

"Her sap attack," I continued, "was the most powerful weapon in all the land. Pinpoint accuracy. Incredible power. It defeated a vicious haint and toppled iron monsters." As I told the story of Gum Baby, I held up the wooden doll in my lap, raising both arms and making it move about like a puppet. The spirit mimicked every movement. Mirrored it. As if...as if there was still a connection.

Gods can't die, not if their stories continued to be told.

But Gum Baby wasn't a god, right?

Right?

"Her legend spread throughout Alke, from MidPass to the Golden Crescent. From Nyanza to Isihlangu. Her reputation as a hero grew, and soon 'The Ballad of the Gummy' was sung by children and adults all over."

The spirit moved closer and closer to me. Telling her story was reuniting the spirit with the doll! I held my breath. She stopped a foot away. So close! But the cluster of haintacles rumbled, and one curled down to collect more sap. It began to return to the ever-expanding upper floors of Old Angola, but then it paused. It returned to wipe the floor of the pit. Then it rose and slowly slithered around the space, as if looking for something.

"Oh no," I whispered, looking at the Gum Baby ghost. While she was standing and listening to a story, she wasn't creating a trail of spirit sap. And no spirit sap meant an angry plantation prison. I had to hurry up. . . . If this was going to work, there was only one thing to do.

"The things I do for friendship," I muttered. Then I began to sing.

"The ballad of the gummy, ballad of the gummy.
Strongest and the fiercest, and her nose is never runny.
Sap attack, back it back, the hero of the hour.
Riding on her bumbly steed, who needs to take a shower."

The haintacle wriggled closer. Any second now and we'd be caught. The spirit of Gum Baby stood over her body, a curious expression on her face. Like she was trying to remember.

WHAM!

But we were out of time. The haintacle crashed into a wall, its tip pointed right at Gum Baby. It shot forward, poised to drag her back to her circuit and force her to give up her sap. Old Angola would grow forever. And my friend would be gone forever.

"No," I said. *"No!"*

I stepped over Gum Baby and stood between her and the haintacle. My fists clenched, and I didn't need to look to know that the akofena shadow gloves had roared to life beside me. The black flames rippled in the purple light of the pit. I wasn't sure what my plan was, but I refused to let Old Angola win. Even if it meant I'd be smashed into a pancake, I would stand my ground.

The haintacle shot forward like a battering ram. If I dodged, Gum Baby was a goner. If I ducked, slipped, bobbed, or weaved, Gum Baby was a goner. I had to stand. Stand strong. With my arms crossed in front of me, the gloves forming a blazing wall of black fire.

Stand strong.

Stand strong.

Stand—

FWOOM!

The haintacle slammed into the shadow gloves. The

impact lifted me off my feet and bashed me against the pit wall, and I slid down in a haze of pain. But through my blurry vision, I saw a black flame leap onto the evil tendril and race along it to the trunk cluster. The haintacle thrashed about, and I groaned and tried to crawl out of the way. But it must've seen me, because it turned toward me. It shivered as if screaming a silent challenge and shot forward once more.

I tried to move, but it felt as if my lungs were filled with mud. I couldn't breathe! A steel band squeezed my ribs, and my movements were so sluggish. The haintacle, sensing weakness, lifted itself into the air for one last whip. A sob escaped my lips. This was it. For me, for Chicago, and for my friends. This was—

WHAP! WHAP! WHAP!

A trio of curiously sticky projectiles smacked the leading tip of the haintacle. The fire already covering the monstrous appendage flared high into the air. The haintacle squealed (squealed!) and changed directions before smashing into the wall of the pit and sticking there.

"Gum Baby's gotta do everything around here!"

I turned to see the tiny doll staggering on her feet, one hand on the pit wall as she pointed at the burning haintacle.

"Don't come looking for the sap, 'cause the sap don't miss!" she told it. Then she turned to me and flipped back a braid that had fallen across her face. "You sing like a toad!"

After that, she collapsed.

32
THE GUM BUDDIES

BUT WE WEREN'T OUT OF THE WOODS YET.

"Stop babying Gum Baby!"

I carried the resurrected tiny doll in my backpack, which I wore slung in reverse so it was on my chest. Gum Baby peeked out of the zippered opening of the main pouch. She was complaining because I wouldn't let her ride in my hoodie.

"Hush," I said, not paying her much attention. More haintacles were starting to take an interest in what was happening in the pit, and I didn't want to get trapped in there. Hand over hand, I climbed the short wall, then pulled myself over the edge and scrambled toward the exit. I hoped it was the same corridor I'd entered from.

"Did you just shush—"

"No," I said, cutting her off. "I *hushed* you. Big difference. Actually kind of polite."

"Oh." Gum Baby thought for a second. "Well, anyway.

Listen . . . Gum Baby's just gonna say it. . . . She came back to life just to save you."

I didn't answer. I had other things on my mind, like making sure we didn't die.

She shifted around in the backpack so that she faced me, and she had a curious expression on her face. I was used to her scowling at me. This was more like . . . affection?

That was it. We were definitely going to die.

"And you sang 'The Ballad of the Gummy.'"

"And?"

"Gum Baby knows it was a bit off-key, and you can't stay on rhythm to save your life, but you still sang it to save Gum Baby. That's . . ."

She paused.

I peeked down into the jagged rubble the haintacles protruded from. I couldn't see anything but darkness and their treelike cluster. No evil engine, or diabolical flywheel, or even an acid reflux capacitor. And, to make matters worse, I'd forgotten which tunnel led to the front entrance. I should've marked it somehow.

SLAM!

I groaned. And *now* I heard doors slamming and the haunted shrieks of Breakers echoing down the tunnel. Make that multiple tunnels—at least two, if not three.

Great, I thought. *Just what we need.* We were out of time, and I was no closer to stopping Old Angola than when I first walked in.

"Well," Gum Baby was saying, "normally Gum Baby doesn't do this, but she has no choice. You saved her life, and she's saved yours (more times than she can count, to be honest), and that can mean only one thing."

"Mmhmm," I said, searching for a hiding space. Maybe if I stood still the Breakers wouldn't see me.

"Gum Baby and Tristan..."

"Yep," I said, holding my hands above my head and wiggling my fingers. I was a haintacle now. Trying to blend in. Not paying attention to the approaching shrieks, or the slinking shadows gathering around the pit. None of that mattered, because I was supposed to be here.

"We're Gum Buddies. Now we can be roommates."

Wait a minute.

"What?" I asked, finally paying attention.

Gum Baby was rummaging around in the backpack headfirst, her tiny legs waving in the air. I tapped one of them, then flicked the resulting sap away. "Excuse me, what do you mean, *roommates?*"

"That's what Gum Buddies are!" Gum Baby's voice echoed with excitement, and she emerged from the pack with a scrap of paper and a pencil left over from school. "Roommates till the bitter end. Of course, Gum Baby needs her space, so you better not be messy or snore or take up too much room in the closet, which is where you'll have to sleep.... Better yet, Gum Baby will bring her costume trunk, and—"

SMASH!

"Oh, thank goodness," I said, and sighed with relief. One of the steel doors had flown out of a dark tunnel entrance and slammed into the pit floor. A couple Breakers I could deal with. Better than contemplating life with Gum Baby as a roommate.

Except it wasn't just a couple.

Breakers poured out of the tunnels like bees protecting their hive. Evil, spirit-stealing bees. They ran along the circular walls, the floor, and even the scorched haintacle. We were surrounded. It was Patty Roller's Wig Emporium all over again.

A giant Breaker leaped down in front of us. Its knuckles scraped the ground and its wide mouth stretched open. Whip-claws unfurled.

I tensed. This couldn't happen again. Gum Baby was on alert in the backpack in front of me. But I couldn't see her get hurt. Not for a second time.

The Breaker flexed, dropped into a crouch, and let out a scream.

So what did I do? I screamed right back at it. It wanted me to be terrified? Fine. But it could have my anger as well. And Gum Baby screamed right along with me. It was just like the barge tow in New Orleans, except this time I didn't care if we burned everything down around us. In fact, I hoped we did.

The Breaker leaped forward.

Once again, I took a step back. But it wasn't out of fear. No, it was to anchor myself. Pull strength up from my legs, into my center, and through my arms, which moved in front of me automatically in a cross-body block. The akofena shadow gloves emerged like firecrackers made of the night sky, and the shield of fire returned once more.

The Breaker's whip claws snapped forward.

"Sap attack!" Gum Baby screamed, and hurled sap at it.

And then a funny thing happened. As the sap flew through the flaming wall, it ignited, bursting into silver flame as it pelted the Breaker right in the chest.

You know what's terrifying? Flaming sap.

The Breaker tumbled to the floor, scrabbling for footing as the silver flames engulfed it. And just like back on the barge, everything the fire touched began to burn.

Gum Baby and I looked at each other.

"Sap dap?" she asked hopefully.

I nodded. "Sap dap."

"Wooooo!" she shouted in excitement as she pointed to the Breakers crowding in all around us. "You butterbeans ain't seen nothing yet! Just wait until the Gum Buddies sap-dap you thistle-heads. You'll be wishing you never heard of us. C'mon, dunderbuns, don't get the shiver knees now!"

Gum Baby's hands were a blur as she skipped sap balls off of my gloves. They flew through the fire, ignited, and landed on her targets. Breaker after Breaker went up in flames, and when the shadow monsters careened off walls and each other, they only made the inferno worse. The pit burned, the haintacles burned, and debris that fell from the walls burned as well. Old Angola was being destroyed from the inside out. We'd done it! And all it had taken was me and a friend.

A friend?

I sighed.

A Gum Buddy.

The Breakers that weren't burning fled down a large tunnel off to my left. That had to be the exit. A section of the haintacle tree trunk crashed down into the pit, throwing sparks everywhere. It was time to make our escape.

"We're leaving, Gum Baby!" I shouted.

She flexed, then pointed after the Breakers. "Cavalry pursuit, bumble-steed."

I glared at her.

"Gum Baby was just joking, jeez."

I raced into the tunnel. Every muscle in my body ached, and it was all I could do to stay on my feet as the prison collapsed around me. At some point the shadow gloves had disappeared. I was exhausted, and whatever powers of Alke I had left were on the verge of petering out, like a candle trapped under a glass. But I could just make out the large entrance ahead of me, and the drawbridge, and it was only a few more steps before...

Pain exploded in my chest. Something knocked me off my feet, sending me spinning to the ground. I felt rather than saw Gum Baby fly out of the half-zipped backpack, tumbling down onto the beach.

And everything went black.

33

THE FINAL FIGHT OF TRISTAN STRONG

DARKNESS. RUMBLING.

Then: "You ain't worth the dirt you're lying on."

Lights. Two of them, like twin candles burning. Or was something on fire? No.

Eyes.

The voice spoke again. "How could you do this to me? You ruined everything!"

A face slowly emerged to contain those burning eyes. I knew that face. Harsh and twisted. Thorns and sharp teeth. Cotton. For a second, I actually welcomed him. It meant I was still alive.

Or did it mean I was dead and those burning eyes would follow me forever?

"Here I thought we had an understanding. Clarity, in a sense, about how the world works." Cotton lunged out of the dark until his face was inches from mine. He grabbed both of my cheeks with stained fingers that tapered into claws. "They were gonna make me king!"

I jerked away from his grip. "You're no one's king," I wheezed.

Light cracked through the darkness, and the rumbling grew louder. We were inside Old Angola, I realized. It was falling apart and we were still inside. Why? How come Cotton didn't drag me outside in front of everyone? The haint was a showman. He'd never pass up an opportunity to make a display of strength.

Unless . . . he'd lost his strength.

The haintacles were burning, as was Old Angola. The Breakers had fled.

"You're alone," I said, interrupting whatever monologue he'd been in the middle of performing.

"What did you say?"

I shook my head and laughed. "You're alone. Just like when we met, a haint from a broken jar."

He growled and then shoved me away. I was on the ground and sore. My body felt like one large bruise. But I refused to just lie there. As much as it hurt, I struggled to my feet, wobbling and dizzy, yes, but still standing.

More cracks of light webbed across the darkness, and bits of concrete began to fall to the floor. A piece about the size of my head dislodged from right above us and hurtled down.

I winced as it smashed to pieces only a yard away. Light stabbed in, revealing a sky smudged with purple and pink. The shadows faded and I finally got a good look at Cotton.

I wish I hadn't.

The empty husks of several haintacles dangled off him, like old, starving leeches. Gone was the fancy shirt and hat, and his pants were stained and tattered. But his eyes still burned with hatred, no longer masked by the costume of a gentleman, like the one he'd worn back in the French Quarter in New Orleans. Now he looked like the haint he was and nothing more. Evil with no filter applied.

"You've ruined everything," he said again with a snarl. "Everything! But I can start over. Find more spirits, gather more power. You'll see. This world has tons of potential. Pockets of hidden stories tucked everywhere, just marinating, waitin' on someone like me to suck the marrow out the bone."

"Give up," I said, my breath rattling in my lungs. "Everyone's seen you for what you are. No way you'd get away with it again."

Cotton threw back his head and laughed. "Boy, you's a twice-born fool. There's always gonna be a Cotton. Always gonna be a need for power. You think I begged them other folks to help me out? To block your progress? Shoot, boy, they were here before me! People always gonna need some-one like me to make them look less greedy. So sit tight, I'm gonna re-up and be back in business tomorrow, you'll see."

No. That couldn't be right, could it?

But I remembered the voices of the spirits fleeing the riots. The stories buried under cities. The violence and destruction hidden beneath the streets and parks. Cotton hadn't done any of that. He hadn't created those stories—he'd just tried to use their power. And if he had his way, he'd continue to devour the past, so no one would ever learn it. People like the Redliners could hide behind their masks and their sanitized versions of history. And creatures like Patty Roller would continue to hunt down children like me and stamp every bit of magic out of them.

No, Cotton hadn't started all this. But I could make sure he didn't take it any farther.

I pulled myself upright, forcing my chin to lift defiantly, and glared at Cotton. When I was sure my voice wouldn't give out on me, I stared straight into his burning eyes and shook my head. "There is no tomorrow for you."

The haint paused. "And who's gonna stop me? You?" He barked out a laugh. "Boy, the only thing holding you up is the breeze."

I limped to the entrance, even as Old Angola shuddered and dust rained down, and shook my head again. "No. This is where it ends."

Cotton's smile faded. "I will flay the spirit from your skin, boy, if you don't get outta my way. I got bigger morsels to chew out there, and you ain't worth the energy."

He took a step forward, and I willed the shadow gloves into existence. They appeared, faint and barely burning, but still, they appeared, and I could've sobbed with relief. I wasn't sure they would.

"Move," Cotton hissed.

I stood straighter and tried not to wince. "No."

"Fine," the haint snarled. "Say good-bye, Tristan Strong."

And as the rest of Old Angola cracked and crumbled around us, revealing the sun-kissed surface of Lake Michigan and the resilient skyline of Chicago, and the gods and Alkeans on the lakefront called out my name, and the community lining the trees held up their smartphones to record, I put up my two fists and prepared to do what I did best, what Strongs did best, what my people had done for centuries when backed into a corner with no way out except the rocky path filled with the obstacles hurled in their way.

One last round in a fight to save me, save my friends, and save the world.

I punched.

Fighting Cotton was nothing like boxing in my first match, or sparring with Reggie Janson, or any of the other matches and practices I'd participated in. It was rough. Dirty, even. There wasn't a ring, just a small clear space amid the rubble of a haunted plantation prison.

And I was losing.

Cotton swiped left and right so fast I couldn't follow his movements. But the pain let me know where his hits came down.

"You done messed up now," he taunted after one of his attacks sent me stumbling backward. "I'm gonna make you famous. Your memorial service will be the talk of the town."

I threw a jab-straight combo. Neither my fists nor the shadow gloves landed, but it forced Cotton to retreat a few steps. That's what I had to do. Keep punching.

"Is that all you got?" The haint laughed. "Boy, you slower than a slug in molasses." He danced around me and clawed at my face. I jerked back but in doing so stumbled over a large stone and fell.

Cotton laughed. "Stay down, boy, before this pile of stones becomes your grave marker. Better folks than you have tried and failed to dethrone the king."

I panted, every inch of my body tired and in pain. I was stressed and suffering. But if I moved one leg forward, put both hands on my knee, and ignored the screaming pain, I could shove myself to my feet. And my arms could lift, and my fists could clench. If I did that, I could keep punching.

Just had to keep punching.

Cotton snarled as I climbed to my feet. "You don't get it, do you? You lost! Give up already."

I inhaled, then let a sigh, or maybe a hiss of pain, escape through my teeth. I shook my head. "No."

The haint howled with rage and attacked. Blow after blow. Punching, kicking, swiping. The akofena shadow gloves flickered as I tried to weather the storm.

Just keep punching.

My jabs were feeble. My straights were worse. I couldn't manage a hook, and an uppercut was out of the question.

Just keep punching.

Cotton was a whirlwind of hatred and aggression, but I noticed his movements were beginning to slow. His attacks came further and further apart. His chest, still covered in the withered remains of haintacles, heaved up and down.

Just keep punching.

Finally, Cotton staggered back. His hands were down at his sides, and he sucked in oxygen like a vacuum cleaner with a leaky hose.

"Why...won't you...give up?" he asked, his snarl more of a whine.

I lifted my fists, ignoring the stinging pain in my arms. Ignored the stitch in my side, the sprain in my ankle. I ignored it all and approached him a step at a time. I had enough energy for one last shot. After that, it was beyond me.

"Keep punching," I said.

"What?"

"We. Keep. Punching."

Cotton swung at me, but I batted it aside. I didn't attack, not yet. He'd tired himself out. He wasn't built to last, not like Walter Strong, not like Nana Strong, not like my family, my community, my people.

"Who?" he asked, and for the first time a trickle of fear slipped through the haint's bravado.

I grinned. Pointed at my heart. Lifted my chin high, and spread my arms wide. "Strongs. Strongs keep punching."

My fists weren't in a guard position, and Cotton saw that. He snarled and lunged forward, throwing his all into an attack that would rip me to shreds.

And I was waiting for it.

Step to the side.

Cotton's momentum carried him past me, and he was off-balance.

Counterpunch.

My right fist, my power fist, knifed through the air and connected flush against Cotton's chin. Just my fist, not the shadow gloves, because I needed them for what came next.

The world is going to hit you hard, son. Clinch and don't let go until you can keep on fighting.

And so I clinched.

Now the gloves winked into existence. The black flames flared to life one more time, with as much energy as I could muster flowing through them. Just as I'd done on the barge, I willed the gloves together, merging six into two shining beacons of black in the light of the setting sun. The fire crept up my arms. The flames wreathed my shoulders, united behind my back, and surged high in the air. For a brief moment, I burned like a black star.

I darted forward and grabbed Cotton.

"What are you doing?" he snarled.

I didn't answer. He twisted, turned, fought, and struggled, but I didn't let go. It was weird, but under the thorns and the snarls, it was like he was barely there. The flames of the akofena spread to him, devouring the thorns and cotton as if they hungered for the hatred binding the haint together.

"Stop! You can't do this! What is happening?"

The flames crackled.

"Do you know who I am?" Cotton screamed, his voice a distorted howl. "I'm King Cotton! King! Cotton! You can't get rid of me, Tristan Strong!"

The flames roared.

"Tristan Strong!"

The haint's voice echoed across the beach, floating over the water. A piece of cotton dropped to the lake as the shout faded away. Just before it reached the surface, a wisp of smoke curled up and it burst into black flames, and the last essence of the haint King Cotton left forever.

Ashes to ashes. Dust to dust.

EPILOGUE

"IT'S BEEN ONE MONTH SINCE THE OAKWOOD BEACH INCIDENT, *and city officials are still at a loss as to how to explain the strange events. The mayor has promised a full investigation and has appointed a task force to lead the charge into unraveling the mystery. And now we turn to a special report: Doctors across Chicago are reporting strange symptoms in the children of the city. Is it really magic, or something else?"*

"Tristan?"

I exited the news video on the SBP. For a few seconds I just stared at the screen. Nyame had given the phone back to me a few days after the battle of Lake Michigan. "Anansi may not be inside," he'd said, "but the Story Box belongs with the Anansesem."

"So . . . I'm still an Anansesem? I haven't been stripped of the title?"

The sky god had snorted and tousled my hair. "No one has seen the stories of the people like you have, Tristan. It would be foolish to deny them your talents. And besides..." He'd slipped his sunglasses back on and turned to leave. "Since when have I ever done as Anansi demanded? He's lucky I even released him."

I'd learned that Anansi had convinced Nyame and the other gods to free him from the SBP, both to get reinforcements for the battle with Cotton and to contribute to the fight himself. I'd miss having him at my disposal.... Maybe. I was still wrestling with it.

"Have you seen him?" I'd asked, clutching the SBP to my chest. It felt... right, having it back. But no one had seen Anansi since the end of the battle, not even Junior. It was a little unsettling, knowing that the trickster god was out in the world, which had been his desire from the very beginning. But Nyame had shaken his head, then gone back to helping John Henry and the other gods clean up the remains of Old Angola (Lake Michigan must've risen several feet from all the cinder-block rubble that had fallen into it).

Eventually, the gods had departed together. Nyame had managed to acquire a giant tour bus, and he planned on giving the other gods a tour of the country while they tracked down more lost Alkeans. He said they'd keep a low profile, but when I saw a picture of the giant golden bus with SKYGOD as the license plate, I knew otherwise.

"Tristan!"

The shout dragged me from my memories, and when the time flashed on the SBP's home screen, my eyes grew wide. I was going to be late! I ignored the triple-digit red number in the lower corner of the Diaspor-app, tumbled off my bed, grabbed my backpack, and threw on a hoodie. School started in an hour, and it would take me forty-five minutes to get there.

"Tristan Strong?" Dad's voice echoed through the apartment.

I dashed into the kitchen, grabbed a bagel and an orange, then hugged Dad and kissed Mom on the cheek. Dad eyed me, checked his watch, and raised an eyebrow.

"I know," I said around a mouthful of bagel. "Leaving now."

He snorted and went back to reading. "Don't think that just because you're getting a ride now you can slack off. If those grades drop, you'll be back on the bus, hear me?"

"Yes, sir!" I tiptoed behind him and snapped off a jab. Before my hand got anywhere close to him, Dad, with his flexibility magic, had somehow snagged my punch out of midair.

"Good-bye, Tristan," he said, and I rolled my eyes. Mom winked at me and I waved, then jogged out the door.

At the curb in front, a black SUV with a crow on the hood honked/cawed. I dodged a mom and her kid drawing chalk sight words on the sidewalk and hopped into the back seat, tossing my bag into the trunk. "How come I never get to ride shotgun?" I complained as I started to peel the orange.

Junior peeked back at me and held out a hand. I sighed and gave him a couple wedges, and he turned around happily. "Easy—you're always late. Can't call shotgun if you're not here when the seats are assigned."

Something scrabbled around in the back, and then a tiny face looked over the back seat. "Gum Baby is sick and tired of riding in the trunk! Is that how you treat your Gum Buddy? Got sap on the windows *one time*, and now Gum Baby's being sappressed. Y'all are mean."

Okay, so hear me out. Yes, Gum Baby and I are roommates. But honestly, where else was she going to go? Not many hotels renting out rooms to a ten-inch sap-covered doll.

But instead of answering her, I held up the SBP screen. Her eyes lit up at the number of Diaspor-app notifications. "More kids with Alkean magic?"

I nodded. "A lot."

"Gum Baby will send out the standard message. Here's how magic works, what Alke was, and what the goal is. Gum Baby really needs to get paid for this, though—her labor ain't free."

I rolled my eyes. "Fine, I'll get you some more espresso. But you really need to cut back."

"Gum Baby needs caffeeeine," she howled as her fingers began blazing across the screen.

Thandiwe looked back from the driver's seat. "Can we go now? Or do you want to debate some more and make us late? Again."

A hand reached out from the seat next to me and rested on my arm. Ayanna smiled and I smiled back, glad that she wasn't alternating between shaking me and hugging me like she had when I'd stumbled onto the beach after fighting King Cotton. She hadn't said anything then, just sobbed and laughed at the same time, and I understood. I really did.

And if our hug had lasted a bit longer than normal, so what?

And if I'd thought that her face had lit up the evening sky and not the other way around, and that the image would stay with me until my dying day, what of it?

And if I didn't really understand or couldn't express what that feeling was, only that I wanted her to help me figure it out, don't even stress.

That's not a part of this story.

"Yeah," I said now. "Let's go."

The princess looked the oldest of all of us, and we needed someone to pretend to drive Old Familiar as we went to school. Self-driving cars were cool and all, but they tended to attract unwanted attention.

Oh, you didn't know? Turns out I had some new classmates going into the eighth grade with me. It wasn't like Junior, Thandiwe, and Ayanna had anywhere else to go, so Mami Wata had pulled some strings to enroll them, and

Granny Z had called in a few favors to get them an apartment down the street in Bronzeville, and the next thing I knew, we were coming up with plans to form an Alke after-school club. Everyone was welcome, of course. Except for haints.

And Gum Baby?

"Do you think Gum Baby can try out for the gymnastics team? She heard them talking about sticking the landing, and that's what the Gummy does best, you know? She can work on her floor routine while y'all in school. Don't look at Gum Baby like that, Bumbletongue! If Gum Baby can't go to kindergarten, she might as well follow her lifelong dream she just thought of."

Yeah. Gum Baby's still Gum Baby.

We arrived at school just before the bell rang. We all had the same homeroom, and we made it to our seats in the nick of time. A few kids were whispering to each other and staring at the door. When I asked what was going on, one of them, an Afro-Latina who was new, too, shrugged. "Mr. Tyson quit. Something about an amazing opportunity in Delaware or something. The new teacher, Mr. Kwaku, isn't here yet, but people are saying he's . . ." She hesitated, and before she could finish, the door opened.

Mr. Kwaku?

"The bell has rung, students. I expect books open and mouths closed."

My hand stilled. Wait . . . wait just a minute. I knew that

voice. It couldn't be.... But when I looked at Junior, his mouth had dropped open as well.

A shadow fell over my desk.

"Come now, Mr. Strong, I've heard about you. Quite the reputation you've got." Two brown hands leaned on my desk, and I looked up to see the twinkling eyes of Anansi staring at me. He winked. "I think we'll have a lot of fun in class this year."

I gulped.

My name is Tristan Strong, and boy am I gonna have a story for you.